I0740138

life in high def

Kimberly Cooper Griffin

Night River Press

The characters, names, and events as well as all places, incidents, organizations, and dialog in this novel are either the products of the writer's imagination or are used fictitiously.

Copyright © 2016 by Kimberly Cooper Griffin

All rights reserved. No part of this publication may be reproduced, distributed, or transmitted in any form or by any means, including photocopying, recording, or other electronic or mechanical methods, without the prior written permission of the author, except in the case of brief quotations embodied in critical reviews and certain other noncommercial uses permitted by copyright law. For permission or additional detail, contact the author at the address below.

Printed in the United States of America
First Edition 2016

Edited by Jamie May

Cover design by Erin Dameron-Hill at EDHGraphics

Author Photo by Bettinger Photography

Night River Press
Denver, CO 80209
NightRiverPress.com

Life in High Def
ISBN-10:0-9972190-1-7
ISBN-13: 978-0-9972190-1-2
Library of Congress Control Number: 2016902563

Visit the author's website at http://kimberlycoopergriffin.com
to order additional copies.

CONTENTS

SYNOPSIS

ACADEMY AWARD WINNING ACTRESS Reilly Ransome has a life that others can only dream about: fame that opens every door, more money than she can ever spend, and freedom to do what—and whom—she pleases. But something is missing, and the harder she seeks to find it, the more evident the absence becomes. She attempts to fill the gap with experiences that become more and more dangerous until one night, she wakes up to find that she has committed the unthinkable. Resolved to live the rest of her life doing penance for her mistake, Reilly withdraws from her whirlwind existence and finally finds what she's been missing when she starts taking yoga from serene and beautiful Drew Tamrin. But finding something and accepting something are two different things, and it is only when Reilly can finally forgive herself that she is able to find her life's meaning.

DEDICATION

To Summer, this and everything.

ACKNOWLEDGEMENTS

I owe the publication of this novel to my writing group; Beth Escott Newcomer, Carrie Repking, and Lake McCleary. I am humbled to have been accepted by you three talented and wildly creative women. You amaze me! Thank you for suffering through countless rewrites and for providing insight into my little story. I hear your voices every time I write.

Thank you, Kit-Bacon Gressitt, for offering the writing class that got me started. I am grateful for your tireless passion for teaching, connecting, and inspiring writers. Some of my favorite memories are sitting in your living room among the eclectic relics of Dia de los Muertos, listening to diverse voices discussing story arcs and tone.

Michelle Dunkley, thank you for being my beta reader. I held my breath to hear your thoughts. You helped me more than you probably know. And, yes, I've told all of my single friends about you!

Jamie May, it amazes me how much better you make my writing!

And finally, many thanks to Skeeter Buck, founder of **Night River Press**, for taking a chance on *Life in High Def*. May this be a successful start of our literary journey!

Not into What You're Offering

IT WAS WEDNESDAY NIGHT, or—to be more accurate—the early hours
of Thursday morning, and the frenetic energy thrumming through the invi-
tation-only nightclub in West Hollywood was just starting to peak. It wasn't
unusual for the club to be open so late in the middle of the week. The clientele
wasn't the normal nine-to-five crowd. But even for an exclusive club that regularly hosted Hollywood's top stars, the energy of the place was off the charts, with
celebrities and their closest friends enjoying the nightlife and partying like there
was no tomorrow. The Academy Award nominations had just been announced
and the lucky few who'd made the coveted list were out to celebrate, while the
rest of the industry was out to be seen. But even that wasn't the main reason
people were still reveling when most of California was deep asleep. The reigning
queen of all party girls, Reilly Ransome was in the house. She'd just received her
second Academy Award nomination. She was high on life. High on being the
center of attention. High on cocaine.

Four-inch heels and a black spaghetti-strapped clingy sheath dress over a
well-toned body gave an illusion of height to Reilly's five-foot nothing frame.
Straightened long blonde hair fell over her face as she danced but she didn't move
it away. The deep thump of the techno-baseline vibrated through her and she let
it own her body as she moved in time with the rest of the writhing mass on the
packed dance floor. A cloud of expensive scents competed with the boozy sweat-
smell of pheromones that amped up the intensity of the drug-fueled crowd. Her
eyes were closed and her arms were raised. Behind the mask of her hair, nothing
existed but the music and the motion.

She was a good dancer, and she knew it. The producer of the movie that she
had just finished shooting had paid a shitload of money to make her that good.

And she had quite literally worked her ass off to get there. Weeks of eight and twelve-hour dance training sessions and a relentless workout schedule had preceded the shoot and it showed. Reilly didn't know how to do anything halfway. She put the same focus and dedication into what her mother insisted on referring to as "that fluff dance movie" as she had put into the role that had garnered her first Academy Award. The dance movie had been a diversion for her between "serious" films, but now, in no small part due to Reilly's intense work ethic, even it was being talked about as next summer's blockbuster. It seemed she could do no wrong. Her life was racing forward at breakneck speed, and the adrenaline rush that came with it was coursing through her body as she moved to the music.

She was alone on the dance floor, surrounded for the most part by strangers and acquaintances that would refer to her as a "dear friend" in the morning. Her co-star in the movie, Cray Layton, had come to the party with her. The media and her studio promoted him as her current boyfriend, and to help support that image, he had stayed by her side for much of the night. However, in the booze-drenched haze of early morning, he was tucked in at the end of the bar dry-humping a muscle-bound guy that Reilly recognized from somewhere—an extra, a bodyguard? It didn't matter. She couldn't care less.

A beautiful woman moved in behind her and wrapped her arms around Reilly, grinding her pelvis into Reilly's ass. Reilly leaned back, pulling the arms closer, so that the roving hands cupped her breasts. The woman kissed the side of Reilly's neck and Reilly shivered. Her nipples hardened under the silk fabric of her top and the woman responded by rolling the hardened flesh between her fingers and sucking on Reilly's neck. Without a word, Reilly turned around and walked off the dance floor, pulling the woman by their intertwined fingers.

They pushed through the crowd and Reilly switched places with her companion so that the taller blonde could fend off the groupies and overzealous hangers-on. They made their way to the bathrooms. There was a line down the long dark hall, but they walked past and went in. No one seemed to mind, and even if they did, neither woman cared. Reilly was Hollywood royalty. The blonde steered them into the mirrored sitting room just inside the door. Two plush couches took up the center of the room and Reilly fell into the woman's lap, straddling her. Her short black dress rode up and the blonde smoothed it down for her, just enough to keep the important parts covered. A long gilt mirror took up one entire wall, and Reilly watched their reflection over the blonde's shoulder. She squinted. She wasn't sure if it was the drugs or the booze, but the woman looking back in the reflection was unfamiliar.

"Fuck, Rye. I get so turned on watching you dance now," said the blonde, breaking Reilly's gaze with her own reflection. And through the fog of energy and drugs, Reilly felt hands on her ass, while she ground into the woman's lap.

"Those dance lessons have unleashed a part of you that… god…"

Reilly moaned into a long kiss and decided that they needed to go home. Now.

"Let's get out of here, Syl." Reilly pulled away, tracing a path with her finger where her lips had just been. The room spun and she couldn't keep track of anything around them, but she was intent on the talented mouth before her, enjoying the low thrum that imagining it on her body caused in her belly. The music from the other room added to the throb thundering deep inside.

"Not yet, lover. I have to pee. And I want to finish off the blow first." Reilly's girlfriend of three years shot her a seductive smile as she shook out her long blond hair and slid out from under her. Reilly settled onto the crushed velvet couch and returned the teasing smile. She wondered how Sylvie could be so steady on her feet when she felt so out of control.

"We can do that at home, baby. Come on," Reilly heard the hollow plea in her voice as Sylvie backed away. The request was just for show. She didn't have to beg. And, if she were honest, she was too stoned to fuck. Though she wouldn't mind being a pillow princess if Sylvie wanted to fuck her.

"I really, really have to pee. I'll be right back, lover," said Sylvie as she disappeared around the corner toward the bathroom stalls.

Reilly ignored the other women who moved around her. Some of them watched her curiously, but none approached her. The people who had been invited to the party were all either in the industry, bored with it, or too worried about image to act like they cared. As far as Reilly went, she was used to being watched, and too high to care. She kicked out of her heels and tucked her legs up under her. From near her waist, she took a credit card-sized pocket mirror from the fashionable tiny club bag that she had strapped across her chest. In a smooth motion born of practice, she slid it open with one hand, while she used the other to uncap her lipstick. She checked her mascara and noted the eyes that peered back were bright, but bloodshot. All the partying didn't help. Red eyes aside, she knew that she was still a beautiful woman. She applied the lipstick and wiped a non-existent spot under her eye before she snapped the compact shut.

The sounds and scents of the small bathroom started to annoy her and she heard Sylvie's voice from inside, near the sinks. She slipped back into her shoes and got up to see who Sylvie was talking to. She was ready to leave. Her first few steps reminded her that she wasn't very sober.

"I don't remember seeing you here before. My name's Sylvie."

Sylvie's voice was low and seductive.

Reilly rounded the corner and leaned against it to steady herself just in time to see Sylvie push a strand of long black hair behind a woman's ear. Sylvie and one of the most beautiful women Reilly had ever seen stood in front of the sinks. The woman faced the mirrors, and Sylvie faced the woman. An attendant stood at a demure distance. Women lined the wall behind Reilly waiting for a free stall. A toilet flushed and the line inched forward. Reilly was aware of the curious eyes on her, but she tuned it all out. The woman with Sylvie drew all of her attention.

Reilly stared at the woman's reflection in the mirror. The woman's presence filled the room. Filled Reilly. The sensation was so intense it felt like a touch, and Reilly realized she was in the thrall of instant attraction. Interesting. The woman hadn't even spoken. She stood there, serene and confident. Her flowing black pants and sleeveless black blouse provided an air of simple sophistication, but Reilly sensed a complexity simmering inside the woman that she wanted to uncover.

So she watched. The woman didn't respond to Sylvie as she finished washing her hands. She accepted a towel from the attendant and patted them dry before she turned to face Sylvie. An amused expression played across her face. The woman sized Sylvie up, and Reilly crossed her arms over her chest as she observed, intrigued. She could tell that the woman thought that Sylvie was attractive, but she remained reserved. Sylvie had found a challenge with this one.

Almost everyone—man or woman—found Reilly's girlfriend attractive. An entertainment lawyer, Sylvie was a classic beauty. She had the face of a model and the body of a centerfold. She was smart and poised, and had a confidence that made people notice her when she entered a room. When Sylvie focused her charms on someone, they didn't have a chance. It was what had brought Reilly and Sylvie together, and if Reilly really thought about it, it was part of what kept them together. Both of them had plenty of other opportunities, but Reilly never worried about Sylvie's wandering eye. She knew that Sylvie was hers without a doubt, even when her flirting became more than that. Even when women came home with them. She wouldn't do it if Reilly asked her not to. But Reilly didn't mind. In fact, she found it exciting, even though her participation—by choice—was usually limited to watching. And that's what she was doing now. All that activity in one bed wasn't her thing. There were too many hands, too many mouths. She couldn't focus.

"I'd love to dance with you," said Sylvie, running her palm up the woman's bare arm. A flutter rose through Reilly when Sylvie's fingers inched under the edge of the opening at the shoulder of the woman's sleeveless blouse and pinched the edge of the fabric. Then Sylvie ran her hand up and down the opening, coming within a hair of brushing the backs of her fingers over the woman's breast. Reilly imagined it was her fingers absorbing the warmth of the woman's skin.

The woman shrugged Sylvie's hand away and laughed. Then she stepped back and gave the towel back to the waiting attendant, along with a tip. The velvet sound of the woman's thank you sent an unexpected ripple down the center of Reilly's back.

The woman dismissed Sylvie with her stance as she faced the mirror again.

"Sorry. It's late. Maybe next time… Sylvia?" said the woman, applying lip balm that she had pulled from the pocket of her pants. Sylvie's answering posture suggested that she wasn't about to give up this chase.

Reilly wasn't let down.

"Close enough. You can call me anything you want when I have my fingers inside of you," said Sylvie, taking a step closer to the woman.

A tall redhead at one of the other sinks laughed at Sylvie's crass remark. Reilly wanted to cringe, but she just lifted her eyebrows when Sylvie glanced at her and winked. Then she watched as Sylvie moved closer, pressing her belly against the woman's hip, resting her hand on the woman's backside. The woman lifted her sculpted eyebrows when Sylvie took the lip balm and applied some to her own lips. Sylvie's eyes never left the woman, as she pursed her lips, and took the cap, replaced it on the tube, and offered it back.

The woman's eyes regarded the tube in Sylvie's hand and then swept up to Sylvie's mouth, which lifted in a smile that indicated that Sylvie was certain that she was going to get what she wanted.

"Keep it. I think your girlfriend is waiting for you," the woman said. Reilly was surprised. Her position as voyeur had made her feel invisible, and she had thought that Sylvie had snared her prey.

Reilly had to give it to Sylvie—her smile never faltered.

"She is, and she likes to play, too."

"Is that so?" The woman turned to leave.

Reilly stood between the woman and the door. She had to remember to breathe when the woman's silver-gray eyes zeroed in on her. Aside from being the most amazing eyes that Reilly had ever seen, there was a smoldering intensity in the woman's gaze that made the room and all of the other people in it disappear. Reilly's heart pounded.

Between Reilly's position and the line of women waiting for an open stall, there wasn't much room to pass without squeezing through. The woman stood, waiting for Reilly to step aside.

"What's your name?" asked Reilly, without moving.

"Drew."

"I'm Reilly."

"I know who you are."

Reilly stood her ground and Drew took her breath away. There was no one in the room except them, as far as Reilly was concerned.

"I can take you home," said Reilly, surprising herself when she lifted her hand to stroke Drew's face. Reilly smiled to see Drew's eyes grow dark at her touch. Even in four-inch heels, Reilly was a few inches shorter. She leaned up and brushed a kiss over the corner of Drew's mouth, lingering for a second to take in the unexpected smell of cinnamon. "It would be fun. I promise," she said against the warm skin.

Drew shut her eyes and Reilly watched a flush edge up from Drew's scoop-necked shirt. Drew's eyes slowly opened again and focused on Reilly's mouth. Reilly knew that she had her.

"Hey, are you in line?" The voice came from behind Reilly, breaking the spell. The sounds of the room around them fell back into her awareness.

"Sounds tempting, but I'm not into what you're offering," said Drew, staring into Reilly's eyes. The dark smolder was gone, but the gaze was far from cold. Reilly had never seen eyes like that before. She wanted the opportunity to study them.

"We have something that might help you out with that," said Sylvie, from behind Drew. Reilly cringed at Sylvie's suggestion. She guessed that Drew wasn't into the drugs that Sylvie offered, either.

"Yeah. I'm even less tempted by that," said Drew, confirming Reilly's suspicion. Drew's eyes remained locked on Reilly's. "Thanks anyway."

With visible effort, Drew broke eye contact and pushed past Reilly to leave the bathroom. Reilly felt a wave of electricity shoot through her at every point their bodies made contact. She shut her eyes and breathed in the faint scent of Drew's cologne—hints of vanilla and sage—and the unexpected cinnamon. Her lips still tingled from the brief kiss.

Sylvie leaned against Reilly, her focus on Drew's retreating form. "That's a shame. She was fucking hot." Sylvie's disappointment didn't last for long. She turned to Reilly and held out her hand. "That just leaves more for us. Give me the stuff."

Wordlessly, Reilly gave Sylvie her purse, and then trailed after her, her thoughts still haunted by Drew's gorgeous eyes.

They made their way back to the couches, where they sat, and Sylvie took a small vial from the bag. Reilly's mouth watered at the sight, but she had other things on her mind.

"I'll be right back."

Sylvie regarded Reilly with a question in her eyes.

"I can't promise there will be any left when you get back," Sylvie called after her.

Without responding, Reilly waded into the press of bodies outside of the bathroom and her skin vibrated with the sensual throb of the music. She surveyed the hall as she pushed through the milling crowd and tried to follow Drew. She spotted her halfway to the exit and rushed to catch up. She ignored the hands and faces that tried to block her progress and kept her eyes on the back of

Drew's head. Drew's hair hung in a brilliant curtain of ebony down her back. The colors of the pulsing house lights reflected in its sheen. Reilly itched to run her fingers through its lengths.

"Drew! Wait!" called Reilly, just as Drew pushed through a door that opened into an alley. There was no bouncer guarding the exit-only door so late into the evening. The door thudded shut and a crash of quiet and dank night air encased them. A couple making out against the opposite wall glanced at them before they went back to their own pursuits. Laughter rose and fell as a group of people passed the mouth of the alley, several feet away.

Drew stopped and turned. Reilly saw surprise on her face.

"I'm sorry about that. You're beautiful, but we shouldn't have—I shouldn't have—been like that," she stammered.

Reilly felt stupid and all out of words. She didn't know why she had chased a stranger through a crowded club and out into the dark ally. She never chased after women. She didn't have to. But she needed to undo what had happened in the bathroom.

Drew tilted her head, a hint of amusement framing her mouth. Reilly stared at the full lips, which lifted into a smile.

"Is that why you followed me? To tell me that?" asked Drew.

God, she was so serene, thought Reilly. All traces of intoxication she had felt with Sylvie in the bathroom were gone. In its place, a deep, hypnotic pull held her. Energy pulsed off of everyone else in Hollywood—good or bad—it was always there. She constantly felt it. Pressing at her, inundating her. But she felt something else with this woman. It pulled at her, raising the hair on her arms with the electric intensity of it, but it didn't invade her. She didn't know if it aroused or comforted her.

"Yes. No. Yes," stammered Reilly. She couldn't think. "I don't know what to say, really. Just sorry, I guess."

Drew studied her. Reilly wanted to kiss her again. Her lips warmed at the thought.

"All right," said Drew with that smile. "Thanks, I guess. My friends are waiting at the car. Good night."

And then she was gone. The door to the club opened as a small group of people drained into the alley, and Reilly walked back into a darkness and sound that felt solid as the heavy door slammed shut behind her. The static buzz of the night infused her once again. She wasn't sure that she liked it, but she was used to it, and the throbbing lights of the techno beat erased the rest of the night.

Rock Stars and Private Jets

REILLY LAUGHED AS SHE STUMBLED up the stairs to the private Bombardier Challenger 601 aircraft that was waiting on the tarmac at LAX. The step lights were illuminated, but it was still hard to see her footing. In the last moments before dawn, the thick velvet darkness seemed to mute all light, but her graceless ascent was more about the countless glasses of champagne and lines of cocaine that she had consumed than about the darkness of the path. Paired with the four-inch heels she wore, hers was not a state for optimal stairway navigation. The rangy man in leather pants and black tee shirt on the stairway ahead of her looked back and laughed before he reached down and helped her navigate the rest of the way up the stairs.

Reilly accepted the help and giggled as she swatted away the other hand that helped her from below—the one that provided balance by cupping her ass. Sylvie just laughed and swatted right back. Everyone was in a good mood and ready to keep the party going.

"Thanks for saving my life, Brady… I mean Bobby? Brandon?" she said, squinting as she tried to remember his name. She watched his face to see if one of her guesses came close. His eyes weren't even on hers, though. They were locked on Sylvie's wandering hands, and even in her inebriation, Reilly fought to keep from rolling her eyes at the display of typical lecherous male attitude. Sylvie played into it, though, by pressing her breasts against Reilly's back as she mounted the top step behind them.

"The name's Brando, Rhonda… I mean, Regina? Rhianna?" teased the lead singer of The Deceased, one of the hottest bands in the world—at least for that week.

"Well, *Brando*, I'll put in a good word for you on the soundtrack of my next movie," she said. She laughed as he took off his small black hat, part of his signature rock-and-roll style, and bowed as they passed. His greasy hair flopped down and covered his face, and from over his bowed head, she could see half of his scrawny bare ass, pale and conspicuous against the black leather pants and black tee shirt he wore. She sneaked a glance at Sylvie who pretended to lick her lips, and she wondered why women across the globe swooned for him. He reminded her of the immature boys who had gone to her private high school, although most of them had probably bathed more often—not to mention grown up in the years since graduation. But, he was fun to hang out with, based on what she'd experienced in the few hours since they'd first met at the after-hours club somewhere on Sunset. Not wanting the fun to stop, she and Sylvie had accepted his spontaneous invitation to fly across the Atlantic to attend the opening concert of the band's European tour.

Reilly had done many things in her twenty-three years of life, but taking off to Europe on a whim, with a band that she had just met, was not yet one of them. It was still enough to make her feel a little star-struck at her own lifestyle, to be honest, which now literally consisted of rock stars and private jets. She hoped that the constant barrage of new situations she found herself in, thanks to her position at the top of the A-List, would never mute the rush she felt in her blood tonight.

They entered the cabin and moved toward the center, where two luxurious leather seats faced another set across a dark, wood-topped table. A plush couch sat along one side of the cabin. The inside of the plane was almost as opulent as the trailers Reilly used on set. On a nearby counter, crystal champagne flutes were nestled in rows of satin-lined indentions in wood boxes lying open next to a silver wine bucket filled with ice. A flight attendant smiled at them as she proficiently popped the cork on a bottle of Dom Perignon and then quickly sopped up the minimal frothing with the linen napkin wrapped around it.

"I can't wait to get you into the bathroom at thirty-five thousand feet so we can re-enact your initiation into the Mile High Club, baby," purred Sylvie into Reilly's ear as they accepted their glasses of sparkling beverage and fell into the leather chairs. Reilly's sex clenched at the suggestion, and she was glad that Sylvie, in an uncharacteristic show of discretion, had said it quietly enough that she wasn't overheard. She pulled Sylvie to her, kissed her on the neck, and was rewarded with a small moan.

It may have been a night of firsts for her, but joining the Mile High Club was not one of them. She and Sylvie had christened a flight to Hawaii earlier in the year, but her first induction into the prestigious club had been on a flight to Vancouver when she was seventeen years old with a pretty businesswoman. Sylvie was under the impression that she had been the one to initiate her though, and Reilly had never tried to correct her.

Brando and another member of the band dropped into the chairs that faced theirs, tossed back the contents of the glasses they held, and motioned for refills from one of the attentive flight crew that hovered near them in the rear of the cabin. Reilly pulled away from Sylvie and fiddled with her seatbelt when she saw Brando elbow his band mate and nod toward her and Sylvie with a grin. She knew that look. It was the look of an entitled male who thought he was going to be invited to partake in some sexy time with her and Sylvie. Boy, was he sorely mistaken. Aside from his unfortunate gender, the greasy hair made her want to gag.

She got downright pissed, though, when she saw Brando grab the flight attendant's ass. Reilly was a little too drunk and high to understand why, but her pulse thundered when she watched him yank the woman into his lap and plant a sloppy kiss on her mouth. The attendant, in an impressive show of professionalism and restraint, tried to mask her displeasure, but Reilly, a master herself, could spot the performance a mile away. She saw a shadow of revulsion flutter across the attendant's face even as she laughed, albeit closed mouthed, and smacked him across his chest, before she pushed herself back up to her feet and went on with her preflight routine. Reilly mentally retracted the soundtrack offer.

"Line it up, Chris. We should all be flying high before the plane even leaves the ground," crowed Brando. He smacked his leg as he watched the other musician retrieve a baggie of white powder from the guitar case that his buddy was strapping into the couch across from him. The guitar got more respect than the flight attendant.

"More champagne, sir?" asked another flight attendant. She topped off each flute and offered them each a linen napkin and a piece of fruit, while she ignored the drugs spread out on the table before them.

"To rock and roll!" said Brando lifting his glass and grabbing the flight attendant's ass as he took a long drink.

"To rock and roll," repeated Sylvie and Chris, while Reilly just held her glass. She was beginning to regret agreeing to the trip.

"That stewardess is going to get a big tip after this flight," said Brando, watching the attendant walk away with the empty bottle.

"Right on, man. A big old tip," smiled Chris, glassy-eyed, as he dumped a generous pile of fine white powder onto the surface of the table in front of him.

Reilly felt the familiar tingle in her gums at the sight of the drug, and her thoughts were redirected from the unwanted leers and gropes as Brando held out a glass tube to her and she leaned over. A minute later, the feel of Sylvie's hand inching up under her skirt as she inhaled her second line of cocaine was the only thing on her mind. It made her forget that she didn't much like Brando, who was watching with a crooked grin on his face, while his fingers traced the length of a pronounced bulge in his leather pants.

The Morning Show

REILLY CLENCHED HER JAW AS the interview rolled on. She should have known where he had been headed as soon as the shellac-coifed host of *The Morning Show*, Tristan Powers, complimented her on how sexy and feminine she appeared.

"You must admit. It's surprising, all things considered," he said, leaning forward to rest his chin on the fist he propped up on the arm of his upholstered chair.

His liquid brown eyes gazed at her across the ubiquitous talk show coffee table between them. His hair was distracting; too perfect, too blond, swept across his brow, just avoiding a too-youthful adolescent appearance. It bobbed en masse as he nodded at his own words. She had to admit, he knew how to dance on the edge of lechery without actually going there, lest he come off as one of the playboys he liked to interview so much. It wouldn't play well with his target demographic.

"You're so beautiful, Reilly. The epitome of feminine. The perfect mix of today's California surfer girl and Sandra Dee," said Tristan. "You have to know about the rumors. It's just so confusing."

Donning an air of deliberate bewilderment, he sat back, wove his fingers together over his crossed knees, and lifted his shoulders, waiting for her to respond. *He should talk about looking feminine*, thought Reilly, taking in his pouty red lips, expressive eyes and perfect unlined brow. Even by industry standards, he wore too much makeup.

She could feel one of her eyelids starting to twitch in annoyance, and she regretted the line of coke that she had done right before going on. But she had needed it to clear the cobwebs. It was barely dawn in New York, making it the middle of the night in Los Angeles where her bed was, and she wasn't used to getting up before noon regardless of where she was. Not between movies, anyhow. Besides, she had stayed up far too late the night before partying it up in the Big Apple. She had been less than coherent as the sun nudged its way above the Atlantic and her wakeup call had pulled her from a catatonic sleep. The little bump of coke she had taken to clear the fog amplified her reactions, and she felt her blood pressure soar at the line of questions that she was getting from the merkin-helmeted morning host.

She smiled and pushed a strand of hair from her forehead.

"Come on Tristan! Doesn't your wife get upset when you flirt like this with your guests?" she teased, shooting a glance at Melinda Powers, who sat in a matching chair next to her husband and co-host. Reilly hoped her good-natured hint would change the path of the interview.

Tristan laughed.

"Oh, Melinda agrees," he said answering for his wife, and favoring the former Miss America with an adoring gaze. He placed a hand on her knee, and sugar dripped from his voice. His teeth gleamed too white against his glossed lips. "We were talking about it just the other day, weren't we, Mel?"

Melinda just chuckled and nodded her spun-gold head—the same color and texture as her co-host's—as she beamed back at him. They stared just a beat too long into each other's eyes, and Reilly heard the collective sigh of five million feminine viewers, clenching their hands to their chests in heartfelt gushiness. She almost threw up into her own mouth.

Reilly wondered how they could stand each other. Their show of adoration was a contrived façade, she was sure. The confusing thing was that they acted no different when the cameras weren't on them. When the producer had brought her by their dressing room when she arrived on set before the show, she had heard them talking to each other as she neared their open door. Her blood sugar had spiked just hearing the saccharine banter. Maybe it was real. Who was she to judge? It didn't matter. It made her nauseous.

At the same time, Reilly knew that Melinda knew exactly what team Reilly batted for. When Melinda wasn't with her husband, she was a different woman. She was smart and engaging. She was funny and had something to say.

Reilly discovered the real Melinda Powers when she sat next to her at a celebrity fundraiser for breast cancer research a few months earlier. As they had waited for the tardy keynote speaker to arrive, they had sat shoulder-to-shoulder at the head table in the fancy ballroom, and Melinda had pointed out each woman in the room and asked Reilly which ones she was attracted to. Reilly had had just enough mimosas to go along with the little game, and she hadn't thought of it since. Until that moment.

Reilly blamed her mother for the media's fascination with her sexuality. Her mother/manager forbade Reilly from confirming or denying it "on the record," and insisted that Reilly accompany her male co-stars to most events, even while the paparazzi snapped pictures of her dancing the night away with her girlfriend. It was an elaborate ruse to keep the public guessing. If it were up to Reilly, she'd be one hundred percent out of the closet. It was who she was. Who she had always known she was. But, Reilly's mother knew a promotional angle when she saw one, and she played the game in a very deliberate way to draw and attract the widest swath of audience.

Autopilot on, Reilly bantered with her hosts and held her sighs of pent up resentment inside.

It wasn't like the world would ever know the real her, anyway. Even if she were the straight, girl-next-door box office cutie everyone wanted her to be. The world saw her the way they wanted to see her, and her mother tugged her puppet strings. It was the way it was, and it worked. Still, it pissed Reilly off. Especially when she had to act the coquette with a plastic tool like Tristan Powers. She hated that the game dictated that she laugh at his ridiculous, and often hurtful, jokes alongside his Harvard-educated wife, who dumbed herself down just for ratings on national television.

She forced her attention back to the interview. Tristan's eyes were locked on her and she could feel him winding up for a fastball.

"We've watched you grow up on our televisions, and now on the big screen. You were our little sister, our daughter, our best friend down the street. We saw you crying when you accepted your Academy Award seven years ago at the young age of sixteen, and soon we'll be seeing you salsa dancing across the silver screen with who *People Magazine* named the Sexiest Man Alive, Cray Layton—the man whom all of the magazines say you've been dating." As Tristan spoke, pictures of Reilly at various stages in her career, culminating in one of her and Cray walking hand-in-hand into the Beverly Hills Hotel, flashed up on the screen behind their chairs. "Then we see pictures in the tabloids of you getting cozy with women at dance clubs." A picture of Reilly and Sylvie dancing extremely close to one another at the club a few nights ago replaced the one of her and Cray, and Reilly held back a smile. "Forgive my directness, but I feel like we know each other well enough for me to ask this: Does it bother you that people wonder about what happens behind your bedroom door, Reilly? Do you see why they're confused?" asked Tristan.

Reilly was used to the questions. It didn't mean she liked them, though. A handful of morning interviews didn't mean she owed Tristan a damn thing.

"It isn't nice to gossip about people, Tristan," purred Reilly, smooth as a pro, and hoping that he saw the warning behind her smiling eyes. If he did, he didn't show it.

"It's in all the magazines, Reilly," laughed Tristan. He leaned forward and patted her leg. "Pictures of you with other women. You have to agree. You don't fit the lesbian description." He glanced at his wife, who gazed back with a vapid smile. "Tell her, Mel."

Tristan encouraged his co-host with a grin, looking for agreement. The two of them had been on the air for almost two decades as the most popular morning show hosts in television history. Hosting *The Morning Show* since the late nineties, America loved them. And Reilly hated them. At least she hated Tristan. She felt sorry for Melinda. She kept her smile pasted to her face as she watched Melinda try to figure out a way to respond.

"Oh, Tristan! Stop already. You're stereotyping," laughed Melinda, apparently trying to ease the moment. Reilly was surprised that Melinda had said anything at all.

"If it's a stereotype, well, you can just call me guilty. You're too pretty to be gay, I'm just saying," whined Tristan, ignoring Melinda's attempt at steering him away from the topic, and facing Reilly with a cheesy white smile. Reilly's irritation rose to a peak at Tristan's treatment of his wife, while Reilly could feel all the housewives in America nod their heads at once.

"Considering that you're my alternative, Tristan," she said between her teeth, and she stood up, pulled the microphone clip from the front of her shirt. She stepped around the coffee table that stood between her and her hosts, took a surprised Melinda's hand, and tugged her up from her seat. She then grabbed the sides of Melinda's face, feeling the thick makeup slide beneath her palms, and kissed her right on the mouth. She lingered there, teasing Melinda's astonished lips, and pressed her breasts against her for a long, drawn out moment. Melinda's eyes were like saucers when Reilly backed away. Reilly mouthed the word "sorry" with her back to the cameras, before she turned to Tristan with a shit-eating grin.

"Suck on that, Tris, my man," she said as she leaned into a smiling double-bird salute directed right at him. "Suck on that!"

Her heart rate, which had shot up during the minutes on stage, started to go down, and the tension in her head eased. The smile on her face as she left the stage was genuine and she felt worlds lighter.

There was going to be some fallout from that little stunt, she knew. Her mother would have a coronary, for sure. At the least, she'd never be invited back to *The Morning Show*. But it had been so worth it. Who cared if it lost her the Academy Award? She already had one.

And maybe it would shut her mother up for a little while.

Hope Comes in Unlikely Packages

REILLY SCANNED FOR PARKING ON the street in front of her favorite Starbucks in West Hollywood. Her head was pounding and she was desperate for a coffee fix, but the line for the drive-thru was a mile long and she was in a hurry. She had already made a pass through the tiny parking lot behind the café, and there was nothing available, but incredible luck provided her with a car pulling away from the curb right in front of the coffee shop, and she pulled out of the lot and slipped right into the prime spot. She parked her white BMW X6, got out during a break in the heavy Sunset Boulevard lunchtime traffic, and mounted the curb near the front bumper of her car, stepping around a homeless man sleeping between a plastic pamphlet dispenser and a blue mailbox near the edge of the sidewalk. She took two more steps and then stopped. Backtracking to the curb, she took a twenty out of her pocket—the only cash that she had on her—and slipped it into one of the man's shoes, which were lined up side-by-side next to his head. His face was buried in a military surplus sleeping bag that featured an incongruous dancing Snoopy iron-on, but the tips of his fingers rested on the toes of the shoes. She had no doubt that he'd wake up if someone tried to take the worn-out boots. She wished that she had more on her to give. Not wanting to disturb him, she moved away and crossed the sidewalk in search of caffeine.

The day had opened with a rough start. After three hours of sleep, she had been awakened at the ass-crack of noon by a call from her agent, Trip, who had somehow booked her on *Ellen*. Someone had cancelled, or Ellen had nixed someone—she couldn't remember, but a slot had opened up, and they had called wanting her. The hitch was that she had to come down that day. If it had been Leno or Dave, she would have told them to fuck off, but Ellen had always believed in her and had booked her before she was big. Reilly really liked her, so she lurched out of bed, showered, grabbed her stuff, and jumped into her car. She had just enough time to pick up a coffee on the way. She didn't want to be late, but no one wanted to deal with her when she was un-caffeinated. Besides, she knew that they'd wait for her. She was the reigning golden girl of Hollywood.

She could smell the tantalizing rich smell of coffee beckoning to her before she opened the door. When Reilly entered, the line was almost to the door, though. She almost turned to leave, but a dark-haired woman waiting in line near the counter caught her eye.

Drew.

She could only see her from the back, but the long black hair and height were just as she remembered. The slight lean in her stance was what gave her away.

Reilly joined the line and watched the woman, seven people away, willing her to turn.

Reilly felt the skin of her palms begin to itch. It was a feeling she knew well, though never in this kind of situation. She felt it when standing behind a curtain that was about to rise, it happened at the start of every new project, and she expected it when she performed live before a group of people. She couldn't help but rub her hands against her thighs, as she stood in the line watching the back of Drew's head. She never got the itch over a woman—at least that kind of itch, the higher itch that signaled fear, and not the lower itch that signaled prey. Women didn't make her nervous like that. But Drew did.

Reilly took a step forward as the line shrank. She watched Drew order, mesmerized. Reilly wanted to dash forward and pay for Drew's order, make her presence known by the gallant gesture. But she was struck motionless, tied in place with unfamiliar ropes of uncertainty. She thought back to the night at the dance club, when she and Sylvie had acted so crass, so entitled, so sure that they could have her. She'd had no problems then. She had put her hand on Drew's face like she had no boundaries, like she owned the right to touch a stranger without permission. The heat of embarrassment spread across her face. The short talk that they had in the alley should have eased the feeling. Hadn't Drew accepted her apology?

But then she thought of the kiss. Her shame paled at the sudden body memory of the surge of energy that she had felt as their lips had brushed. She remembered smelling cinnamon.

Reilly stepped forward again. Her eyes never left Drew's back. She'd hoped that Drew would turn to face her once she moved to the counter to await her order, but without so much as a glance Reilly's way, Drew went over to the nearby newspaper rack to study the headlines. An impatient tap of Drew's foot made Reilly pause. It was so discordant with the graceful peace that Drew had worn even when faced with the predatory mating dance of two stoned women in a dance club bathroom.

A touch on Reilly's shoulder surprised her. Reilly turned to face one of the baristas.

"Your order is ready," said the young woman with a shy smile. Reilly recognized her from her numerous trips to the coffee shop before. She wasn't surprised that they'd already made her coffee. She always ordered a non-fat vanilla latte. Half of the time, they had the drink already waiting when she got to the register.

"Thanks. I need to order another Venti house blend and a couple of blueberry muffins, too, if that's okay. Make that one blueberry and one orange-cranberry," said Reilly, backing toward the counter where the barista had pointed to her latte, already waiting. Steam rose in an inviting, thin stream from the drinking hole in the cap.

"No problem!" replied the cheery barista. Reilly watched her walk back to her post on the other side of the counter, where she poured the additional cup of coffee. She waved away Reilly's card when Reilly stepped up to the counter and held it out. "This one's on us, Ms. Ransome."

"Hey, thanks," said Reilly. The on-the-house thing wasn't a first, but she always felt grateful when it happened. She wished she had cash for a tip and made a mental note of the name on the barista's nametag, intent on doubling the tip the next time she came in.

Reilly took a few more steps toward the pick-up counter and her heartbeat increased when she saw Drew turn toward her at the same time. Before Drew had fully faced her, Reilly turned away and pretended that she hadn't yet seen her. She leaned over to take the two pastries and the second cup of coffee from the barista, and then turned back with a smile.

Reilly's heart dropped into her stomach. The woman with Drew's hair was not Drew at all. The woman wasn't even a woman, but a tall girl. Reilly couldn't have been more disappointed.

Deflated, she left the store and wondered what she would have done if it had been Drew. She realized that she had no idea.

She placed the extra coffee and the two muffins next to the man sleeping on the sidewalk and went to her car. A folded slip of paper was tucked into the rubber seal between the door and the driver's side window. Thinking it was the work of a roaming flyer dropper, she picked it out and got into her car. She had twenty minutes in which to make it over to Ellen's studio. Hoping for light traffic, she tossed the paper onto the passenger seat and started the car. The light behind her turned red and she merged into traffic. When she reached for the cup of coffee that she'd placed in the beverage holder in the center console, she saw the scrap of paper on the seat beside her. Writing in dark ink peeked from between the folds. Accustomed to random notes from fans, she wondered what it might say this time. Holding it against the steering wheel she read the scratchy words on the torn scrap of paper.

Hope comes in unlikely packages. God bless pretty lady. God Bless.

Reilly wasn't a believer one way or another, but she appreciated the intention of the note. The coffee and the bit of money she had given were a small price for the gift of hope.

Did We...?

REILLY ROLLED FROM HER STOMACH onto her back and moaned. Her mouth felt and tasted like the wet sludge under a leaking port o' potty. Something raked across her right eyeball when she tried to open her eyes. She rubbed at it, winced, and then peeled her false eyelash the rest of the way off. The relief was immediate, and she kept from rubbing anymore. She was just coherent enough—and, just recently, experienced enough with rough mornings after—to know that the glitter-infused eye shadow that she had not bothered to take off before going to bed the night before was still in place, and it would feel like sand if she smeared it into her eyes. She peeled the other eyelash off and squinted at the sunlight reflected onto the high bedroom ceiling.

Claustrophobic anxiety rushed into her amid the pillows piled around her head and the bedclothes that wound around her. With a frustrated groan, she kicked at the sheets to get some air. But the more she kicked, the more the sheets tangled around her legs. She reached down to remove them, but the motion inspired a throbbing pulse that shot a spear of fire through her temples and down the back of her neck. Her stomach churned.

"Sylvie. Move over. I can't get the sheets off," she whined, falling back into the suffocating mass of pillows, while she pushed against the leaden weight of the body that pressed along her side, trying to find some room. It was a fucking king-sized bed, why did she feel so crowded?

Defeated, she sighed. Something was always in the way. She closed her eyes and rubbed the base of her skull. Shit, her head hurt.

She couldn't remember much of the Academy dinner party that she and Sylvie had attended the night before. Billed as a party, the event had actually been work for her, and she had self-medicated in order to get through it. As a result,

21

most of the night was a blur to her that faded into a cold unknown blankness.

The press party that had preceded the event was clear in her mind. The studio car had dropped her and Cray off, and later, Sylvie had arrived with Reilly's best friend and first co-star, Hank in Reilly's private car. Reilly frowned at the memory of all the glad-handing and promotional activity she and Cray had submitted to, although Cray didn't seem to mind it at all. Pictures and autographs, smiles and name-dropping, hugs and air-kisses. She had posed for a thousand pictures, with more people than she would ever remember.

Reilly hated that part of her job more than anything else. More than the occasional over-exuberant fan, even more than the loss of anonymity. She hated making small talk and pretending to enjoy meeting and talking to total strangers as if she knew them. Trading inside jokes, enduring droll commentary, watching others pretend to be above what they were all there doing—it created a mass of poisonous resentment in her chest that grew and hardened throughout each event.

When she had first realized the resentment within her, it had been but a faint discomfort after the novelty of stardom had worn off. It had gone away as soon as whatever event she had been at was over. When she had first met Sylvie, it disappeared, and she enjoyed watching Sylvie's excitement about being a part of it. But in recent months the dark feeling had come back. It ebbed a bit between events, but resurged as soon as she attended another one. She knew that it would eventually consume her if she didn't learn to accept the parts of fame that flexed her comfort, but in the meantime, it was buried inside where only she knew it pulsed. No one seemed to suspect that it existed under her bright smiles and practiced warm eyes. As much as she hated some of it, work always came first.

When the dinner was over, and she had stayed more than was required to be considered a polite amount of time—after she had kept it to just one too many glasses of champagne—she had signaled to Hank and Sylvie that it was time to leave. Cray had left before Hank and Sylvie had even arrived, having another commitment that evening. Somehow their car was called, and she collapsed into the dark interior onto fine leather seats. Only then had she been able to breathe again. The plastered-on smile cracked away, and the tired muscles in her cheeks and jaw felt the relief of relaxation. She had been so glad to get out of there, just wanting to go home. But she had promised Hank that if he'd agree to be Sylvie's date, they would go out to a private dance party after the dinner. He hated the events. But he loved the parties. It was the least she could do to repay him for being Sylvie's beard, so she could be Cray's. Or was Cray her beard? It didn't matter. She didn't care.

She remembered arriving at an unassuming storefront on Wilshire Boulevard. The crowd had receded and the people stared as they got out of the car. The doorman had come out to meet them and had helped them cut through the waiting nobodies, had ushered them through the velvet rope and escorted them through the unadorned black metal doors that opened to a din of voices, dance music and laughter. As she passed the waiting crowd outside, an unfamiliar feeling of connection hit her. Instead of ignoring them, she smiled at the faces waiting in line, and the ghost of an idea occurred to her that there wasn't a whole lot of difference between them and her. She didn't have the time, nor the inclination, to explore that feeling, but as she passed, she took one woman's hand, helped her under the rope that separated them, and led her in, but she didn't remember seeing her again after they made it through the immediate press of bodies and into the less crowded roped-off section near the private back bar. She remembered dancing. But then the memory ended. She had no memory of how they had gotten home, let alone climbing into bed.

Head throbbing, she stopped trying to remember, removed the arm that she had draped over her eyes and squinted at the clock next to the bed. Almost noon. Depending on what time they had stumbled in, it meant that she may or may not have had enough sleep. If she had to guess by the lead in her bones, she hadn't had enough.

She felt worse than shit. She dropped a hand onto the sleeping form next to her.

"What time did we get home last night, Syl? I think we need to ease up on the partying," she groaned, as she tried to roll over and pull a pillow over her head. But her legs were still trapped and she couldn't move. Claustrophobia welled up again and she kicked her legs with a convulsive panic.

"I was wondering if you were ever going to get up today," said Sylvie from the doorway.

Surprised, Reilly peered between two pillows toward Sylvie's voice and saw her walking into the bedroom from the bathroom. She was in her bathrobe, fresh from the shower, holding a cup of steaming coffee.

Reilly pushed aside the pillows, clawed away the tangle of hair that was strewn across her face, and glanced at the sheet-covered form beside her. Then she turned to Sylvie.

"What the…? Who is…?" she said, struggling to sit up to gape at the stranger with Sylvie's hair lying next to her. It wasn't the one from the door line. The hair was all wrong.

"It's Parker, you goof," laughed Sylvie, tugging on a corner of the sheet, and in an instant Reilly was untangled. Sylvie sat down on the bed next to Reilly, who struggled to sit up. Sylvie took a sip of her coffee. The aroma made Reilly's stomach churn, and she clutched a pillow to her chest.

"Parker, as in Parker Stevens?" asked Reilly, knowing that there was no way that it was Parker lying in the bed next to her. No fucking way. They hated each other. Had always hated each other.

The feud had started over a decade earlier as a publicity campaign dreamed up by the studio that they had both worked for, though they had been starring in different shows. The campaign had placed the new child stars in a trumped up competitive spat for ratings sweeps. Reilly's show had catapulted her to stardom, while Parker's show had tanked. Since then, Reilly's star had kept rising and Parker had starred in a couple of forgettable movies and landed spots in a number of TV shows, most of which had silently sank after the pilot aired. Now, Parker, who had grown into a beautiful and charismatic woman, kept her career afloat by moving from one reality show to another.

No one had thought to make sure that the impressionable young women knew that the publicity spat was just that—publicity—and the feelings that had been manufactured for entertainment value somehow became part of their reality. Ten years later, the animosity was as much a part of Reilly as her ability to smile through an event that she'd rather skip.

Though Parker's star wasn't near as bright at Reilly's, she had managed to remain a part of the Hollywood scene and had built up a large, almost cultish following, and while Los Angeles was a large city, the entertainment industry was small enough that Reilly managed to run into her around town far more often than she would have liked. Having been the lucky one, and the one in a position of comfort, Reilly would have been happy to ignore her, but Parker couldn't seem to. She never let it drop. Any chance she had, she went out of her way to let everyone around them know about the bad blood between them. As a result, when Parker showed up somewhere, Reilly usually just left.

Apparently not last night, though. The hazy memory tried to elude her, but Reilly remembered running into Parker near the open bar at the dinner. They hadn't talked, but they had stood a foot apart, facing away from one another. Reilly had felt Parker's darkness behind her and she'd waited for the comments, the long glowering stares. But they never came. Parker had ignored her as Reilly waited for Sylvie to get her drink. That was all Reilly remembered. Even without Parker's usual antagonistic commentary, however, it was almost inconceivable that they would have interacted enough to have resulted in Parker sharing their bed.

Reilly shook her head, ignoring the way the motion made her brain feel like a sodden sponge that had been placed by mistake inside of a snow globe.

"No way."

"Yeah. Way. You two were like long lost best friends last night," said Sylvie with a mischievous expression on her face, reaching over Reilly to run her fingers down the side of the sleeping woman. The motion slid the sheet down, exposing more of Parker's bare skin. Parker arched into the touch and pulled the pillow off her head, but continued to sleep. All Reilly could see was a bare back and mussed up blond hair.

"No way," repeated Reilly in a whisper. She pushed her bed-mussed hair away from her face. The trapped feeling was back. Sylvie sat on one side of her, and their unexpected bed guest was pressed against the other.

"Way," repeated Sylvie with a sly smile and a slap on Reilly's foot.

"Did we…?"

"Kiss and make up?" asked Sylvie. Her eyes sparkled with suppressed entertainment over the rim of her raised coffee cup. Reilly wanted to punch her.

"Sylvie…" she said. She had to know.

"Yes. And then some."

Bile burned Reilly's throat.

"Did you initiate it, or…?" asked Reilly, unable to finish her question. Her eyes slid down the bare back and over the curve of naked hip that disappeared beneath the sheets. She thought of her own hands traveling those lines and dread spidered through her.

She imagined Sylvie casting her net over Parker in a dark corner of some club out of sheer mischief and wondered how Parker had fallen for it. Shit, she wondered, how *she* had fallen for it.

"Oh. That was all you, lover," said Sylvie with a wink, and Reilly's stomach turned over.

"Hank would have never let me—"

"Hanky took off right after midnight like his coach was about to turn back into a pumpkin," scoffed Sylvie, who had never even tried to hide her dislike of Hank. The feeling went both ways, but Hank was better at hiding it. Reilly had a hazy memory of trying to talk him into staying, but she didn't remember how it played out.

"Shit. That's it. I think I'm going to throw up," said Reilly, clawing at the sheets, kicking at Sylvie to move. She scrambled to get out of the bed.

"You seemed pretty into it last night," said Sylvie, standing up quickly, trying to keep her coffee from spilling.

"No, seriously," said Reilly kicking her legs. "I think I'm going to throw up. Help get these fucking sheets off of my legs!"

Reilly barely made it to the toilet before she expelled whatever was left in her stomach from the night before, which wasn't much. Actors never ate anything substantial in public. It was an unwritten rule. She heard voices in the other room. Great. Parker was awake and here she was puking up her guts like a teenager that couldn't hold her drink. At least she'd have an excuse for how the night had ended. Reilly spit the last of the bitter remnants into the bowl and shuffled to the shower.

Business Brunch 1

IT WAS BEFORE NOON, AND Reilly trailed her mother into Dwight's Deli, rubbing her temples and cursing the noise around her. The restaurant was a long-time local favorite for Reilly and, due to her frequent patronage, was now one of the current obsessions of the expanding group of trend-setting Hollywood foodies. All the publicity had even landed the chef her own show on the Food Network as well as the lead judge position on a reality show, where non-professional cooks vied over the course of a season for a chance at winning his or her own restaurant. Reservations at Dwight's were booked for months in advance. But there was always a table open for Reilly, and she and her mother were seated as soon as they arrived.

Reilly navigated the circuitous route behind the host toward their table, paying no mind to the curious eyes that watched her pass. She held onto a sigh and continued on when her mother stopped to say hello to a man with an impeccable beard and meticulous clothing that was chosen to convey a casual appearance. Hipsters repulsed her, and feeling the residual effects from the hangover that had kept her on her knees for much of the day before—not to mention the shock over whom she had found snoring beside her—she just didn't have it in her to engage in vapid small talk.

She took her seat and accepted the menu that the host offered her, wishing that she were still home in bed. Alone. As much as Reilly loved Dwight's, she resented her mother's insistence on meeting there. When Reilly had suggested meeting at one of their houses, her mother, who was also her manager, had reminded her that they weren't going out for a casual mother-daughter brunch. It was their weekly business meeting. And as usual, her mother had her promotional hat on. Reilly was out to be seen.

Reilly hadn't been able to summon the energy to protest.

She slumped low in her chair and opened the menu. Her mother, a moment behind, sat down across from Reilly, and shot her a look that Reilly felt rather than saw. Reilly sat up, just managing to not roll her eyes. She pushed her tousled hair away from her face and tucked it behind her ears.

"Really, Reilly. You could at least try to be friendlier—and a little more careful with your appearance. Someday a role might depend on Ron's input, and it wouldn't do for him to remember the day that you walked right by him without stopping to say hello. At sixteen you can get away with it. At twenty-three you don't get many do-overs, even if you do have an Academy Award and another on the way."

"You're going to jinx me if you keep talking that way."

"That's where you're wrong. The law of positive attraction works. Think it, and it shall become," said her mother with a sage lift of her eyebrow.

Reilly just nodded and studied her menu. She wanted to believe her mother, but she wasn't in any mood to acknowledge it.

Although they sat in the shade of an awning, Reilly was grateful that she had remembered her sunglasses. The sun was bright and high. A gentle breeze kept her cool, and the scent of honeysuckle arrangements on the surrounding tables masked the smell of baking cement. It was another gorgeous Southern California day. Even through her annoyance at having to be there, Reilly could take pleasure in the dependable beauty of the region found all around her. It was something that she kept to herself. She didn't want to give her mother the satisfaction of knowing that the meeting wasn't a complete inconvenience to her.

The erratic SoCal topography contributed to the non-linear road layout of towns located in the hillier regions and often resulted in an eclectic display of architecture. Dwight's Deli was one of the more prominent examples of that brand of unique design. Located on the corner of two streets that come together at the base of a hill to form a raised pie-wedge lot in downtown Hollywood, the small restaurant featured a glassed-in, wrap-around dining deck, much of which could be seen from the street below. With interesting walls and the strategic placement of potted plants, each table provided the impression of seclusion; celebrities could be seen but were well out of the reach of over-eager fans.

Reilly and her mother sat and studied the menu without talking. It didn't matter that they always ordered the same thing. It was part of their routine, and it eased them into talk of business.

They were a striking set. Reilly's appearance had been inherited mostly from her mother, and side-by-side, to any casual observer, they resembled the before and after picture of a beautiful woman in an age-defying makeup advertisement. It was in the unconscious grace of her gestures that Reilly took after her father, whereas Melissa planned every one of her movements.

"The pomegranate mimosas sound good," said Melissa, dropping her menu to respond to a text message on her phone. She gave the impression that she was the wired-in celebrity manager that she was.

Reilly studied her mother and wished, not for the first time, that Melissa were just her mother. She wanted to throw the phone over the edge of the deck.

"I'll just stick with water," said Reilly, subduing the urge to fling the phone. She dropped her head and rubbed her temples. She debated whether she should forgo her usual egg white omelet for plain toast. She desperately needed the protein, but her stomach was protesting the mere thought of anything but water.

"Nonsense, Rye. Brunch isn't the same without a mimosa or a Bloody Mary," laughed Melissa, putting her phone down after keying in a short reply to the text. She cast a meaningful glance at Reilly's hand on her head. "Feeling a little green today, are you? Did you go out last night?"

"No. We stayed in. At least I did. I'm still feeling the effects of the press party dinner from Friday night," admitted Reilly, brushing her fingers through her hair.

"You don't get hangovers, darling. Are you sure you aren't coming down with something?"

"Yeah. I'm sure," said Reilly. She raised her head and smiled at the trace of concern in her mother's voice. It was something that she hadn't heard in a very long time.

Her smile faded when her mother started in on business.

"Good, because you need to be in top form and stay visible until after the awards. A nomination is money in the bank and sets you up for the best projects. A win is that, times ten. So you have to stay out there and keep your name on everyone's lists. We can't have you holing up in your house, or letting your appearance go. Let's schedule a cleanse with that spa up on La Brea. You need to stay healthy for at least the next six weeks. And I'll line up some handsome men to escort you to some of the events. In fact," said Melissa, picking up her phone again and swiping to reveal a page on her calendar app, "I have your schedule lined up for the next few weeks. We need to get a hold of Cray or Zac's people. Hank, if neither of them is available, though he's a very last choice since no one remembers him anymore. He is a pretty face, though. I really want Cray, since everyone thinks you two are an item."

Reilly slid down in her chair and watched the cars drive up the hill, away from the restaurant, zoning out as her mom continued to discuss her suffocating schedule. When the waiter arrived, she didn't say anything as her mother ordered for both of them, including the mimosas. Reilly felt acid fill her stomach just thinking about it. Between her nervousness about the award and her partying, her stomach was a mess.

Her mother recited appointment after appointment as the waiter brought their drinks. Reilly wanted to ask for coffee, but her mother waved him away before she had a chance to ask.

"You know what they say, a little of the hair of the dog," said Melissa with a smile, as she exchanged her phone for a glass and tapped her champagne flute to the rim of Reilly's. Melissa's eyes scanned the area around them to see who was watching.

Reilly raised her glass in a dutiful toast but put it back down without taking a drink. The moment reminded her of too many times when her mother had made them mimosas the morning after a night of partying. It had been a while since Melissa had gone out with Reilly, though. She had stopped accompanying Reilly to clubs after a series of tabloid headlines declared Melissa Ransome the Worst Mother of the Year, in response to a picture of a then sixteen-year-old Reilly passed out against her mother's shoulder. The photo was just a terrible picture taken out of context. Reilly had been mid-laugh, and the shot had just caught her with her eyes closed. But the truth was that they had both been drunk, and with the bright light of judgment shined square in her face, Melissa had decided that her participation in Reilly's life had to appear more responsible—at least to the public. Since then, Melissa had worked hard to regain a more appropriate reputation, and Reilly had been subjected to her mother's constant criticism. In some ways, she missed those old days.

Melissa had never explicitly explained it to Reilly, but Reilly knew that a big part of the image that her mother tried to promote was one of Reilly as the consummate party-girl. It was that image that kept Reilly in the spotlight, even when she was between films, like she was now. As long as it didn't impact the quality of her work, affect her appearance, or lower her box-office standings, Mellissa encouraged the behavior and was gratified when it made headlines. And because it gave her freedom, Reilly exploited her mother's business strategy.

So when Reilly had snuck away to go to nightclubs with her older, more famous friends when she was just sixteen, it had surprised her that her mother hadn't confronted her when the pictures appeared in the papers. Her mother reacted with appropriate motherly concern when asked about her daughter's behavior by the press, but in private, she had ignored it. Her father had had some things to say about it at first. But even he stopped when her mother continued with a nonchalant attitude. At first it vexed Reilly. Part of her still wanted her parents to set the boundaries. But when her mother had flipped her lid over a picture that had shown Reilly with a cigarette dangling from her mouth, she finally realized that there were boundaries—inconsistent and quite often arbitrary—but boundaries, nonetheless. Drinking and partying were okay with her mother, but the smoking wasn't. It took a while for Reilly to realize the method to her mother's madness. The party girl reputation was news worthy and her mother turned a blind eye to certain behaviors in order to get the free publicity. Drinking was scandalous, but newsworthy, smoking was ugly and not newsworthy. It would have been easier for Reilly if her mother had spelled it all out for her. It was several years later that it dawned on Reilly, that talking about it would have underscored the hypocrisy.

Then there was the lesbian thing.

"Is Cray excited about going with you to the awards ceremony, darling?" asked Melissa. She sipped her mimosa as she asked the not-so-innocent question. Her eyes made another sweep of the area around them.

Melissa never could turn a blind eye to Reilly's romantic life. Although Melissa refused to acknowledge it in public, many a private battle had been fought over that subject. Even when the conjecture over Reilly's sex life became a huge magazine seller, Melissa hadn't let up. So, Reilly had learned not to bring it up and not to respond when her mother did. And while the struggle over it had subsided a little over the years, as long as Reilly made occasional public appearances with a handsome man by her side, Melissa kept her displeasure with her daughter's lifestyle at a low simmer. When Reilly had agreed to go to the awards ceremony with Cray, who also needed a cover, the nagging over Reilly's relationship with Sylvie had stopped—until the incident at *The Morning Show*.

Reilly sighed and spun her spoon on the tabletop a few times before she responded.

"Mom," she warned, knowing exactly why her mother was bringing it up. Her mother's passive aggressive game playing never ceased to push her buttons.

"Don't get upset at me, darling. You know that I'm just thinking about your career. Somebody needs to think about it. After that stunt you played on *The Morning Show* with Melinda Powers…"

And there it was. Reilly knew that she'd never hear the end of the kiss, and she hadn't. Her mother brought it up every time they met.

Reilly knew that she should let go. It had been so long since she had engaged with her mother on the topic. All she knew was that she couldn't let it drop one more time.

"I already play along with your little games, Mom. You don't need to rub it in."

"I'm not rubbing—"

"You know you are," Reilly interrupted. "And you know that who I take to the awards ceremony won't make a bit of difference to my career."

"You're delusional if you believe that, Reilly," responded Melissa. She put her mimosa down and scanned the room to see if anyone was listening to their disagreement.

"I'm not discussing this with you, Mom," said Reilly. Her mother had always tried to make her objections to Reilly's sexuality seem like concern over preserving her daughter's career, but Reilly knew that it was something far more insidious. And she had no intention of giving her mother an opportunity to pretend that it was anything else.

"I'm just trying to remind you—"

"Not now," said Reilly, surprising herself with the finality she heard in her own voice.

The waiter, who had stood a discreet distance away during the quiet, but intense interaction, took the pause as an opportunity to deliver their food. Mother and daughter sat in silence as their plates were set in front of them.

When the waiter left, Reilly concentrated on her omelet, though she wasn't the least bit hungry. They sat in tenuous silence, picking at their food. Neither wanted to be the one to back down or to light a fuse.

Melissa was the one to finally break the silence. She always was.

"I saw something interesting on the way over here today."

Reilly knew that her mother's tone could go either way, and she was wary. She watched as her mother scooped up a small forkful of the food and ate it as if it were the most delicious morsel she had ever tasted.

Reilly pushed a piece of omelet around her plate and tried not to show emotion one way or another.

"Oh yeah?" she asked. Melissa didn't do small talk during their meetings. It was always work, and when she used the word *interesting*, it usually meant that she wasn't happy about something that Reilly had done. Reilly scanned her memory for what it might be. There was a smorgasbord of possibilities.

"It's certainly something I never thought that I'd see in my lifetime," Melissa intoned dryly. She put down her fork and lifted her Gucci messenger bag into her lap.

Reilly's curiosity was piqued, and she braced herself for round two.

Melissa pushed her plate away, pulled a stack of trade papers and magazines out of her bag, and started to leaf through them. She invested a small fortune on celebrity papers and magazines and spent a good portion of time searching on-line, tracking any and all mention of Reilly, in an effort to stay on top of rumors, stories, and publicity opportunities. A one-time computer illiterate, Melissa had become a search engine expert. If Reilly's name appeared in any context, Melissa would find it. If she hadn't been Reilly's manager, she would have made a great private investigator.

Happy to leave that part of her career to her mother, Reilly usually tried to stay away from gossip about herself. She had learned long ago that respectful reporting didn't sell, and truth held no commerce for the publications that bartered in the fame game. Reilly was pretty good at ignoring the unflattering things she heard about herself, but sometimes things got under her skin, and she ended up expending unnecessary emotional energy on them, even when she knew they weren't true or were taken out of context. So, for the most part, she let her mother handle that aspect of her career. Her mother told her what she needed to know and silently kept tabs on the rest.

Reilly took a sip of the mimosa that she didn't want and impatiently watched her mother thumb through paper. With a grimace, she pushed the bubbly drink aside, as well. She signaled to a passing waiter to bring her some coffee, hoping against hope that she'd be able to drink it.

Finally, Melissa found the trade paper she was looking for—Reilly noted that it was on the top of the stack—and she held it so Reilly could see the front page. On it was a picture of Reilly and Parker standing next to each other with drinks in their hands. Parker had her arm looped through Reilly's. An innocuous picture. Hardly worth her mother's declaration of interesting.

Except that Melissa capitalized on the bad blood between the two women when there was a lull in promotional opportunities.

"When did this happen? It's all over the place. Not the headlines. But pretty much everywhere. I took one day off from the internet and I get treated to this," said Melissa. She dropped it on the table and pushed it toward Reilly.

"We sort of buried the hatchet the night of the press thing. Don't ask me how it happened," said Reilly, downing half of her mimosa before reaching for the paper.

She lowered her sunglasses to study the picture. It didn't appear altered. She didn't even know why she searched for the signs that it had been. After all, Parker had been in her bed the next morning, real as life. There was no doubt about that. Reilly still had some interesting marks etched on her body as reminders. Her clothes may have still been in place, but she knew that she'd had sex that night when she went to take a shower the next morning. Thank god that Parker had been gone by the time she'd finished her shower.

Reilly remembered how relieved she had been to see the empty bed as she'd emerged from the bathroom, but it had left a host of unanswered questions. And a lot of conflicting emotions. A roll in the sack didn't just erase years of vicious animosity. For a second she wondered how the sex had been, and then, like she had every time the thought had crossed her mind, she pushed it away. The knowledge that she had lost time made her crazy, but not knowing some of the details was a relief.

"The tension between you two has always been a good thing to spike interest when you're between projects," mused Melissa, confirming Reilly's suspicion for her mother's focus on the subject. She could see the cogs spinning in her mother's head as she tried to see how to use the new development.

"It's not like Parker and I are now BFF's, Mom," said Reilly, deliberate in her use of the adolescent slang to irritate her mother. She suppressed a smile when she saw her mother's eyes narrow. "We managed to get along for one night. Who knows how things will go from there?"

"Well, forgiveness is a good thing. It saved your dad's and my marriage after that little fling he had with that intern at his firm years ago." Reilly knew that her mother hadn't forgiven him. She had held it over his head for the past fifteen years. But Reilly wasn't about to bring that up. She and her mother never spoke about anything that really mattered. "At least it isn't another picture of you with that Sylvie creature," said Melissa, signaling for another round of mimosas, though Reilly hadn't even finished her first one.

Her mother's comment about Sylvie was filed away for later. Reilly inspected the picture again. She and Parker were almost back-to-back. Parker was laughing with someone out of the frame, and Reilly could see that her own eyes were vacant and her smile was forced. The picture didn't indicate that they were on their way to waking up in bed together the next morning.

It didn't seem possible to make the leap from battlefield to bed in just one night. She wished that she could remember how it had happened.

St. Bart's

"GOD, I'M SO GLAD WE decided to come down here, Syl. I so needed this,"
said Reilly as she sprawled out on the towel-covered beach lounge next to her
sunbathing lover. She shook out her long blond hair, playfully spraying Sylvie
with salt water. Sylvie laughed and threw a fruit rind at Reilly from the drink she
was sipping.

The conversation with her mother on Sunday had exhausted Reilly, and after
an afternoon spent stewing over it, in a moment of spontaneity, she had decided
to take a mini-vacation. Now, they were relaxing on a white sand beach at a private resort in St. Bart's after having flown in the day before. With no eyes on her
and no pressure from agents, directors, or managers, Reilly couldn't remember a
time when she had felt so carefree. Ever.

She settled into her chair and let the fragrant, tropical breeze dry her skin
and hair. At home she wouldn't have dared let her hair air-dry in public, but on
the private beach she didn't care. She had just come in from the water, and the
gentle waves and warm water still called to her, but even with the most effective
sunblock, her pale flesh burned if she wasn't careful, so she had to monitor her
time out in the sun. And even though she tried to tune it out, her mother's voice
whispered cautions about leathery skin and premature wrinkles.

"You mean that you're glad that *you* decided to come down here. This had
nothing to do with me. I'm still shocked, babe," said Sylvie, slurping down the
rest of the rum and coconut concoction she held in one hand.

"You didn't have to come if you didn't want to, Syl," said Reilly. Something
in Sylvie's response put her off. It wasn't unlike Sylvie, who had a tendency to
go along with things and then complain about them. But Reilly had hoped that
Sylvie, of all people, would support her need to escape.

"It was such a spur-of-the-moment idea, that's all. Plus I'll get to hear you bitch about your mother's reaction for the next month. Not to mention that it was tough to reschedule my caseload. That's all. I'm not complaining!"

Reilly watched Sylvie out of the corner of her eye. Sylvie was little more than a figurehead at her firm, lining up work for the other attorneys at the entertainment law firm. She worked cases, but as the primary partner, her main focus was to bring the business in and take the big cases. Right now she was between clients. A few days off wasn't a hardship for her.

"Good. Because this is just what I needed, I think," said Reilly, stretching out on the lounge with a sigh.

Sylvie put down her Kindle and flagged down one of the hovering attendants to order another drink. Reilly cringed at the condescending tone in Sylvie's voice as she also had him adjust the umbrella to move the shade over Reilly's chair and ask for a few more towels.

"Are you sure you don't want to try one of these coconut rum things, babe?" asked Sylvie, setting down her empty next to her chair. "They're so yummy."

"Ugh. Pass," frowned Reilly, as she settled back into her chair and closed her eyes. "I'm sticking to juice and water on this vacation. My body needs a serious detox."

Sylvie took the new drink that appeared as if by magic beside her.

"I hope that doesn't mean *all* fun is out. The bellman said he can hook us up with party favors. I'll need them when we go dancing tonight," said Sylvie, lowering her glasses to peer over the top of them at Reilly for emphasis on what she just said.

Reilly rolled her eyes at Sylvie and then shut them again, slinging an arm over her face. Her gums tingled at the suggestion of cocaine.

"I might take a pass on that too, babe," said Reilly, debating whether she'd just do one or the other. Maybe if she just stopped drinking for a while it would be enough to avoid the more frequent bouts of lost time that she was starting to experience. She watched from beneath her arm to see Sylvie's reaction at her statement.

"Dancing or the blow?" asked Sylvie. She lowered her drink along with her sunglasses to favor Reilly with an expression as if she had just said that she was thinking about marrying one of the monkeys that ran wild around the resort.

"Both maybe," replied Reilly. She lowered her arm and gave Sylvie a look that said *deal with it*, although in her head she was pissed by the doubtful expression on Sylvie's face. "I kinda like being chill."

"Well, I'm sure I can find someone to play with tonight if you pull an old lady on me," said Sylvie. Her words sounded casual, but Reilly heard the challenge in them.

"I'm sure you can," said Reilly, and she swallowed back a pang of resentment. She knew that Sylvie would have no trouble rustling up company if Reilly didn't go out with her. And, to be honest, Reilly really didn't care if she did. But Reilly was irritated that Sylvie couldn't summon up just a little support for her need to get away from all of that for a while.

Back to Reality

REILLY FASTENED HER SEATBELT AND accepted the cranberry juice that the flight attendant in first class held out to her. She took the copy of the *Celebrity Rag* she had picked up at the airport at St. Bart's out of her bag and laid it across her lap. Though she usually let her mother watch the press about her, she didn't like going too long without at least checking in. The magazine she held was exactly what it marketed itself to be—a rag. But it was the only one the small airport carried. She'd never admit it, but she was a little starstruck when it came to some celebrities, too.

Last week's *Rag* had featured her on the cover after the Academy Award nomination. In the current edition, she had a small teaser picture in the corner of the cover, which showed her in a beach chaise. It was a strange feeling. The resort had felt private, and she hadn't seen anyone taking photos of her, yet there she was. The sand was barely rinsed from her feet and the pictures of her frolicking on the beach in her bikini were already circulating.

She studied herself in the tiny photo. Thankfully, she wasn't too critical about her body. Her mother had been good to her in that regard, encouraging a healthy self image—at least as far as her physical attributes went. She still worked hard to keep a toned body, though, and it didn't hurt that good genes had provided her with nice curves and full breasts that she didn't have to buy. But it was hard to pull off wearing a bikini when you didn't tan. The color and the background had to be just right to make skin as pale as hers photograph well. She was pleased that the photographer had captured her in a flattering light.

Something wasn't right though, and she examined the photo closer. It took a minute for her to realize what it was, but then she noticed that she was holding one of the coconut drinks that Sylvie had liked so much, complete with a straw and umbrella sticking out of the top. Several empties were on the sand around her. The picture suggested that she had been on a coconut-rum binge.

"Sheez! I never touched one of those vile concoctions while we were there. Though you certainly drank enough of them," said Reilly, teasing Sylvie, who was nursing a pretty severe hangover. She inspected the pictures. "They aren't even trying very hard to pretend that these pictures aren't doctored," she said, flipping to the pages where they showed more pictures of her lying in the sun and walking on the beach. Each and every one had her holding a drink of some sort in her hand. Her mother would be proud. "Sylvie, check this out. They just cut and pasted that there. I think I was holding my Kindle before they added the drink. This one's not too bad, but you can see the shadow on my thigh is different than the beer bottle they put in there."

"You sound shocked."

"These people are professionals. That's shoddy work. They should take their craft more seriously."

"I can't believe you just said that," said Sylvie without opening her eyes. Her head was leaned back against the headrest and she didn't move her head. "The media likes their party girl. Besides it could have been worse."

Reilly laughed, and Sylvie peeked out of the corner of one eye at her with a raised eyebrow.

"You are so right," Reilly snickered. Their sex life had always been good, but the tropical surroundings had brought out a streak of adventure in both of them. She smiled as she remembered the hammock on their private patio where they had taken a nap and woken up to have sex. And the quickie that they had snuck away for among the banana plants while walking on the beach one evening. And the one time they had done it standing up against the trunk of a frangipani tree. Sylvie had even taken her in the center bathroom stall of the bathroom off of the main restaurant. Reilly laughed when she remembered Sylvie putting her hand over Reilly's mouth as someone entered the bathroom just as she came.

"Uh-huh," nodded Sylvie watching Reilly's face, with a knowing smile. "It could have been worse. At least they aren't saying you have a baby bump."

"That's true," laughed Reilly, as she flipped through the pictures again.

Sylvie leaned her seat further back and closed her eyes. "Now let me sleep. Have I told you that I hate it when I have a hangover and you don't?"

"Welcome to my life, Sylvie, welcome to my life."

So Much for the Detox

"SO MUCH FOR THE DETOX," sighed Reilly, as she took one of the shot glasses from the tray the server brought to their table. She had already tossed back two shots of Patrón Silver and the backs of her knees were feeling the warm tingle that always crept up on her when she was on her way to getting buzzed off of hard liquor.

"Hey, you managed five days," said Sylvie, holding her shot glass up in the way of a cheer before she tossed the clear liquid back and put the glass down on the bar. "And what can you expect right now? Everyone wants to celebrate your nomination. You'd have to lock yourself away for the next couple of weeks to avoid it."

Sylvie bit into a lime slice and tossed it on the bar behind her.

"My mom would kill me if I decided to go on the wagon right before the awards," said Reilly, accepting a drink from another waiter who pointed to a dark-haired woman across the room. Reilly smiled and raised her glass in thanks to the woman who returned the salute and smiled back. The woman reminded her of Drew. She wished it were.

Where had that come from? She never daydreamed about women like that, especially women she didn't know. She shook her head to clear her thoughts and tried to pick up the thread of discussion she and Sylvie were having.

"She has commanded me to hit every A-list event that I get invited to. Do you know how many parties that is?"

"Poor baby. So many people love you. Don't pretend that you don't like it," said Sylvie, turning to see who Reilly had been smiling at. "She's a cutie. Wanna see if she wants to play?"

"Nah. Too nice," said Reilly, laughing at the glint of challenge that brightened

Sylvie's eyes at the comment. Sylvie was on the prowl and the woman had been marked. "Seriously. Not her. We can corrupt someone else tonight. Anyway, it's not that I'm not flattered and it's not that I don't like going to all of the parties." She narrowed her eyes at the unwanted vision that appeared behind the woman who'd sent her the drink. "It's just that I could do without some of the bullshit."

Parker stood about ten feet behind the dark-haired woman. Reilly hadn't talked to Parker since that night when they were supposed to have buried the hatchet and she didn't remember any of it. She didn't know how to feel. She couldn't seem to summon the feelings that a truce should have elicited, let alone anything like the ones she should have for someone she'd had sex with. There was no denying that Parker was gorgeous, but thoughts of exchanging bodily fluids with her made Reilly feel a little sick.

"Like what?" asked Sylvie.

"What?" asked Reilly, confused. She had lost track of the conversation. Parker had stopped to talk to the woman who had sent her the drink. A flare of irritation warmed Reilly, even though she'd never even met the dark-haired beauty. She felt like going over to warn her.

"What bullshit could you do without?" repeated Sylvie, with an impatient sigh.

"Oh… the predators that lurk among us," responded Reilly, knowing that she sounded vague. She watched Parker flirt with the dark-haired woman across the room.

"That's rich," said Sylvie. "Seeing as you like to hunt as much as I do. Come on. I see Parker. Let's get her and hit the dance floor. It appears that she's helped us do some of the reconnaissance work with your admirer."

Reilly finished her drink and signaled for another shot from their waiter as she rose and followed Sylvie to the other side of the bar. All of her dark thoughts were gone by the time they hit the floor and she had the dark-haired cutie pressed against her front and Sylvie draped across her back in a techno grind.

Santa Monica Pier - Take 1

"…THE FUCK OFF ME!" said Reilly, rolling away and slapping at the hands that were grabbing at her. Her head pounded and her back was killing her. Where the fuck was she? And who the fuck was touching her?

The light around her was too bright to open her eyes, but from the noise and scents around her, she thought that she might be outside. That couldn't be right. She put her hands over her face and peered through the cracks.

She was at the beach.

The sun was just coming up and she was lying on a bench. Ocean air had settled on her in a thin layer of dampness, making her feel heavy. She swung her legs over and sat up. Someone with unfamiliar hands was trying to help her up. She couldn't focus clearly enough to see who it was and she batted the hands away. A dark blur was all she could take in and she blinked her eyes and tried to get used to the sunlight. Various parts of her body protested the movement. The worst was her pounding head. Whoever was with her finally took a step back. She surveyed the area around her. There, several feet away, was her car, parked across three spaces in the otherwise empty pay lot.

She recognized her surroundings. She was at the Santa Monica Pier. Her hands steadied her on the worn bench beneath her. The grain was smoothed by use and so many seasons in the sun, but she could still see her name, faint but legible, carved by her into the wood more than a decade earlier. Her fingers traced the mark that she had made so long ago. A family outing. Cotton candy. Happy times. It seemed like another person's memory.

"Ma'am. Are you all right?"

Reilly roused herself from the past. A police officer stood beside the bench, a cautious foot or two away. The officer seemed relaxed, but Reilly noted that her hand rested on the Taser strapped to her belt. Was the cop really afraid of her?

"Just peachy," mumbled Reilly, having a hard time keeping her eyes open, and not just because of the light. She was tired. She felt it in her bones. The contents of her stomach churned, chasing some of the sleepiness away. She was disoriented and fear started to creep over her. The fact that she had just woken up outside with no memory of getting there sank in.

"That your car over there? The white one?" asked the officer. The officer used her elbow to indicate Reilly's white BMW with the driver's side door standing wide open.

It was the only car in the lot.

"Yes," said Reilly, fighting back the fog that muddled her mind.

"Did you drive it here?"

"Not that I can remember," replied Reilly. It was the truth.

"Well, it's parked in a pay lot without a permit, not to mention that the lot is closed from midnight to 5:00 AM." The officer studied Reilly for a moment, sizing up the situation. "Because I didn't see you in it, or it parked there before 5:00 AM, I won't haul you in on a DUI or cite you for being there during the off hours, but I'm going to have to ticket you for not paying for the three spaces you're taking up."

"I'll just move it," suggested Reilly. She was feeling a little put off by the officer's attitude. Did she seriously think Reilly would be grateful for the slap on the wrist?

"You get behind that wheel, and I'll have to take you in for driving under the influence," replied the officer, shifting her weight across her feet.

Reilly rolled her eyes.

"Could you just move it then?"

Reilly felt in her pocket for her keys.

When the police officer didn't respond, she glanced up. The stare that met her eyes exuded an air of cold regard, and Reilly knew that she had said the wrong thing. Even though her head hurt like a motherfucker, her stomach was threatening to revolt and she was feeling the spins like she might still be a little drunk, she was smart enough—and scared enough—to know when to kiss a little ass.

"Never mind, officer. That was stupid of me to ask. I'll be happy to accept the parking tickets." Reilly leaned back on the bench and closed her eyes. This was so fucked up. And she was so tired. The steady rhythm of the waves rushing up onto the sand was lulling her to…

"You can't sleep here," said the officer, cutting through the encroaching velvet that was falling behind Reilly's eyelids. Reilly sat up with weary deliberation. Tired as she was, she didn't want to sleep at the beach. "Is there someone you can call?"

She was surprised to find that her cell phone, identification, and cash were still tucked away in the pocket of the light jacket she was wearing. With a great effort toward concentration, she called a cab. She couldn't call her driver, Alison. She didn't want anyone she cared about to see her like this.

While the officer finished writing up the tickets, she contemplated her car, which, she realized, was still running. She tried to remember how she had ended up at the beach. Her complete loss of time scared the hell of out of her. A list of terrible things that could have happened streamed through her mind. She scanned her surroundings again. There was no one near, except a motionless mound under an army green sleeping bag that rested in the crease between the sidewalk and a cinderblock wall housing two battered trash bins about fifty yards away. Two shoes were lined up next to the covered head of the bag's inhabitant.

When the cab arrived, the officer retrieved the keys from the ignition of her car and shut the door. She didn't say anything to Reilly as she handed her the key ring, but Reilly could see the reproach in the officer's eyes. Embarrassed and chastised, she talked the cab driver into repositioning her car, which she'd have to arrange to get later on, and then she got into the cab.

Fighting a migraine on her way back to her house, Reilly attempted to focus on the screen of her phone as she checked to see if Sylvie had called her or left any messages. There was nothing. Worried, she dialed Sylvie's number. It went straight to voicemail.

Her phone signaled a received text message and she squinted to see Hank's name before she opened it. A photo taken while it was still dark filled her screen and she was surprised to see a picture of her sprawled across the bench the night before. It accompanied a short article that she couldn't read in the taxi without getting even sicker. A cold shiver ran through her, caused only in part by the nausea. She shuddered to think of how long she had been on the bench and who had been skulking around her unconscious form. She was lucky that she hadn't been robbed… or worse. The vultures in the celebrity press were a secondary thought.

On the verge of vomiting, Reilly paid the cab driver when they got to her house. Her access card let her in through the locked gate and she took a few deep breaths as she walked down the long driveway to her house. The walking helped clear her head a little.

She used her keys to let herself in. Her house was quiet and dark when she entered. The pleasant scent from the giant floral arrangement in the middle of the foyer enfolded her, and some of the rigid stress in her shoulders melted away, though she was still wound up tight. She resolved to tell Camille, her live-in housekeeper, how much she appreciated the flowers. Aside from them, the house lacked life even when she was in it, she realized. It was a sterile monolith without a heart. In some respects, Camille had an easy job, since Reilly was rarely home, but Reilly wasn't an easy person to live with when she was, so she didn't envy the woman's life. She'd tell her thanks for the flowers and give her a bonus.

Clutching her cell phone, she headed to her room. The trip up the stairs took an extreme effort, as weariness settled deep into her bones without warning after the first few steps. At the top, she paused and leaned against the railing to regain her strength, and then dragged herself down the hall to her room where the promise of feather pillows called to her. When she entered the room, the neatly made bed confirmed that Sylvie hadn't been there the previous night. Irritation clenched Reilly's jaw.

She had no recollection of the last evening beyond when she and Sylvie had left the first bar, on the way to another party. Parker and Natalie, the dark-haired women from the first bar, had been with them. She had a hazy memory of a short squabble with Sylvie before they got into the car. The others were already waiting inside. It seemed that it had been over Parker and the way she had been hanging all over Natalie. She didn't know why that would upset her. Maybe it had escalated after she had gone past the point of no return with the drinking, where fights never seem to have a real reason. Had they even gone to the other party? Reilly didn't remember ever getting into her car. She wondered how she had gotten to the beach and where the others had gone. Sylvie had probably gone back to her own seldom-used apartment.

Her cell phone rang. She answered it without looking at the screen to see who it was. It better be Sylvie and she better have an excellent apology ready.

"Where the fuck did you go last night?"

She leaned her shoulder on the doorjamb and waited for Sylvie to respond.

"Um," replied a familiar male voice. "You're okay."

"Hank?"

"Yeah. You were expecting Sylvie, weren't you?"

"Yeah."

"And you're angry about the picture in the trades this morning, aren't you?"

"Sounds like you saw it," said Reilly. "Wouldn't you be?"

"Yep. I gotta say, even for you I'm shocked. I was thumbing through the feeds on my iPad while waiting for my venti, skinny, quad vanilla latte and, bam, there you were. My sleeping beauty. I'm glad that your mouth wasn't hanging open."

"God," moaned Reilly, pressing her forehead to the cool, white wood in the doorframe.

"Is it at least a good story?" asked Hank.

"I wish I could remember."

"Seriously?"

"Yes. Seriously. I think I blacked out. Don't tell anyone, okay?"

"From your lips to my ears, no farther. You know that."

Reilly did know that, and it made her feel better to be able to take for granted that at least one constant in her life wasn't either fucked up or spiraling away from her. She loved her best friend for understanding when she needed him most.

"Why don't we meet up this afternoon? I'll tell you everything I can remember. But right now I think I need to lie down."

"I'll bring miso to your house at three-ish. How's that sound?"

"Perfect. You are my prince, you know that, right?"

"I know. I know. You owe me."

"I'll do anything for your miso. Later, skater."

Feeling a little better after talking with Hank, Reilly pushed off from the doorway and unbuttoned her pants with clumsy fingers. She let them slide down her hips, walked out of them, stumbling slightly in an unusual display of clumsiness, and kicked them away as she approached her bed. She was desperate to lie down. The heavy drape of sleep pulled at her. But her irritation at Sylvie—for not being there, for not watching out for her, for letting her pass out on a bench at the end of a night in which they should have gone home together—kept her drooping eyelids from making the final descent, even as she dropped like a rock onto the bed. Her mind was foggy but still racing, refusing to process that for the second time in as many weeks she had blacked out. So, instead of sinking into sleep, her thoughts chewed away at her irritation at Sylvie, and she leaned against the headboard and pounded a pillow into place behind her.

She checked her phone for messages. Still, there were none. She threw her phone down on the bed beside her and reached for the laptop that sat on the bedside table. She rested the computer on her lap and logged on before she picked up her phone again. She hit the speed dial reserved for Sylvie. As her Mac booted up, she listened to the phone at the other end of the call ring into voicemail. She hung up and hit the redial button rather than leaving a message and repeated the action several more times as she browsed the internet. She sighed as the calls she made to Sylvie continued to fall into voicemail, and she found what she was hunting for on her computer.

She could always count on Randy Candy's celebrity gossip site. There she was, amid the garish gifs and obscene use of too many fonts. In all her glory. Passed out on the bench with the lights of the Santa Monica pier twinkling in the background. The photo had been taken hours earlier, when the moon was still hanging low in the cobalt sky and casting a reflected swath of incandescence across the calm surface of the ocean behind the pier. She looked like she was relaxing. The scene was rather beautiful, if you didn't know that Reilly was passed out cold. And in case the reader didn't come to that conclusion on his or her own, Randy had captioned the picture "Reilly Ripped!!!!"

Her head throbbed as Sylvie's phone rang several more times and then dropped into voicemail again. She still didn't leave a message. She just ended the call, pushed her laptop onto the bed beside her, and succumbed to the nothingness of sleep.

I'm Not Your Mother

THE NEXT NIGHT, IGNORING HER aching head and roiling stomach, Reilly slid her laptop onto the bed beside her and sat up when Sylvie walked into the bedroom. Exhibiting poise that cost her more than she'd admit, she crossed her arms over her chest and flipped her hair away from her face. She hoped the look on her face told Sylvie that she'd fucked up and had some major explaining to do. Instead, Sylvie exuded her own displeasure, which just made Reilly's anger over Sylvie's disappearing act on Friday reassert itself with vigor. It felt like a stand-off and Reilly didn't know if she had the stamina to withstand it, let alone win.

"So, you've been here all weekend?" demanded Sylvie.

"As if you give a shit. Where were you Saturday morning? Where were you when I called? Where do you get off coming in here all pissed off?" Reilly responded. The feeling of abandonment that she had woken with on the bench erupted into a full-blown fury. She'd expected Sylvie to cower under her wrath, not come in spitting fire.

She was wrong.

"After your tantrum outside of the club, I have every reason to be pissed off."

Sylvie stopped at the side of the bed and regarded Reilly with a critical stare. The information was new, but Reilly was still too angry to be intimidated. She waved an impatient hand.

"What are you talking about?"

"I'm talking about you accusing Parker of being a predatory slut."

"What? Besides, who cares? She is." It felt good saying it out loud. She didn't like Sylvie's new friendship with Parker and now she was even more pissed off that Sylvie seemed to be aligning with the interloper.

"Oh, you don't remember the hissy fit that you threw after you found Parker kissing Natalie in the bathroom? You practically chased them out of the club."

Reilly didn't want to admit to the total lack of memory she had of the night.

"Who the hell is Natalie and why would I care who Parker fucks?"

"You sure did then. You pulled them apart and told Natalie to escape. Except you kept calling her Drew."

"I have no memory of this."

"You were blotto. That's the only reason I came over here. I turned off my cell and was going to wait for you to come over to my place to apologize. But after not hearing from you for two days, I came over here tonight to make sure that you weren't dead."

"Oh, after two fucking days, you decide to check on me? I'm the one who should be waiting for the apology. I was wasted and you let me drive away! For all you know I really was dead."

"You're twenty-three. I'm not your mother. When you refused to go to the next club with us, I told the valet not to give you your keys. I called the cab myself."

"Well, somehow, I ended up driving to Santa Monica that night. Haven't you seen the papers?"

Reilly saw something pass over Sylvie's face and she hoped that she had finally succeeded in making her feel bad. The response that came was not what she hoped for.

"I have better things to do than keep up with the banal details of Hollywood's finest," said Sylvie dismissively.

Reilly was beyond pissed by Sylvie's casual disregard of the frightening events that had shaken her so badly. Reilly knew that Sylvie wasn't completely to blame, but she wanted her to at least acknowledge some part in it.

"I woke up on a bench. Outside. At the beach!" screamed Reilly, hearing her voice growing shriller but unable to control it. "The fucking, goddamned beach, Syl! Anything could have happened to me out there! I count on you to make sure that I don't do stupid shit like that. I count on you to protect me from fans, from the press, hell, even from myself!"

Sylvie stared at Reilly with a strange blank expression that Reilly couldn't decipher.

"How is that my job?"

Reilly gaped at Sylvie. She would have understood if Sylvie's response had been angry or defensive. But the apathy was a surprise.

"It's how it's always been with us. You can't go changing the rules without telling me!"

Reilly heard the out-of-control tone to her voice and knew the words coming out of her mouth were juvenile, but she wasn't about to back down.

Sylvie crossed her arms over her chest.

"Oh, I see. So I'm the bad guy? Next thing you'll be saying is that I ruined Valentine's Day."

"Valentine's Day? What the fuck does that have to do with anything?"

"It was yesterday."

Reilly was confused. "We've never celebrated it before."

"Exactly my point. We never talked about not celebrating Valentine's Day. We simply never have. We never talked about your expectation that I watch out for you, either. But I always have. Maybe I'm tired of unexpressed expectations."

What the hell was Sylvie getting at? Reilly felt like she was being mind-fucked by a prosecuting attorney in a high-profile court setting. In a way, she was. She hated it when Sylvie acted like a lawyer with her during arguments. Reilly wanted to kick her.

"Whatever. You let me take off when I was in no shape to be left alone."

"I didn't want to leave you, but you refused to stay with us. I did the only thing I could. I left you with a valet. He was supposed to put you in a cab. Maybe I should have insisted you go with us. Or maybe I should have stayed with you, but I was over arguing about it."

Sylvie sounded tired.

Reilly was tired, too. And the yelling match wasn't getting anywhere, so she offered a branch. She sighed and ran her hands through her hair. "I guess we both fucked up, then."

"Yeah. I guess so," said Sylvie. The fire left her eyes. She sat down on the edge of the bed. Reilly figured that they'd made some headway, since she no longer wanted to kick her.

"So…"

"I'll have that valet fired for letting you drive away."

Sylvie's declaration made her feel better, but she didn't want anyone else to suffer the fallout of her issues.

"I guess it's not his job to babysit fucked up actresses."

Sylvie rested her hand on Reilly's comforter-covered leg. The heat of her hand helped Reilly let go of more of her anger.

"You still feel like shit?"

Reilly remembered the headache that she couldn't shake, and it started to pound in her skull with a vengeance. She rubbed her temples.

"I do. I was camped by the toilet for most of yesterday."

"Want me to call Hank?"

"He already brought me some of his magical miso."

"Well, I'm here now. Let me take care of you," said Sylvie, unwinding her scarf and kicking off her shoes.

"Thanks, Syl. Sorry I'm such a bitch."

"It comes with the territory, love."

Business Brunch 2

IT WAS UNCHARACTERISTIC AND UNINTENTIONAL of Reilly to be
early, but she was—thanks to the unusually light late morning traffic in North
Hollywood. Ignoring the valet, Reilly parked her car and waited across the street
from the Ova Café on Santa Monica Boulevard. Although the restaurant catered
to celebrities, she was reluctant to arrive before the person she was meeting
because it would be more difficult to ignore fans who might approach her while
she was waiting. She had a reputation for being very gracious with her fans, but
it always took a large amount of energy. So she waited in her car and watched the
front entrance.

She didn't have to wait long before she saw her mother enter the sleek
building. Unlike her, her mother was always early, a habit that Reilly assumed
was acquired just so her mother would have one more thing to complain about
when Reilly showed up later than her. She should have gone to meet her mother,
but she sat and watched her disappear into the restaurant and emerge a moment
later on the patio following a host.

From her car, Reilly observed her mother's social façade with an unexpected
resentment. Taller than Reilly and confident, she strode among the outdoor tables, chin up, shoulders back. She nodded and smiled at one table but didn't stop.
Even if the people seated at the tables she passed through didn't recognize her,
her mother definitely put off an impression that she was *someone*. Reilly watched
as heads moved together and eyes followed, while her mother pretended not to
notice. It was a performance, but it was subtle. A soft smile. A tilt of the chin.
A shake of the head. A scan of the area to see if anyone else of importance was
already there. Reilly hated the feeling that welled up in her as she watched her
mother. She didn't want to feel this way. She wanted to let it go. But she couldn't.

Her mother followed the host across the café's sunlit patio. She fluffed her coifed hair and ran her manicured hands down the front of her tailored blouse as she waited for the host to pull out a chair at *the* table. The owner of the Ova Café kept staff out in front to deter autograph seekers, but anyone with a decent camera phone could take a picture of the people who sat at that table. It was expected. It was where celebrities went to be seen without being approached. The food was good, but it felt like work to dine there. And it was.

Reilly hated the meetings, but today she dreaded the topic that was certain to be at the top of her mother's agenda: the incident at the pier. So she sat in her car and put off going in. Although they'd discussed some of it after her mother had called her screaming the day the photo had come out, Reilly hadn't told her mother the whole story. How terrified she'd been when she woke up on the bench, still half-drunk and with no memory of anything that had happened the night before. Even after Sylvie had tried to bump her memory, she remembered nothing after the first line of coke and the first shots of tequila. Instead, she had told her mother that she had gone to the pier to sit on the bench to think and had just fallen asleep. Her mother, of all people, should have understood that.

The Santa Monica Pier had always been the one place in Reilly's life where she felt safe and whole. When she had been a little girl, it was where her parents had gone to celebrate life's little moments, so it was the setting of many of Reilly's favorite memories. The pier had started its long run as "their place" when her father had proposed to her mother there. The photo that her parents took that day still hung in the family room, and in it, they were young and blissful, the rides at the end of the pier filling the background with a testament to their joy and happiness as they smiled into one another's eyes. Right next to that photo on the wall was a picture of them in the same spot, this time with Reilly, who was then four years old. Her mother and father looked like they still loved each other, and Reilly remembered how happy and secure she had felt standing between her parents on that sunny day.

Since then, the pier had become the destination for all celebrations, small and large. Reilly remembered how they had gone there after her first day in kindergarten, and the day that she had lost her first tooth. They had visited it every time friends or relatives had come to town. And the last time they had gone to the pier as a family was the day that she found that she had won the role of Dusty in the television show that had made her star rise like a firework.

After the television series, though, they couldn't go there without being mobbed. The show had been an instant hit, and so had Reilly. Now, Reilly was confined to sneaking down to the pier at night, when people were less likely to recognize her.

The days since, of spinning the pier incident into a photo taken out of context, had taken more emotional energy than she had to spare, and she was tired. Reilly pulled off her glasses and threw them onto the seat next to her. She shut her eyes, blew out a breath, and steeled herself for the meeting. Her fingers clutched and unclutched the steering wheel in front of her as she tried to imagine floating in the warm water at St. Bart's. She conjured the gentle rhythm of the undulating water buoying her prone body, the sun's heat prickling her skin. Minutes passed. The meditation helped. Peace hadn't suddenly descended upon her, but she did feel calmer. She opened her eyes and took a few deep breaths. She pulled a tube of mascara out of the Hermès bag on the seat next to her and applied some to her already thick lashes. Then she applied a light coat of lipstick and ran her hands through her hair before she put her sunglasses back on and opened the car door. She'd get through this meeting.

Moments later, Reilly followed the host to the table where her mother sat scanning the menu.

"I thought you might have beat me here today. Isn't that your car across the street?" Her mother lowered the menu and tilted her head toward the street. No complaints for keeping her waiting. No accusing stare. A first.

"Phone call," lied Reilly, grateful for the dark tinted windows on her car. She felt eyes from the other diners on her. If her mother confronted her, they'd be seen by anyone who was watching. "I was hoping to sit inside today. I'd rather eat where it's quieter."

"Nonsense. Did you see that Anne Hathaway is here?" Reilly had seen Anne in the restaurant. They'd exchanged smiles and waves. Reilly nodded and her mother continued. "I'm glad she isn't in the running this year."

Reilly was relieved not to be going against Anne, too. Despite knowing other-wise, Reilly wondered if she'd only won the first Academy Award just because the competition had been weak that year.

"It's so nice outside. Besides, you need a little *normal* publicity after that vagrancy thing earlier this week," whispered Melissa. The sunlight was bright on the patio, and she cast a glance at Reilly while lowering the sunglasses that she had earlier pushed to the top of her head. Some of the calm that Reilly had pulled together fled.

"Vagrancy?" asked Reilly, trying to keep her expression mild, while yanking her own chair out with a little more aggression than she had intended. "Seriously, mom? If you can't even back me up, who can I rely on? You know that photo was taken out of context, just like everything else said about me in the media. You know I go there to think."

"I know that, honey," said Melissa, using an endearment that Reilly hadn't heard in a very long time. Her mother reached across the small table to pat her arm, making Reilly feel guilty for not telling her the truth. "That's just what the papers called it. I won't say it again. Now stop frowning before the lines become permanent."

The shred of warmth that had started to grow in Reilly at the endearment evaporated.

"I feel like a Bloody Mary, how about you, darling?" asked her mother, setting aside the leather-bound menus. Here, too, they knew the bill of fare by heart.

"I think I'll stick with water today," said Reilly without picking up her own menu. She didn't feel like a drink. She would have the Southwestern omelet, just like she always did.

"Oh, come on, darling. I don't get out as much as you do. Have a drink with me."

"I just don't feel like it," said Reilly. She wished that she could talk to her mother about the blackouts and how scared she was that her life was spiraling out of control. But they didn't have that kind of relationship. That knowledge, though always there, darkened her mood even more. Surprised, Reilly felt angry tears rise within her. She stared at the drink menu willing the tears to go away. The anger she could handle.

"Someone call the press, my daughter is passing up a drink!" laughed Melissa. Reilly rolled her eyes at the joke that wasn't really a joke. "Next thing, you'll be telling me that you aren't a lesbian anymore."

Reilly knew the last comment was more hope than humor, a topic of contention between them older than any other argument. It stoked her anger and she was able to stuff down the tears. She was back to familiar territory that she could navigate with ease.

"Nope. Still a homo, Mom," said Reilly. Her mother's comment pissed her off more than usual, but she refused to be baited. Melissa had gotten pregnant with Reilly at the height of her own sitcom stardom and had somehow linked the risk that she perceived from Reilly's lesbianism with her own thwarted acting career. Reilly would forever be making up for it. Her current stardom and being on the brink of a second Academy Award didn't seem to earn her any slack. And being aware of it didn't make her resentment go away, either. Reilly had too much going on to deal with any of that so she let it drop.

"So, what are your plans for the weekend?" Melissa asked with practiced innocence. Reilly wanted to scream. Her mother knew full well that the upcoming weekend was the Academy Awards. Melissa herself had planned out Reilly's every waking minute between now and the night of the show, down to wardrobe changes and bathroom breaks.

"Cofton Hughes gave Sylvie and me his house up in Big Bear this weekend. I thought that Sylvie and I could do some snowboarding to take the edge off before the ceremony. We'll be back in time for the show, though," said Reilly with a straight face. She thanked the waiter and accepted the Bloody Mary that her mother had ordered for her, despite her opposition, and took a sip. She watched her mother's face over the rim of her glass. The reaction was immediate, and Reilly got a sick satisfaction from her mother's anger.

"You most certainly will *not* go snowboarding this weekend," demanded Melissa. She put down her drink and stabbed at the table with her manicured finger. "I've gone to too much trouble assuring that you were invited to all of the important events. Did you get the list I emailed to you? I filtered through at least a hundred pre-parties and cut it down to a dozen, the first of which are tonight. Then there are three events after the show, where it is *critical* that you appear. Mitzi has your dresses ready, except for the diamond inlaid Gino Tivati that you'll wear for your acceptance speech at the actual show. And Liz and Doltz are on for makeup and hair—"

Reilly couldn't hold her laughter any longer. Her mother sat back and glanced around them. People at nearby tables turned their heads back to their meals. Melissa dropped her hands into her lap, leaned forward again, and lowered her voice to a harsh whisper.

"That was not funny, Reilly Tatum Ransome!"

"It was so easy, though," Reilly laughed. Tears formed in her eyes. She was on the edge of a manic laughing fit but most of the anxiety that had burned in the center of her back for most of the morning started to fade. "You should have seen your face!"

"You're terrible!" said her mother. Reilly gasped for breath and willed the muscles in her face to resume their normal expression as she watched her mother's eyes roam the area, noting who might be watching. The display didn't irritate her like it had earlier.

She sat up and cleared her throat, trying not to laugh. Back to business.

"I have the lists, and the tailored outfits came two days ago, along with the jewelry. Everything fits and Liz and I have settled on the hairstyle. We'll be hitting up the parties you lined up for me starting tonight. But don't talk like that. Like I've already won. That's bad luck. Besides, it would be greedy of me to win again. Someone else should get a chance," said Reilly through a smile, finally subduing the laughter. As tired as she already was from the excessive running around that she had been doing, the anticipation over the weekend's events, let alone the ceremony itself, had butterflies battering the lining of her stomach. And despite her words, Reilly wanted to win.

"You'll be the end of me, Reilly!" her mother said, with an arched brow and a half-smile as she lifted her Bloody Mary. "You are going to win. Just tell me that you won't be taking that Sylvie with you to any of the major events."

Reilly's laughter died immediately.

The Academy's Next Best Actress

"CHRIST! I CAN'T DO ANOTHER line tonight, Sylvie." Reilly shook her head back and handed Sylvie the glass tube that she had just used to bump her high.

Reilly's sinuses burned and she sniffed, hoping that the tickle she felt deep inside didn't mean that she was going to get a nosebleed. It had only happened to her once before, and it was after she had overdone it—much like she was on her way to doing that night. In a brief moment of clarity, she wondered why she did it at all. It didn't give her the same, sensual buzz that it had in the beginning, when she'd do a line and want to fuck all night long. Now, snorting coke was more like a super shot of caffeine that made her horny. She decided in that moment that she would cut down. She was serious this time. Really.

"More for me, then," said Sylvie, leaning over the dresser where the lines were laid out.

Though they could hear the party going on on the other side of the door, Reilly and Sylvie were alone in a guest bedroom at Cray's Mulholland Drive house. Getting ready to rejoin the party, Reilly performed a quick check in the enormous gilt mirror above the mahogany dresser, the sprawling canopied four-poster bed behind her reflected in the background. She couldn't do anything about the glittery, glassy eyes that stared back at her, but she wiped away a thin line of powder rimming one of her nostrils. Always hyper-vigilant of appearances, she vowed not to be the next starlet featured in the pubs under a headline that read "Rehab!" The bench incident had been bad enough, but she had explained that one away. The stories of overwork and exhaustion had worked like a charm.

Sylvie inhaled the last line and then moved behind Reilly to press up against her. She ran one of her hands along Reilly's ass, and slid the other through the slit opening of Reilly's dress that ended high on Reilly's thigh. Sylvie's fingers skimmed the edge of her thong, causing a pulse to ripple through Reilly's center.

"You seem tense. Maybe I can help take the edge off, lover."

Warm lips trailed up Reilly's neck.

"Later, Syl," she laughed and bumped Sylvie away. The contact made her nipples hard, but she wasn't in the mood.

"Come on, Rye. It's been over a week. Plus, I've done enough coke to give a whale perma-wood," whispered Sylvie into Reilly's ear, as she leaned into her, and then took Reilly's earlobe between her teeth. "I'll probably explode as soon as your lips wrap around my clit."

Reilly shivered from the vibration of Sylvie's deep voice and the warm mouth on her skin. The thought of her own mouth on Sylvie made her mouth water. Maybe she was in the mood. But she grabbed Sylvie's wrist just as fingers slid under the barely there thong she wore.

"I don't want to walk out of this room looking like I just got laid, Syl. The rag-trolls are out in force this weekend. I'm nervous enough as it is."

"They think that's what we're doing anyway," said Sylvie with a smirk, though she stepped away, smoothing her lipstick with a finger.

"I'll take care of you later, babe. Promise," said Reilly with a smile. She gave Sylvie a quick kiss and headed toward the door. She watched Sylvie wipe away the vestiges of dust they had left on the dresser and put the nearly empty vial back into her bag before she opened the door. She hoped that Sylvie didn't make her follow up on the promise. Reilly was still a little raw about Sylvie's absence the Saturday morning before, though Sylvie's side of the story had gone pretty much the way she had predicted. They had made up that night—kind of. Reilly still carried resentment, but she tried to put all of that behind her as they rejoined the party. She didn't want the negative attitude to affect the night's fun.

Back in the main rooms, where everything was well under way, Reilly and Sylvie pushed through the crowd to get to the bar, which was near doors that stood open into the backyard. Reilly took in the scene and let her eyes roam over the partygoers on the temporary dance floor installed over an elaborate flagstone deck. Next to it was a huge pool that had been covered with a thick floor of Plexiglas. Flowers and candles in clear bowls floated on the surface of the lit pool below. Strings of white lights had been strung across the yard, and footlights illuminated the tropical foliage that gave the yard a lush intimacy. Beyond the crowd, toward the back of the yard, a deck jutted out over the steep slope that fell away from the house. The lights of the valley shimmered below. The crowd was full of Hollywood's biggest players. Even Reilly was impressed with the star-studded view.

Reilly surveyed the crowd looking for Cray, but she didn't see him. Her eyes did land on someone else, though. Why was Parker suddenly everywhere she went?

"What's she doing here?" Reilly asked. She knew that she was supposed to have mended fences with Parker, but that was before the fight with Sylvie, and now her feelings were all over the place. Reilly was struggling to figure out what she was supposed to feel about Parker's presence just as Parker spotted them and headed their way.

"Who? Oh, Parker. Why wouldn't she be?" retorted Sylvie after following Reilly's gaze. Sylvie smiled and gave Parker a hug in greeting. Reilly wondered again when Parker and Sylvie had become so friendly.

Reilly knew Sylvie well enough to know that she wasn't applying the artificial sweetness that glazed most Hollywood greetings. She seemed genuine in her happiness to see Parker. Something about it rankled Reilly, but she tried not to let it show. The weekend was too important and busy for an argument. She filed the thought away with an internal reminder to confront Sylvie about it later.

She dragged her eyes off of the two women and was shocked to see someone else that she never expected to see there. Drew was standing right behind Parker, and her eyes were already on Reilly. A small smile played on Drew's mouth and Reilly's eyes moved to her lips. A memory of the light kiss she had given Drew in the bathroom filled her head and other parts of her anatomy. Her irritation and angry tension suddenly fled.

Reilly heard her name being called, and realized that she had been staring. She pulled herself from the hypnotic gaze with Drew and turned toward Sylvie, who was now beside her.

"Hmm?"

"What do you want to drink, Reilly?" repeated Sylvie. "Parker wants to do a shot to celebrate your nomination. Patrón? Sambuca? Both?"

Reilly tried to remember what Sylvie had just said when Drew stepped closer. An excited flutter filled her stomach. Drew was dressed in a long silk sheath dress with a plunging back. The dress fastened around Drew's neck accentuating the length of smooth skin that was exposed by an upswept hairstyle held by two chopsticks in the back of her head. Reilly admired her strong yet sensual shoulders and toned arms.

"Reilly? Drink? Patrón or Sambuca?" repeated Sylvie.

"Uh, I think I'll stick with the tequila. I'd like to at least try to avoid a headache tomorrow morning," replied Reilly, distracted. She really didn't want any more to drink. She wanted to stay sharp now that Drew was around. She'd do one more shot and that would be it.

Reilly's thoughts of Drew were interrupted when Parker's hand encircled her wrist.

"No kidding. I was a mess Saturday morning after all of us went dancing."

Parker laughed. She leaned toward Reilly and lowered her voice. "Hey, sorry about the drama last weekend. That was completely my fault. We haven't really talked about—stuff, and—well, I know that things are still sort of new for us."

Reilly glanced at Parker's hand. Although Parker sounded sincere, she wanted to step away and shake out of her grasp. She ignored the sense of distorted anger she felt and smiled back at Parker. She was an actress. She could fake it until she figured it all out. Besides, it seemed silly to perpetuate a feud that she had never been the one to fuel in the first place. They were adults now. Maybe it was time to bury the hatchet.

"No worries," she said to Parker. She was thankful when Parker let go of her wrist.

"Are you nervous about tomorrow? I'd be shitting bricks. But you're probably used to it, since this is the second one, right?"

"I'm pretty nervous," admitted Reilly. "I'm not sure if you can ever get used to being under this kind of spotlight."

"I'd like to give it a shot, though," laughed Parker. Reilly doubted Parker would ever be in the running for an Academy Award, but she was being petty and she held her tongue.

Sylvie moved closer to Drew, and Reilly lost track of what she and Parker were talking about.

"Drew, right?" asked Sylvie, fixing her sights on the beautiful black-haired woman who stood beside Parker. Reilly recognized the tractor beam intensity in Sylvie's stare, and an unfamiliar jealousy swept through her—and it wasn't over Sylvie. She watched Sylvie run her hand up Drew's bare arm in a re-enactment of their bathroom meeting. "I remember you. What's your pleasure?"

Drew ignored the innuendo, which pleased Reilly more than she would ever admit.

"Just soda water for me tonight. I'm the DD."

Her smile was polite, but not inviting.

"That's why God invented car services, Drew," coaxed Sylvie, circling a finger on Drew's bare shoulder.

Drew stepped away from Sylvie's touch and looked around as if she were looking for one of the wandering wait staff. Reilly hid a grin. She knew a practiced move to avoid unwanted attention when she saw one.

"Thanks anyway. I have a class to teach tomorrow morning. I'll stick with water tonight." Drew smiled and pointed to a waiter with bottles of water on his tray. Some of the tension inside of Reilly eased.

"Maybe I should stick with water, too. It seems to work for you," said Sylvie, glancing up and down Drew's tall frame. "It works very well."

"Jeez, Sylvie. Roll your tongue in," said Reilly, sidling up to Sylvie and pushing her toward the bar, embarrassed and irritated by the lascivious come on.

Parker punched Sylvie in the arm as they walked away, and Reilly lifted her eyebrows at Drew in an apology as she turned toward the bar and placed their order.

Reilly stood next to Sylvie and tried to control her vacillating emotions.

"Parker said she was going to bring a date, but I had no idea that she knew that beautiful creature," said Sylvie, as they waited for the shots.

"You knew Parker was coming?" asked Reilly, wondering when Sylvie had stopped being her protector. The old Sylvie would have warned her.

"Yeah. She told us both last weekend. Remember?"

Reilly had no memory of that, and Sylvie's tone indicated that Reilly should feel bad for doubting her.

"I must have forgotten."

"Sounds like we need to take another vacation when this craziness is over," Sylvie said with a hollow laugh. Sylvie signaled for the others to move over to the bar, and she distributed the shots that the bartender had lined up for them.

A few other people joined them, and the bartender poured more for them. Reilly watched Drew sip her water and wondered what the serene woman was like when she let her hair down.

"This is it for me tonight," said Reilly, lifting her shot glass at Sylvie's suggestion. "I mean it. Don't let me get stupid tonight."

"I'm not your conscience, Reilly. Besides, I'm not sure I'll be a suitable chaperone after a couple more of these," Sylvie smirked. Then she held her shot up and addressed the small circle of people that had gathered around them. "To Reilly! Here's to the Academy's next Best Actress!"

Reilly felt like the toast was for someone other than her, but she smiled and nodded with what she hoped was a graceful acceptance.

The small group tossed back their shots and then slammed their glasses down on the wooden bar.

"Yum!" declared Sylvie. "Now let's dance!"

The small group went outside to the dance floor.

As Reilly stepped onto the parquet surface, strong hands grasped her hips from behind and she was led with a rhythmic sway into the middle of the floor. Like a scene from a movie, the crowd parted, the first notes of a familiar song played, and confident arms pulled her back into a hard body. Reilly was loose from the tequila and amped from the coke. She eased into a slow grind with her dance partner, letting the music build. It felt easy and right, and she loved the feeling of the appreciative eyes on her.

She hoped that Drew was watching. A low thrum filled her belly thinking about Drew watching her dance.

"You ready for this, sexy lady?" asked the deep voice from behind her, and the song picked up the tempo.

"Bring it, hot daddy," she purred, and then she laughed as Cray pushed her away and then snapped her right back to him in the beginning of a spicy salsa.

They must have performed the dance a thousand times in rehearsals, and there were times that Reilly thought that she would scream rather than hear that song one more time. But tonight, when it was just for fun, she let her body respond and her feet do their thing. Gone was the cu-cum…pa, cu-cum…pa repetition of her dance coach's voice in her head. It was just she and Cray and the salsa beat. She let go.

The emerald green dress her mother had selected for that night was perfect for the dance. Simple, strapless, and light, with a slit that ran from foot to hip, showing flashes of her toned thigh and calf as she took the long graceful strides that embodied the sensual dance. The black suede heels with thin straps that wound around her calf could have been treacherous, had she not been forced to learn to move with practiced confidence in heels during her hours of rehearsal and training. She and Cray danced better than they ever had before. The music became part of them; the dance an extension of their sensuality, and all Reilly could think about was the silver-gray eyes that she felt watching her. She danced like she was showing Drew the secrets of her body.

When the song ended, she and Cray separated to a roar of applause and requests for another dance. But they knew to leave the crowd wanting more, and Cray made her promise to save another dance for him even as his eyes tracked a beautiful young man across the floor. He kissed her cheek and left.

With a smile, Reilly made her way to where she had left her friends, turning down a few requests to stay on the dance floor. The performance had filled her with a sense of anticipation that bordered on craving. Her eyes scanned the crowd for Drew, though she didn't know what she would do or say once she saw her. There seemed to be so much in the way. Still, Reilly's eyes sought her out.

She found Parker and Sylvie on the edge of the floor, dancing and laughing at a joke one of them had made. A shadow of disappointment fell over Reilly when Drew wasn't with them.

Then she saw her.

Drew danced near the middle of the floor, one of many on the crowded parquet, but alone, while Parker and Sylvie performed a racy grind several feet away. Reilly slowed her approach as her eyes slid over Drew, and she felt the music moving through Drew's body as if it were her own. Drew's eyes were closed, her arms were raised, and she swayed in sensuous rhythm. A small smile sculpted her mouth and Reilly once again remembered the kiss. Though no more than a brush of skin, it was still vivid in her memory, and she wondered how a real kiss would feel.

Reilly's fingers went to her lips and a buzz filled her from head to toe. Something more powerful than she had ever experienced pulled her to Drew.

Under normal circumstances, when another woman caught her eye, Reilly enlisted Sylvie's efforts to arrange for the woman to go home with them. Reilly would do more than just watch this time. The thought filled her with a restless ache as she watched Drew dance. But when Parker and Sylvie moved closer to Drew, who didn't seem to notice them, Reilly realized that she wanted Drew to herself.

That was a problem.

She and Sylvie were a couple, and they played as a couple, but it was part of their agreement that they wouldn't play on their own. Early in their relationship, after they both realized that they enjoyed the dynamic that other women brought to their sex life, Sylvie had made Reilly promise not to sleep with other women without her. Sylvie had said that she didn't like the thought of Reilly coming while another woman held her if she wasn't there to see it. Reilly had agreed to Sylvie's request, even though she didn't care if Sylvie had sex with other women, with or without her there. Just as long as Sylvie came home to her. Reilly knew that the agreement was unconventional, but she also knew that their relationship wasn't a forever thing.

So, feeling like a cheater, she stood in the crowd and watched. She had no idea how long Drew had been watching her in return, but when she realized that the silver-gray eyes were locked on hers, her body responded and she instantly forgot all of the things that had just gone through her mind. She found herself moving toward Drew. Without touching her, she began to dance with her. It was as if they had danced together a million times before. Reilly was so in tune with the energy emanating from Drew that she knew exactly where each part of Drew was in relation to her own. The awareness allowed them to move together in a seamless flow. Still, they didn't touch. There was nothing but the connection of their eyes and the music in their world, and Reilly let the sensation fill her up.

The music changed, but Reilly didn't notice until arms wrapped around her from behind, breaking through the trance that she was in. She kept dancing though, unwilling to break from the power of Drew's gaze. But when she saw hands wrap around Drew from behind, and Parker's face appeared over Drew's shoulder, Reilly felt the loss of connection like a cold stream of water, and she turned to face Sylvie. Containing her disappointment, she continued to dance, though she could barely feel the music anymore.

"That was hot, baby," purred Sylvie, nuzzling her ear. "I never get tired of watching you dance. Drew has some moves, too. I wonder…"

Reilly watched Drew over Sylvie's shoulder and was relieved to see Parker let go of her and walk toward them.

"Hey, Drew is going to head home. I'm going to walk her out, but I told her that you guys would take me home. Is that okay?" It was the first time that Reilly welcomed Parker's presence.

Then it hit her. Drew was going to leave.

"You can't talk her into staying?" asked Reilly.

Sylvie's eyebrow rose in a knowing smirk, and Reilly decided that she wanted Drew to leave rather than let Sylvie near her.

Parker rolled her eyes.

"I already tried. Apparently, she really does have a class tomorrow, and I want to cut loose tonight. She's a yoga instructor or something. I really don't know her very well. She did on-set yoga classes on a pilot I just shot and one of the producers who knows us both hooked us up. She's hot, but not my type, it turns out."

Reilly was glad to hear that last part.

"Well, I'm sure we could get her to loosen up a little," said Sylvie, and Reilly didn't like the reaction she had to Sylvie's insinuation. "Besides, Reilly has decided to go all old lady on us tonight. Maybe we can convince them both to cut loose."

"Let her go, Syl. I want to party after all. We don't need to have a sober judge watching over us," said Reilly.

Getting her party on was the last thing that she wanted, but Reilly would rather let Drew leave than watch Sylvie drool over her all night.

"Okay. We'll be by the bar when you get back," said Sylvie, with an impish smile, her scheming mind off of bedding Drew for the time being, which gave Reilly a measure of relief.

Reilly and Sylvie watched Parker escort Drew back into the house so that Parker could send her on her way. Reilly tried not to think about kisses goodbye.

"Hey, was that Parker Stevens?"

Reilly turned to Cray, who had come up behind them.

"Yes. As a matter of fact it was. Why did you invite her?" asked Reilly, turning to him. She didn't mean to sound shitty, but she was annoyed about the goodbye kisses that she didn't want to think about.

"I didn't. You hate her, and tonight is all about you, babe," said Cray, draping his arm around Reilly's shoulders and giving her a squeeze. "I just noticed that she's with my friend Drew. Drew's someone I've wanted to introduce you to for ages. I asked her to come to the party, but I didn't think she would. I never would have guessed she'd be with Parker."

"Why's that?" Reilly could guess, but she wanted to hear it from someone else.

"When you meet her, you'll know why."

Reilly didn't feel like explaining to Cray that she had already met Drew, but she was glad to hear Cray's assessment.

"I don't hate Parker. She just annoys me. If you didn't invite her, why is she here?"

Reilly thought it would be just like Parker to crash a party thrown for her.

"I invited her," said Sylvie, sounding irritated. "Jesus, what's the big fucking deal? You two made up. I'm going to get a drink."

Reilly watched Sylvie walk toward the bar and order another drink. She hated the confusion that filled her. She and Parker had allegedly made up, but it didn't feel like it. And Sylvie was so hot and cold all of a sudden that she couldn't keep track of the shifts. Reilly decided to let it go until after the award show the next day, and then she was going to have it out with her. Maybe it was time to move on.

Santa Monica Pier - Take 2

"HEY, LADY! WAKE UP!"

The voice came from a million miles away. Reilly recoiled from whatever, whoever it was that was grabbing at her, shaking her. She needed to protect herself, but she was trapped in a swamp and couldn't rise to the surface.

"Get off!" she moaned, struggling to breathe through the haze of pain threading through her brain. She wondered if she had even said it out loud. Or was it still queued up in the back of her throat, an echo of an idea that never left her head?

The groping hands shook her again. She reached out to slap at them, but her arms were too tired and leaden to obey her, and they fell back to her sides. She struggled to tear through the gauze of sleep, to chase the angry intruder away.

"Wake up!" The voice was louder and the hands were rougher.

"What?"

She managed to open her eyes, though her lids threatened to close with every long blink. It was dark. She was outside. And it was cold. Lights cut through the darkness. Busy people moved all around. She tried to sit up, failed, and then tried again. The man who had roused her pushed her into a seated position. She struggled with her legs, which were tangled in a sheath of fabric. Someone helped her to swing her legs down over the edge of the seat.

"I know. I know. Can't sleep here," she said through thick lips, grabbing the bench on either side of her legs to keep from tilting off.

The familiar sound of the ocean acted as a backdrop to her awakening and muted the noise of the people moving around her. An overwhelming sense of déjà vu enshrouded her. Was it a nightmare? She groaned and her teeth chattered in the frigid sea air. She was at the pier on the bench. Again. She closed her eyes.

The hands, warm against the night air, grabbed her again, jostled her shoulders.

"Ow! Leggo!" she tried to yell, but even through the fog of confusion, she could hear that the words were garbled and not very loud. Movement hurt her head. Her brain felt bruised in the tight confines of her skull. The fatigue that held her was like a rope net pulling her down. A terror over not being able to move tried to claim her, but it was chased away by the overwhelming need for sleep. She willed the nightmare fueled by bad memories to end. She reached for blankets but her arms were too tired.

"Lady! Open your damn eyes!"

It wasn't a dream. The hands were real.

She was able to get her eyes open, and this time, a police officer crouched in front of her, holding her shoulders, shaking her. She was sure that he'd start slapping her if she closed her eyes again, so she worked to keep them open.

"Stay right there," he said, and stood up to assess the activities behind him. He kept a hand on her shoulder to keep her from moving, but her body wouldn't have obeyed her if she tried to go anywhere.

A woman in a light blue uniform shirt and dark blue pants came over and draped a blanket over Reilly's bare shoulders. Shivering and scared, Reilly pulled it around herself, hoping to shrink away.

She tried to peer around the officer. There were several cars parked nearby and people milling about. The lights and movement around her reminded her of a night shoot on location.

A few feet away, through the space between the officer's legs, Reilly saw a pile of sheets. There were several people standing around them. She realized the rhythmic strobe lights were from emergency vehicles, and that most of the people around her were officers and firemen. The flash of cameras pierced her brain as a man with a professional-looking camera circled a concrete parking pylon and snapped pictures, not of her, but something behind the officer in front of her.

Something very wrong was going on. She tried to stand.

"What happened?" she asked.

"Sit down, ma'am," said the officer, who was still standing in front of her. His hand remained on her shoulder, and it was enough to keep her seated.

"Tell me what's going on. Is Sylvie okay?" she asked. Her tongue was thick, but as if a switch had been flipped, she was hyper-aware of everything around her.

She watched two paramedics lift the sheet onto a gurney and realized that there was a person under it. A tennis shoe lay on its side where the sheet had been. A dark puddle flowed from the concrete structure and shimmered next to it.

"Where's Sylvie?" she screamed.

"Sylvie, Sylvie, Sylvie…" muttered a voice in a sing-song cadence behind her.

The officer in front of her shifted his attention to over Reilly's head and stepped to the side, with his hand on his weapon.

"This is a police scene, sir. You need to leave the area." The police officer signaled to his partner to deal with the interruption, and Reilly watched a cop that had been standing next to the gurney move around the bench to escort a homeless man with a sleeping bag draped over his shoulders away from the scene. The officer was not gentle with his guidance and the vagrant fought to juggle the small array of possessions that he carried in his arms.

"Sylvie, Sylvie, Sylvie…" muttered the man as he shuffled away.

"Who's Sylvie?" asked the police officer, and he crouched down in front of her. She focused on his eyes. It did nothing to ease her fear, but it helped her to concentrate.

"My girlfriend. Where is she? Is she—is she all right?"

"Is she supposed to be with you?" asked the officer, and Reilly began to cry. He would have told her if the person on the stretcher was Sylvie. Wouldn't he?

"Was—was that her?" asked Reilly, when the officer returned her stare but didn't say anything.

"No, ma'am. Was she here at one time?"

"I don't know," said Reilly, relief that it wasn't Sylvie falling on her like a heavy wrap. She slumped into the blanket, the edges of which she held to her chest, twisting the corners. Someone was under that sheet, though. The last thing she remembered was doing another round of shots and going back into the bedroom at the party with Sylvie and Parker to do more coke. She shut her eyes and tried to think beyond that, but nothing more came to her.

"You'll have to come with us," said the officer.

"I'm okay. I don't think I'm hurt," said Reilly. She needed to find her phone and call Sylvie. She needed to know that Sylvie was okay.

"That's good. But you'll have to come down to the station with us and answer some questions."

"But I didn't see anything," said Reilly as she got up.

That was when she saw her car parked on the sidewalk. The front fender was just a couple of feet from where the sheet had been.

"Oh, god—" she said, and the world went dark.

Keep on Breathing

REILLY OPENED HER EYES AS the paramedic wrapped his fingers around her wrist. She was half-sitting, half-lying in the back seat of a squad car, and the paramedic was sitting in the seat next to her, the doors to the car open wide. He stared at his watch while he took her pulse.

"I need to check her pressure, but she seems fine," he said, placing her hand in her lap and reaching for the stethoscope that was draped around his neck. "If you think we need to take her to the hospital, the other unit will be here in a few minutes. You should keep an eye on her, make sure she doesn't—"

Reilly leaned away from him before she vomited out the opposite door. All over someone's shoes. Embarrassed, but too exhausted to care, Reilly lifted her head to see the startled face of the police officer that had been with her on the bench. Great.

"—get sick," finished the paramedic who held her by the elbow so she wouldn't fall out of the car.

"Sorry," said Reilly, sitting back up and wiping her mouth with the edge of the blanket that was still draped over her shoulders. Her head was spinning and her stomach threatened to revolt again. The last thing on her mind should have been whether there were reporters around to have seen her retch up her guts, but that's exactly what she thought about.

Then she remembered the sheet and the tennis shoe. The concrete barrier. And her car parked on the sidewalk.

"Ohmygod, ohmygod, ohmygod—" She squeezed her eyes shut and rocked. All she saw behind her eyelids was the white sheet lying on the gray cement sidewalk. And the tennis shoe.

Her eyes flew open and she grabbed the police officer. With an irritated grunt, he brushed her off and stepped away, trying to kick off the mess that she had spewed on his feet.

"What happened? Oh my god. What happened? Please tell me. Did I…?"

She couldn't say it. It was too horrible.

"Ma'am, just sit back in the car. You need to calm down."

The officer looked disgusted as he blocked her from exiting the vehicle, pulling his soiled pant leg away from his skin.

Reilly tried to sit back, but her head was a swirling mess, and she needed to get up and move. The paramedic tried to wrap the blood pressure cuff around her arm and she shook him off.

"I can't handle that. Please… please don't touch me."

"Ma'am, try to be calm," said the paramedic, attempting to capture her arm to take her blood pressure.

"Get off!" she yelled, pulling away.

"I'll have to cuff you or he'll have to sedate you if you don't let him do his job," said the officer, ducking his head inside of the vehicle. Reilly saw the paramedic shake his head.

"Um. I don't think we need to do that. Maybe Lisa can help," suggested the paramedic. He swung his legs out of the car door. "Lisa! Come here. Can you…?"

The paramedic slid out of the car, and all Reilly felt was relief that she had more space to breathe. Her relief was short-lived when another light-blue uniformed paramedic moved in beside her. It was the woman who had given her the blanket earlier. Reilly tried to breathe but couldn't seem to take a deep enough breath.

"Hey, hey. You're going to be okay," said the paramedic. Her voice was low and soothing.

"I just can't catch my breath. I need a little space. If I get up and walk—"

"You have to stay in the car. But try to lean your head back. Take a deep breath."

"I c-can't. I can't breathe," said Reilly, as tension built in her head. Her peripheral vision narrowed. All she could see was the paramedic's serious face, her dark hair pulled back in a severe ponytail

"Yes, you can. You can breathe. It's natural. Shut your mouth and take a deep breath. In through your nose."

"I can't—"

Reilly's vision filled with dark spots and the edges started creeping in. She needed to get out of there.

The steady voice beside her helped to anchor her, but she felt like she was sinking.

"You can do this." Reilly heard the voice at the end of a tunnel, and a hand clasped her own. "Can you feel that? Think about me squeezing your fingers. Good. Now lean your head back." Someone cupped the back of her head as Reilly tried to loosen up enough to lean back. "Keep your eyes shut. Breathe in through your nose and out through your mouth. See? You're doing it."

Reilly's head cleared a little as she concentrated on doing what the paramedic told her to do—in through her nose, out through her mouth. There was still the sensation of weight on her chest, but she was able to fill her lungs with air.

"Not too much. Okay? Slow, easy breaths. In… now out… good. Feeling a little better?"

Reilly let go of the hand. The sinking feeling was starting to go away, but her head was beginning to spin.

"Yes. Thanks. I'm just a little dizzy."

"Keep on breathing. In. Now out. Lower your shoulders." Reilly felt a hand on her stomach. The touch calmed her. "Relax your chest and stomach. Feel that? My hand on your middle? Breathe into that. You have it. Good."

Reilly felt the oxygen filling her lungs, and her vision began to clear. Her limbs felt heavy and thick. She concentrated on the warm hand resting on her stomach.

"Okay," said the paramedic. "I'm going to take your pulse. That's better. Now I'm going to put the blood pressure cuff back on. Chances are, you've had that done a few times."

Reilly nodded her head. She was so sleepy.

The cuff went on and she didn't fight, even when it tightened around her arm.

Not a Monster

SHE LEANED AGAINST THE BATHROOM counter. The smooth marble
was cold even through her pajama bottoms. The small plastic bottle felt hard and
foreign in her palm. She tried to think back to the last time she had taken any of
the medication that it held. The days had all blended together since she had been
released on bail. She had no idea what time it was, or even what day. The clock
next to her bed was broken. She remembered throwing it after waking from a
nightmare, but it seemed so long ago. All she'd done was sleep. Nothing had
fractured her numbness since she'd retreated so far into herself that she wasn't
sure she'd find her way out. Her sense of disconnection was complete. With the
blinds closed, all she could tell was that it was daylight by the lines of sunlight
that bordered the darkened windows. Or maybe it was the landscaping lights.

Reilly squinted at the label on the bottle but couldn't focus enough to read it.
She was tired, yet she had done nothing but sleep for over a week—or had it been
two?—seeking relief through nothingness. It didn't work. Even in sleep she saw
the sheet and the orphaned shoe. She wondered if anyone had picked the shoe
up, or if it had remained on the sidewalk for tourists to walk around. She spent
hours thinking about that shoe.

She opened the bottle and poured the contents into her hand. She tried to
count the small blue pills, but lost track after starting over several times. She
lifted her hand and then lowered it, lifted it again. She thought about tossing the
pills into her mouth like a handful of popcorn. Her hand shook. She closed her
fist around the pills and turned on the water. She opened her trembling hand and
examined the pills sitting on her damp palm. She rotated her wrist and watched
them fall. A straggler, caught in the crease between her fingers, had to be shaken
loose. The water swept the pills down the drain. She let the water flow to make

sure they were rinsed far, far away. She did the same thing with the Lithium and the Valium. They were too tempting to keep taking.

Too tempting to take too many.

She reached over and switched on the light over the vanity.

The woman that contemplated her from the mirror was a surprise.

Dark circles under vacant eyes and greasy hair made her appear haggard. She leaned forward to see beyond that, to find the signs of the monster that she had become. But there were no horns, no scales, no weeping sores. Her expression was flat, but her eyes were clear. She had no new lines to mark the day when she had become a murderer. Where was the sign that told the universe that she was someone to hate?

Greasy hair aside, the woman in the mirror was still beautiful, but Reilly didn't feel beautiful. She didn't deserve to be. She didn't deserve anything, except to be punished. *That* she understood, *that* she deserved. She felt like an empty husk. It wasn't fair. She shouldn't be standing there, gorging on the gift of self-pity, when a man was dead because of her. She wrapped her arms around herself and tried to see through her reflection.

"Reilly?"

She heard her mother's voice in the bedroom behind her, from the room in which she had spent her childhood. She didn't respond. She realized the water was still on. She made no move to shut it off.

She stood in the bathroom and released the hold that she had on her own arms. Angry red prints marked where her fingers had tried to dig into her flesh. There would be bruises there eventually. She rested her hands on the marble countertop and saw the raw tips where her nails were bitten down to the quick. If she hadn't chewed them down, she knew that the red marks on her arms would be accompanied by bleeding crescents.

She didn't feel any of it.

A shadow moved behind her and she saw her mother's reflection over her shoulder.

"There you are. You're out of bed. Sylvie's here to see you. Do you want me to send her away again?"

Reilly tried to reply but her unused voice came out in a croak. She cleared her throat and tried again.

"Can you ask her to wait a few minutes?" asked Reilly around the lump that seemed to have lodged permanently in her throat.

"Are you sure? I can tell her to come back tomorrow," said Melissa. Reilly had never seen the expression of concern that had been on her mother's face the last several days.

"No. I'll see her. I just want to take a quick shower."

"Well, that's one thing I'm glad to hear, honey. I'll have her wait downstairs."

Reilly wanted to scream that the person under the sheet would never be able to shower again. Instead she turned off the water running in the sink and hoped that the pills were far, far away.

Can't Do This Anymore

"GOD, YOU LOOK HORRIBLE, RYE!"

Reilly stood in the doorway and watched as Sylvie rose from the sofa in the family room and walked toward her. Self-conscious, Reilly ran her fingers through her still-damp hair. Conflicting emotions rose in her. She hoped that Sylvie would reject her, while at the same time she yearned for Sylvie to wrap her in her arms. She didn't deserve to be comforted, yet she craved the warm balm of sinking into someone familiar so she could forget everything, if just for a few minutes.

Sylvie halted several steps away, her eyes searching, her expression full of something that might have been sympathy or pity or another emotion that was equally upsetting, equally unwanted. Reilly averted her eyes.

Since Reilly was offered neither comfort nor rejection, she didn't know what to do. So she stood there, eyes cast down while hot tears ran down her face.

At the top of the stairs, she had felt closer to normal than she had in days. The shower had helped. Her resolution to stop taking the mind-numbing pills had helped. Anticipating Sylvie's visit, and being reminded of who she once was, had helped. But by the time she had reached the bottom of the stairs, it occurred to her that she didn't have the right to feel better. She had killed someone. She would live with that forever.

Sylvie's distance—both physical and emotional—confirmed the judgment.

They stood like strangers, each uncomfortable in the other's presence.

"Why don't we sit down?" suggested Sylvie.

Numb, operating from a remote place deep inside, Reilly obeyed. She followed Sylvie into the room and sat, sinking into the corner of the sofa. Sylvie sat at the other end. Reilly watched her fumble with her purse, first setting it in her lap, and then placing it on the floor beside her feet. When Sylvie glanced at her, Reilly had to look away.

"Your mom said that you haven't left your room since you've been home."

Reilly didn't answer. She watched Sylvie chew her lip and cross and uncross her legs.

"That isn't healthy. She says you won't eat."

Reilly shrugged and shoved her hands under her thighs to keep from biting her nails. Her thoughts were buried and unreachable.

They sat for a few minutes and silence made a fragile wall between them. From her inner bunker, Reilly watched Sylvie fidget. Sylvie never fidgeted. As an attorney, she was always poised and in control. It was one of the things that had always made Reilly feel safe.

"You haven't returned any of my calls," said Sylvie. "I've tried to call you. I've come by to see you," said Sylvie. "Has your mother told you? I didn't want you to think that I haven't tried. I've been worried about you."

Reilly regarded Sylvie. The fidgeting became worse. Reilly noticed that Sylvie appeared tired and thinner. Reilly hated what she had done to the people around her.

"It's funny. I've talked to your mother more in the last five days than I have in the last three years," said Sylvie with a nervous laugh, glancing at the doorway. Reilly wondered if Sylvie thought that Melissa might be listening to the conversation. Or maybe she just wanted to leave. Reilly didn't blame her and wondered if Sylvie had just come to see her out of obligation or guilt.

"I killed a man."

Reilly wasn't sure if she said it, or thought it. She lifted her head.

Sylvie watched her with wide eyes. She must have said it.

Sylvie seemed to register her words, and the uneasy fidgeting stopped. They sat silently and Reilly watched Sylvie trying to figure out what to say next.

Finally, Sylvie spoke.

"I know this isn't good timing. But I don't think that I can do this any longer, Rye. I didn't come here to tell you that. I swear. I came here to see you. To make sure that you're okay," said Sylvie. "But, you're not even talking to me. As I try to carry on this one-sided conversation, all I can think of, all that floats through my mind is that I can't do this anymore. I can't. I'm sorry."

Reilly had never seen Sylvie cry. She would have thought it would have made her feel something, but it didn't.

Sylvie stood up and Reilly sank deeper into the couch.

Reilly could feel Sylvie watching her, but she couldn't meet her gaze.

Sylvie stood for a moment just watching her. Reilly sensed more words dangling from Sylvie's lips, but Sylvie didn't give them voice. She just stared. Reilly stared back without blinking, a steely chill holding her still. The air felt thick and flat, the space between them a chasm filled with expectant silence. Then, taking her unspoken words with her, Sylvie pulled the strap of her bag over her shoulder and walked out of the room.

Reilly felt nothing.

Having a Tough Time

"REILLY, COME ON. YOU HAVE to eat," said Melissa.

"I feel like I have something stuck in my throat," said Reilly, pushing the mashed potatoes around her plate.

"You should at least try. Besides pot roast with carrots and potatoes are your favorite."

"Thanks for making it, Mom, but I just don't think I can eat anything right now."

Reilly kept her eyes on her uneaten food, but out of the corner of her eye, she saw her mother lower her fork and lean back in her chair. Reilly didn't have to see it, to know that her mother's face wore an expression that spoke of last meals and disappointment. The old Reilly would have had something to say about the lack of support, the inability of her mother to at least try to fake encouragement. But that Reilly was buried deep inside, in a small space set aside for who she used to be. The new Reilly, the Reilly that felt nothing and thought about nothing, couldn't muster the energy to engage. She just kept on pushing food around her plate.

"Where's Dad?" she asked after a few minutes, her eyes still on the circles she had drawn in her uneaten potatoes.

Her father's absence was another guilty sentence to her—a sentence she had already given herself. She didn't need to wait until the next day, when the verdict would be read. She already knew.

She closed her eyes and the pictures that haunted her dreams flickered like an old-time home movie across the inside of her eyelids. She wanted to open her eyes to stop the show, but like the ads before an internet clip, it had to finish before she could do anything else. First the running shoe. Always the running shoe. On its side on wet pavement. The laces still tied. Flash to the horrible photo that had been presented as evidence, of a man slumped over a round concrete parking barrier, propped up between the hood of her car and the immovable object. Then, there was the white sheet covering the shape of a man, a red patch spreading along one side as the fabric absorbed the blood, all the blood. So much blood. Then, the portrait the prosecution had used as an emotional weapon by displaying it every day at the trial. Next to the witness stand, the full-length framed painting of the little Traynor family, all four of them, blond-haired and blue-eyed, stood there, the epitome of the American family. Matt Traynor, still alive, smiling, with his wife Lydia, and his two daughters, seven-year-old Paige, and nine-year-old Taylor. It had worked—at least on Reilly—who now had the picture forever imprinted in her mind, except that her traitor mind had added a bonus—when their faces morphed into glares of accusing hatred, even though the surviving Traynors had never once met her eyes from their seats behind the prosecution's table.

Melissa's voice broke through Reilly's dark thoughts. Reilly lifted her head to see her mother's lying face.

"Your father had to stay late at work tonight."

Reilly doubted her father's architectural firm required him to work long nights any more, especially since he was a primary partner. If he'd wanted to, he could have been home. Her father's neglect, so unfamiliar, would have hurt more than her mother's, if she could feel it. But she didn't, so she stored it away.

"Will he be there tomorrow?"

Melissa regarded Reilly for a moment, and for the first time in a long time she wasn't wearing her manager's face.

"I don't know, honey," she said. "He's having a tough time with this."

The old Reilly would have had an angry retort, but the new one told her that she didn't have any right to be angry after the chaos and pain that she had caused her family and friends.

"I hope he comes," she said, drawing another circle.

The Verdict

"FOR THE CHARGE OF VEHICULAR manslaughter while under the influence of drugs or alcohol, we find the defendant guilty as charged. A date for sentencing will be…"

Just as she had done throughout the weeks of emotional drama that had been whipped into a frenzy during the highly publicized trial, Reilly sat still as the verdict was read. She fought the urge to stare at the hands she had folded in her lap, and followed the instructions of her attorneys by watching the jury foreman as he read the verdict, but she did all of this as if from a distance. She sensed the disappointment that rolled toward her from every direction after it was read. While none of the feelings that she would have expected to feel seemed to make it through the fog that continued to dampen her thoughts and emotions, she was aware of the disappointment of her attorneys over the fact that she hadn't been cleared. At the same time, disappointment came from the prosecution team because they hadn't been able to get a second-degree murder verdict. Reporters and those who had been watching the trial closely exuded disappointment that the trial hadn't been more dramatic. Matt Traynor's family continued to show no reaction, but Reilly watched them silently move out of the courtroom, protected by their own attorneys from the army of reporters that tried to ask questions. She imagined their disappointment that she was alive and their husband/father/son was not.

The sense of numb detachment that she'd felt for so long held its place within her, and she took the announced verdict in as if she were listening to a lecture. But even though she didn't feel much about it as it pertained to her, she couldn't help but try to understand the thoughts and emotions that were battling within everyone else around her. The team of attorneys that her mother had hired to defend her was the best in the business, and they had been so certain of a verdict of not guilty. They had already been successful in reducing the charge from second-degree murder to vehicular manslaughter, and they had gone into the trial confident that they'd win the not guilty verdict, as well. Her testimony had been the Achilles' heel, though. They'd tried to keep her off the stand, but the prosecution had pressed, and the judge had agreed. She'd followed her attorney's guidance, but her eyes must have projected the guilt she felt. The energy of optimism was notably subdued in the days after her testimony. Still, the verdict was less than what the prosecution had asked for, and she felt the disappointment from them, as well.

She felt the gazes of her parents behind her. Her father had finally come, but she didn't have any feelings about that. Wiping away a tear she avoided looking back so they wouldn't see how empty she was, what a waste of time it had all been for them. As the courtroom cleared she sat. What happened next was out of her hands. But wasn't that the story of her life?

Sentencing

"**WE HEREBY SENTENCE THE DEFENDANT,** Reilly Tatum Ransome, to twenty-three months at Ral-Rutherford Women's Correctional Facility, to begin immediately."

Reilly never lifted her head. She stared at the table in front of her and wished for nothingness. She heard the clamor of a hundred feet shuffling to stand up in the small courthouse. Other than that, there was no sound. No one spoke. There was no loud noise to signal the agreement of the universe, no outraged denial from a bereaved loved one. Just the shuffle of feet, and the rustle of belongings as the collection of personal items was accomplished.

A shadow fell over her, and she raised her head. One of her lawyers shook his head in apology. She hoped her eyes conveyed her thanks, because she was unable to speak. An officer appeared next to her and led her from the defendant's table to the bailiff, who put handcuffs on her.

She glanced at the seats where the Traynor family had been sitting throughout the trial. As usual, not one of them would return her gaze as they filed away. She didn't know if she felt relief or regret at the lack of vindication that she had expected to see in their faces. She tried to tell herself that the universe would even the score, would set things right in its inalienable ways, but she knew that there would never be punishment enough for what she had done.

She was taken to the nearby jail—the same one into which she had been booked the day of the accident—and put into a temporary holding cell to wait for the bus that would take her to Ral-Rutherford Women's Correctional Facility, a medium-security prison located in the middle of the Mojave Desert. The guard looked at her with pity in his eyes as he shut the door to the cinderblock and steel-barred cell.

"The bus to RR only runs twice a week. The good news is that it runs today, so we don't have to process you into here. The bad news is that the bus don't leave until after dinner, so it's gonna be a long wait. You might as well get comfortable."

The guard wrapped his beefy fingers around a bar, tugged on the door to make sure it had latched, and turned away with a sad shake of his head. Through the bars that spanned the front of the cell, Reilly watched him walk back along the way they had just come.

His words sank into her reality like acid and she took a seat on the metal bench at the back of the cell.

She was going to prison.

As the guard predicted, the wait for transport took most of the day, and Reilly began her long relationship with learning patience.

Reilly had been one of the first few women placed in the holding cell that day, but as the hours drew out, about two-dozen women joined her in the twelve-by-fourteen foot space. By then, there were more women in the cell than there were seats, and women sat on the floor against the wall and bars. She watched larger and more menacing women enter the cell and stand next to other women who wordlessly gave up their spots. Reilly was surprised that she was allowed to keep her perch on the hard metal bench, pressed into the cinderblock corner, and she waited for the moment when someone would cast their shadow over her. It never happened.

With a manufactured air of detached disinterest, she watched the sporadic business of the receiving desk across from the cell. Prisoners were processed through the facility all day long, like packages on a loading dock. Despite the stress that had to have been simmering under the surface for many of the women in custody, there was little emotion displayed—if you didn't count the one woman who started screaming for a cigarette break late in the afternoon.

Bag lunches containing an apple and a peanut butter and jelly sandwich were handed through the bars just after noon. Reilly wasn't hungry, so she ignored the press of bodies toward the bars and focused her unseeing eyes on the gray cement floor. A small, oily-haired woman with sunken eyes and missing upper front teeth stepped in front of Reilly and dropped a bag in her lap.

"Take it. They might not give you dinner."

Reilly looked up, but the woman just shrugged without meeting her gaze and moved over to the wall, sliding into a seated position. The woman attacked her lunch with a gusto that turned Reilly's stomach. The toothless maw smacked open to reveal each new churn of food between decaying teeth. Reilly tried not to look and dutifully sampled her sandwich, but her throat wouldn't open for her, and the bread scraped down in a painful gob. Water was provided via a leaky water fountain that Reilly couldn't bring herself to use for two reasons: she had seen no less than four women spit hocked-up mucus into it, and requests for restroom breaks were received by the guards with hostility. When Reilly hadn't been able to ignore her bladder earlier in the day, she was chaperoned into a dark and dank closet-sized bathroom, where the stainless steel toilet had no seat and there was no toilet paper. Fragrant puddles of urine spotted the concrete floor. The guard stood just inside the door facing Reilly, her arms folded across her chest. They were shin to knee as Reilly dropped her pants and hovered over the dripping toilet rim. She stared at the expensive heels she wore and wondered if the designer ever imagined them flanking the piss streaked basin of a prison toilet. Though Reilly had to pee worse than she ever remembered, the guard's stare filled her with a performance anxiety that turned the urgent need for release into a hesitant trickle that took forever to cease. The impatient look on the guard's face had only made it worse.

As the day wore on, she studied her cellmates. The group was quiet and Reilly tried to determine if it was because the cell was across from the booking desk, where two stern guards stood post, or if the women just wanted to keep to themselves. Like her, each new arrival took a seat and waited. There was minimal interaction among the incarcerated. It wasn't until several hours into waiting that Reilly noticed the wordless communication that was happening all around her. Body language and attitude conveyed quite a bit, and Reilly studied the silent dialogue.

Some of the women were dressed in civilian clothes, as if they had woken in their own homes that morning, just like her. Of those, she could tell who were first timers like her, and those who were making a return trip just by the way they sat. The first-timers were nervous, fidgety, eyes darting around the room. Those whom she suspected had been through it all before took their seats with what were probably practiced airs of indifference, but Reilly could tell that they still took in every detail around them.

Late in the day, two women were brought in wearing orange jumpsuits. The rest of the women made room for them and kept their distance. Until then, Reilly had felt removed from everything around her, like it was happening to someone else. When she saw those jumpsuits, Reilly felt the first real fear about what waited at her destination. It was then that she realized that she would have a rapid learning curve ahead of her. She cursed the days of catatonia between arrest and sentencing, when she should have been preparing for life in prison. She didn't speak the language. She didn't know the rules. A cold anxiety grew within her. After preparing for roles her whole life, this was a role that needed the most preparation, and she was not ready. Reilly tried to assume the demeanor of the ones who had been through the system before.

She kept to herself all day. Surprisingly, it seemed like no one recognized her.

Finally, a police officer stopped at the cell and called out a list of names, one of which was hers. As the women were summoned, they lined up at the door. When the officer stopped calling names, he unlocked the holding cell, and they filed out in a slow shuffle. They followed him down a long hall to a metal door that opened to the outside. Single file, through diesel fumes and humid Los Angeles night air, they streamed like broken and beaten cattle into a white bus that was idling next to the building.

"Reilly! Over here!" called an unfamiliar voice.

Reilly kept her head down, even when she saw the flashes of light from the cameras out of the corner of her eye. Part of her wondered why anyone would want a photo of her. She was no one now. She had spent the last several months, prior to and during her trial, out of the public eye, and she hadn't done a single interview. The reporters and her publicist had been relentless, but she had stead-fastly refused. Even after she won her second Academy Award. To her mother's consternation, she had even stood her ground when the studio had threatened to sue when she refused to do publicity for *Salsa Nights*, which was about to be released. Somehow, publicity hadn't been a required part of Reilly's contract, so the suit was dropped. The studio sent her a stern letter, though, telling her they'd have to think long and hard about hiring her again. Reilly hadn't cared. To her, her career was the last thing on her mind.

That part of her life seemed so far behind her now. Shame welled within her when she thought about the shallow focus she had had on her trivial life.

Reilly slid into the first empty seat on the bus and leaned into the metal side near the wire-screened window. Her head lolled against the smudged glass, and she stared without seeing at the brick building across the way. She wondered if she would get used to viewing the world through the inside of a cage. When the last woman took a seat, the bus roared into gear, and Reilly was relieved to find that she was still sitting by herself.

The bus ride was silent, aside from the roar of the engine and the hot, dry wind that rushed in through the mesh-covered open windows. The smell of fuel and exhaust blended with the moldering smell of the old bus. Reilly looked out through the windows and felt numb as the city streamed by and the desert took its place. When the lights of the city faded away, her eyes peered out at the empty black night. Perspiration accumulated on her back in the plastic-covered seat. By the time they arrived at the low, gray complex of buildings that constituted her new home for the next twenty-three months, the thin fabric of the blouse she wore was plastered to her, but she didn't notice, didn't care.

Through her wakeful catatonia, Reilly learned a few new things:

Body cavity searches are embarrassing and thorough.

Prison food does suck.

A cell is called a house.
The door to the house stays open during the day, no exceptions.
The door to the house stays closed during the night, no exceptions.
Prisoners do not enter other prisoner's houses.
She could hear, see, and smell everything anyone did—or did not do.
She could be silent for three days and no one would ever notice.
The clock in the day room controlled everyone's life.
Time in prison moved when it felt like it.

Fish

FISH.

That's what people on the inside call a new prisoner.

Fish.

That's what Reilly felt like the first few days she spent in prison.

Underwater.

Learning to breathe.

Avoiding bigger fish.

Reilly felt the humidity of the showers before she ever saw them. The sound of running water was a welcome thing after her first two full days in prison. She was grungy and dusty, and she wanted nothing more than to rinse the last two days of being treated like an unwanted package from her skin.

The showers were located at the opposite end of the wing from the cell that she had been assigned. She clutched the towel and small bag of generic toiletries she had been issued to her chest, and she winced at the loud slap of her cheap shower shoes against the polished cement as she walked through the common room that stood between her cell and the showers. Though she was acutely aware of their presence, she pretended to ignore the three lounging inmates watching a crime show on the television that was mounted near the ceiling. She felt their eyes on her as she passed. The smell of soap and steamy water were her focus as she approached the showers.

A half-dozen steps from the doorway, fear tried to take possession of her limbs. During processing, she and the other new prisoners had been given a short list of suggestions intended to help make shower time as uneventful as possible. The list, and the fact that the facility even took the time to address it, told Reilly all she needed to know about the vulnerability of new prisoners in the shower area. Her senses were on high alert.

Somehow, she made her legs move, taking a hesitant half-step before resuming her steady gait. She found herself in a large tiled room where she made a quick path to the nearest row of benches and put her small bundle of bath gear down. In an effort to appear relaxed, she scanned the area through the corners of her eyes.

The bench area was almost empty. By the sound of running water and voices, the majority of the women were already in the showers.

Reilly kept her eyes on her gear, took a deep breath, shrugged out of the blue work shirt she had been issued, and then pulled her tee shirt over her head. She dropped both shirts in a pile next to her gear. She reached back to unhook her bra, but hesitated when she sensed that she was being watched.

Without showing her unease, she discreetly knocked her shower bag with her knee, making it fall to the tile floor. She crouched to pick up her stuff, chancing a casual glance around to assess the situation.

A nude woman leaned against the tile wall near the showers, slowly unwinding a long, thick braid of black hair that was streaked with gray. From what she could take in from the quick scan, Reilly saw that the woman was of average height, well-defined muscle, and wiry build. A twisted rope in the shape of a pretzel decorated the pale skin of the woman's out thrust hip. Reilly felt the woman's eyes roam over her like a greasy caress. Chancing another peek, Reilly saw the woman's eyes flick to a place behind her, and she knew that the woman was working with a friend. A malicious intent filled the room.

"Shit," Reilly said, as she picked up her shirt and shower bag, making a show of going through her gear. Then acting as if she had forgotten something, she picked up her belongings and turned to retrace her steps. Two enormous women that Reilly hadn't noticed lurking near the sinks eased their way toward the door, but she escaped before they had a chance to block her retreat.

"Hey, fish! You can use my soap," she heard, as she walked quickly back to her cell, shaking from the thought of what might have happened.

Footsteps approached from behind. Reilly double-timed her step.

"Ransome, put your shirt on!"

She sprinted the last ten feet into her cell. Behind her, a presence filled the doorway and she tossed her things onto her bed. She pulled her tee shirt back on over her head. In her panic, she made the strategic error of getting tangled up in the fabric and struggled to get her arms through the armholes, all the while anticipating hands grabbing her from behind. Finally, her arms free, breathless from fear, she spun around and saw a guard standing just outside of the cell door. *Ferguson*, the badge read. Reilly recognized her from processing. The guard was huge. She was at least a foot taller than Reilly—and all muscle. Reilly didn't know if she should be relieved or afraid.

"Shirts, pants, and shoes are to be worn in all areas, at all times, Ransome. Except for bathing and changing. No exceptions. Next time it's a tag. Got it?"

Before Reilly could respond, the guard walked away. Reilly watched her massive back disappear through the common room and then sank onto her bed.

She wished that she could close the door to her cell. But all doors stayed open until lights out. It would be hard to get used to, but she had her own room—at least for the time being. Reilly pulled her legs up onto the bed and lay back on the scratchy wool blanket.

Still trembling, she smelled her armpit and wondered how long she could avoid the showers.

Warden Wants You

REILLY'S FIRST DAYS IN PRISON were a fog as she tried to remain anonymous while navigating an invisible path through a place where landmines were hidden at every turn. She still hadn't grown accustomed to the smell, a smell that was almost a taste. It was the way she thought that dirty pennies mingled with pine cleaner would be if she rolled them around in her mouth. That was, when she wasn't assaulted by the funk when she stood too close to some of the other women. The frequency in which she was treated to that pleasure was more often than she would have predicted, as her plan to remain aloof, separate from everyone else, was more difficult to realize than she thought it would be. Somehow it seemed that she had avoided being recognized, at least. And she hoped that she'd be able to make that last.

Every day followed the same routine, yet every day seemed to bring with it new challenges. The first meal found her sitting at the wrong table, as did the second, and the third. Just when she had almost resigned herself to taking all of her meals while standing, Reilly found a woman who would let her sit next to her as long as she handed over her dessert. Yard time, an event that was almost as fun as shower time to Reilly, happened for an hour, twice a day. It was a sweltering torture, until Reilly found a sliver of shade next to the building's sewage exhaust grate that no one wanted to fight her for.

But no amount of study showed Reilly how to avoid the braided woman, whose eyes followed her with a predatory hunger wherever she went.

It was her fifth day in prison, and Reilly squatted with her elbows on her thighs against a wall in her sliver of shade, breathing through her mouth so she didn't smell the sewer, hiding as best she could from the woman. She counted the number of bricks that ran up the side of the wall across from her. Every so often she'd let her eyes wander around to take in the social dynamic of the women who congregated in groups within the cement yard that made up the center of the prison compound. She took care not to let her eyes stay in one place too long, or to let them wander across the same women too many times. Observation had helped her avoid having to learn that lesson through firsthand experience.

"Ransome! Warden wants you."

Reilly turned toward the voice and her eyes landed on the enormous guard, Ferguson, who, like the braided woman, always seemed to have an eye on her. The guard turned and Reilly followed her into the prison. Inside was dark compared to the relentless sunlight out in the yard, but the guard didn't pause to let her eyes adjust. Reilly followed Officer Ferguson through the main entrance of the facility and into a section that she hadn't been before. When they stopped at an open door, the guard stood to the side, indicating that Reilly should enter by herself. Reilly was nervous and her eyes scanned the room when she entered. She found herself standing in a dark paneled room with heavy wooden furniture that was buffed to a high shine. The head of an elk was mounted on the wall behind the desk, and framed hunting-themed pictures covered the wall all around it.

The sound of the door closing made Reilly turn. A man in a well-pressed gray suit, with French cuffs and cufflinks, stood next to the door. His hair was impeccable and neat. His fashionable shoes were shined to a high sheen. A handkerchief that matched his yellow tie poked out of the breast pocket of his suit jacket. The man seemed out of place in the colorless, hard world within the prison walls. Reilly couldn't see him in the uniform worn by the other officers, and even less so, the camouflage of hunting gear.

He smiled and approached Reilly with his hand offered in greeting. His teeth were whiter than those of most actors she knew.

"What a pleasure to meet you, Ms. Ransome. Though we're meeting under, well… unusual circumstances, I'm delighted to welcome you to Ral-Rutherford."

Reilly didn't know what to say, so she said nothing and took his hand and felt hers encased in a dry, limp grip that lasted a beat too long as the eyes before her scanned hers. It was a strange greeting, after months of self-imposed exile and the last several days of institutionalized alienation. Aside from that, she hadn't said more than a dozen words in the last four days, so she wasn't sure her voice would work if she tried. She managed to smile and nod her head in the way of a greeting.

"I'm Alexander Rutherford—the warden here," he added inanely. Reilly could tell that he expected a certain response. It felt like a first meeting with the head of a new studio. Her actress kicked in out of habit. She smiled at him in what she hoped was a demure way, in a way that she thought he would expect. It seemed to work. He beamed back and finally let go of her hand as he offered her a seat. His gestures were over-effusive and embarrassing. The tall, leather chairs sat at an angle to each other in front of the large desk that dominated the office. When Reilly sat, he took a seat in the chair next to it and crossed his legs in an almost feminine fashion. Because of the angle at which the chairs sat next to one another, Reilly had to twist in her chair to face him.

"Nice to meet you, Warden," she said. She was surprised to hear that her voice sounded almost normal and that she could summon the courtesies of her former life. She surveyed the office again. "Do you greet every inmate personally in your own office like this?"

A flash of discomfort passed over the warden's face before his practiced smile settled back into place.

"No. Not every… inmate. Our population is quite large. Though I do make myself familiar with every jacket." Another look of discomfort crossed his face and he corrected himself. "I'm sorry. File. I read every file."

Reilly smiled, taking note of the way he hesitated at using the prison slang in front of her, as if it would offend her. She knew the term "jacket" from processing. A question about why she was an exception danced on her lips, though she already knew the answer. She didn't know why she had thought she could blend in among the prison inmates without being recognized. Reilly knew an enthusiastic fan when she met one, although she was unfamiliar with how to deal with it in the present circumstances. If the nervous, expectant look on his face as he watched her hadn't been a giveaway his next words clinched it.

"I have an admission," said the warden. He watched his fingers pinch the crease in the leg of his suit pants. "I'm a bit of a fan."

"Thank you. I'm flattered, I guess," she said, and wondered if her response had sounded disrespectful. She was well aware that knowing her place in every situation was a survival skill inside the cinderblock walls of Ral-Rutherford. Pissing the wrong person off could make or break her chances of getting out in one piece. Other prisoners might hurt her physically. The warden could make her life uncomfortable in other ways.

"Please call me Alexander, Ms. Ransome. May I call you Reilly?"

"You can call me whatever you want, Warden. You seem to have all the power around here."

Reilly didn't know why she played such a risky game with such disregard.

A fleeting expression of discomfort clouded the warden's face again, but he was fast in replacing it with his plastic smile. He didn't dispute her comment, though.

"I admit that I wish I could have met you under different circumstances, Reilly. But, seeing as you're here and I am a big fan, I thought that I would alter the routine a little. Being warden does come with its advantages. If you ever need anything, please don't hesitate to let me know. I'm bound to a certain level of procedure to make sure that I treat every… person… here with the same amount of… protocol. But, if you need anything, I'm sure you and I can come to an understanding."

When the warden touched her knee, Reilly understood what any special consideration would cost her. She struggled to keep from slapping his hand away, and it was only because she was an actress that she was able to mask the feeling of disgust that hovered under the serene façade of her expression. Distant memories, retrieved from what she felt was an even more distant lifetime, flashed through her mind, and she saw again the look on Drew's face when Sylvie had taken the lip balm from her hand, the response of the flight attendant that time when the boorish rock star had gotten grabby. Now she wished that she had hit the greasy singer with his own guitar when she had had the chance. On the opposite side of that memory now, she maintained her best smile and hoped that her violent fantasy didn't show.

"Thank you, Warden. I'll keep that in mind."

"Good. Good. Well, you better get back to your day. I have a group of underwriters coming out for a tour, otherwise I'd have reserved more time for us to get to know each other better," he said as he showed her back to the door. When he opened it, Officer Ferguson stood in the same spot that she had taken when Reilly had gone in. The warden stopped Reilly before she left, just out of hearing range from the guard. He spoke in a quiet voice. "And Reilly, I know how the shower situation can be. But please don't let it force you into making hygiene a lesser priority than it should be. I can let you use my private shower if those perverted dykes become too much of an issue."

Reilly felt her face color with anger as she nodded her head and walked away. She clenched her fists and shook with indignation. She didn't even realize that it was she who led, and Officer Ferguson that followed, on the way back to the wing where she lived.

Where she lived.

It was true. Like it or not, this was her home for the next twenty-three months. The other prisoners called their cells their houses, but she knew that she would never refer to hers that way. And she stank. A tear ran down her face before she had a chance to wipe it away. She walked toward the door that led to the yard and waited for the guard to unlock it so she could go out and become a shadow again.

She stood in front of the heavy metal door in front of her, but it didn't open. She turned to the guard, but couldn't hold the large woman's challenging gaze, and her eyes skittered to the ground.

"Ransome, do you read?"

"What?" she asked, glancing up at the guard's face and away again.

"I asked you if you read."

"Is that a trick question?" asked Reilly, before she could filter herself. She glanced up to chart the response to her impertinence.

The guard waited without changing her expression. It was scarier than if the guard had worn a mask of anger.

"Sorry. Yes, I read," said Reilly, studying the floor.

"You want to be the wing librarian?" asked the guard.

"There's a library here?"

"Yes. But it's a mess. No one uses it."

"So, I'd have to clean it up?"

The guard nodded her head. Reilly wondered what the catch was.

"I already have a job in the chow hall. I do dishes after dinner."

"You'd have to do both for a while."

"You mean extra duty? Why would I want that?" asked Reilly, wondering why the guard was asking, when she had the authority to just order her to do the work.

"Most people wouldn't."

"Then why ask me?"

The guard just stared at her again.

"Why doesn't anyone want to be the librarian? What's the catch?" asked Reilly, trying another approach.

"Besides having to clean up the library, you lose one of your hours in the yard each day. Plus, you miss half of dinner if you want to take a shower, since you have to be in the library during showers. That's when it's open."

Reilly didn't know how to answer.

"Look, you can check in, too," said Officer Ferguson, her voice cold with something worse than impatience, and Reilly knew that the guard was done with the conversation. Reilly's lawyer had told her about checking in, which was a prisoner's request for protective custody. She'd thought about it off and on ever since she had gotten there. The thing was, she wasn't sure that she could bear the solitude, though she could care less about the disdain that other prisoners had for inmates that chose checking in over general population. "I'm sure the warden would accept your application, considering your situation."

That comment settled it for Reilly. She didn't want to be isolated, with the guards—and the warden—as her only contacts.

"I'd get to shower alone?"

"No. The laundry crew showers at the same time."

"Just them? Are they the ones that come into the chow hall after everyone else does?" asked Reilly, understanding the gift that the guard was offering her.

"Yes."

Reilly knew who those women were, and as far as she could tell, most of them were short-timers, just biding their time before being paroled. They kept to themselves and didn't do anything to get into trouble.

"I'll do it. When do I start?" Reilly knew that the guard would expect something in return. She didn't care.

"Today, if you want."

"Show me where to go."

Twist

REILLY HAD HER ARMS ELBOW deep in hot, gray water, scouring the bottom of one of what seemed to be a never-ending supply of huge pots that had been used to cook dinner. Though she had dish gloves on, her flesh stung from the heat and from the water that ended up sloshing in over the tops of the gloves. Steam from the sink engulfed her, adding to the rivulets of sweat that trailed down the sides of her face. Every so often she wiped some off with her shoulder, but she couldn't find it in her to pay much mind to her surroundings or what she was doing, other than to just get it done. She attended to her dish duty the way she attended to everything else these days—like an automaton.

For the past three nights, she had reported to the kitchen after dinner and had taken the station pointed out to her by the woman who ran the place, the woman the guards called Bird. The first two nights she had spent washing the glassware that only the guards and administration got to drink from. The prisoners had plastic cups. This was the first night she had been on pots and pans. Reilly knew that Bird was an inmate by the standard issue clothing, but the guards treated her with respect. And, when it came to the kitchen, Bird was the one in charge.

The woman was rough in every way, from the wiry gray hair that stuck out around the edges of her hair net to the sandpaper skin of her hands. The riprap gravel texture of her voice when she barked out an expletive-laced command to one of the kitchen crew said that she didn't put up with any shit. She expected the crew to do what she told them to, when she told them to do it. And they did. Under her command, the kitchen ran well, and the work got done.

The intermittent sound of Bird barking out orders over the constant clatter of dishes receded into the background as Reilly retreated into her mind and went over the conversation she'd had that afternoon with the guard who the other prisoners called Fergie.

Reilly had soon stopped wondering why Fergie had singled her out for the job. So much happened in the prison that didn't seem to make sense that figuring out what motivated the people around her was a waste of time. It was easier to just take things as they came, to try and stay under the radar.

While she scrubbed the stubborn film from the bottom of a soup pot, Reilly mulled over the work that she'd soon be doing in the library. It didn't seem like it would end up being much work, since calling it a library was a generous description for the walk-in closet sized space that Fergie had showed to her. It held a dismal but eclectic array of ancient books and out-of-date magazines, arranged in haphazard piles on dusty shelves. An unplugged computer sat on a pile of books in the corner of the room.

Reilly's thoughts skidded to a stop when one of the pots she had just washed was tossed, with no warning, back into the sink, causing a tsunami of dishwater to cascade over her. A short burst of laughter echoed off of the bare gray walls in the large room.

"Shut your holes, bitches!" snapped Bird to the other women whose laughter stopped as fast as it started. She focused her anger on Reilly. "You'll clean this right, or you can start scrubbing shitters tomorrow, princess."

Without a word, Reilly nodded, wiped the dishwater from her eyes with her arms, and began to scrub again. Bird walked away and Reilly heard her yell something at someone else out in the service line area of the kitchen. A small knot of anger pulled together in her chest. Aside from the overarching cloud of fear and depression that had been her constant companion since the accident, the knot of anger building inside of her was the first sign of emotion aside from sadness and fear she had felt in months.

She had several seconds to consider it before she sensed someone approach her from behind.

"I like my women wet," purred a voice close to her ear. It was the voice that had called after her from the showers, and the humid smell of rank breath that accompanied it, strong enough to be discerned over the stench of dirty dishwater, made Reilly's stomach turn. She cringed inside when the person behind her reached up and picked something from the front of her hairnet.

"Yeah, limp cabbage is a definite turn-on," mumbled Reilly, glancing at the fingers holding something slimy a few inches from her face.

"Shut up, snatch. I didn't ask for your opinion," spit out the voice behind her, and Reilly was smart enough not to turn. She knew it was the braided lady who had been watching her since she had arrived.

A loud buzzer pierced the air and Reilly's eyes shot up to the speaker mounted in the corner of the kitchen. The small metal boxes were mounted throughout the facility, and she was beginning to get used to the sound of them going off at intervals during the day. They measured the cadence of the lives inside. They signaled the beginning and end of each day, announced each meal, and warned the inmates of the end of each period of outdoor time. Once, they had signaled the beginning of an announcement by the warden. This time it called the guards to action.

"All Charlie Guards to Station 12. All Charlie Guards to Station 12."

The two bored guards that stood near each door to the kitchen came to life and left the room.

"Nothing to concern you, ladies," growled Bird to the room. "Just keep doing your fuckin' work. I'm not gonna miss my TV shows because you decide to dick around when the guards ain't here."

"Well, well, well," smirked The Braid, and Reilly felt the woman press up against her from behind. "Now we have an opportunity to get acquainted, since you don't seem to like to shower with us."

"Twist, just do your work," said Bird from across the room.

Reilly felt relief with Bird's words, and she had a name for the woman with the braid at last. If the situation hadn't been so scary, the cynic in her would have observed how very, very *prison* the name sounded. But the feel of the wiry woman at her back and the awareness of the very serious situation she was in just made her freeze.

"Mind your own business, Bird. This is between the little lady and me."

"Anything that goes down in this kitchen *is* my business," barked Bird, her voice closer. Reilly wondered who would win in a fight, Bird or Twist, and for a fraction of a second, Reilly hoped that the territory skirmish would save her. But the rapid negotiation that followed dashed that hope.

"You can take your pick of showerheads the rest of the week," offered Twist, and she didn't make any move toward going away.

"Four weeks. No time limit. And a good towel," countered Bird.

"Done," said Twist.

"Just be finished with her by the time the guards get back," said Bird, and Reilly's heart leapt into her throat as she heard the hardened woman walk away.

The pressure from behind Reilly increased and the rank smell of Twist's breath made the meal that had been hard enough to stomach in the first place threaten to come back up. Reilly's hand tightened on the handle of the heavy pot she'd been washing. She tried to calculate the logistics of using it as a weapon if it became necessary. Filled with water, it would be too heavy to lift quickly, let alone swing around.

"I expected to see you in the showers by now, Movie Star," purred Twist, trailing her fingers up Reilly's arm along the exposed flesh between the latex glove and her rolled up sleeve. "I've been dying to see those tits in real life. They only show us the edited version of your movies in here."

There was now no question about whether the other inmates recognized her, making her skin crawl with the familiarity she heard in Twist's voice. By the sound of it, at least some of them had seen the one in which she had done her first and last nude scene. She was glad that it was the edited version that didn't show the full nudity that she had consented to during the rehab scene that had garnered her a second golden statuette. The way that Twist had been leering at her, she didn't want those visions fueling her imagination.

"I bet the rest of you is pretty tasty, Movie Star," said Twist, and Reilly felt a warm tongue slide up her neck. She shuddered with revulsion. "I've staked my claim, so you'll be mine starting tonight."

The terror that had been building in Reilly since the moment she had entered the gates of Ral-Rutherford welled up in her and she moved without thought. She whirled upon Twist and pushed her away. Though the woman wasn't large, she still outweighed Reilly by at least fifty pounds and most of that was muscle, so the motion that provided Reilly with a moment of space was successful only because it was unexpected. Through her fear-shrouded eyes, Reilly saw black fury take possession of Twist's face. The terror that infused Reilly as she realized the fate that was about to claim her, almost paralyzed her. With nothing to rely on but the talent that she used to make her movies, Reilly did the only thing she knew. She fell into character. The same character that Twist had referred to. Excavating the emotions that she had used to bring a young, gang-influenced drug addict to life on the screen, she became the character, Deuce.

"Back the fuck off, motherfucker," she spit out at the advancing Twist, and her own unrecognizable voice enhanced her performance, as she braced herself for the imminent physical confrontation. She could feel every muscle in her body tense, and she prepared herself to spring at the menacing figure.

"The fuck you say, bitch?" asked Twist. Rage contorted her face, as she paused for a second to assess the unexpected turn of events.

"You fucking heard me. Back off," snarled Reilly, bracing her hands on either side of her as she leaned against the steel sink behind her.

Reilly focused on Twist, the danger in front of her. The circle of women that had formed around them was a remote concern. She didn't have time to think about what a hyped-up group of women with access to sharp and heavy objects might mean. She'd never seen a riot.

"Oh, bitch, you gonna figure out your place around here real quick," threatened Twist as she threw herself at Reilly.

Reilly trusted the sink behind her to hold her weight as she kicked both feet up as Twist advanced. They landed in the center of Twist's chest. Then Reilly pistoned her legs back and out, throwing Twist backward.

A surprised and angry growl erupted from Twist as she fell, and Reilly flew after her without thinking. She landed on Twist with both knees, knocking out what wind Twist still had in her after her abrupt fall onto the concrete and tile floor. Reilly scratched at Twist's face and tried to punch her, but she couldn't land a solid blow. An awareness of what she was doing descended upon her, and the energy that had powered her limbs in the last minutes evaporated as she realized that she didn't have much left with which to attack. At the same time, the slack-jawed and dazed expression that had been on Twist's face as she gasped for air morphed into a crazed anger. Reilly's mind clambered to figure out her next move. She didn't know what else to do. Her adrenaline was depleted and her arms were weakening. Without thinking, she bent low and bit into Twist's hate-filled face. The coppery taste of blood filled her mouth and the rubbery pop of her teeth breaking skin echoed in her skull. Growling like a dog, she sat back and watched as blood poured out of the round mark she had left on Twist's cheek.

The sight of blood sobered her, and she coughed up the blood that tried to go down her throat. She saw Twist's eyes narrow, and before she knew what was happening, Twist's face came flying at her. Reilly's head flew back as Twist head-butted her. She saw stars as she corrected her fall backward and started to fall forward, stunned.

With an abrupt yank, someone grabbed her by the shirt, and she was lifted off her knees. Her arms and legs thrashed weakly in the air. Comic in their vibrant color and size, she realized that she still wore the thick yellow dish gloves. Long strands of dark and gray hair were tangled in the rubber fingers. The guard dropped her several feet away from Twist, and her legs, in typical post-adrenaline retreat, threatened to give way as the last ounce of energy fled her body. She wiped her face. The blood that she saw on the glove when she pulled it away made her bile rise and she threw up.

"What the hell?" cried a guard, stepping with athletic speed out of the way of the vile splash.

"Okay, ladies, backs against the wall. Move back!" yelled another guard who ushered the circle of prisoners away from the immediate area.

The half-dozen prisoners retreated. The blackness encircling Reilly's vision opened up, and she took note of her surroundings.

"She fucking bit me! The bitch fucking bit me!" Twist screamed as she sat on the floor, legs splayed in front of her, holding the side of her face. Blood dripped down her arm, onto her lap, and splattered onto the white-tiled floor. Reilly's stomach churned again at the sight.

"Take them to the infirmary."

Reilly was led away on wobbling legs, the tastes of vomit and blood in her mouth.

In Reilly's House

A FEW DAYS LATER, REILLY sat on the uncomfortable chair in her cell
after having spent two days in the infirmary for a concussion resulting from the
head-butt Twist had given her. Although the doctor had scared the shit out of her
about hepatitis C, Twist had tested negative, which had been a huge relief. Other
than that, the stay in the infirmary had been uneventful and almost relaxing.
Twist had been stitched up and released, and the separation had been a welcome
reprieve for Reilly, who knew that she had made a dangerous enemy. The best
thing about her convalescence was the shower that she had been able to take for
the first time since arriving, an act that made her feel far more human than the
two days of rest.

Back in her cell, Reilly stared at a blank piece of paper on the desk in front
of her and tried to gather her thoughts. It would be her first letter home, and
she couldn't think of anything to say. She rolled a cheap pen between her hands,
which were poised as if in prayer in front of her, with her elbows propped up
on the cool metal surface of the desk. There was nothing she wanted to tell her
parents about her first few days in prison, and her depression was so thick that
no words drifted through her mind.

She glanced at the low metal-frame bed beside her. She longed to curl up on
the rough wool blanket that covered the thin mattress and go to sleep. But she
knew that the feeling of vulnerability that would keep her from falling asleep
would only lead to frustration. Even with the rule that prisoners stay out of
each other's cells, she felt too insecure to let her guard down enough to sleep
while the door was locked open. Two of the other women in the infirmary had
been shanked in their own cells. She pined for the sterile, safe sick hall, where
the mattresses were a little thicker, the blankets were a little softer, and nurses

watched over her, so that she didn't have to worry about being attacked as she slept. She closed her eyes and traced with her finger the edge of the bandage that covered the four stitches she had received just over her eyebrow.

A thick silence damped the already leaden air of the space within her cell, and Reilly's eyes flew open. The skin between her shoulder blades tingled and she turned in her chair.

Someone stood inches away. Reilly only had time to take in the up-close view of a prison work shirt and the sinister glint of something sharp held in a tight fist.

Reilly stood, but the person behind her pushed the chair to the side and leaned into her, pinning her forward against the desk. She tried to get away, but only succeeded in bashing her thighs into the sharp edge of the desk in front of her before an arm wrapped around her head and clamped a dirty hand over her mouth. Another arm wrapped around her and pinned her arms to her body. The pen that she had been holding was knocked away. Too late, she realized it was the one weapon that she might have used. Her neck protested the unnatural angle in which it was held, and she could hear the raspy breath and rapid heartbeat of her captor. Reilly tried to move her lower body to ease the lancing pain of the desk edge cutting into her thighs, but the women held her tight and pushed her harder against the desk. It had happened with nauseating speed, almost without sound, and Reilly felt panic rise in her chest. A terrified sweat sprang from her every pore. The tangy scent of Irish Spring soap wafted in the air.

Without loosening her hold, the woman that held her leaned to the side and swiveled just enough to show Reilly the two large women who stood sentinel in the doorway to her cell, blocking what was happening within. Standing with feigned casual disinterest, shoulders propped on either side of the doorframe as if they were there for a visit, were the two women who were never far from Twist. A flame of terror rose in Reilly's chest.

Reilly knew that to anyone observing, it would have appeared to be a social call—if it had been anyone other than the two visitors that were standing just outside the door, that is. Everyone knew that the presence of Thing One and Thing Two was never a sign of anything good. Reilly hoped that someone would come investigate, though she knew that everyone in her wing was more likely to turn their heads than try to help, glad that the goons weren't visiting them.

The full weight of the situation descended upon Reilly, accelerating her heartbeat to a thunder that pounded through her head. A stone seemed lodged in her throat. Twist could kill her and be out of the cell before anyone knew what happened. And even if they did witness something, they wouldn't tell. A closed mouth was a survival skill in prison. A chill replaced the flame inside of Reilly, freezing her. If Twist had let go, she wasn't sure that she would be able to move.

"Listen to me, you pathetic fuck. You're going to pay for what went down in the kitchen."

Reilly felt as if she were a spectator, above the scene, peering down through thick glass windows. Twist's voice came from a distance.

"You think you're tough?" asked Twist next to Reilly's ear. "You're shit. You're less than shit. I call the shots around here. Whether you live or die is up to me. Are you hearing me?" asked Twist, wrenching Reilly's head even more to the side. The pain was almost unbearable. Reilly could barely hear through the pounding of the blood in her ears, but she took in every word that Twist said. A strange feeling of calm descended upon her, along with the knowledge that she was about to die. In a way, she almost welcomed it. Not just because it would take away the immediate issue of the excruciating electric pain that was radiating from the contorted position of her neck, but because Reilly was sure that she would never survive the gray hell that she had landed in. If she didn't die in the next few moments, it was just a matter of time.

"I asked if you heard me, you fucking cunt!" whispered Twist in a harsh rasp, pulling Reilly up so that she had to stand on her tiptoes or risk having her head ripped off in the tight grip that Twist had around it.

The additional pain made her gasp and she choked on the mucus building in the back of her throat that she couldn't swallow because of her awkward pose. Her tears, now from pain rather than fear, made it worse, and she couldn't speak. Her mouth was still covered. She knew that she would have bruises where Twist's fingers bit into her skin, and the corner of her mouth stung. She tasted blood. Her jaw ached from the crooked way it was being held to the side.

Reilly grunted, though it sounded more like a moan, and she tried to nod her head.

"Feeling tough now, bitch?"

Reilly grunted again and tried to shake her head.

"What's that?" asked Twist. Reilly felt Twist's jaw work against the side of her head. Miraculously, Twist released her mouth, and Reilly drew in a deep and ragged breath.

"I asked if you're still feeling tough," whispered Twist against Reilly's hair.

"No," said Reilly, her voice thin and weak in her own ears.

"What? I couldn't hear you."

"No, I'm not feeling tough."

Twist laughed.

"Good. I think you get it, now. I'm the boss, you're the dog. It's that simple. You just needed some training. It would be a shame to waste such a tasty morsel."

Reilly was fighting the black spots that floated in her vision and wasn't sure she heard Twist correctly. Was she being spared? The swing of emotions that ensued erased the last vestige of energy in her, and she slumped against the vile woman behind her.

"That's right. Don't try to fight it," purred Twist against her head. "So this is how it works. You talk to no one else but me. You look at no one else but me. I tell you what to do, and when to do it. That means that you don't eat unless I say you eat, you don't piss unless I say you piss. You don't do nothin' unless I say you can. I am your boss in everything. Got it?"

Reilly nodded her head again. The bones in her neck ground together painfully. Tears streaked her face and snot filled her sinuses.

"Are you crying?" laughed Twist. "Are you really crying?"

Twist turned again just enough to show the goons Reilly's face. Reilly saw the eyes of the woman on the left flicker and wondered if she saw a little bit of reluctant shame. Reilly was an expert at reading body language. She studied it for her craft. She saw something in the woman's face that said that she did not want be part of what was going on. The emotion was there and then it was gone. And Reilly knew that an effective game face was just another survival skill learned in the bowels of forced penitence in which they lived.

With a glimmer of hope over a possible advocate, she glanced at the other shadow that darkened her door. There, she saw something different. That woman stared at her with abject hatred. Reilly understood, in a stomach dropping second, exactly what that woman's motivation and focus were. It filled her with a sick, terrified doom, and all hope vanished. Twist owned *that* woman, and at the moment, Reilly was competition. If Twist didn't kill her, that woman might.

Reilly was relieved when Twist turned back, taking the two women out of her view.

"I've decided not to fuck you up. At least, not just yet. While I was laid up, all I could think of was how I was going to hurt you, kill you. But now that we're here, I think I have other plans."

Reilly heard Thing One clear her throat, while Thing Two laughed uneasily.

"Yes. I think that I'm going to spend a little time getting to know you better before I decide whether I should kill you. Or maybe I'll just cut up your pretty little face. Either way, I'm going to let you wear my brand until I decide."

Reilly heard a whimper and then cringed when she realized that the pathetic sound was from her.

"Don't worry. I won't touch your face. Not yet. Maybe other places that don't show too much, but I'll leave your pretty face alone. I'll cut your face when I'm done with you, my sweet piece."

Twist tightened her grasp on Reilly and shook her head from side to side at each of the last few syllables, and Reilly heard the bones in her neck crack. Reilly withdrew from her body, receding from what was happening to her. She heard the words, understood the meaning, but somehow they didn't seem to apply to her. She wished Twist would just kill her.

A sound near the door made Twist snap around, tightening her hold on Reilly's head. Reilly whimpered again, and this time she didn't care. Twist dug a thumb into the soft flesh of her cheek.

"Step back, Betts. The guards will come if you're inside the door, you idiot," said Twist over her shoulder. "Turn around and watch for guards. Both of you."

Reilly heard the two women move out of the cell, and Twist relaxed. Her hold on Reilly loosened a little.

"I'm going to enjoy fucking you, you know. I'm no dyke, but beggars can't be choosers in here."

Reilly felt a warm wet tongue slide across the side of her face. Bile rose in her throat.

"When you do me, I'll tell you how I like it," whispered Twist, pulling Reilly against her and smashing her crotch into Reilly's ass. "If you make me come, I won't mark you."

Reilly nodded her head, feeling that it was the appropriate response. It seemed to work, because Twist loosened her hold again to stroke Reilly's face with the back of her fingers.

Reilly caught another glimpse of the pike.

At least that was the word that came to mind that described the weapon that Twist held in her fist. It solved the mystery of the soap smell. A rusty length of thick wire, which may have come from a wire coat hanger, was embedded at one end in a bar of soap that was shaved down to form a thick makeshift handle. The other end of the wire was sharpened to a lethal point. The shiny surface of the sharp end put off a threatening glint that contrasted with the rest of the rusty length.

Anything that Reilly had felt until that point was nothing compared to the terror that washed through her then. She shivered. Her remaining strength evaporated. The pounding of blood in her head quickened and her awareness of her surroundings dimmed. She knew that she was on the verge of passing out.

Twist's voice pulled her back from the blackness that threatened.

"I might let you kiss me if you suck me off with that beautiful mouth of yours," said Twist, close to her ear. Twist turned Reilly around so that they faced each other. The edge of the desk cut into the back of Reilly's thighs, and fear made her stiff. Reilly couldn't meet Twist's gaze, but she could see a white bandage on Twist's cheek in her peripheral vision, and she wondered what kind of hell she had called down upon herself for provoking this crazy woman.

Reilly squeezed her eyes shut and held her arms rigid down her sides as Twist buried her face in her neck.

Twist straddled one of Reilly's legs, and Reilly suppressed a cry as Twist pushed her crotch into her, rubbing it with rough thrusts against Reilly's denim covered thigh. Reilly could feel the moist heat through the fabric and the smell of unwashed flesh wafted up. The pain of the edge of the desk cutting into the back of Reilly's legs was the only thing that kept Reilly from blacking out.

"If you hold still," breathed Twist. "I'll come right now. That will give you some points. I won't have to mark you… fuck…"

Twist grunted, her breath heavy and dank on Reilly's neck.

Reilly tasted bile again as Twist moved with a quick rhythm, panting, until she rocked with a violent shudder. Just when Reilly thought she could take no more, Twist blew her hot, foul breath out in a shaking exhale. The hold that Twist had on Reilly loosened as she slumped against her.

"That's a good girl. I guess I'll let you eat dinner tonight," sighed Twist with a little laugh into Reilly's hair.

Twist eased back and inhaled deeply, as if to gather in the smell of Reilly's hair before she stepped away. Reilly wasn't sure what to do, and even though she was no longer shoved into the painful edge of the metal desk, she stood like a statue, her eyes squeezed shut.

It was easier to breathe again, but Reilly still had a hard time catching her breath. The places where Twist had held her throbbed. Her jaw clicked when she set her teeth together to close her mouth. She hoped that if she made no sound, and didn't move, Twist and her two thugs would leave.

Instead, a gentle caress swept across the side of her face. It might as well have been a slap. The vomit she had held back bubbled from her throat. She tried to seal her lips against its escape, and only a little trickled out before she swallowed it back. The thin hot stream that snaked down her chin felt like acid etching its way across her skin.

"Oh, yes. I'm going to enjoy you, movie star," sighed Twist, as she took a step back. "I'll see you at kitchen duty tonight. You'll wear my brand before lights out."

The chuckle Twist uttered as she turned to leave sounded like the harsh rasp of a dry branch on splintered wood.

Reilly kept her eyes shut and listened to Twist and her minions' footsteps as they left her cell.

"Oliver! Did I see you just leave the cell of another inmate?"

Reilly wiped her chin with a shaking hand and slouched in relief at the sound of Officer Ferguson's voice.

"I was just checking on Ransome, Boss," she heard Twist say. "I figured she'd want to see the results of her handiwork."

Reilly opened her eyes and all she could see of her attacker was her back through the doorway. But she saw Twist's arm rise, and she imagined Twist moving her fingers over the bandage covering her scarred cheek.

At the same time, Reilly saw Twist pass the pike behind her to Thing One. Thing One tucked the pike into the waistband of her own pants and pulled her shirt over it.

"You have any complaints in there, Ransome?" asked Ferguson without taking her eyes off of Twist.

Reilly remembered Twist's warning and struggled to think of a response that would keep Twist from coming back later to mark her—or worse. She hesitated, and Twist turned toward her. She knew that it was a test.

"Cat got your tongue, Ransome? Say something, or Fergie will think I offed you."

"No complaints," said Reilly, her voice sounding foreign and rough in her own ears.

Officer Ferguson stepped closer to Twist. They were toe-to-toe and the guard was five inches taller. Twist didn't so much as flinch.

"Sanderson and Betts, step back and to the side," ordered the guard, motioning with her baton. "Oliver, raise your arms to your sides so that they're parallel with the ground."

"Oh, for Christ's sake, Fergie. I was just visiting the newbie," complained Twist.

"Do it."

"For fuck's sake," said Twist, but she complied.

Officer Ferguson completed a pat down of Twist that would have done any TSA agent proud. Finding nothing, she motioned for Twist to lower her arms.

"You three move along," said the guard.

"Did you enjoy feeling me up, Fergalicious? It's okay by me if you use the memory to get off on tonight when it's just you and your trusty baton," laughed Twist as she and her shadows strode away.

Reilly studied Fergie, who stood just outside her door watching the three women disappear down the corridor. When the guard turned to look at her, Reilly felt like she had done something wrong.

"There's yoga in the media room. Starts in ten minutes. Do you some good to get out."

Then the guard turned and walked the other way. Reilly collapsed into the nearby chair as all of the strength left her.

People Eat In Here

IT WAS HER FINAL SHIFT in the kitchen, and Reilly was trying not to think about the awful interaction with Twist in her cell that morning. She turned her thoughts to her new job as librarian. Trying to figure out ways to acquire more books was easier than trying to figure out how she was going to get through the rest of her incarceration being the lap dog of an insane woman. Deep in thought, she found herself alone in the empty dining hall, walking down rows of tables, wiping them down.

"Hey, fish."

Reilly hadn't even heard her approach. She spun around and Twist was right there, six inches from her face. Thing One and Thing Two hovered just over her shoulder. Reilly was blocked in, between rows of tables. She calculated her escape and turned to leave the other way, but Thing Two was already circling around to block that route. Reilly lifted her foot to the bench, ready to vault the table, when Twist grabbed her arm.

"Where you going, movie star?"

"I have to finish wiping down the tables in here," Reilly said. Her voice trembled and she tried to hide her fear.

"Are you scared? You don't need to be scared. I'm gonna be nice to you. Nice, like you were to me in your house this morning." The thumb brushing Reilly's wrist in a suggestive manner made her want to scream. But if she screamed, the women would probably do something worse than what they already had planned.

Reilly flicked her eyes between the three women, trying to assess the situation.

"Oh. They just watch."

"People eat in here," said Reilly, hoping to negotiate a rain check on Twist's promise to treat her nice.

Twist's lips curled into a malicious smile as she peered past Reilly to Thing Two.

"You hear that, Betts? People eat in here."

"Eat pussy," snorted Thing One—the one called Saderson. Twist shot a derisive glare at Thing One, who wiped her nose with a self-conscious frown. "Sorry. I thought it was funny."

Twist's gaze returned to Reilly.

"I guess this is appropriate, then."

"Right here?"

"I'd suggest that you meet me in the bathroom, but something tells me that you wouldn't show."

"You never know."

"Oh, I think I do," said Twist, reaching up to run a thumb over the bruised cut that she had left on the corner of Reilly's mouth that morning.

"But the lights will go out soon in here."

As if on cue, the fluorescent overheads went out in the dining hall with an ominous thunk. The room was illuminated with the ubiquitous low light that kept the inside of the prison bathed in a constant gray glow at night.

"That's a bonus," said Twist, stepping closer. Reilly backed away, and into the large body of Thing Two, whose hand landed on her shoulder.

Twist reached out and grabbed the front waistband of Reilly's denim pants. The feel of unwanted fingers touching the bare skin of her belly made Reilly's panic break free. She tried to get away. Before she knew it, she was lying on her back on a table with the rag that she had been using to wipe the tables pulled taut across her mouth and nose. The musty smell of dirty dishwater made her gag. Thing One stood at her head, holding her head firm against the table with the filthy cloth. Reilly was suffocating. Her arms and legs flailed, and she felt one of the others trying to grab her ankle. She reared up, her legs swinging up over her, and she kicked Thing One in the face. With a crunch she felt, rather than heard, her feet found satisfying purchase, and the rag loosened. She rolled away from her attackers, falling off the table. Her side struck the edge of the bench on her way down, and she landed hard on the floor. She strained to regain the breath that had been knocked out of her, and she grabbed her side when a lance of pain cleaved her in two.

She heard angry whispered words and the sound of rapid footsteps between the tables. The creak of the table under tremendous weight told her one of the goons was climbing over to get to her. She forgot about her painful ribs, and she rolled under the bench to get beneath the table. She crawled down the length as fast as she could. Her focus was to get to the end of the row of tables, hoping that she'd somehow be able to make it into the kitchen where there were other people. Metal braces made navigating under the tables difficult.

A large hand wrapped around her ankle and pulled her backward. Her arms slipped out from under her and her hips landed on the bars that she was halfway through. She tried to hold onto them as she was yanked backward, but she lost her grip. Her shirt rolled up as she passed through, and the metal tore at her exposed skin. Streaks of fiery pain made her cry out.

One of her attackers grabbed the back of her shirt and heaved her up. Her head slammed against the underside of the table, and she was thrown to the ground between the two rows of tables. A fist slammed into her jaw and another pummeled her stomach. Bile rose in her throat. Through a curtain of stars, she saw Betts above her, her face contorted into a fury that bordered on insanity. Dark liquid poured from the giant's nose, and a cut separated one of her eyebrows. The huge woman straddled her, using her knees to pin Reilly's arms to the ground. The pain Reilly felt as the bones in her arms were pressed into the cement floor under the full weight of the enormous woman was more than Reilly could bear. She wailed.

"Betts! Betts! Get off her!" Twist's harsh whisper was close.

"Fuckin' bitch! I'll kill her!" spit Betts, and a fist hit Reilly in the temple. Lights flashed behind her eyelids as Reilly fought to remain conscious.

"Get off!"

The rain of punches ceased and the weight across Reilly's midsection was gone.

Reilly groaned at the relief of having her arms free, but she didn't have any strength to fight anymore. She shut her eyes and curled into a ball on her side. She tasted blood, and waited for the next onslaught. She disappeared into her head and hoped that whatever they did to her physically wouldn't get through to who she was inside.

She was lifted and carried somewhere. Bright lights tempted her to open her eyes, and Fergie's face was floating above her. A train of bright florescent lights flowed past her head.

"Fergie?"

The guard glanced down at her.

"If you ever want a job outside of here. Come see me when I get out. I mean that. You… you're…"

Reilly forgot what she was going to say, and her lip, split and bleeding, hurt when she talked. But Fergie was there for her. She always was. Reilly closed her eyes. She opened them again as she was lowered onto a stiff sheet on a high bed. The smell of rubbing alcohol and bleached linens rose to greet her. She was back in the infirmary.

Dodged a Bullet

SHE MAY HAVE HAD A FRIEND in Fergie, but the warden was another story. It had taken a few months of Reilly being summoned to the warden's office as well as an increase in subtle innuendo before his intentions became overt, but when it became clear, Reilly shouldn't have felt surprised. Even so, she couldn't believe how it went down. After weeks of indirect references and insistent, but timid attention, the warden didn't simply ease into opening his heart, he jumped right in.

The whole situation had been surreal at first, what with his calling her to his office for tea and reading poetry to her. Most disturbing about it was that he had never even acknowledged the strangeness of the situation. The sense of expectation that came from his attention had exhausted her. Every time she had received a call to his office, she wondered if she could still pull off her act of ignorance over what she very easily guessed was a slow process leading to his asking her to have sex with him. In the weird ways of irony, she suspected that it was his sense of decorum that had kept him from pressuring her, or outright forcing her, into sex right away.

Then, one day, a little over three months into her sentence, Reilly had responded to the call to his office and had just taken her usual seat in the oversized chair in front of the expansive desk when he dropped to one knee before her, taking her hands in his.

"It would make me the happiest man alive to make you my wife, Reilly. Not right away, of course. It wouldn't do to make our love public while you're a guest here, obviously. But we can be discreet. The couch is a sofa-bed—"

She'd barely heard his words, her focus was on his sweaty hands over hers. She was slightly behind him in comprehending what was happening, but when he mentioned the sofa-bed, she had almost jumped up from the chair. He beat her to it, though. A phone rang and then a knock sounded at the door. He stood up quickly, backing up a few steps. She'd never been more relieved in her life, and she hadn't realized that she had been holding her breath until the warden's assistant opened the door a crack to tell the warden that the Governor was on the line.

She left his office that day feeling like she had dodged a bullet, but the kiss he had brushed across her surprised mouth before he opened the door to let her out had been a portent of things to come.

Different From the Others

FERGIE STOOD IN THE DOORWAY to the library, causing the small space to feel smaller than it already was.

"Ransome, warden wants you."

Reilly felt like a trapped animal. The warden's last words had haunted her.

"But the library is open for another twenty minutes," she said, looking up from the stack of books that she was sorting. She'd spent her first few weeks as librarian applying for grants, and the rewards of her hard work had paid off with boxes of books, most of them used, as Reilly tried to stretch the limited funds as far as she could. The shelves of the little room were filling up.

"Everyone out. Library's closed," said Fergie, taking a book from the woman standing next to Reilly and placing it on the desk.

Abject impotence washed over Reilly as she locked up the library. She was crying by the time she arrived at the warden's office. She never cried. She had tried to hold it in, but the feeling of helplessness was overwhelming. Fergie didn't look at her as she took her normal post next to the door as Reilly went in.

He was near the door, hovering as he always did, awaiting her arrival, his hands fluttering near as she moved past him. She kept her face averted, and wiped her eyes.

"Reilly! Are you okay?" he asked, standing too close behind her. She heard concern in his voice, which made it even worse.

She stood in the middle of the room and nodded, but she didn't turn toward him, not trusting herself to speak. His presence was a greasy shadow behind her and her stomach churned.

"Did someone do something to you?" he asked, shutting the heavy door and following her into his office.

She shook her head.

His arm fell across her shoulders and she struggled to keep from shaking it off. He led her to one of the chairs in front of his desk and pulled the other one close. He kept one hand on her leg and took the handkerchief that matched his tie out of his breast pocket to offer it to her. She accepted it, but did not use it. It was scented with his cloying cologne.

Reilly watched her fingers twist the handkerchief in her lap. She felt cornered and was too exhausted to keep on fighting the warden's advances. She didn't see a way out of sleeping with him without making him an enemy.

"What is it, Reilly? What's the matter?" he asked. The worry in his voice sounded genuine. And she hated him even more for it. She wanted to shove his reeking handkerchief down his throat. "Has your… situation gotten to you? It's understandable. You've been so strong."

She decided that making him an enemy was the lesser of two evils. She'd rather him lump her in with the "perverts and dykes" than let him touch her. She pulled her anger up and used its strength for courage.

"It's this," she said, motioning between them. "I can't do it."

"I don't understand," said the warden. The confused expression he wore made her want to claw his eyes out.

"You and me. I don't want to make you mad, but I just can't do it!"

Reilly didn't expect to see the countenance of resigned agreement that transformed the warden's face. He nodded his head and removed his hand from her knee.

"Does this have to do with Cray?"

"Cray?" She was confused.

"It does. I can see. I should have known."

Reilly watched the warden run his fingers through his hair. It was the first time she had ever seen him lose his composure. Hope filled her at the thought that she might have found a way out.

"How… how did you know?"

The warden gave her a sad smile, and her hope grew. She didn't break character, though. She maintained the expression of the distraught lover.

"I'm just relieved to know that I was right. If it can't be me, I'd rather it be another man. You had me wondering, though, since he has never been to visit you. But one of the guards saw him leaving yesterday. They said that he wore a hat and sunglasses, and he used an alias. I looked it up. He hasn't been linked to any other actresses since you've been here."

The information confused Reilly. Cray had never come to the prison. She had made it clear that she didn't want anyone to visit. The only visitors she'd had were the ones she couldn't persuade to stay away—her mother, Alison, and Hank.

Hank. Hank had visited the day before. The warden thought that Hank was Cray in disguise. She didn't try to correct him. Maybe she had an out.

"We… we're private," she said.

"Of course you are. You're a decent and complex woman, Reilly. I never knew what to think of the stories about you in the papers. But you haven't taken up with any of the dykes in here. If you were that way, you would have by now. They can't help their perverse nature. I was glad to know that the homo rumors were untrue."

Anger burned Reilly from the inside out, but she had had enough practice with her mother that she was able to just sit there and stare over his shoulder.

"I'm sorry. I didn't mean to offend you," said the warden, misunderstanding her lack of response. "You must be tired of the stories. I shouldn't have mentioned that horrible gossip. The indignities that you must have suffered from those obscene rumors."

"You have no idea," said Reilly through clenched teeth.

"I know. I know. Rumors can be mean-spirited. It must be hard to hear such disgusting lies." The indignation he displayed on her behalf just fueled her anger.

"You think that they're lies?" Why couldn't she keep her mouth shut?

He just nodded his head.

"I'll admit that for a while I wondered if they were true. Everyone knows that Hollywood has more than the normal share of perversion and sin running rampant through it."

Reilly was beyond angry.

"What?"

He mistook the source of her anger, which saved her, but goaded him on to increase her rising agitation.

"No. No. Not you. I know that now. When you didn't respond to my attempts to court you, though, I have to admit that I started to wonder if the rumors were true. I wondered if you just needed a real man to show you what you need. But— but I can just look at you and see that you aren't that way," he stammered. "You don't act like those dykes. For a while I thought maybe that you were just playing hard to get. But it finally occurred to me that you're in love with someone else. I just didn't want to believe it until I saw how upset you were today."

Reilly lost track of how many times the warden had just offended her. Her continued silence was the result of disbelief as much as it was anger now. Did the world really grow this kind of asshole anymore?

"I don't want to sound arrogant, but most of the women here would jump at the opportunity to be with me. You've always been more reserved. That's why I like you. You're different from the others. It's obvious that you don't belong here."

Reilly wanted to remind the warden that she had killed someone. She wanted to tell him that she deserved to be there more than many of the other women. She wanted to scare him with her soullessness. But she finally knew when to keep her mouth shut.

"Can you do me a favor?" asked the warden.

Reilly tilted her head, wondering what she could ever possibly do for him. He had all of the power.

"Let me know if it doesn't work out between you and Cray. I can be a good man to you, Reilly. I know that these long distance things don't often work out. And if he can't wait, please let me know. I'd like a chance to treat you the way a woman like you deserves to be treated."

After that the warden had backed away from his relentless pursuit. And in doing so, he acted as if he had committed a noble deed. Although he never tried to touch her again, and he didn't call her to his office after that, she had often felt his oily eyes upon her. Once, he'd left a book of poetry on her bed. She'd known it was from him when she'd noticed the marked page on, "How Soft this Prison Is". Her love of Emily Dickinson had been tarnished since then. But she'd been afraid to throw the book away. If he'd noticed it was gone, there was no telling what his reaction would have been. So, she'd endured its presence in her cell. A reminder that she was never alone. As if the excessive trips past her cell hadn't been enough. She shuddered at the memory of the metal taps on his shoes tap-tap-tapping by her cell late at night when she was supposed to have been asleep, slowing as he approached, and quickening again once he had passed.

Fuck You, Warden

EIGHTEEN MONTHS, SEVENTEEN DAYS, SIX hours and twenty-three minutes. That's how long it had been since she'd been brought to this place. Not quite noon, and the temperature in the shade already tipped past a hundred and ten. Reilly took a cautious step from the stale, air-conditioned chill of the gray building that had been her home. Pausing to get her bearings, she stood beneath the long, steel awning that jutted like a middle finger from the structure behind her. It did little to shield her from the glare of the midday sun. A dry heat wrapped around her, tightening her skin, creeping beneath the edges of her once-favorite clothes, clothes that now felt foreign. Her emerald eyes squinted against the wind and glare, as her lanky blond hair, held back by a well-worn black bandana, whipped against her neck. Unrelenting bright light assaulted her from all sides, and arid wind swept down from the barren landscape to pepper her with a fine spray of grit. She licked her dry lips, the chapped skin rasping against her tongue.

Footsteps followed from the dark doorway behind her and stopped. The hiss of the automatic security door clanged shut. Her eyes darted to the side, but she did not turn. She was going against instinct by keeping her back turned, but she knew who—and what—was behind her. What mattered now was what stood before her. Freedom. And although she would never escape her past, she didn't have any intention delaying putting some physical distance between her and the last months of her life. Eyes forward, and ignoring the guard behind her, she descended the two steps in front of her and moved down the cement pathway that led away from the tangent her life had taken.

Steel-linked fencing spanned the sides of the awning like a cage. A feeling of uncertainty fluttered in her stomach as she took her first hesitant steps, heeding the impulse to increase space from what lay behind her. Her back twitched with each step, as she felt the invisible links of a chain anchored to her spine. She tensed when she conjured the image of someone on the inside holding the other end of the chain in their fist, waiting for her foot to cross over some unseen demarcation point, just so they could yank her back with a just-kidding smirk.

When the fencing beside her rattled with a burst of wind, she almost broke into a run. Fighting that urge, she channeled the woman she used to be, the woman who had walked with poise down more than a few red carpets. She ignored her roiling guts and moved, even-paced, through the channel of wire fencing. Her pale unmanicured feet, clad in worn-out plastic flip-flops, slapped an even cadence across the cement. The footsteps of the guard who followed close behind were almost silent. A whispered shadow that reminded her that someone was always there, always watching.

Away from the building, the heat only intensified. The smell of dry sand and burned pavement swept over her. As she emerged from under the awning, next to the parking lot, the direct sunlight beat down on her. Its needle-like intensity scoured her, and she squinted out across the sun-bleached blacktop through tear-obscured eyes.

The synthetic fabric of the light blouse she wore flapped against her skin, and she was aware of the faint smell of her own stale sweat. Her gaunt hips, which had become used to the broken-in, denim pants that she had worn for the last eighteen months, felt strange in the once fashionable skin-tight capris that were now a size and a half too big. She was grateful for laser hair removal, as the warm air caressed the bare legs she wouldn't have been allowed to shave. Out of nervous habit, she lifted a hand to chew on a thumbnail, and dropped it as soon as it touched her lips. Beyond the cloistered walls, she was unsure who could be watching her. Inside, she had gotten used to it. She knew there were prying eyes and hadn't cared, as long as they had kept their distance. But she was on the outside now. It felt different when she didn't know whose eyes might be on her. Aside from the bored guard behind her, it could be anyone. She had to assume it was everyone, although she was sure that none of her fans would recognize her now.

She squared her shoulders, pulled them back, and tilted her head back and to the side. She knew that the posture accentuated her defined jawline. Just the way the camera liked it. The pose had once come natural, now it felt uncomfortable and arrogant. She softened her stance and sighed.

Her eyes scanned her surroundings. A small parking lot sprawled before her with three-dozen or so cars baking in the sun. Not a person was in sight. Relief and disappointment shared a moment within her.

Fergie towered behind her, cleared her throat, choosing to remain in the shade. Reilly had heard the sound a thousand times. At one time, it had scared her. She had worried about its intent. Now, it was a backdrop to her metered days, familiar in its gruffness, comforting in its steadiness.

She realized she would miss it.

She swiveled to meet Fergie's eyes. Clear, blue, and unwavering, they stared back at her. Reilly held them for a moment, even though her conditioned response was to avert her gaze. For once, the guard's eyes held no challenge. A small thing, really, but enormous to Reilly, who had faced what seemed to be a lifetime of challenges while under the watchful gaze of the taciturn giant before her.

The guard's hand, strong with short, neat fingernails, held a limp, white plastic bag out to her. Reilly regarded it with numb detachment. Fergie flicked a glance at the bag and then nodded. Reilly took the bag and dropped her clenched fist to her side so that the sad package hung along her thigh. She searched the guard's expression for a clue about what came next, but the eyes were already scanning the parking lot. Reilly thought she had become accustomed to being ignored, that so many months of not mattering had hardened her a little more. But the dismissal stung.

Reilly turned back to the parking lot to see what caught Fergie's attention. Nothing had changed. Just the bright sun, still glaring off of windshields and the dusty metal of the cars parked in three neat rows.

A pumpkin-sized tumbleweed blew a lazy path across the faded pavement. She watched as it skipped up the broken curb and lodged itself against the base of the razor wire topped chain-link fence that wrapped around the prison. A second fence stood inside of that, forming a double-dare canyon. A dozen other tumbleweeds cowered in scattered groups along the outer barrier, and Reilly knew that by dinnertime, there would be an even skirt of dried weeds, two or three deep, pressed against the fence. She also knew that the short-timers would be out to clear them in the morning. Her nose itched at the memory of the dusty baked wood scent of them, and she ran her fingers over the half-dozen fresh and healing scratches she had on her own forearm.

The plastic bag next to her leg twisted in the wind. The heel of a very expensive shoe poked through and stabbed her leg, and then the bag spun the other way.

Standing there at the mouth of the tunnel-cage, she wriggled her toes in her pressed out flip-flops. Reilly had been relieved to shed the state-issued pants and work shirt, but she hadn't been able to bring herself to slip into the four-inch heels that she had worn during the entrance march into the facility all those months ago. Instead, she opted for the plastic shower shoes that the other inmates called rice paddy racers. She was sure the term was born of racism, but on the inside, everything had an element of some sort of –ism. It was the way the population defined itself. If you didn't belong to one of the groups, you wouldn't survive. Somehow though, Reilly had defined her group of one and had survived her stay, but not without serious impact to the way she saw herself and the world around her.

Looking down at her toes, she thought about the no-brand tennis shoes she had thrown, along with an unread book of poetry, into the trash bin next to the battered desk in her cell. Who was going to empty the bin now that she was gone? The thought of the abandoned shoes, a ghost of her former life, elicited a memory that she pushed away, leaving in its stead the shadow of a dull pain that she had learned to live with.

The metallic clank of the heavy security door closing behind her preceded the quick-paced, tooth-grating sound of footsteps that grew closer with the signature tap-scratch of metal against cement. Always a precursor to punishment or unwanted attention, the steps made Reilly's heart race. Her first response was to feign sleep or find a corner to hide in, but now neither option was available to her. Before she had come here, though, she had learned to hide her fear, and she didn't allow a muscle to twitch in her too-thin frame. She stood still and tracked with her ears the person approaching from behind.

"Ms. Ransome, your car is running a few minutes late. Have a seat inside where it's cooler." His voice was clipped and professional, but she knew it was a façade.

Reilly, who hadn't said a word all day, maybe all week, swallowed and turned toward the voice. There was no fucking way that she was retracing those steps again. Not in this lifetime. She didn't want to acknowledge the man who had spoken, and she willed him to disappear. Instead, she concentrated on a point just past his shoulder. She opened her mouth to decline the offer, and then shut it. A year and a half of words roared back into her, filling her throat, choking her with their volume. Her chapped lips formed a thin white slash on her face. She was afraid that the words she withheld might be as dangerous as the feelings that fueled them. Despite her struggle to refrain from letting her words free, they pressed against her lips, stronger than her resolve, and she knew that she was about to lose the battle. The low rumble of an engine and the crunch of wheels rolling over sandy pavement saved her. She turned toward the interruption and watched a long, black car pull up to the sidewalk in front of her and stop. The desert seemed to recede, and a shroud of vertigo enfolded her. The familiar sight in such an unlikely place turned her senses on their side, and a poignant sense of surrealism filled her. A sudden breath of fine sand scoured her ankles, restoring Reilly's sense of reality, and the ground upon which she stood felt solid again. She took half a step toward the car and rested her hand on the smooth black paint.

An attractive woman wearing mirrored sunglasses and an expensive suit emerged from the driver's seat and walked with a brisk gait to the passenger door of the limousine. When the driver opened the door, the smell of fresh lavender and fine leather swirled around Reilly from the air-conditioned interior. The cool whisper of chilly air and the remembered scent brought back a flood of memories, and Reilly felt the tension that had been her companion longer than she could remember begin to slide away. A little of who she knew herself to be came back to her, and she closed her eyes to regroup. When she opened them again, the driver had her hand out. Reilly offered her the limp plastic bag, and the driver took it as she lowered her dark glasses with her other hand and smiled.

As one of the few people Reilly had allowed visit her in prison, the driver's familiar face was a welcome sight for homesick eyes, and Reilly smiled back. It was the first time she had smiled in months. Her even, white teeth showed against her chapped, full lips. She turned back to the guard, her smile disappearing, and in a gesture she would never have tested before, rested her palm on the Fergie's beige uniform sleeve. The guard glanced down at her hand, but when the eyes returned to Reilly's face, there was no warning in them.

"Thanks for everything, Fergie. If you're ever in the Valley…"

"Ms. Ransome, I don't think that's within protocol—" began the warden, shifting from one foot to the other beside the guard.

"Fuck you, Warden."

Reilly was surprised she said it, but she didn't stick around to take in his reaction. She just patted Fergie's arm, which felt strong under the stiff sleeve, and turned to get into the town car that idled at the curb, noting the slight smile that twitched in the corner of the guard's mouth before she turned away.

The feel of her driver's hand on her elbow as she ducked into the waiting car shocked her. That it was brief, and that Alison was both her friend and her driver, was all that kept Reilly from shaking it off. She would have to learn to live with casual touch again.

Relief was not an adequate enough word to describe the emotion that over-took Reilly as she settled into the soft leather seat. The tinted windows created a shadowy refuge, and the soft scent of lavender enveloped her. Out a little over four months early for good behavior, she was beyond ready to leave the shithole that had housed her for so long.

She wouldn't miss a thing about that place. As soon as she thought it, she realized that wasn't completely true. In an unexpected way, she found that she would miss Fergie and the yoga classes she taught. At first the classes were a way to stay in a safe place, away from menacing inmates during free time, but after a while, they became a ninety-minute escape from the tedium. That was something Reilly would miss. If she never saw the warden again, it would be too soon. She squeezed her eyes shut against the memories as they played through her mind.

Turtle Shell

FAMILIAR AND DEPENDABLE, THE INSIDE of the car enclosed Reilly in a sense of safety she'd forgotten. Reilly sighed and closed her eyes, letting it sink in, not quite ready to believe she was free. When she opened her eyes, her eyes had adjusted and she found that she wasn't alone. Her best friend Hank was waiting in the dark interior. She had asked Alison not to bring anyone with her when she picked her up, but she knew that Hank would be there anyway.

She was glad that he was.

He started to hug her and then stopped. Less than a foot separated them, but it felt like a mile. At one time, they'd touched and hugged without restraint. But since the accident, she had pulled away from everyone in her life, emotionally and physically, even Hank. Prison had built a chasm where physical touch was forbidden, and even embraces between inmates and visitors were not permitted. She had been relieved with the simple spoken hellos and goodbyes that she was allowed. Prison had honed her protection of personal space, and she knew that her body language warned against any intrusion into it. When she saw Hank, in this familiar place, she felt a hunger for a sense of her old self. But she couldn't break down in minutes what had taken her eighteen months to build. So they just sat there and stared at each other. She watched his eyes take in her split ends and ratty headscarf, the prominence of her collarbones and bony wrists, her unadorned toenails. At one time, she would have cared what he thought of all of that. Now she just wondered if she radiated the jagged wariness that she felt. Whether he could see the Reilly that he used to know under this unfamiliar shell.

Finally, Hank reached over and took her hand. They sat like that as the car pulled out of the prison parking lot and sped down the desolate highway that would take them back to the Los Angeles Basin.

As the miles accumulated between her and the prison, Reilly fought the sensation that someone would chase her down and drag her back. She wondered how long it would take for her to feel comfortable in her own skin outside of the prison, how long it would take her not to feel like a turtle out of its shell.

Hank broke the silence, and the uncomfortable tether snapped.

"Hey, Rye. I see you're rockin' the refugee look. You look good," he said, waving his free hand to indicate her clothes. "Aside from that outfit. It's so two years ago."

Hank squeezed her fingers and let out a self-conscious laugh as his eyes searched her for a reaction. Reilly smiled and tried to think of something to say in response. Her months in prison had atrophied her conversation muscles, and as she searched for words, she had a strange feeling of sliding backward.

"The scarf makes it all work," continued Hank, filling in her awkward pause. She knew him well enough to know that he'd keep on talking until she said something. That he'd probably resort to harsher teasing to get a response. That her continued silence would make it harder and harder for him to act normal—if normal and Hank could be used in the same reference.

"I'm glad you came, Hank," she said, finally.

Hanks eyes were glued to her flip-flops. He had been getting ready to say something else, but he paused. His smile stayed, but his eyes took on an earnest gaze as they shifted back to her face.

"You do look good, Rye. You always look good. Could be better, but nothing a spa treatment can't correct, you know," he said with a sincere smile. "Al almost didn't let me come. I had to threaten her with—"

"Hank," warned Alison from the front seat.

"What?" asked Reilly, wondering what Hank, who was all of five-foot-six and small-boned, could ever threaten the six-foot-tall, muscle-bound Alison with.

"Al is in love and I told her that I would start telling people about it if she didn't let me come," said Hank in a stage whisper, his hand ineffectually blocking the sound from traveling to Alison.

"Really?" asked Reilly, pulling herself up closer to the front seat. In the rearview mirror, she saw Alison glare at Hank. "Is it true, Al?"

"She made me promise not to say anything. But everyone knows that I can't keep a secret," laughed Hank, warming up to the topic.

A kind of relief swept through Reilly. She realized that hearing about her friend's love life helped her to get out of her head. It had been so long since she had anything else to focus on outside of the bleary existence of her incarceration. She was beyond bored with thinking about herself.

"That's a lie. You've kept many of mine," Reilly reminded him.

"Self-preservation. You have just as many on me as I do on you," responded Hank.

"Who is it?" Reilly asked Alison. She slid up so that she could lean over the front seat. "Why didn't you tell me when you visited, Al?"

"Yeah, Al. Why didn't you say something?" teased Hank.

"I'm gonna kick your skinny twink ass, Hank!" growled Alison, shooting him daggers over her shoulder as she drove. With an abrupt yank of the wheel, she changed lanes and Hank thumped into the door next to him, which just made him laugh harder.

"Ow! Al, you used to have a sense of humor!"

"Are you going to tell me what you two are talking about?" laughed Reilly. She had missed Alison and Hank's habitual, mostly good-natured bickering. "Why didn't you want me to know?"

"Alison is in love with a certain paramedic."

"Hank…" Alison's voice was low with steely warning.

Reilly scrutinized Hank for information, but his face held no clue as to why Alison didn't want him talking about her new love interest. She touched Al's shoulder. It felt weird after so many months of not touching another person, but she was desperate to feel a connection with her friends.

"That's great, Al. It's about time. I was afraid that your lesbian card was just for show. Wait—" said Reilly, pausing. "A female paramedic, right? You didn't switch teams did you?"

Hank hooted.

"That's hilarious. Al? With a guy? I think I just peed myself!" he said, slapping his thighs, rocking back and forth.

"Shut up, Hank!" growled Alison.

"What the hell is so funny?" asked Reilly. She felt the sting of disconnection that came with being on the outside of an inside joke. It wasn't a feeling she had experienced much until she went to prison. And then it had become a daily part of her life. She hadn't expected it to continue once she got out.

Alison glared at Hank in the rearview and she saw them silently argue about whether to explain.

"Fuck you both," Reilly said, sitting back in her seat. The strength of her reaction surprised her, but she was pissed. "What is this? High school? Keep your secrets. I could give a—"

"She's dating the paramedic who took care of you that night at the pier," explained Hank, cutting her off.

Reilly watched Alison's eyes, moss green and serious, studying her over the rims of her mirrored sunglasses via the rearview mirror. Alison was obviously worried how she would react to the news. Reilly didn't know how she felt about it.

Hank cleared his throat to break the silence.

"In case you want to change, I brought you some things." Hank pulled a bag up from the floor and rifled through it. It was just like him to start shit and then try to change the subject when things got uncomfortable.

"Is that why you didn't want to tell me, Al?" asked Reilly, ignoring Hank, her eyes intent on the eyes in the rearview mirror. A parade of emotion flew across her friend's face. "Is it serious? Are you happy?"

"Damn you, Hank! I wanted to tell you on my own, Rye, after you settled in. It sounds bad, but…"

"Are you happy, Al?" repeated Reilly. The answer mattered to her. Alison studied her from the rearview, and she gazed back, waiting. Alison's eyes softened.

"She's awesome, Rye. I knew Lisa was it for me as soon as I saw her," said Alison, a trace of her old Brooklyn accent coming out. Any ambivalence Reilly would have felt at Alison's unfortunate choice in girlfriends flew away at the expression she saw on her friend's face. Reilly had never heard Alison's voice sound quite like it did, dreamy and happy. Her heart, which had felt dead for so long, began to beat again for her friend's happiness.

"Her name's Lisa? Tell me about her," said Reilly.

"Yeah. Lisa Ruiz. Captain Lisa Ruiz. She's in the Air Force Reserve and works for the Santa Monica Fire Department. I met her at a coffee shop two months ago. Totally random. She'd just got back from her second call up to Afghanistan. It felt like I already knew her, you know? It wasn't until she found out that I was friends with you that she told me she was there that night. She didn't have to. She could have not said anything. But she thought it was important. That's the kind of person she is, Rye. It made things weird. But I couldn't stop seeing her. I just couldn't—"

"Al, I'm happy for you."

"I've been worried about how you would feel about this. My gut has been a mess. I was gonna tell you after—"

"Al, it's okay. Really. You're in love. That's more important than… all that other shit."

"I can't wait for you to meet her," said Alison. The tension that had built in the car dispersed. "I know you technically already met her… I mean…"

"I know what you meant, Al," said Reilly, rubbing Alison's shoulder. The touching thing was coming back faster than she expected. "I don't really remember much of what went on that night anyway."

Reilly didn't know why she denied her memories. Although there was a big blank between Cray's party and the moment the police officer had woken her on the beach, she remembered more than she wanted to about that night. The sheet.

The blood. The shoe. How she acted. How she felt. The way the officer and some of the others around her had treated her like a scumbag—a celebrity scumbag, once they realized who she was—but a scumbag just the same. She'd deserved it, though. But sometimes, in her darkest moments, she also remembered the one and only kindness.

She could still feel the pressure of the paramedic's hand on her belly, helping her to focus on her breathing. In fact, she had gone back to that memory over and over since then, anytime she needed help controlling her anxiety, especially when she woke up in the middle of the night, the image of an abandoned running shoe fading from her mind, a cold sweat coating her body. It had been the one thing that had kept her from screaming out when the nightmares would rip the gauze of numbing sleep from her eyes, and she'd find herself sitting up in her dark cell, unable to catch her breath.

Reilly shook her head to clear her thoughts.

She needed to lighten her own mood.

"Too bad I didn't know about your thing for women in uniform, Al. There's a guard at the prison who I think might give Lisa a run for her money."

"I'm sure there are several," scoffed Hank, holding up a pair of stenciled khaki capri pants.

Reilly slapped his arm and then grabbed the pants.

"Are these yours, Hanky?"

"Yes, they're—"

"Dressing a bit femme these days, aren't we? Even for you."

Hank contemplated her for a moment before he answered, and Reilly knew that she had crossed a line with him. It had always been that way. He could dish it out, but he couldn't take it.

"As I was about to say, yes, they are mine. I designed them. They are part of the women's board apparel line coming out this month," he said as he pulled more clothing from the bag.

"I was just kidding, Hank. I think being away from normal people—I have to learn how to talk to people again. I'm sorry."

Hank's haughty attitude disappeared with her words and he leaned over to hug her.

"Oh, my poor Rye. I was just messing with you. That's what we do. Remember?" asked Hank.

The hug was off-balance and pinned Reilly's arms to her sides. Awkward as it was, Reilly absorbed it. She missed touching people. In prison, every touch came with questionable intention, every glance held a warning message. Reilly had learned self-preservation, though. Especially after the encounters with Twist. After that she had managed to keep to herself and avoid confrontation.

Reilly clung to Hank and willed the awful memories away. She never had any problems with the three women who had attacked her after that night. No one had, at least not in the wing they lived in, because soon after, Twist and her two thugs had vanished. It was weeks before word got back to Reilly that the trio had been transferred to the other wing of the prison. Since the two sides of the facility didn't interact, Reilly never saw them again.

"Hey, hey. They're just capris."

Reilly wiped her eyes. She had no idea when she had started crying.

"Huh?"

"Try them on, Rye. I made them for you."

"What?" asked Reilly, leaning out of the tight embrace. She pulled herself back into the present.

"The capris, Rye. Quit your blubbering and try them on. I designed them for you."

Reilly, who had been Hank's model in countless private fashion shows, and often the guinea pig for his design ideas, changed into the capris. They were a little too big, but since they were meant to be baggy, it didn't matter. The hand-painted long-sleeved tee shirt that Hank held up next fit her perfectly.

"I love them, Hank," she said, running her hands over the fabric on her thighs.

"Now for the pièce de résistance," he said, reaching into the bag again. "Voilà!"

He produced a pair of stenciled Converse to complete the outfit.

"Oh, Hank! What would I do without you?"

"You'd do other women, love. Just like you always have," laughed Hank. A snort from the front seat told Reilly that she was on her way home.

Think They Missed You?

THE CAR ROUNDED THE LAST bend before Reilly's property, which was situated high in the Hollywood Hills. All she could think about was her own bed and a long hot bath, although it kind of felt like she was coming home to a hotel. Her house had never felt like a home, even before she had left for prison. She was glad that her mother had kept Camille, her housekeeper, so at least she wouldn't be coming home to a closed up mausoleum.

Still lost in daydreams about the softness of her bed, she wasn't prepared for the scene when the car pulled up to the gate at the entry to her driveway and they were met by a mob of reporters and fans. Alison inched the car forward as the gates swung inward, forcing the crowd to part. Metallic raps echoed through the car, as hands pounded on the car as it passed. Faces pressed against the windows trying to see in. It had been three years since she had vanished from the public eye, after she'd locked herself away immediately following the accident. Part of Reilly wished they had forgotten her. Another part of her was glad that they hadn't. All of her was scared either way. She slouched low in the seat even though she knew that they couldn't see through the tinted windows.

"Holy shit, Rye," said Hank. "Think they missed you? This is why I left acting, you know. Too many people want a piece of you. Literally."

"Liar," she said. She knew Hank had left acting because he hated having to be on all the time for his fans. He hadn't had the energy to live up to the hyper—but cute—kid brother that he'd played on the show, when, in reality, he'd been a sulky—but still, cute—kid with a secret. "You always liked the guys who wanted a piece of you," said Reilly, trying to remain calm, although she'd broken out in an anxious sweat. She hadn't expected a crowd. She hadn't thought beyond the daydreams of her own bed. Out of respect for the life that she'd taken, she'd tried so hard not to focus on her own ruined life. She told herself that it was because of that, and not the prospect of a shattered future, that she hadn't put any planning into what she would face when she left the prison. Her only plan was to live life one day at a time, and to atone for her past mistakes. Regardless of why, she hadn't anticipated facing a crowd of fans and reporters.

A face appeared on the other side of the window next to her, and Reilly recoiled. She had to remind herself that they couldn't see her. "I should have taken your lead and ditched acting to go into the career that I dreamed about when I was thirteen, too," said Reilly sarcastically, feeling claustrophobic and nauseous.

"I thought that you always wanted to be an actress, chica," Hank replied, pretending to poke a nose pressed to the window next to him. Reilly laughed, and some of her panic eased. She was happy that he was there with her.

"Pretty much," she admitted. "But for a minute, I wanted to be a cowgirl. Maybe I should reconsider."

"I can see you rocking a pair of chaps," agreed Hank.

They laughed until they drove through the gate that opened with infuriating slowness. A loud thump sounded on the back of the car, making Reilly jump. Alison slammed on the brakes and yanked open her door. She stood up right outside of the open car door and uncoiled to her full height of six-foot-three.

"Back the fuck up!" she shouted. Gone was her normal soft voice. Her growl echoed against the eleven foot, vine-encrusted wall that surrounded Reilly's house and yard. "That means you, asshole! You're trespassing now. Don't make me get all Make My Day on your asses!"

Reilly imagined Alison's face as it appeared to the mob over the roof of the car and laughed at the threat. She knew full well that Alison didn't carry a gun. She was her driver, not her bodyguard.

Sirens sounded close by. Alison pounded the metal top of the car.

"That's right! The police are here now. Get the fuck back and leave the premises! We will press charges on anyone caught on the property!"

Alison got back in the car and pulled up to the house.

"The police have it all under control, Rye. No worries," said Alison, glancing at them in the rear view mirror.

"Thanks, Al."

"I wonder what would have been waiting for you if your mother hadn't done the bait and switch," said Hank, gathering his bags.

"What?"

"She put out a press release saying that you were getting out next week. Otherwise, there probably would have been a mob a hundred times bigger out here today."

"She did?" asked Reilly.

"Yeah. She's been working the rags, keeping your name in the papers."

Alison parked the car and Reilly sat in the back seat, not wanting to leave the safety of the car. With the police there, no one would have followed them onto her property, but the experience had shaken her. She had spent the last year and a half deliberately not thinking about her life when she got out of prison. Had she really thought that she'd just go home and live a life of reclusive regret?

Business Brunch 3

"HONESTLY, REILLY, YOU NEED TO get out of this house."

Reilly and her mother were on the pool deck at Reilly's house, where Reilly had insisted on meeting. For once, her mother had relented when she'd said that she didn't want to meet at a restaurant or café. How could she not? The brunch meeting they'd had just the week before—the first since Reilly's release from prison a month and half earlier—had been a circus. They'd had to sneak out of Café Ova through the kitchen, and even then, two cars had still followed them all the way back to Reilly's house, where the guards that she'd had to hire to keep people from camping at her front gate had to warn them away. Her mother had no choice. It was either meet at Reilly's, or don't meet at all. Reilly had a twinge of guilt over taking one of her mother's pleasures away, but she just couldn't face being in public yet.

"I get out," said Reilly as she watched her mother brush non-existent dust from the cushion on a wicker chaise lounge before she sat down. Melissa was dressed too formally for the poolside meeting, wearing slacks, a tailored blouse, and perilously high-heeled sling-back sandals. She shed her designer jacket, draped it across her lap, and dropped the leather messenger bag she'd been carrying next to the chair. Reilly, on the other hand, was dressed in hemp lounge pants and a tank top. Her freshly pedicured bare feet—some things had come back to her easily enough—were propped casually on the low, glass-topped wicker table that sat between their chairs. Reilly placed her coffee cup on the table, wrapped her arms around her bent legs and rested her chin on her knees. Camille topped off Reilly's coffee with more steaming liquid and placed a plate of croissants on the table. Reilly thanked the quiet woman who had done such a wonderful job of maintaining Reilly's home while she was away, and who had, on her own accord, placed fresh flowers in every room so Reilly would have something nice to come home to. Reilly's eyes filled with tears as she thought about it, and she thanked her again, knowing her sudden newfound appreciation of the woman embarrassed her. She watched the woman blush as she poured Melissa a mimosa, and then retreated into the house, leaving the women alone.

It was 11:00 am and Reilly had been up since 6:00 am. She had already worked out in her home gym, had gone through her correspondence, and had read through most of a script that she was considering. The jasmine was in full bloom and the breeze up the canyon was cool and filled with the briny smell of the ocean mixed with the green smells of new growth. Everything around her was vibrant and soft. She was relaxed and happy. It was even nice to see her mother.

"Work and appointments. I wouldn't call that getting out."

"Mom, I get out. I just don't party anymore."

"I'm not saying you have to party. But you do need to socialize. It's part of the job. It's what the image consultant said."

Reilly sighed at the thought of the high-strung consultant that her mother had hired.

"I fired Antoine, Mom."

"So I heard."

"He was full of shit," said Reilly, trying to hold on to her feeling of ease, even as she remembered the condescending prick that had tried to tell her how to live her life in the days just after her release from prison. At first she had accepted it. She had needed the help. Not only had she lost the art of how to act in public, she was forced to change the entire way she coped with having to do it. It was disconcerting how hard it was to socialize without the courage of drugs or alcohol. It wasn't just the anesthetic quality that she missed, the crutch she'd leaned on to help ease the mood, which had always seemed necessary, but she missed the use of them as a prop or a distraction most of all. Reilly hadn't realized how often she had relied on the excuse of finding another drink to ease her out of an unwanted conversation until she wasn't able to.

"He called me himself to tell me all about it. He was in quite a state."

"He was always in some sort of state. That was another thing I couldn't stand. Everything was always so dramatic with him. It was exhausting."

"People pay a lot of money to work with Antoine."

"I don't know why. He's full of shit."

"Reilly! He is one of Hollywood's—"

"Overpaid bags of wind," Reilly finished her mother's sentence with a laugh. "You don't tell someone who's in the program to go out and *yust hold a dweenk. Pweetand to seep eet*," said Reilly, in Antoine's over-the-top French accent. For someone who had lived in California for the last twenty years—if she could believe his resume—the guy was still almost impossible to understand. "Antoine is most definitely full of shit."

"You aren't in the program," said Melissa, shaking her head in frustration.

Reilly paused a moment. She was still in a good mood but knew that would change if they moved into an argument about Reilly's lifestyle, so she refrained from reminding her mother that part of her sentencing had mandated that she attend Alcoholics Anonymous every day of her prison sentence, or until a counselor said she didn't need to attend any longer. The counselor provided clearance well before her term was up, but Reilly had attended meetings until the day she was released from prison. She had gone for the interaction. It was the only place she had felt connected. It was the only place she ever talked.

"You're right, Mom, I'm not. I'm lucky. I don't have a problem with drugs and alcohol. It turns out that I can stay away from them if I try. But I'm grateful for what the program taught me. For all that clueless consultant knew, I do have a problem, though. And he still suggested that I go to parties and just hold a drink to fit in. He was a jerk."

"He's the best in the business, Reilly."

"And that's scary."

"You can't stop socializing, Reilly. You have to be seen. You have to—"

Her mother had hit the trigger. The mood Reilly had been holding onto dropped immediately.

"That's the thing, Mom. I don't have to do any of that. I was away for almost two years, three if you count the time during the trial—"

Reilly's mother gestured for Reilly to stop, but Reilly wasn't about to let her mother keep avoiding the event that had changed her life.

"Mom, just because you don't like to hear it doesn't make it any less true. I was in prison for almost two years, and no one has forgotten about me. I have more offers for work than ever before. The press still stalks me. You can't say that my lack of *being seen* has affected me in a negative way."

"I guess that me busting my backside to keep your name in the papers all of this time had nothing to do with it."

"That's my point, Mom. There are other ways to keep my name out there rather than me having to go to parties and playing the social diva thing. I can't do that anymore."

"It's part of the job—"

"Not anymore. You already proved that my career could survive my physical absence."

"You can thank the second Academy Award for that. And that ridiculous dance movie that came out after you… went away. Who knew that tripe would turn out to be a summer blockbuster? For once, I'm grateful you didn't listen to me. There. I'll give you that. But you got lucky. You can't rely on those things holding you in the spotlight forever. They won't keep you on the lists. You need to get out there."

"That's what I'm trying to say, Mom. I don't need that stupid image you think works for me. It doesn't anymore."

"Luck doesn't last. That award will only carry you for so long—"

"Mom. Stop."

"—and then one day you'll wake up and no one remembers who you are—"

"Stop."

"—and what will you have then?"

"Stop!" screamed Reilly, balling her hands into fists on her knees. She was so frustrated that she wanted to throw her coffee.

"What?" asked Melissa, feigning innocence and inflaming Reilly's anger even further.

"I can't have this conversation with you anymore! If you can't hear that, well, maybe we need to consider adjusting our arrangement."

"What? Is this because of the book?"

Melissa took a thick sheaf of paper from her bag and set the manuscript on the table between them. The title page blew open in the breeze. Reilly grimaced at the title, *Growing Up Reilly*. It was a book that Melissa had written while Reilly was in prison. It was about Reilly's rise to fame. Reilly had read the first couple of chapters and had to put it down. She had been embarrassed by the way her mother had written it from the perspective of an adoring and supportive mother who had orchestrated her daughter's every move—some of which was true. But the overall tone embarrassed Reilly in its blatant and smarmy attempt to make Melissa sound like a wonderful and caring mother. When Reilly couldn't get through the second chapter, she told her mother that there was no way that she would allow it to be published. They had argued about it, but Reilly had been adamant.

"The book?" asked Reilly. "No. Like I said, there will be no book. It's beyond that."

Melissa smoothed the top page down on the manuscript and looked up at Reilly.

"What are you saying then?"

"I'm saying that if we can't begin to work together in a more collaborative way, I don't think that we can continue to work together at all. I want to take a more active role in my career. And not just by showing up at parties and falling all over directors and producers with my tits hanging out. I don't want to just show up anymore. I don't want to play those games. I can't. Not anymore."

Her mother sat back in her chair, seeming to take in what Reilly was saying. The insecurity that washed over Melissa's face tugged at Reilly's heart. She didn't like to see her mother feel uncertain or hurt. Softer words formed in Reilly's mouth, but before she could say them, an expression of petulance swept over Melissa's face, and the feelings that Reilly always felt when she knew that her mother was manipulating her took over.

"I never—I wouldn't—" started Melissa, leaning forward in her chair and then sitting back again. "I should have seen this coming when you asked me to stop coming to visit you. When you were—away," said her mother, mustering the crocodile tears that always tore Reilly in two. Reilly knew the tears were fake, but to see her mother cry made her stomach churn even when she knew she was being played. Shame made her shrink back into her chair. She wanted to take back the tits comment. Her mother had never asked her to use her body to get a job, though the expectation that she hide her sexuality made her feel the same way that she would have if she had. A swirl of confusing emotions swam through her.

"I only asked you to cut back on the visits, Mom. Just for a few weeks. You were driving me crazy with all the talk about what was going on outside, when I was having a hard time adjusting to being inside," said Reilly, trying to soften things, to ease them back into a less emotional discussion.

Even as she spoke, Reilly's thoughts slid back to that day over a year earlier in the visitor's room at the prison.

A low, gray cloud of angst and despair hung over the visitors and visited in the sterile prison meeting area where Reilly sat facing her mother across a plastic expanse of white. The ubiquitous institutional gray of the surroundings seemed to steal the life from everything in it, including the people. Even the army of fluorescent lights that hung from the ceiling did little to chase away the shadows that clung to the edges of the room. Reilly slouched in the plastic chair, her unattended hair tucked behind her ears and her hands tucked under her thighs. The low, monotone drone of voices from the conversations going on around her made Reilly's head hurt. Between that and volatile emotion choking the air, it was hard to concentrate on what her mother was saying, so she watched her mother's lips move but didn't follow what she said. She didn't even try. It was always the same. Work and gossip. Reilly felt so removed from all of that, and it was just a reminder of the life that she had lost. It was easier to just tune it out.

"…and that Sylvie creature. I don't know how they get invited to the functions where they show up together. You have to admit, Parker Stevens has got to be the hardest working B-Lister in town."

Reilly's eyes shifted from watching the crease next to her mother' mouth lengthen and shorten as she spoke up to her mother's green eyes. The familiar names caught her attention. Some of the fog cleared in Reilly's head, allowing her to focus on some of her mother's words.

"Sylvie? Parker?"

Melissa leaned forward, a sudden, renewed energy in her story, now that she had Reilly's interest.

"I know that you two mended fences, but I think it's disrespectful how they carry on."

"Carry on?"

"Flaunting their relationship. Shoving it down everyone's throats. Even you displayed some class by not making such a big deal about your… lifestyle," explained Melissa. She made a dismissive gesture and wore an expression as if something smelled bad. "I'm sure it's just for the publicity. Celebrity lesbian couples seem to be the new 'in' thing."

"Relationship?" It surprised her that she cared less about Sylvie and Parker being a couple, and more about her mother's reaction to the news. She wondered if her mother was upset because lesbians were getting more mainstream acceptance, or if it was residual bitterness over the fact that Sylvie used to fuck her daughter. Either way, Reilly fumed at her mother's homophobia. Her recent meeting with the warden, where he had referred to the showers as a hotbed of dyke-lechery, was still churning in her mind. And her old triggers over her mother's bigotry seemed to be just as sensitive as ever. Reilly felt hot anger flash within her. After being numb for so long, in a way, the anger that she was starting to experience was a comfort, welcome even, and Reilly allowed it to build to a level that probably wouldn't have flamed in another situation.

"Yes, they're together. That's what I said. Honestly, Reilly. You could at least try to listen. It's like talking to the wall sometimes."

"I'm sorry that I haven't been able to keep up with the important things, Mother. I've been a bit… preoccupied," spat Reilly, aware that she was picking a fight, but unable to stop herself. As far as her mother knew, she was still in love with Sylvie. But her mother didn't seem a bit concerned about how Reilly would take the news that her former lover and ex-rival were now together. The lack of sensitivity made Reilly's head pound and it was a good enough excuse to goad her mother.

"I know it's tough, darling. But if I'm going to drive for two and a half hours each way every week to see you, it would be nice if you tried to engage in the discussion."

"Tough?"

"Well, yes. I imagine hearing that your… friend is moving on is hard."

Reilly thought about that. Her mother was right. It was hard to hear about the lives that were going on without her. But it always came back to the fact that she had absolutely no right to mourn the loss of her own life when she had been the cause of loss to people who were far more innocent than she. She had no right to feel sorry for herself. And with that, her anger evaporated, only to be replaced with an exhausting sense of disconnected loss and self-loathing. Even her mother's homophobia was no longer an outrage that she could claim. As her mother continued to talk, Reilly sank further into her shell. She wished that she could crawl into a corner and let the world fade away.

"Mom. Maybe you should hold off on coming out here again for a little while," Reilly suggested, even as Melissa continued to talk. She heard the hollow sound of her own voice, flat and toneless, coming from a distance that was made from emotional barriers rather than physical space.

"—can't be that difficult, though. I mean, even a nod every once in a while would be better than—" Melissa continued, focused on her nails, an expression of being wronged etched across her face. Then she dropped her hands to the table as she absorbed what Reilly had just said. "Not come out here? That's ridiculous, darling."

"Just for a few weeks. I need a break. I can't deal with much of anything right now."

Reilly stood up and turned away before she lost the will to do even that, but not before seeing a kaleidoscope of emotions flash over her mother's face as she sat stock still in the plastic chair. Reilly felt a pang of guilt over having caused her mother to look so unsure of herself, sitting in the middle of the stark surroundings, among the eclectic array of humanity that gathered in prison visiting rooms. She was certain her mother had never expected to be here. Reilly was ashamed that her actions had inflicted it on her mother, and she hesitated in her retreat. She turned back, ready to recant her last comment. But the petulant expression that greeted her stopped her cold.

She turned and walked across the room to the guard who unlocked the door that led back into the cellblock. This time, Reilly didn't look back.

That discussion was never brought up again, and Melissa had never come back to the prison to visit again. In a way, that had been a relief for Reilly. It had been hard enough for her to summon the energy to visit with the people who still came out to see her even after she had asked them to stay away—mainly Hank and Alison. But her friends didn't drain her like her mother did, or push her buttons the same way. Reilly had written her mother letters, though. And even though she couldn't bring herself to talk about the real horrors of prison life, she spoke of her jobs and superficial things. And, eventually, Melissa had written back. Reilly had even started to look forward to the twice-weekly letters that were covered in her mother's elegant cursive once they became regular. She found that it had been easier to take in the inane accounts of existence of life on the outside when she read about them.

Now, sitting across from her mother, basking in the sunshine that splashed across her own backyard, all of that seemed like another lifetime. It was part of her, but different. Was it wrong of her to own that existence when it suited her, but store it away when it didn't? How was it any different when her mother asked her to do the same?

"I was just trying to keep you informed. I thought that it would help you keep close to things, you know, stay in touch."

"It just reminded me of how cut off from things I really was, Mom. You coming there, visit after visit, telling me about a life that wasn't mine anymore. You have no idea what I was going through and you never even asked."

That's what it was really about. But Reilly didn't mean to say that. She didn't really want to get into it, but, there, it was out. She had said it. Her mother had never once asked about her life behind the walls. It shouldn't have surprised her, since her mother had never even asked her anything about the night of the accident, how she felt about the knowledge that she had killed someone, how she was holding it all together. Not once. Reilly thought that any other mother would have worried about how her child was coping. But Melissa hadn't. She never even acknowledged it.

"I can't imagine that it was very interesting, darling," Melissa said. Her mother's response was like a punch in the stomach. Reilly didn't try to hide the fury that swept through her. She saw it reflected in the surprised look on her mother's face, and then her mother immediately tried to back pedal. "That came out wrong. I didn't mean that it wasn't important. I—I just didn't want to remind you of your—your confinement. I mean, what with you having nothing to do but hang out in your cell."

Reilly didn't respond immediately, but when she did, her voice was shaking with emotion.

"You wouldn't have been reminding me, Mother. I was in it every day. It wasn't a confinement. It was a prison sentence. I was a prisoner. And, by the way, on the inside they don't call it a cell. They call it a house. And I didn't just sit in my house all day long. I had a job. I had a routine. I had things to—to deal with," spat out Reilly. She wanted—no, she needed—her mother to understand what she had been through, even though she knew that no one had the capacity to understand the fear and isolation that she had felt, without actually having survived it. But she couldn't bring herself to tell her mother the details about the horrors she'd faced. "I lived it. I breathed it. I survived it. And it will always be part of me. I won't let you pretend that what happened doesn't exist. By avoiding it, you avoid part of who I am."

"I don't know why you want to bring attention to it. It—it's—" Melissa searched for the word she needed.

"It's what, Mother? Embarrassing? Uncomfortable? Distasteful?" suggested Reilly.

"Reilly—" But Reilly wasn't about to let her mother try to diminish what she had gone through. She was done letting her mother's experience be more important than her own.

"Yes, it's embarrassing and uncomfortable and distasteful. It's also something I will live with for the rest of my life. I've let you avoid other things about me, but not this, not anything else, not anymore."

The air hung like a brittle piece of cellophane between them.

Melissa sighed. It wasn't a sigh of exasperation, but a sound of letting go. And she surprised Reilly by not defending herself or propagating the argument.

"So, where does this leave us?" asked Melissa.

Reilly took a deep breath and tried to ignore the pounding in her ears. She summoned the calming mantras that she had learned in the prison yoga class. Finally getting to release the core of her anger on her mother should have made her feel better—or at least relieved. But, instead, it made her feel hollow. Suddenly, she knew that the relationship she had with her mother was only a part of the unnamed cancer that had riddled her life. She'd taken responsibility for the horror that she had committed. She'd made some wise changes by eliminating the out-of-control parts of her life. Now, she had faced down her mother and shifted the power. But there was still something out of tune in her life, something that drifted just out of reach. Something that she still needed to fix. But she didn't know what it was. She rubbed her temples and looked at her mother.

"I want to be more involved with my own career," repeated Reilly. Her voice sounded dull in her own ears. She was exhausted, and she dropped her head into her hands.

"Okay. That shouldn't be hard. You could put your degree to use."

Reilly was surprised that her mother remembered the online business degree that she had pursued while in prison, even though Reilly had mentioned it several times in the letters. Reilly had only pursued it to keep busy, to keep from obsessing over her ruined life. And though the pursuit of the associate's degree had been nothing more than a diversion for Reilly, she was proud of it. It had been something that she'd done on her own. And it had been one of the only safe topics that she could report home about, so she made more of it in her letters than she felt.

"I'm sure that what I learned online doesn't come close to your vast experience, but I'd love it if you showed me a few tricks," said Reilly, offering a branch. She wondered if she and her mother could start over.

"Does that mean that you'll keep me around? You're not kicking me to the curb?"

"Of course I'm not kicking you to the curb, Mom," said Reilly, feeling tenderness toward her mother in the face of her mother's uncertainty.

"Good. Because I didn't want to remind you that we have a contract."

Reilly felt a stone grow in her heart and she stood up. She hid the disappointment over the comment. Her mother had simply reminded her that she was incapable of being her mother.

"I hope it doesn't come to that. But contract or not, I'll still take care of you and Dad. I'm tired. You know the way out."

Reilly walked into the house.

Hank's Warehouse

"WHO WOULD HAVE THOUGHT THAT those pictures taken of you coming back from prison in my clothes would have resulted in this, Rye?" asked Hank, as they strode through the warehouse that now worked as his design studio and retail hub. It was a far cry from the much smaller strip mall storefront and one-man show that had been Hank's business just two months before. Even then, Reilly had been impressed with the small fashion house that Hank had grown. Today, she was blown away.

The dusty smell of industry wafted around them as they walked across the gritty cement floor. The enormous metal doors on the front of the building reminded Reilly of the sliders that opened into the studios on the large movie lots. They were wide open, and the mid-day sun tried to infiltrate the cavernous space with light, though it didn't quite make it to the very back, where high metal shelves were piled with cardboard boxes and massive bolts of fabric. The section in front of the shelves was filled with industrial sewing machines, several of which were in use by incongruous appearing young people who seemed like they would fit in better at the local skate park. In the center of the large open space were huge tables littered with works in progress and stacks of silkscreen templates. The corrugated steel walls of the space were covered in colorful graffiti. Mannequins peopled the workspace, many in interesting poses. One mannequin seemed to fly through the air like Tarzan from a long chain attached to a metal I-beam that spanned the building.

Artifacts left behind by the previous owner took up the entire front section of the giant warehouse, and Reilly knew that they were the largest determining factor in Hank's decision to set up shop in the space. A small skateboard park complete with an empty fiberglass pool, several rails, and a professional-sized half-pipe filled the space. Punk music blared from an overhead speaker system. The place reeked of creativity. Reilly loved it.

"This place is amazing, Hank! I bet you can't wait to get to work each morning," she said, speaking loud enough to be heard over the music.

Hank just smiled and nodded.

Reilly watched a dozen kids dart about on their skateboards in the half pipe, and Reilly knew that she had grown up a little when she wondered if Hank had enough insurance to cover a nasty fall. As if she made it happen with her mind, she saw one of the skateboarders shoot into the air, miss his landing, and slide the rest of the way down the slope. He was up like a spring, though, seeming to be no worse off for the fall. When she heard the kid laugh, she realized it was a girl, and she smiled to herself.

Reilly stepped over to one of the tables and watched as a young man with a pierced lip and a tattoo sneaking up the sides of his neck drew an elaborate dragon design on a piece of thick paper, which was then taken to a nearby table by another tattooed kid, who cut it into a stencil. The focus they had on their work was impressive. Neither of the artists looked older than fifteen.

Hank stood behind them and watched.

"Awesome work, Skeet. Great cuts, Lucia. I can't wait to see the shirts when they're finished," he said, with an encouraging pat on each back.

Reilly watched Hank talk to his helpers and smiled. Hank had always been a positive person, even at his lowest moments. And between the two of them, coping with the pressures of Hollywood and dealing with coming out to not-so-very supportive parents, she had seen Hank at some pretty low points in his life. But he always responded with an upbeat attitude, and she was impressed to see it reflected in his work and in the people he worked with.

Reilly picked up a small stack of stencils and sorted through them.

"I'm not gonna see you on a documentary anytime soon am I, Hank? *Sweatshops in America: From Skateboard to Sewing Machine*," she teased. She watched through her lashes for his reaction. She was only half-kidding.

"Only if it's good for business," Hank teased back, smacking the bottom of the stack of stencils Reilly held. She almost dropped them, juggling them back into a neat stack that she placed back on the table. Then she trotted after him as he made his way to another set of tables.

"Aren't you a little worried about having so many kids hanging out here? Do you think that it might bring some unwanted elements into your work?" asked Reilly when she caught up to him. She tried to sound casual, but in her own ears she sounded judgmental—and not at all unlike her mother. She cringed and wondered if there was a way to take back her last words. His glance told her that he had heard it, too.

"Actually, no. Just the opposite. Everyone knows that this is a drug-free, attitude-free zone. They bring that shit in here, and they're out. No exceptions," said Hank, slashing the air for emphasis.

"You sound like such a badass!"

"You say that like it surprises you!" Hank said as he stopped abruptly and faced her with his hands on his hips.

Reilly just laughed.

"Yeah. You are such a badass, Hank. You. The guy that hid behind me when that muscle-bound guy at the frozen yogurt place caught you drooling over his boyfriend's ass!"

"I wasn't drooling. Besides, I couldn't help it. It was right there, asking to be looked at. And that giant had muscles on his eyeballs, Rye! His eyeballs!" said Hank, taking his hands from his hips and pointing at his eyes.

"So you used me as a shield?"

"Okay. I admit, it wasn't my finest hour," conceded Hank as they watched the skaters zip up and down the concave pipe. "So far, the kids have policed themselves. You'd be surprised. They rise up to the expectations that are set for them. If you expect them to act like punks, they will. If you expect them to be cool, they're cool. Besides, the majority of the kids here aren't even kids. They might act like it, and dress like it, but most of the people you see here are twenty, or older. Most of them are our age, if you can believe it. Skeet, the guy who just drew the dragon design? He just turned thirty-one." When Hank saw Reilly's raised eyebrow, he laughed. "I've been begging him for his secret. I'd be a gazillionaire if I could bottle that shit!"

Reilly continued her tour of Hank's warehouse and grew more impressed with her friend's work. When demand for his designs outgrew his capital for the raw materials and space he needed, Reilly had loaned him the money to grow his operation so he could keep up. With that decision, not only had she become the unofficial spokesmodel for the clothing line, she had become a silent partner in one of the hottest niche fashion houses in California.

"Hank, I'm so proud of you! You've done so well with all of this."

"Thanks to you, Rye. I did okay before, but you wearing my stuff has taken it to another level. Plus the loan. I can't thank you enough. I just hope you keep liking what I put out."

"A few years ago your stuff was a little too punk for me," admitted Reilly. "Either you've tamed it down, or my taste has changed. But I do like the edgy vibe of the stuff that you design for me."

Hank inspected the tee shirt Reilly was wearing. Scoop-necked and three-quarter length sleeves, the distressed material had a carefully stenciled image of a woman holding several shopping bags, as well as a Chihuahua in a designer carrying tote—both the woman and the dog were living voodoo dolls. Reilly's cargo pants were also part of Hank's collection, with a small voodoo doll Chihuahua stenciled on the back pocket. The pants came with a detachable chain that hung from one of the front belt loops and ended in the back pocket, but Reilly wasn't comfortable with that statement, so she had taken it off.

"To be honest, I don't think you could have pulled it off before the—a couple of years ago," said Hank, hesitating over giving voice to the moment when her style had changed. Even Hank had a hard time defining Reilly by the heinous mistake she had made. Reilly appreciated the sensitivity, but at the same time, she knew that she didn't deserve to be given an easy out. She wanted to put it out there, take responsibility for it, but at the same time, she didn't want to make the whole thing about how she felt or how she was doing. That would have been disrespectful in light of what she'd done. So she didn't say anything as Hank continued. "No offense, you've always been fab, Rye. But you used to have that girl-next-door-growing-into-a-sophisticated-lady thing going on. Sleek and put together. It was nice. Maybe too nice. But, now, you have a little edge going on. It's a little bad-girl, and a lot sexy, and it definitely suits you."

"Thanks, Hank," she said regarding him out of the corner of her eye. "I think."

Hank just laughed and put his arm around her shoulders as they walked toward the front of the building.

"So, I've been meaning to ask you what you want to do with your car. I kept it at my place for a while. Now I'm storing it here, out back," said Hank. His words were casual, but the arm around her shoulders told her otherwise. She was sure he felt her back stiffen.

The car.

When the trial was over, and all of the evidence had been returned to her, she had been in prison. Her accountant had paid the impound fees, and Hank had picked up her stuff. Her mother had asked her what she wanted to do with the car during one of her visits to the prison, and Reilly had asked her to see if Hank would deal with it. Since then, when Hank or her mother brought it up, she changed the subject. The stuff was meaningless. She had no idea what had been in the car. A jacket? A pack of gum? It was nothing important. As for the car, she wasn't sure that she would ever drive again. If she did, she certainly would never drive that car.

"I can keep it here for you as long as you want," added Hank when Reilly didn't respond. "Or I can get rid of it for you, if you want. You know—make it disappear," he said in his best Al Capone imitation.

"Would you?" responded Reilly after another pause.

"Sure. I can do that."

"Thanks. You can just sell it, though. No need to find car-sized cement boots."

"Where's the fun in that?" asked Hank before they were interrupted by a familiar voice.

"Hey, you two!"

Reilly was relieved to drop the topic and turned to see a sorely missed friend coming toward them.

"Cray! I didn't think that I would see you until shooting started," she said, referring to *Dare to Dream*, the sequel to *Salsa Nights* that they were scheduled to start filming in a few weeks. She threw herself into his arms when he got close enough. "What are you doing here? Researching a role?"

Cray was so clean cut that he'd literally been the poster boy for BYU before he caught his big break in Hollywood. Standing in the workshop, he stood out like a missionary among the punks and skaters that wandered the premises. She wondered what the parents of the innocent sheep who attended that hallowed institution would think if they knew the recruiting model that graced the literature they held during freshman orientation would have been excommunicated for what he had done with the photographer after the photo shoot.

"Why not? It seems to fit *you* pretty well," said Cray, stepping back to inspect her. He gave a playful tug on the belt loop of her baggy cargo pants. The form-fitting tee shirt she wore stopped a fraction of an inch above the waistline of her pants, showing off a little skin. He pulled down the fabric as if he were trying to cover her up. She smacked his hands away.

"What really brings you down here? I can't believe I haven't seen you since I've been back. It seems we kept exchanging messages."

She saw Cray and Hank exchange a look.

"I was out of the country. Hank said you'd be down today, and I thought that I'd surprise you."

"You guys know each other?" she asked scrutinizing one, and then the other.

"Shaw. Totally," said Hank nodding his head, in his best imitation of a surfer.

"Really? How'd this happen?"

"Well, if you must know," began Hank, teepeeing his fingers in front of his face, a la Dr. Ruth, "when two men who love other men meet up in the dark hallway of a sex club—"

"Shut up! Shut up! I don't want to hear this," said Reilly. She covered her ears and walked away.

"Just kidding, Rye! Just kidding!" Hank grabbed her arm.

"Let's go to lunch and we'll tell you over some chicken vindaloo," said Cray, catching up to them.

Lunch with the Boys

TWENTY MINUTES LATER, AT HANK and Reilly's favorite Indian restaurant, the three of them had settled into a half-circle corner booth and returned the menus to the waiter who had just taken their order. Reilly broke off a piece of fresh papadum. She dipped it in the sweet and spicy sauce and sized up her friends.

"So," said Reilly, waving between them, encouraging them to tell the story of how they knew each other.

"We met at the premier of *Salsa Nights*," said Hank, winking at Cray.

"*You* went to a movie premier?" asked Reilly, pinning Hank with her gaze. He hated things like that. It was one of the reasons that he had given up acting.

"What can I say? He was hot! I mean so, so *hawt!*" crowed Hank, shooting his finger up in a dirty reference to what the *hawt* guy did for his penis. Reilly hated it when Hank brought his penis up in conversation.

"That he was, my friend, that he was," agreed Cray, mimicking the gesture.

Reilly was confused and a little grossed out by the penis bonding, but she had to wait for the waiter to refill their water glasses to ask what they were talking about.

"One more order of papadum?" asked the waiter, unknowingly imitating Hank's and Cray's finger gesture.

The waiter looked confused when they all broke out laughing.

"Yes, please," said Reilly, nodding her head as she tried not to choke on the sip of water she had just taken. When the waiter was out of earshot, she whispered: "You guys are awful!"

Hank and Cray just laughed more.

"Who was the hot guy?" she asked, after the guys got their laugher under control. She looked at Hank, who looked at Cray. "Cray?"

"No. Not Cray," said Hank, rolling his eyes at her, as if she were clueless. Reilly was irritated at his response—how was she to know?—but she was relieved that she wouldn't have to hear about what Hank and Cray would do with their penises together. Then Cray, who was sitting next to him, smacked his arm, and Hank amended his response. "I mean, yes. Cray is hot. Beyond hot, actually. But I was talking about Noah. The guy I was dating at the time—no, make that the guy that I was *doing* at the time. He was a gaffer or something on the movie."

"He was an assistant producer, you dork," corrected Cray.

"That's just what he said to get in your pants," said Hank, raising his eyebrows and lowering his chin to stare at Cray.

"You lost me. I thought you were dating—I mean, *doing*—him, Hank? Wait. Did you both…?" she asked, without completing her question, waving a pointed finger between them.

"Yes," they answered in unison.

"Gross," said Reilly. She didn't want to imagine the two of them with some random guy like that. She knew that she had no room to talk, though.

"But not at the same time," added Cray.

"Though, if it had come up, I'd have been all over that action," said Hank with another obscene hand gesture.

"Stop!" said Reilly. Then she realized that she was being hypercritical. She and Sylvie hadn't been so different about their conquests. They just hadn't talked about it openly to other people. At least she hadn't.

"But that's all over with now. Hank is it for me," said Cray.

Reilly set her glass down so hard that she sloshed water onto the tablecloth.

"What? Wait! You two are together? You're dating? How long?" she sputtered.

"Long, as in gay years? Or long, as in straight years?" asked Cray.

"She doesn't know straight years," said Hank to Cray before turning back to Reilly. "We might as well be married, Rye."

"What does that mean?"

"Well, like I said, we met at the premier. That was, what? Right before Memorial Day the year the movie came out? Three years?" Hank turned to Cray for affirmation. Cray nodded and took a sip of his water.

"*Three* years? How did I not know? Why didn't you tell me?"

"I know, right? That's, like, twelve years in gay years. Anyway, you had so much going on," said Hank. With a smile and a nod of thanks, he took the new order of papadum from the waiter who delivered it to the table.

"You were a bit tied up with the trial at the time," said Cray. He reached across the table and petted her arm. "You couldn't even do the promotional stuff with me, remember? I had to do most of it by myself. Thank the gods that someone filmed that dance we did at that award party I threw for you. Holy crap, that dance was hot! You were on fire that night, babe."

"Oh, yeah!" said Hank, glancing at Cray with a smile. "That video has over a hundred million views on that video website that everyone uses when they aren't watching porn."

"I just saw the video a few weeks ago," said Reilly. "Internet access was limited to certain websites on the inside. A hundred million views, though? Wow!" Reilly smacked Hank on the shoulder. "Okay. I was busy with the trial. But what about when you came to visit? Why didn't you tell me about you and Cray then?"

"You mean when I came out to visit you in the Big House?" asked Hank. "You were so quiet whenever I visited. We didn't talk much. We just sat there most of the time. And when we did talk, I didn't know what to tell you that wouldn't make you feel bad."

"That's what my mom said." Reilly had a sudden revelation about how she had forced people to walk on eggshells around her. She wondered if they still did. Shame welled up inside of her. She studied Cray to see how he was responding to all of this.

"Don't look at me. You told me not to visit," said Cray, studying the food the waiter had just set down before him.

Reilly had seen a glimpse of hurt in Cray's eyes before he glanced away.

"I'm sorry, Cray. I was embarrassed and depressed. I didn't want people to see me like that."

Reilly wondered how the topic had gotten around to her and wanted to change the subject. But she also knew that they needed to acknowledge a few things before they could all feel comfortable around each other again. Again? Maybe for the first time since she'd been back, she thought. She hadn't really talked about her experience in prison, except to give the sterile version when anyone asked: that she had kept to herself and that she had read a lot. Partly because she didn't want to relive it through the telling, but most of it was that she didn't want to feed the curiosity of most people who asked her about her experience. It was intensely personal. That didn't apply to her close friends though. Some people probably wanted to know because they loved her.

"It's okay, Rye. I wouldn't have known what to talk about if I had visited, anyway," Cray said. Reilly took some comfort in Cray's affirmation.

"I never knew what to talk about, either. I know that I didn't act like it, but I loved hearing about what was happening on the outside. It helped to get my mind off of what was going on inside."

Reilly realized that they were having the exact opposite discussion of the one that she had with her mother by the pool. She wondered why it had been so different when it had come from her mom.

"Was it awful?" asked Hank. He lowered his fork to give her his full attention. A rare action on his part, so she knew that he was concerned and she couldn't just brush it off, as she was accustomed to doing. Cray continued to eat, but he was also watching her intently.

"Sometimes. On the good days. Most of the time it was worse than awful," Reilly admitted, feeling herself pulled back into memories that she had a hard time connecting to the person that she was now. It just didn't seem like some of it had anything to do with her. She felt like there was somehow a separate part of herself that had lived that part of her life back then, or that it hadn't really been her. It was a disorienting sensation. She couldn't describe it. "I want to tell you about it, and I will, but maybe right now isn't the best time. Is that okay?"

"Sure, sweetie. No problem. Whenever you're ready," said Hank. He didn't joke about the lack of spa services, non-designer clothes, or that there probably wasn't any bottled water. Somehow he knew how precarious she felt right then. She knew he'd go there one day, but for now, he just accepted her answer, and Reilly's heart filled with even more love for him.

"You're a good friend, Hank." Reilly saw Cray trying to be unobtrusive beside Hank, and she reached over and patted his arm so he didn't feel left out of the conversation. "You are, too, Cray. But Hank has been my family since the day he made me spew milk from my nose during our screen test together when we were—" she looked at Hank, "What? Ten-years-old?"

"You were ten, I was eleven," Hank explained for Cray's benefit. "All I had to do was lift my eyebrow and she would burst out laughing. Good thing they were looking for comic chemistry. Otherwise you'd be eating lunch with a couple of baristas right now."

"I owe you my career, Hank."

"Yes, you do," he responded, with a teasing twinkle in his eye. Then the top of his nose wrinkled in a frown. "I still feel so bad about telling you about Sylvie and Parker, though."

"I'm the one who should be sorry, Hank," said Reilly. "I was embarrassed. I should have told you that I already knew. I felt as though I didn't deserve anyone's love or loyalty, and I tried very hard to convince other people of that for a while. You didn't deserve my reaction. I'm sorry."

A thousand thoughts rose to the surface for Reilly at the reference to the time when she had tried to put herself into emotional solitary confinement. It hadn't been enough that she was already behind bars. She had tried to sever all ties. The incident with Hank had happened the same week as the one with her mother. When Hank mentioned Sylvie and Parker a few days after Melissa had, Reilly had just stood up and walked away from the visitor's table.

She had immediately regretted her actions, feeling a cold sadness sweep over her as she walked back to her cell. The feeling of wanting to push people away, yet still longing for connection had been disorienting and she'd felt so confused. She also knew that the disconnection she felt had started well before she'd gone to prison. She had written letters to both her mother and Hank that day, apologizing, even though she didn't try to explain what she was going through. Hank had responded first. Her mother had taken longer.

As Reilly sat there with Hank and Cray all these months later, she still didn't understand it, but she knew that she was starting to live her life in a better way, and one day, she would understand the crisis that had driven her into the abyss that she was still trying to crawl out of. This knowledge made her grateful for having Hank in her life, and tears worried at the back of her eyelids. She concentrated on her food.

"No biggie, Rye. We're past that. I'll always love you. You can't ditch this queen that easy," said Hank, rubbing her arm. And just like that, she knew that he would understand when she had the courage to talk about it.

She cleared her throat and turned to face Hank. As she spoke, she punctuated her sentences with swats at his arm.

"Back to you two, then. What about the past three months? We've been hanging out at least once a week, Hank. Surely, it would have come up by now. Why haven't you said anything about you two hooking up?"

"Ow!" squealed Hank, dropping the fork he'd been using and grabbing his shoulder. "You're a witness, Cray. The hag battered me!"

"Don't you change the subject, Hank! Why have you two been hiding this from me?"

"We haven't, Reilly. I swear," said Hank, retrieving his fork. "It just hasn't come up. Cray's been shooting some Kung Fu thing overseas for the last five months. He just got back a couple of days ago."

"Check this out." Cray lifted his shirt to reveal solidly defined abs. "That's from Kung Fu. I followed Bruce Lee's workout regimen to the letter. And, yes, I did my own stunts."

"Nice! Your six pack is now an eight pack," admired Reilly, leaning forward to see over the table.

"And I get to go home with that," said Hank proudly.

"I can't believe that I didn't know. What kind of friend have I been?" Reilly sat back and pushed the food around on her plate.

"Relax, Rye. We're cool," said Hank. He rubbed her arm and smiled. "You need to stop beating people up—especially yourself."

"God, I wish I could," said Reilly. "I'm just a little tense. Our new movie starts shooting soon. It'll be weird seeing people again. You know, since I got out."

"What have you been doing?" asked Cray. "I can't imagine you sitting at home reading."

"That's pretty much it," admitted Reilly. "I mostly read scripts and work out in my home gym. Gotta get ready for the new movie." She patted her own abs and thought about asking Cray for the Bruce Lee work out. The costumes would be revealing if they were anything like the last movie.

"You don't go out at all? What about interviews?"

Reilly shook her head. "To my agent's chagrin, I'm still living in the cone of silence as far as the press is concerned. I guess that will have to change when we start filming, thanks to the new language in my contracts. But for now I'm laying low. It's tough, since they've been hanging around like gnats—staked out at the gate to my house and following me everywhere. So that's made going anywhere but work tough—or tougher than normal, I guess. But I've gone down to the studio a few times to talk about *Dare to Dream*, and Hank and Alison have come over to the house a lot, but, other than that, I've been a hermit. To be honest, I'm starting to crawl out of my own skin, but I'm just not ready to answer the inevitable questions."

"Have you tried yoga? Maybe it will help if you get out to do that. You could be around people without having to interact. There's this one class that I go to that's just amazing," offered Cray.

Reilly thought back to prison and how yoga had been her lifesaver there. Since she'd been out she had tried to find an instructor or class even half as good as the one Fergie had taught. She'd almost given up.

Reilly lifted a cynical eyebrow. People in the Valley referred to everything as amazing. "I've tried a few classes. Is this class you speak of amazing, amazing? Or is it L.A. amazing? Because, seriously, I can't deal with going to another hyped-up, *amazing* yoga class just to end up stuck in a room with a bunch of Barbie doll wannabes more concerned about the newest yoga pants than they are with the exercise. I want to go to a class where everyone is serious about it and the vibe is right."

"Trust me. It's amazing, amazing," said Cray. "Besides, lots of industry folks go there, so you don't have to worry about groupies eyeing your ass during downward dog. You'll be able to get your chakra on there. Trust me."

Reilly rolled her eyes but Cray ignored it.

"Besides, I think you'll like the instructor. She's a hottie. I'll sign you up and give you the address."

Downward Dog

THE NEXT DAY, REILLY FOUND herself on a quiet street in West Hollywood. It wasn't more than two miles from her own house, but she'd never been down these particular streets. From the back seat of the car, Reilly surveyed the bucolic neighborhood as Alison pulled the car to a stop at the curb next to the address Cray had texted Reilly. The next text said that he had signed her up for the yoga class because he knew that she probably wouldn't do it herself. She'd texted back denying it, but, secretly, she had to admit that he was right. Reilly had forced herself not to cancel. But now that she was there, she was excited about the class and hoped that it was as good as he promised. At the same time, she was a little apprehensive about venturing out in public. The unassuming location and large trees that arched over the streets helped ease her discomfort, though, and after telling Alison that she'd see her in an hour and a half, she pushed open the car door.

She stepped out onto the gently buckled sidewalk—the product of the roots of the mature magnolia trees lining the streets—and breathed in the scent of the large white flowers. The scent mingled with that of the lavender that grew along the front of the tall picket fence that ran next to the sidewalk. The sounds of the nearby city didn't penetrate the tranquil street, and the dense but neatly trimmed foliage provided privacy to the homes. Most of the 1920's built structures had been well kept, and in a town of constant makeover, it was surprising that most had retained their original architecture.

An unobtrusive sign engraved with the name *Anahata Yoga* hung from the gnarled branch of an old pepper tree, and it was the only indication that Reilly was standing in front of the studio Cray had recommended. She could barely see a house beyond the hedges that stood behind the fence. A low gate opened through a vine-covered arch, and she made her way up the raised wooden walkway that meandered through the deep front yard and up to the front of the house. She was early, so she took her time and admired her surroundings, which were landscaped in a style that was a mesh of Japanese serenity garden and forest glen. Several large trees kept most of the yard in shade, and even on the warm June day, Reilly felt the air drop to a comfortable temperature as she walked beneath them. A small fountain, fed by a recirculating stream bordered by mossy rocks, ran from the porch and then under and along one side of the walkway. She paused about halfway to the house to watch the brilliant flashes of colored koi swimming amid the cover of water lilies in the shallow water. Lush vegetation all around provided an abundance of flowers and shadowed greenery. A wooden bench invited her to sit on a clover-covered mound under one of the trees on the other side of the stream. A small stone bridge provided access, and Reilly was tempted to wander over and sit there for a little while and just… be.

As she stood contemplating the fascinating and peaceful area, a group of three women stepped through the gate. Their conversation was held in respectful low voices as if they, too, felt the quiet peace that held Reilly enthralled. She stepped aside to let them pass, and a man with a yoga mat strapped to his back turned into the yard from the street. She was reminded that she was there for a class, and she turned to follow the group down the path, which split to run alongside the house and up to a studio that was located in a structure behind the main building.

A scaled-down version of the wide porch on the main house provided the threshold to the studio, which was accessed by wide French doors. The wood was rough-hewn, but heavily lacquered, providing a rich glow to the entryway, which flowed into a large open room to the right. The space was open and airy, sparsely furnished with clean lines and flat surfaces. Wood and brushed steel gleamed in the natural light spilling in from the many windows. A hallway to the left led to the back of the building.

Continuing to follow the lead of the other students, Reilly put her shoes, silenced cell phone, and keys into one of the highly polished wooden cubbyholes that lined one wall. She then spread her mat in the corner near the back of the room. No one talked. As if by an unspoken agreement, each person's movements slowed and became deliberate once they entered the studio. Ambient music played low in the background. Reilly took her seat in the half-lotus pose on her yoga mat and closed her eyes. She soon drifted into a state of relaxed but heightened awareness. She aligned her center and shut her eyes, focusing only on her breathing.

She had no idea how long she sat like that, but she opened her eyes when a subtle shift in the energy of the room occurred. A pleasant ripple of tingles flowed across her back and along the length of her limbs. The natural light had been dimmed by bamboo shades that had been lowered since she had taken her seat, and she scanned the space around her. More people had entered the room. It wasn't crowded, but it was filled to a comfortable capacity. When her eyes moved back to the front of the room, pulled by the source of the energy that she felt buzzing through her, a shock of recognition hit her. A light flutter filled her chest and stomach. The woman's eyes were closed, but Reilly didn't need to see them to know the silver flash that danced behind the lids.

"Eyes closed. Head high. We summon peace and focus from the space around us."

The class had started and Drew's smooth voice flowed down Reilly's spine.

Reilly tried to subdue the reaction she had at seeing Drew again, and though she wanted to continue watching the lovely ghost from her past, she forced herself to close her eyes. She concentrated on her breathing and tried to summon the meditative state that Drew guided them toward.

Despite the underlying current of her distraction with Drew, the class ended up being everything that Reilly wanted it to be. Drew was serene and focused and showed no indication that she recognized Reilly. She took the group through the first few poses without saying much at all. In a voice imbued with velvet warmth, she said a few words to get wandering minds centered on the exercise, and then transitioned from one position to another. Most of the students were seasoned practitioners, and Drew was able to conduct the first part of the class from her mat, but when the poses became a little more difficult, she moved through the class to help reposition or align hips, shoulders, and limbs. Reilly could feel Drew's proximity as if the air between them was solid, constricting and expanding with every step that Drew made toward or away from her. She had to fight to concentrate on the exercise and not to follow Drew's path through the room.

The class was moving into *parivrtta parsvakonasana*, a pose that Reilly often had trouble breathing through, when she smelled the faint scent of cinnamon. The tingle that had danced along her skin earlier grew stronger. Warm hands encircled her ankle from behind and rotated her back foot just a fraction of an inch. The hands then moved up to realign her upward arm, and Reilly fought to keep her eyes pointed at the ceiling. The adjustments were enough to ease Reilly's breathing, but the sensation of Drew's touch almost overshadowed the relief. When gentle fingers next cupped her chin to tilt her head further, her breathing became difficult again, and it wasn't at all because of the pose. Then the fingers were gone, and Reilly could breathe again. She felt every point on her body that Drew had touched long after she had moved on to the next student, but it was amazing what a difference the small changes had made.

From there, they went into simple lunges, and Reilly felt the strength of her body in a way that she never had before. She was strong and pliable, focused on maintaining her stance, and the distraction of Drew's proximity added an exciting dimension to her workout. Eventually, the blend of emotion and physical exertion became a powerful focus for her, and the enfolding energy made her feel vibrantly alive. The concept of being in the moment never made more sense to her then it did right then.

When she raised her head for the final motion of the last lunge, she almost over-balanced in surprise when she found Drew watching her. The silver eyes seemed to bore into her. Reilly moved into position but held her eyes.

"From high lunges, we go to low lunges, or *anjaneyasana*."

Reilly felt the timbre of Drew's voice flow over her skin as she stepped forward, reached up, and dropped low. Drew nodded with a small smile and moved to correct the posture of the man in front of her. Reilly felt a twinge of jealousy that Drew's attention had been averted, but the smile became an invisible focal point in her mind as she moved through the poses that Drew guided them through in her soft, low voice.

It seemed that the class had barely begun when Drew called out the last pose and instructed the students to lie down in the *savasana* position for the last minutes of class. The corpse pose was Reilly's favorite part of the workout, and even with the distraction of Drew and the disappointment that the class was nearly over, Reilly was able to succumb to a place of peace that floated between awake and asleep. Then the gong sounded, and the prone bodies around her began to reanimate themselves.

"Namaste," offered Drew in her low voice.

"Namaste," replied the class, along with Reilly.

Reilly rose slowly, feeling the loose strength in the long muscles of her back, sides, and legs. Her mind was sharp from the closing meditation, and she felt amazing. Cray had been right.

The yoga class was perfect, and just what Reilly needed, despite the unexpected presence of Drew. She still held most of the sedate invigoration brought on by well-worked muscles and a focused mind. She glanced around the room, looking for Drew, but she didn't see her. The other students, in their post-yoga experience, displayed the peace that she felt, and while some of them spoke in quiet tones to one another, the rest remained silent as they left the studio to carry on with their days. She gathered her things and made her way out through the French doors.

Moving slowly, she was the last one out, and as she closed the door, she felt a hand on her arm. She knew who it was before she turned to see Drew. The same gaze that had startled her that first time so long ago, when the clear silver eyes had stared back at her, transfixed her again with their power. She didn't know what to say or do. The life in which she had known Drew was buried in a past that Reilly had left far behind.

"I'm not sure if you remember me," began Drew, letting her hand drop from Reilly's arm.

Reilly continued to feel the place where Drew's hand had been. She hoped her smile looked relaxed.

"Of course I remember you, Drew."

Drew's smile was as beautiful as Reilly remembered.

"Good. I wasn't sure. I didn't want to be uncool and assume."

Reilly wondered if Drew was capable of being uncool.

"I'll admit that it was a surprise to see you teaching the class. We have a mutual friend, Cray—he signed me up. He didn't say you were the instructor, though."

"I'll have to thank him for sending you my way. Did you enjoy the class?"

"I did. It's the best I've ever taken," responded Reilly, and she meant it, although she wished that she didn't sound like a breathless school girl saying it. Drew's smile in response eased her discomfort.

"I'm flattered. I can tell that you've been practicing for a while."

"A little while," admitted Reilly. "My last instructor was exceptional."

Reilly didn't know why she added the last part. She wished that she had just said thank you. Instead, she had just opened herself up to questions about where she had attended her previous classes, who her teacher had been. There was no doubt in her mind that Drew knew about her time in prison, but it wasn't a topic she wanted to discuss with anyone—most of all Drew. The impression that Reilly once had of Drew being somehow above the seedier aspects of life—herself included—was validated. Reilly had observed Drew in her natural environment. The pure and peaceful energy that Reilly always felt in her presence made sense now. Drew wouldn't have any interest in a person like her, unless it was pure curiosity.

"I'm lucky that you chose to change instructors, then," said Drew. Reilly relaxed. No questions.

"I suppose that I'd still be going to her if I could. But that's a story for another day."

Again with the allusion to a time that Reilly didn't want to discuss. She mentally smacked her own head. She had been in the clear, but then she had to go and dangle another invitation for questions at Drew. What was it about Drew that made Reilly want to ramble?

"Well, I hope you come back."

Another bullet dodged. Drew was so easy to be around. It was such a departure from most people she knew.

"I think I will," she said with a smile.

"Call me if the classes are full when you go to sign up. I can open an additional slot."

"I wouldn't want to impose on you or crowd your other students," demurred Reilly.

"I keep the classes small to retain the intimacy," explained Drew. "One more wouldn't hurt."

Reilly saw Drew's eyes slide down her body and felt the heat through her form-fitting yoga clothing. Her mind told her that the quick glance was a professional assessment, but she wished that it were something else.

"Do you… do you teach all of the classes?" she stammered.

"I do. I'm the only instructor here."

"Cray told me that your classes were very popular."

"Well, I can't complain about how good business is," Drew said, without a trace of arrogance.

"It looks like you picked the right career." Reilly saw a shadow cross over Drew's face and then disappear. She wondered why her comment bothered her.

"I have my mom to thank for that. But that's a story for a different day too, I suppose," said Drew with a wink and a smile, recovered from whatever had caused the brief frown.

"I look forward to it," said Reilly. With her recent past, she doubted that Drew was really interested in exchanging the stories they both hinted at, but she hoped for it all the same. The cynic in her decided that it was time to go before she found out that Drew's attention to her was merely part of a good marketing campaign. "I'll see you soon."

"And *I* look forward to *that*," replied Drew.

Reilly turned and walked back to her car. She felt Drew's eyes follow her down the path. The image of Drew's smile and unbelievable eyes was imprinted on her mind. To Reilly's out of practice ears, Drew's last comment sounded a lot like flirting. Before her inner cynic took control again, Reilly relished the flare of excitement that the thought gave her.

She Could Hope

TEN MINUTES LATER, ALISON MANEUVERED Reilly's car through rush hour traffic while Reilly sat in the backseat, mumbling aloud in frustration as she found the next two days of Drew's classes already full. She tossed her phone aside, hard enough to make it bounce from the leather seat and onto the floor. Ashamed at her immature response, she retrieved the phone and signed up for the next available openings. She would have to be satisfied with that. She wasn't comfortable about taking Drew's offer to make room for her in the full classes. The temptation to call her, to hear her voice on the phone, to move their acquaintance to a different level, was compelling. But without a script, she didn't know what she would say, and the fear of coming off badly—or worse yet, discovering Drew was just being a good businesswoman—was too much to risk.

After all this time, it was interesting to know that Drew still had that crazy pull on her. Surprised at her reaction, and mulling over her disappointment about having to wait to see her again, she leaned her forehead against the window. She watched the billboards flash by along Santa Monica Boulevard but didn't see them. Alison's tuneless voice sang along with a sappy love song on the radio. She smiled at her friend's uncharacteristic behavior. Alison was in love. The old Reilly would have teased her. But the present Reilly was happy for her. For the first time since she had awakened on that bench at Santa Monica Beach, Reilly thought about her own vacant bed and wished that she wasn't alone.

She'd seen Drew just twice before that day, but both times, the power she had felt in Drew's presence had caught Reilly by surprise. She knew very little about the woman—she hadn't even known her last name until she'd signed up for the classes—but there was something about Drew that captivated Reilly more than any woman ever had. Maybe it was because they were so different. Maybe it was because Drew seemed unimpressed with her, or maybe she was just out of her reach. Reilly's thoughts landed on the first meeting in the bathroom of that dance club. She couldn't remember the name of the place, but she remembered Drew in high definition.

In particular, she remembered that kiss. It was just a whisper, the brush of lips against hers, but Reilly recalled how her skin had buzzed with the connection. Thoughts of Drew, a woman she didn't even know, had filled her head for days following that kiss.

Reilly's mind lingered on the pleasant memory for several minutes, and then her thoughts focused on the excitement that had filled her when Drew had shown up at Cray's party. An electric thrill coursed through her when she remembered dancing with her. With her head still pressed against the window of the car, Reilly felt Drew's mysterious pull.

Reilly hadn't tried to get Drew to stay at the party that night. Instead, she had encouraged her to leave rather than let Sylvie try to bed her. She wondered if that selfish gesture had changed her own life for the worse. Because just hours later, after she had said a reluctant goodnight to Drew, and after she had continued to party with Sylvie and Parker, late into many more shots of tequila and lines of coke, the unthinkable had happened. Now, an eternity of regret and guilt claimed her. Any hope for something meaningful happening with Drew had been erased forever that night.

Following the accident, Reilly had pushed all thoughts of Drew from her mind. In her own heart she knew that she was no longer free to dream about her own happiness. Not when she had ruined the lives of an entire family. She'd wasted her own life in the car that night, too, and she was unwilling to inflict her negative influence on another person.

The old feelings of shame and remorse swept over her, and she leaned back in the leather seat with her eyelids squeezed tight against the memories. She was caught between absorbing the guilt of her reckless mistakes and the temptation to allow herself the feelings that Drew elicited in her. Just for a few minutes. Only in her head. But she knew that she'd never be satisfied with just a few minutes. And even if they were only in her head, it was more than Matt Traynor would ever have again. Thoughts of all the things that the man she'd killed would never again get to do filled her with self-recrimination.

But, damn, Drew was attractive. Very attractive. Reilly's stomach fluttered as an image of Drew took form in her mind. The striking combination of long black hair and silver-gray eyes gazed back at her. Reilly remembered standing next to Drew that first time, so close she could feel her heat. The air between them had seemed to vibrate, and she hadn't been able to help herself as she had touched Drew's face. A warm wave of heat filled Reilly, remembering the smolder in

Drew's eyes and the feel of the soft planes of Drew's face beneath her fingertips.

An unexpected wedge of shame edged its way into Reilly's heart. She'd acted like an entitled brat that night. Had she behaved much better the second time? She replayed those meetings, seeing herself acting with imperious ego and taking her celebrity for granted. She groaned aloud. Who had she thought she was? The memories paralyzed her with embarrassment. Suddenly, she was relieved that she wouldn't be seeing Drew so soon, after all. Drew didn't need Reilly Ransome in her life for more reasons than she could count. Maybe a little distance was a good thing.

Reilly thanked the universe that filming for the sequel to *Salsa Nights* started soon. It would be her first work after getting out of prison, and all of the dance rehearsal was sure to keep her focus away from raven-haired beauties with extraordinary eyes.

She could hope.

She Does Location Work

"SO? WHAT, EH? AN ACTAH of yah calibeh don't associate wit da suppoh'tin' cast? Yah think yah kin treat us like scale playehs? Two measly Academy Awah'ds, and yah act like yah too good for us!" accused an angry voice in a bad Boston accent.

Reilly stopped pacing and lowered the script that she was reading. She turned toward the voice and smiled at the man storming toward her.

"And that, Mr. Layton, is why they don't cast you outside of your genre."

"I don't know what you're talking about. I play a wide range of parts," countered Cray in his normal voice. His storm became a saunter and his scowl became a smile as he came near and fell into a nearby director's chair.

Reilly, who had been pacing the area memorizing her lines, felt the tension between her shoulder blades ease. She swatted Cray on the chest with her rolled up script.

"Let's see. Studs, action studs, Kung Fu studs, studs with a heart of gold, and, of course, the dancing stud," she acknowledged, ticking off on her fingers the roles that she knew Cray had played. "But you'll need to study up on sociolinguistics to make the stud with the accent work out for you."

"Sociowhatchamacallit?" asked Cray. But he waved his hand with a dismissive flick. "Whatever. I've done accents. Inspector Clouseau in the *Pink Panther Strikes Again*. Senior year. Redondo Beach Senior High School. I rocked the part, as stated by Betsy LeChart in the review posted in the *Redondo Beach Tattler*. LeChart. That's French, so she would know, being an expert."

"I stand corrected, then," laughed Reilly. "You do have the anger part down, though."

"I knew it! You jumped, just a little," said Cray, holding his thumb and forefinger about a centimeter apart in front of his squinted eyes.

"Okay, I jumped a little. On the inside," said Reilly, trying to sound serious.

"That's what I thought," he said, smacking the arm of the chair with a triumphant hoot. "So, seriously, why are you over here all by yourself, pacing? You're making me stressed just watching you. Everyone else is over at craft services. They have a taco bar today. You should love that. Tacos. Pink tacos. Get it?"

Reilly rolled her eyes, ignoring Cray's crude joke.

"I'm waiting for Marty to get back," explained Reilly, referring to the set masseuse. She rubbed her neck. "He's going to devote an hour just to my neck and shoulders."

She didn't mention that when she had been on her way to join everyone for lunch she had run into a woman she and Sylvie had partied with before. Jill, who worked in lighting, had pulled her aside to offer her a hit of coke. It had freaked Reilly out. Not because she wanted it—she didn't—but because she had almost done it without thinking. She remembered the casual interaction, the ducking between two plywood sets, the reaching out for the proffered silver bullet-shaped container with hands that weren't even controlled by her. Like it was an everyday thing for her. Like it used to be. Reilly remembered Jill's raised eyebrows when she had frozen, realizing what she had been just about to do, and then the confused, "What the…?" Jill had uttered when Reilly shoved the bumper back at her. Reilly hadn't even tried to offer an excuse before she spun around and walked back toward the trailers. She should have found Jill to explain, but she didn't want to get into it.

That's when she had run into Marty. With his signature messenger bag strapped across his chest, he looked like he was on his way out to run an errand. He stopped dead in his tracks when he saw her, though. With well-trained eyes, he had read the stress that was coiled around Reilly like an invisible snake and told her that she was his next subject. He promised to be back in twenty minutes. She had been going through her lines near his trailer since then, trying not to obsess over something that hadn't even happened.

"Did you try out the yoga studio I signed you up for? Hey, come here," instructed Cray. He stood and spun her around so that he was behind her. Strong hands kneaded her shoulders. "Sheez, you *are* tense, girl."

"I know," she said dropping her chin and letting him have access to more of her shoulders. "God. You don't know how good that feels."

"So, did you?" prompted Cray after a couple of minutes. It took Reilly a beat before she realized that he'd asked her about the yoga class. In fact she'd gone every day in the past three weeks since that first one, save for the two days that had been full. Now that set work had started and she'd be working crazy hours, she was going to miss going.

"Yes. I've gone a few times," said Reilly, closing her eyes. A small groan escaped her as the tight muscles in her neck responded to Cray's ministrations. An image of Drew crept into her mind and a little of the excitement that took over every time she saw or thought about Drew fluttered in her stomach. But ever since the first session, she had bolted out of the class as soon as the last gong sounded, just to avoid interacting with her. Reilly couldn't keep herself from going to Drew's classes, but she couldn't bring herself to talk to Drew, either. It was a new feeling, being timid with women. She'd never felt that she wasn't good enough for someone. The fear of Drew's rejection prompted her to keep her distance.

"Well, keep going. It should help with some of this tension," said Cray. Reilly could hear the concentration in his voice as he continued to work on her shoulders. "Drew is pretty great though, am I right?"

She nodded. In so many ways, she thought to herself. There was the peace that she exuded, the power in her gaze, the intelligence that she seemed to have, not to mention her beauty and killer body. Reilly could list a thousand things that she liked about Drew, and she barely even knew her. "It's the best class I have ever attended. But, you know how it is. I won't get to go now that we're shooting. Eighteen hour days don't leave much time for other stuff."

"She can come on set and give private sessions."

"Yeah, right," said Reilly. An unexpected spike of excitement hit her stomach, even as the thought of being one-on-one with Drew terrified her. "Besides, I'm sure she's booked up."

"She does location work all the time. Can't hurt to ask. I'll call her," said Cray, finished with his shoulder rub and patting Reilly's shoulders. He spun her back around to face him and pulled his cell phone out of his pocket.

"No. Don't do that," argued Reilly. She reached for the phone, but Cray stepped out of her reach.

"She's a friend. And these gigs pay huge," said Cray, with a smile. She took a step after him, but stopped when he spoke into his phone.

"One ringy-dingy… two ringy-dingies… Hey, Drew. It's Cray. Interested in a studio gig?"

He wagged his eyebrows at Reilly, and she wanted to throw something at him. Having nothing on hand but her script, which she needed, she threw him a dirty look instead.

Cray smiled and turned toward craft services with the phone to his ear and a sassy swing of his hips. He was just out of range for Reilly to hear him, and she wondered what they were talking about. She hoped that he didn't tell Drew that the call had been her idea. She prayed that Drew was busy, and then changed her mind, then changed it back again. She was waffling yet again, when Cray slid the phone back into his pocket and smirked over his shoulder.

"She'll be here tomorrow at 3:00. Wear something cute. I'll tell Wes to break for dailies then, to give you the time you need. You know, to take care of all that tension."

Reilly did throw the script at him then.

People Are Staring

"HOLY FUCK, MOTHER! HOW DO you expect me to feel after you expose me to the world like this?"

Reilly paced across the bare cement of the studio floor with an agitated stride, twisting the ends of the towel she had draped around her neck. With an irritated flick, she whipped it off and snapped it at one of the ubiquitous director's chairs that were set up next to the set where she had been rehearsing dance numbers for most of the day. Her voice carried throughout the building with unsuppressed anger.

"Reilly, calm down. People are staring," whispered Melissa, casting an uncomfortable glance around the studio. Several stagehands that were moving props turned away when her eyes swept over them. The best boy dropped a bundle of cables and rushed away like he had forgotten something important on the other side of the lot.

Reilly didn't care who was paying attention. She was too angry to think about anything else other than her mother's betrayal. But she did feel a familiar buzz rush up her spine and flutter to the edges of her skin. She didn't need to see her to know that Drew had arrived on set. Reilly almost lost her train of thought until she saw her mother shake her head at one of the producers, insinuating that Reilly was being unreasonable again. It was the last straw.

"Isn't that what you want?" she asked, wiping perspiration from her forehead. She stopped her pacing and stood in front of her mother, waiting for an answer. "Isn't that what you've always wanted? To be seen? For people to notice?"

"Not like this. Hush!" said Melissa, anger replacing the surprise in her voice. "I am your mother, after all."

"Really, Mother?" asked Reilly, her eyes narrowed as she crossed her arms over her chest. Melissa's face lost its cloud of anger, and Reilly grew even angrier at the expression of indignation that replaced it. "Really? Is that how mothers treat their daughters? By publishing their personal letters in magazines?"

Reilly waved toward a crumpled paper on the seat of one of the chairs as she spoke. It was a letter from an editor at Doubleday asking if she'd be willing to loan them the rest of the letters she had written to her parents from prison. He wanted them for a book idea inspired from a letter that had been provided by her mother and printed in *Watch This!,* the nation's most circulated celebrity gossip magazine.

"Letter, Reilly," said Melissa, holding up a forefinger to underscore her point. She didn't seem to notice the warning in Reilly's body language telling her that she was on fragile footing. She continued in an angry voice. "A single letter. And I knew it was a mistake as soon as I saw it in the magazine. I never let them publish another one. I told you that I was sorry."

"Yes, you did. But for what, Mother? What are you sorry for?" demanded Reilly. She lowered the volume of her voice. Even she felt the ice in it. A producer, who had been lingering nearby, walked away like an animal fleeing a wildfire.

"I'm sorry for making you feel like this, of course," Melissa stammered.

"No, Mom. I don't think that's what you're sorry for at all. I think you're sorry because you misjudged my potential reaction. And that you let someone publish a letter that talks about things you won't even talk about yourself. Why did you give them the first letter? What possessed you to do that in the first place?"

"I don't know. Things were so weird for a while. I didn't want anyone to forget you. It was a misguided action. I said I was sorry. I don't understand why you're so angry," breathed out Melissa, a weary surrender in her voice. Her shoulders lowered. Reilly wondered if her mother was backing down or if her sudden change in demeanor was just another manipulation tactic.

"Of course you don't," said Reilly. Something new inside of her replaced the anger. She'd lost all of her steam. Her voice was quiet and her arms hung at her sides. "And it doesn't matter. Not anymore. I'm done," she shrugged.

At last, Melissa seemed to understand the depth of her daughter's disappointment. Reilly stood as her mother's eyes searched hers. She kept her gaze steady.

"Done with what?" asked Melissa, when she realized that Reilly wasn't going to elaborate.

Reilly paused, gathering her thoughts. She hadn't been sure either, until just that moment.

"Done with this," said Reilly, gesturing between the two of them. When she saw the confusion on her mother's face, she knew that she needed to be specific. She couldn't let her mother misunderstand what she was saying. "I can't work with you anymore."

A parade of emotions swept across Melissa's face as she tried to determine her next move, and Reilly felt a cold sort of detachment as she wondered which of the emotions were real and which were manufactured.

"You can't do this, Reilly. You need me," said Melissa, squaring her jaw. She shook her hair back and adjusted the strap of the Louis Vuitton bag that hung from her shoulder. Reilly almost felt sorry for her mother then. The bravado seemed so thin.

"I have an agent to get me jobs, Mom. I have an accountant to deal with my finances. Shit. I even have a personal chef to feed me, and a best friend to dress me," Reilly laughed, but there wasn't any amusement in her eyes. "I guess that I'm old enough to take care of myself—or at least to pay people to do it for me."

"You need someone who knows you, to promote you, to hone your image. Someone to line up fashion lines that don't make you look like a hoodlum." To prove her point, Melissa reached over to the back of the chair that Reilly had been sitting in earlier and picked up a black hoodie with a zombie poodle embroidered on the sleeve. She examined the garment with a look of distaste and tossed it back onto the chair.

Reilly ignored her mother's jibe at Hank's clothing. She knew that her mother still blamed him for encouraging Reilly's choice of gender in bed partners. He had come out of the closet first, and therefore, he bore the sin for Reilly's journey into the world of forbidden love.

"I think I can figure out how to promote myself," replied Reilly.

"You haven't done such a—" began Melissa, and then reconsidered her response. "There is far more to what I do for you than you know, Reilly. What you see is just a small part of it."

"I know there is, Mom. And I'm sure that I'll miss some of it. But I can't do this anymore," said Reilly. Her shoulders dropped, and she heard the tone of resolution in her own voice. She spoke in a quieter tone. "We'll talk about arrangements later. And I haven't forgotten the contract. Even if there wasn't a contract, you and Dad have nothing to worry about. You're still my mother. I love you. But I just can't work with you anymore."

"Reilly—"

"Mom. Please," said Reilly, interrupting her. She glanced toward Cray and Drew who stood on the other side of the studio pretending not to notice. "We'll talk later. I have an appointment right now."

Reilly stood, silent, and willed her mother to leave. She had been stretched to the breaking point and she needed some space, at least from her mother. Melissa snapped her mouth closed and searched Reilly's eyes before she turned away without another word.

Reilly wanted to feel something, to understand how much damage this fight was going to have on them, but she felt nothing. The sting never came. She watched Melissa walk away, her silhouette getting smaller in the sunlight framed by the massive open studio doors. Soon her mother turned the corner and was out of sight. The sounds of the busy production set filtered back into her awareness. She looked around and people were busily doing their jobs as if nothing had just happened.

A deep sigh escaped her, and Reilly shifted her gaze to Cray and Drew standing near the open doors, talking. There was no doubt that everyone in the building had heard the argument. She wondered if Drew saw her as a callous diva, a person who treated her own mother like an employee. Only Sylvie and Hank knew how much she had tried to build a relationship with her mother. As soon as she thought that, though, she knew that she wasn't being truthful, even to herself. She had wanted the relationship, but she hadn't tried very hard, often letting her childish responses take over their conversations. She was no better than her mother.

That sudden realization hit Reilly like a punch. Cloying guilt upset her stomach. The relationship she craved with her mother would never exist. It was then that the pain set in. Losing what she had with her mother was not painful. But losing the mother that she wanted to have was devastating. Tears threatened to come, and Reilly used all of her will to push them down.

The Memories Are Still There

REILLY DIDN'T WANT TO FACE Drew in her emotional state, and she wondered if she could beg out of the yoga session. She mustered a smile as Drew approached, a few tactful moments after Melissa's exit, and hoped that her acting ability would get her through the next few minutes.

"Hi, Reilly. You look amazing," said Drew. Her eyes traveled over the skintight dance costume that Reilly still wore from the scene that she and Cray had just rehearsed. The unexpected glance and compliment helped to distract Reilly's spiral into a burgeoning breakdown.

"Thanks," said Reilly. She ran nervous hands down her flat stomach. She was glad for all of the practice that she'd done to get in shape for the strenuous part. "It's good to see you, Drew."

Drew smiled, and things tilted a little more back to right. The serenity that Drew always carried with her seemed to surround Reilly in a calm embrace. Reilly gladly succumbed to its thrall.

"Are you ready to get your yoga on?" asked Drew.

Reilly, who had been less than a minute earlier trying to figure out a polite way to ask Drew to leave, now didn't want Drew to go.

"Definitely," replied Reilly. "I'm amazed that you'd come out here at the last minute to do this. Thanks."

"I have a big gap in my schedule most afternoons, so it works out perfectly, actually. It allows me to do location work. And Cray told me to remind you that the studio pays very well."

"Do they? Because I can—"

Drew rested a hand on Reilly's arm and Reilly forgot what she was saying.

"They really do. You can relax. This is far from an inconvenience for me."

Reilly stared at Drew, entranced by the smile in her eyes. She forced herself to look away so that she could continue the conversation.

"I guess I need it. Especially after that thing with my mom," Reilly groaned. She couldn't even explain how she felt about the argument with her mother, but she was compelled to share it with Drew, knowing that, somehow, Drew would make it better. And she did.

"Mothers! They aren't doing their job if they aren't making us crazy," Drew laughed. A simple, undemanding response.

In just a few minutes, Drew had calmed the storm of emotion in Reilly. Not completely, but enough to get through the next hour or so without a breakdown.

"Do you have a place in mind to do this? A room? A trailer? Anywhere without distractions will do," said Drew, scanning the area.

Reilly had long since accepted the fact that Drew would always be a distraction to her, but she didn't mention that. She considered their options. She had expected to use the trailer that Marty used for massages, but when she asked, he told her that the break for dailies was his busiest time. There was only one place she knew that would be quiet enough.

"How about my trailer? I think we'll have room."

Drew shrugged.

"Sure. I've done it in trailers before."

Reilly knew that she was feeling better when her inner twelve-year-old snickered at the unintended double entendre. Struggling with restraint, she turned before Drew could see her smile. She led them toward her trailer without comment.

Apparently she hadn't turned quickly enough.

"Yes. I just said that," said Drew, with a slight blush and an impish grin. "Sorry. I blame it on Cray. He was being, well, being himself earlier when we were talking. It rubs off. I'll smack him when I see him next."

"That's our Cray," Reilly said, through her own blush. "I can't imagine you smacking anyone, though."

"Why? I can give a good smack down when the situation warrants it!"

"Like, let's see, when stoned assholes hit on you in restrooms?" returned Reilly. It came out as a surprise, even to her. Her heart beat out of tempo at the reference to the first time she had seen Drew. An unexpected memory of Drew's lips touching hers made her stomach flutter.

"Yes. But, in that particular kind of situation, I prefer to slay them with my wit, rather than with violence," replied Drew.

"I'm fortunate that you held back with me, then."

"Oh, you were never in any danger, Reilly. That Amazonian warrior you were with, though. She was treading pretty close to summoning my slayer," said Drew.

She lifted an eyebrow when Reilly glanced at her.

Reilly was glad that they arrived at her trailer right then, because she didn't want to think about Sylvie and Drew in any common context, even if it were with Sylvie as the victim. She only smiled and opened the door. She tried not to stare at how well Drew's yoga pants fit as she followed her up the short set of steps. When she closed the door, silence fell over them, and the only sound in the space was the sound of their breathing. Some of her nervousness came back. It intensified when she brushed past Drew, who stopped just inside the door to scan the open room.

As one of the leads in the movie, Reilly's contract stipulated a private trailer. She sometimes felt like it was an extravagance, but she was grateful for it when her work required eighteen-hour days and she needed to slip away for some much-needed quiet between takes. Cray had a similar set up next-door. At thirty-one feet long and eleven feet wide, the trailer had plenty of space, with a bedroom, bath, kitchen, and a small sitting area. It was outfitted with all of the amenities she needed to be comfortable between shoots, and more. She appreciated the state-of-the-art sound system, which she used a lot, but the wide-screen televisions in each room were wasted on her. Slide-outs provided additional space in the sitting and sleeping areas. For one person, it was more than enough space, and for two women doing yoga, it was big enough.

"Is Cray going to join us?" asked Reilly, wondering if they would have enough room with him there.

Reilly couldn't read the expression on Drew's face. Was it disappointment?

"He made it sound like you wanted a private session. Did I misunderstand?" asked Drew.

"No. Um. Well… I didn't even know that you did this sort of thing. Cray suggested it. I just thought that he—" Reilly stammered.

"Do you want me to text him?"

Reilly didn't want him there, but she didn't want Drew to know why. Hell, she didn't even know why.

"He knows where we are. If he wants to join, he'll come over."

"Sounds good," said Drew, looking relieved. She took a rolled-up yoga mat out of the colorful cloth bag she kept it in. "Is here okay?"

"Anywhere is fine. I'm going to change into different clothes and take off some of this Spackle," said Reilly, indicating the thick stage makeup that had been applied for lighting checks earlier in the day. I'll be out in a minute. Help yourself to anything you need. There's water in the fridge."

Reilly shut the door to the bedroom, and her awareness of the woman on the other side of the door was acute. It took but a few minutes to wipe off the makeup and get changed into the exercise clothes that she had brought with her that morning, but she took a few extra minutes to compose herself. Between the emotional discharge with her mother and the simmering sense of expectation that Drew inspired in her, her barriers were feeling weak.

When she re-entered the common area, Drew was examining a red-spiked fruit that she had found in the basket on the counter.

"I'm always finding interesting things on my step when I'm filming," said Reilly coming up behind Drew. Drew twitched and Reilly knew that she had startled her, but Drew didn't give any other indication of her surprise. "That fruit basket is courtesy of the car service that picks me up and drops me off every day, since Alison is on vacation. The one with all the chocolate in it on the table is from the studio."

"This thing looks like a sea anemone," said Drew, turning the red fruit with long, bristle-like spikes in her hand.

"That's a rambutan," said Reilly, resisting the urge to touch the fruit that Drew held.

"It looks dangerous. Are they good?"

"Their looks are deceiving. They're very good. Sweet. Slippery, like a ripe grape. Be careful of the seed, though. It's large, but easy to swallow. It won't hurt you. It's just a weird feeling going down. And if you believe the father of a friend of mine, it will grow in your stomach. Don't let that scare you from trying it, but be warned."

Reilly remembered the first time she had tried the delicious fruit and how the seed had slipped down her throat while she was sucking the attached flesh from the large almond-sized stone. She'd panicked at the feeling, but had laughed when Angel, the set security guard, had teased her about the fruit growing in her stomach.

Drew studied her for several seconds, an unreadable expression on her face. Then she smiled.

"Warning acknowledged. Maybe I'll try it after we're done. How did you get so knowledgeable about the—Rambo-ton fruit?" Drew made a final inspection of the fruit and placed it back in the basket.

"Ram-boo-tun," Reilly pronounced it carefully, over-exaggerating both the pronunciation and her facial expressions in a parody of the stage training exercises she had studied. It had the desired effect and made Drew laugh, which made Reilly smile in turn. Drew's company, while definitely distracting, was just what she needed to help her forget the heated exchange with her mother. "They're native to the Philippines. I saw a lot of them on one of my first location shoots."

"Oh, yeah," said Drew. "The one where you played the kidnapped daughter of the missionaries. You were so young."

Reilly smiled. Drew knew her movies. And not just the blockbusters.

"Yeah, *Sampaguita Mists*. It was my first movie and the first time I had been out of California, let alone the United States. My mom didn't want to go and tried to get my father to go with me. She was worried about the bugs and the danger of being kidnapped. In that order," laughed Reilly. "My dad couldn't go because of work, as usual. So, she ended up going with me anyway. She stayed in the trailer almost the entire time we were there. Being in the Philippines was like being in another world. I loved it there."

"I hear it's beautiful."

"It's gorgeous. But it was the people that I remember the most. They were so hospitable, more so the farther we traveled outside of the cities. Everywhere we went, we were offered gifts. Fruit, homemade food, things they made. They'd offer you the last morsel of food they had in the house, even if they were starving. And they'd be offended if you didn't take it. I had to buy another suitcase for the presents they gave me while I was there. But what I liked best was the way they listened. Like they were really interested in what you had to say. They expected nothing in return."

"I'll bet you treasure the gifts that you brought home."

"My mom called it junk and threw it out when we got back."

Drew paused in her inspection of the other fruit in the basket and glanced at Reilly. Reilly didn't know why she'd offered the last bit of information. It was true, but full of too much baggage to lay on someone new. Maybe she said it so Drew wouldn't judge her so harshly about the argument that she had seen.

"Too bad you lost those memories."

"Oh, the memories are still there," said Reilly, picking up the unique fruit and rolling it in her palm.

A montage of images fluttered through Reilly's mind as she was transported back to a time and place that she hadn't thought about in years. Suddenly, she was a thirteen-year-old girl again, experiencing the tropical island of Luzon, the largest of the Philippine islands, situated where the Pacific meets the Indian Ocean.

The memories, so long ago tucked away, came back with a vivid clarity that amazed her. She could almost feel the humid stickiness that had coated her as soon as she stepped from the airplane when they landed; the smell of jet fuel, frangipani flowers, and sewage tickling her sinuses as she accepted the flower necklace of the airline attendant on the tarmac at the bottom of the steps; the crazy cab ride from the airport to the hotel—a dingy place in contrast to the ones she had stayed at in the States, but opulent when compared to the others in the area; downtown Manila, where a hodgepodge of buildings crushed together around a swarm of people dressed in odd clothing and bizarre vehicles that moved in all directions; sleek glass office buildings separated by tarp-covered caves full of vendors selling anything and everything, exploiting every crack and open space. Then, there were the roads, cram-packed with pedestrians, bicyclists, and motorists, with no regard to any obvious rules. She relived the bone-jarring drive to the outer-barrio village where the film was being shot, and the relief that came when the streets had opened up and the dare-devil driver didn't have to honk his horn to edge into impossible spaces to inch forward. Reilly remembered the awe that she had felt when she finally took her hands from her eyes during the drive long enough to watch the colorful birds that flitted through the greener-than-green branches of the trees that overhung the roads. Pieced-together houses constructed from cinderblock and metal roofs had flown past, and children ran with sticks and straps of fabric in dirt yards. Everywhere her eyes had landed, strange plants and stray animals had amazed her.

Even more vivid were her memories of the village in which she and the crew had stayed during shooting, in a section rented by the studio from the inhabitants, who were delighted to lend their homes in exchange for what to them was a fortune. There, the smell of damp earth, dust, and green things competed with the smell of open fires, meat cooking, and bread baking. Her mouth watered as she thought about waiting near the barbeque stand for the skinny fresh pork skewers marinated in tangy sauce that went so well with the warm, sweet rolls that melted in her mouth.

In her mind, she was standing next to a sari-sari store, drinking Coke from a bottle, staring down the village's one paved street that was comprised of more holes than street. She was walking down dirt paths, careful to avoid the open trenches where human waste flowed. Her eyes examined cinderblock houses, most in various stages of construction, where extended families lived and built on as they could afford it. The more solid structures were a step up from the bamboo shacks with tarp or plywood roofs that comprised some of the other homes.

Every afternoon, a torrential rain had fallen, with drops so fat and heavy that afterward she had looked around in disbelief that the surrounding foliage hadn't been crushed under its thrashing battery. She had watched, at first in near-horror, and then in amused interest, as the armies of walking—not hopping—frogs covered the landscape amid fairytale tendrils of mist that rose from the evaporating rain.

She remembered picking up her shampoo bottle in the shower one day only to have her fingers wrap around a squirming gecko that had somehow breached the screens on the trailer and taken residence in the shower stall. Reilly thought about the trailer that she and her mother had stayed in, and how she had longed to sleep in one of the bamboo houses. It wasn't long before she was grateful for the raised accommodations with screened doors and windows, though, because, to her mother's disgust, the geckos and rice bugs seemed to outnumber the villagers by a million to one. The cockroaches were ten times that number.

She thought of all of that, and more, in a fraction of a second, and a sense of sweet nostalgia hit her hard. The small village had been her home for just six weeks, but it had felt like so much longer.

A long-forgotten face filled her mind.

Imelda—the daughter of Angel, one of the guards from the local village, hired by the studio to protect the set.

Imelda. Beautiful Imelda. With the grownup name, the big smile, and the eyes like melted milk chocolate. She spoke with her hands and twirled in her bare feet, always moving and always laughing. She could climb a tree to the top quick as a flash and without fear, but refused to cross the small stream that ran close to the village for fear of the ghosts that lived between the rocks. She was responsible to a fault when she took care of her six younger siblings, and like a child when she was unburdened from that chore. Reilly had never known a girl so full of contrasts.

Reilly had first seen Imelda near the craft services tables on the first day of shooting. Because Imelda's father worked for the studio, she had been one of the few children from the village allowed on set. Imelda had trailed after her security guard father as he attended to his important job, and Reilly had watched her for half of a day before she got up the courage to talk to her.

Imelda spoke Tagalog with a smattering of English, while Reilly spoke only English. But despite the language barrier, they had become fast friends. Reilly showed Imelda around the set and inside her trailer, and Imelda took Reilly through her village during breaks in shooting. Fast friends, from that first day, they went everywhere together.

With Imelda, it didn't take long for Reilly to understand some of the feelings that had confused her about girls for most of her life. A frown darkened the grown up Reilly's face when she remembered how Angel had found them kissing behind the local sari-sari store.

Reilly still carried a rock of guilt around with her over what happened that day.

Imelda had led Reilly behind the tiny cinderblock building that served as the village convenience store. Reilly couldn't remember why. To catch a gecko? To look at a flower? It didn't matter. She would have followed Imelda anywhere. But before Reilly knew what was happening, Imelda was kissing her. It was Reilly's first real kiss, and it had been a revelation. The softness. The warmth. The feeling of butterflies in her belly.

The memory turned painful, as she thought about the sudden absence of Imelda's body against hers when Angel had lifted his daughter by the back of her shirt and carried her away. Reilly had just stood there, hot with shame and confusion—and something more, something that made her body shake. She remembered how her lips had still been tingling from Imelda's kiss as she stood there for so long after Angel's angry departure, wondering if—hoping that—Imelda would sneak back to her. She never did.

Reilly had returned to the set and waited for Imelda there, but she hadn't come back there, either. When Angel came back to work the next day, Imelda wasn't with him, and he wouldn't respond when Reilly asked where she was. The once warm and smiling man had become a closed off stranger. For the rest of the shoot, his eyes slid over Reilly, never again acknowledging her. Reilly went to Imelda's house, and her grandmother had only shooed her away with an angry scowl, using sounds and gestures meant for a stray dog.

Reilly had never seen Imelda again. But she had overheard one of the set designers tell the director that Angel had taken Imelda to a bar near one of the bigger cities. She hadn't understood then, but years later, after hearing about the thriving prostitution trade in the Philippines, fueled by the sale of adolescent females by their families into the bar trade, Reilly hoped with all of her heart that Angel hadn't punished Imelda by selling her into that life.

The sound of music mingled with running water brought Reilly back from her reflective journey, and her eyes once again focused on the fruit that she held in her hand. Drew adjusted the volume on a portable device and the gentle sounds filled the room.

"Ah. There you are. I felt you disappear for a minute there," smiled Drew, as she squeezed Reilly's arm and moved past her to stand next to her mat.

The brief contact was like an electric current that helped to anchor Reilly back in the present. She shivered and wondered if Drew felt the same electric charge when they were together.

"Sorry. I just had a moment of perspective," said Reilly, dropping the fruit back in to the basket. She picked up her yoga mat and unrolled it on the floor across from Drew's.

Drew smiled but didn't ask for more explanation.

"I brought some things to help set the tone. Atmosphere plays a large part in bringing your mind and body into balance," said Drew as she lowered herself with a graceful ease onto her mat.

Reilly noticed a light scent of lavender and saw a few fresh branches lying on the counter. Two candles were lit beside it, and a small gong sat on the floor near Drew's yoga mat. Drew had already drawn the shades and turned off the lights so that the trailer was in partial shadow.

"I like it. It's very zen. I might keep the trailer like this all the time," smiled Reilly, as she lowered herself onto her own mat.

"Ready?" asked Drew with a smile. She pulled her shoulders back to strike the perfect lotus position.

"Always," said Reilly, doing the same and closing her eyes.

Not a Date

"SO, TOMORROW'S THE LAST DAY on set," said Reilly, her voice little more than a whisper. She was lying on her back on her yoga mat, eyes closed. Drew had been coming out to the set four days a week for the past five weeks. Long enough to have developed a comfortable routine, and for Reilly to have almost gotten used to the constant buzz she felt in Drew's presence. The familiar scent of the shampoo that Drew used wafted near. If she wanted to, she could reach out and touch her. Instead, she kept her arms where they were, stretched out along her side, palms up, completely at ease. It was how they ended their sessions now. Lying on the floor, head to head, in the corpse pose. Reilly didn't want the best part of her days to end.

"Does that mean that you'll start coming to my studio classes again?" asked Drew, rolling onto her left side, easing out of the pose. Her voice was still low and relaxed, the same tones she used as she guided Reilly through the poses of their sessions. It travelled through Reilly's skin and settled in her stomach with a flutter.

"As much as I can," said Reilly, rolling onto her left side, too. "When my schedule allows it. We still have a little location work to do."

"So, you'll be travelling?" Reilly wondered if she heard disappointment in Drew's voice.

"Malibu resembles Cuba, it turns out. So most of it's pretty local. Then after that, things get a little hectic at the beginning of editing as they figure out what needs to be done. Reshoots, voiceovers. And there's always the publicity shoots. The director gets most of that during filming, but there will be some things to redo. There always are."

"Why don't we go over your schedule, and see where we can align it with mine? Maybe we can work in some ad hoc on-site stuff if you'd like."

"Are you this accommodating to all of your clients?" asked Reilly. She tilted her head to see Drew.

Drew tilted her head too, and smiled. Reilly's stomach did a somersault.

"Only the ones whose studios pay out the ass for on-site visits."

Reilly's spirits sank at the statement. She didn't know what she expected, but after five weeks of one-on-one sessions, she realized that she wanted Drew's special attention to be more than just part of a job.

Drew must have sensed her thoughts.

"That doesn't mean that I won't miss having you to myself. I've enjoyed these sessions."

Reilly's disappointment disappeared and she smiled at Drew.

"Me too," said Reilly.

They lay on the floor for a few more minutes, and then Reilly sat up. She reached up in a lazy stretch and watched Drew do the same. Drew moved in ways that made Reilly want to stare.

"So, I was wondering—" Reilly started, but then chickened out. She ran her finger along the edge of her yoga mat and grew embarrassed at the lengthening silence.

"Wondering what?" prompted Drew, when Reilly didn't continue.

Reilly had tried to muster the courage to ask Drew to a studio event for the last week and had given up. She was surprised when the invitation had just come partially out of her mouth, and now she still didn't know how to finish asking her.

"Well, I have this thing that I have to go to."

"What kind of thing?"

"The kind of thing where I have to dress up and bring someone with me. You know, the kind of thing where people pay ghastly amounts of money to eat over-rated food, at over-rated places, so they can rub elbows with over-rated people. The studio makes me go to pose for pictures with people I barely know. That kind of thing."

Reilly realized that she wasn't painting a very appealing picture of the event and wondered why she was trying to talk Drew out of going with her before she even asked.

"And?"

"Well, I know this will sound weird, and don't hesitate to say no if you don't want to, but I was wondering if you would go with me. I've seen how comfortable you seem to be at Hollywood things. And well… I… well…"

"When is it?" asked Drew, standing up and rolling her mat.

"This Friday. I know it's last minute. It wouldn't be a date or anything," said

Reilly, rolling up her own mat, and hoping that Drew's question meant that she was at least thinking about it. She didn't know if she could bring herself to go if Drew didn't go with her.

"Sure."

"Really?" Reilly asked, looking up, surprised. "Because you don't have to. You aren't obligated or anything."

"I know that, Reilly. I'll be happy to go with you. Even if it isn't a date."

Reilly felt like twirling around in circles, but just smiled. She thought about Drew's last words for the rest of the day.

Lunch with Cray

CRAY LEANED OVER AND TOOK one of Reilly's sweet potato fries. Reilly
swatted at his hand, though she knew that she wouldn't eat them all, anyway.
They had spent even more time hanging out together outside of work than they
had during the first film they had worked on. Their friendship had blossomed
since she had found out about him and Hank. He was so much like Hank in
some ways, and she was happy that they had found each other. Cray looked like
he was finally settling down. And Hank seemed happier than she had ever seen
him. Hank was out of town, so she and Cray were eating lunch without him after
a morning interview to promote the release of the movie.

They sat on the patio of an out-of-the-way little vegan restaurant off of Santa
Monica Boulevard near Hank's warehouse. Even though they wore sunglasses
and ball caps, the number of double takes by the infrequent passing pedestrians
had increased, so Reilly knew it wouldn't be long before fans approached them
for autographs. She lowered the bill of the ball cap she was wearing and slouched
down a little more into her chair.

"You don't have to go with me to that thing on Friday," she said. "I found
someone else to go with me. You can do your skater thing down in La Costa, or
wherever it is Hank wanted to take you."

"It's a fashion show. Excellent! He'll be so—"

Reilly raised a hand as if to block his voice.

"Stop! Don't you say *stoked*," interrupted Reilly, lowering the wrap that had
been halfway to her mouth. There was one thing that Reilly didn't like about
Hank's influence on Cray. Cray's vocabulary had degraded at an alarming rate
since he'd started hanging out at the warehouse. Hank didn't even talk that way.
But the kids who were always there had somehow rubbed off on Cray. She had

been listening to him talk in skater slang all morning, and her jaw ached from grinding her teeth to keep from saying anything. She couldn't stand it any longer. "Don't you even say *stoked*!"

"What? I wasn't going to say *stoked*. Who says *stoked* anymore? It's so… so…" Cray searched for the right word.

"So what?" asked Reilly when Cray just stared at her and didn't answer. "Huh, skater punk? If you weren't going to say *stoked*, what were you going to say?"

"I was going to say amped."

"Oh my god, Cray!" she said, sitting back in her chair and laughing. "Don't you hear yourself? You talk just like them!"

"I do not!"

"You do, too!"

"Do not," said Cray, taking another fry. "Anyway, what's so bad about talking like them? They're Hank's crowd. Hank's supposed to be your friend."

"He is. And I like the way he talks. But it suits him. It doesn't suit you."

Reilly didn't have the heart to tell him that he had taken it to an extreme level, that even Hank sounded like a Rhodes scholar compared to Cray.

"What do you mean?"

"Hank and the people he works with dress the way they talk. They look the part," she gestured at him. "You're more of a Calvin Klein model. You can't talk like that. I almost peed my pants when you told Ellen that the wrap party for *Salsa Nights* was *super dope*."

"I did not!" he said, covering his mouth. "I did? How embarrassing."

"Come on! You didn't pick up on her making fun of you with that exaggerated Valley Girl accent just afterwards? Seriously?"

"Hey, you're one to talk."

"What do you mean?" asked Reilly with her mouth full, wondering how he was going to switch the tables.

"Ms. *I need to focus my energy*. Ms. *I feel so Zen*. Ms. *My chakras are all out of alignment*."

"What?" asked Reilly. She was the indignant one now. "I have never said that chakra thing!"

"Well, you might as well have." He leaned toward her with a glint in his eyes. "You, my friend, are starting to sound just like Drew."

Cray threw her off by mentioning Drew. She was always on Reilly's mind and she wondered if Cray could tell.

"I thought you liked Drew," she asked after a pause.

"I do. I love Drew. She's my other favorite lesbian. But she's a yoga teacher and you aren't," replied Cray with a shrug of his shoulders. He took a bite of his tofu burger.

"Whatever."

"Don't you mean *touché*?" he asked in a smug manner as he set his burger down.

"I mean bite me," she said as she chomped down on a fry.

"I love you, you know," he smiled as he took another bite of his burger.

"I know you do. I love you, too," she said, as she lifted her plate and dumped the rest of her fries onto his.

"Okay," said Cray, sitting back in his chair. "So, I don't have to go with you, but who are you taking to the shindig? Do you have a real date? Have you decided to emerge from your cave? Is the real Reilly getting ready to come out and play? Tell me!"

"Give me a break," said Reilly. "This *is* the real Reilly."

"I mean the fun Reilly."

Reilly just stared back at him. She couldn't believe that he had just said that.

"You know what I mean," laughed Cray. "The Reilly that used to go dancing with me. The Reilly who made all the ladies cream their thongs when she walked into the room."

"Gross," said Reilly, a little upset that he thought that she was boring now. "I'm still that Reilly, Cray. The dancing one, not the creaming one," she clarified. "I've just been working. And before that I was… readjusting."

"Well, I'm glad that you're back," he said and leaned forward to give her arm a reassuring pat. "Who are you going to the dinner with?"

"Drew."

"I knew it!" he crowed, pounding the table so hard that the silverware clattered.

"Knew what?" asked Reilly. She pretended to right her silverware, but knew full well what he was talking about.

"That you were totally hitting that!"

"I am not *hitting that*."

"Yeah. Uh huh," said Cray, nodding his head to tell her he did not believe her.

"I'm not!"

"Okay. You're not. But you want to."

Reilly was quiet for a second. She didn't mean it to be an affirmation, but that was how Cray took it.

"I'm right, aren't I?"

"Yes and no," admitted Reilly. She did want to be with Drew. She had since the first time she had met her. But it was more than that, and so admitting to Cray's suggestion that she wanted to *hit it* wasn't it at all.

"Well, if you want to, you should go for it," said Cray.

"I don't know—"

"This is so weird, Reilly. Seriously. You used to dive without fear into things—especially women."

"This is different," said Reilly. Then it hit her. She knew why she was so afraid of Drew. It wasn't about potentially being turned down as far as sex went, though there was a little bit of that. It was mostly her heart that she was afraid for. Drew mattered to her, and she had never put her heart on the line before.

"If it makes any difference, I'm pretty sure she's into you, if that's what you're scared of," said Cray, still thinking that Reilly was just out of practice in the scoring department.

"I'm not scared that she'll turn me down," lied Reilly. "You really think that she's into me, though?"

"Hell yes," said Cray. And his emphatic affirmation made Reilly's stomach flutter. "It is most definite that she has a thing for you."

"She does not. Does she?"

"Totally. The entire time I've known her, she has always been so… so…"

Cray struggled to find the right words while Reilly could think of a thousand words that would accurately describe Drew.

"Serene? Composed?" she suggested, sticking to words Cray would use, as terms like "enticing", "sexy" and "delicious" floated in her head.

"Yeah, both of those," he said, his furrowed brow smoothing. "When you're around, she's not serene or composed. I've never seen her like this. She gets nervous and kind of twitchy. It's pretty cute."

Reilly digested what Cray told her. It took a moment for her to get up the nerve to ask him what she was wondering.

"She doesn't date?"

"Oh, she dates," said Cray, as if that were a stupid question. The previous feeling of encouragement that Cray had given her evaporated. Her mind filled with images of the line of women Drew probably had waiting around the corner for her. "She dates a lot. But I've never seen her like she is with you."

"A lot, huh?" asked Reilly, wondering why she had asked. She didn't want to know the truth. That Drew had her pick of women. Nice women. Women without a past.

"Yeah. You've seen her. She's gorgeous," said Cray. He had no idea how his response affected Reilly. But when he continued, she wished she hadn't asked. "The ladies dig her. And she has an endless supply to choose from in the line of work she's in."

"Oh," responded Reilly, feeling dejected and wishing the conversation had never taken place.

"I'm telling you, though. You should go for it," advised Cray, taking a sip from his water and trying to pretend that he didn't see the growing group of people that milled around the front of the restaurant.

Reilly hid her disappointment and hoped that they'd be able to slip out the back.

"We'll see," she said as she gathered up her bag.

Wish Me Luck

IT WAS LATE DUSK ON FRIDAY night, and Reilly's car pulled up in front of Drew's house. The branches of the pepper tree swayed in a slight breeze and the string of path lights leading up to the lighted porch cast a warm glow over what little of the front yard she could see through the low front gate. Some of the light reflected from the surface of the dark water in the tiny stream, changing the lush area from a verdant picnic spot to a romantic grotto in Reilly's imagination.

She sat in the car for a moment trying to settle her nerves as she watched the rosy light in the sky beyond the swaying branches. One of the reasons that Reilly had asked Drew to accompany her to the dinner was because of the calming effect Drew had on her. She needed Drew's peace to give her the confidence to face her first working social appearance since the accident. But it appeared that her plan was backfiring. The prospect of going on a date-that-wasn't-really-a-date with Drew was more frightening than the event itself. She tried to remind herself that it wasn't supposed to be a date. But it sure felt like one.

She smoothed the flat front of the simple black dress she wore and adjusted the strap to her shoe, knowing that she was killing time, avoiding making that scary walk up to the front door.

"Rye? You okay?" asked Alison. Reilly saw concerned eyes watching her in the rearview mirror.

"I'm fine, Al. Just getting up my nerve."

"Jeez, girl! You're the hottest game in town. She's the one who should be nervous," said Alison, and Reilly loved her friend a little more.

"Thanks, Al. You're a bit biased, but I'll take the encouragement," said Reilly grabbing the handle of the door. "Wish me luck."

"You got it. You don't need it, but you got it."

Reilly got out of the car, took a deep breath of the August evening air, and made the short walk up to the front door of Drew's house, where she hurried to ring the bell before she lost her nerve. Her finger hadn't even left the button before the door swung open and Drew stepped out.

Reilly took a breath and didn't know what to say. It wasn't a date, but Drew had dressed like it was. She was seductive and elegant, in a diaphanous black wrap-around tunic, and flowing pants. The sleeveless top showed off her toned arms and her only jewelry was a thin black bracelet with a single silver charm dangling from it. Her hair was swept up into a knot on the back of her head, accentuating her long neck, and inviting Reilly's mind to wander. Reilly was glad that she had put some thought into her own outfit. As simple as the dress was, she had tried on at least two dozen before she found the perfect fit. She knew the halter top with plunging neckline showed off her shoulders and the bare back was sexy as hell, or so Alison had said when she had picked her up.

"You are stunning," said Reilly, and she realized that she had never said those words to another woman.

Drew smiled.

"It's impossible to compete with you, but I'm glad that you think so," said Drew, and Reilly felt a light blush creep up her chest and neck.

Drew smoothed her hair and shifted her weight to her other foot, but she didn't drop the hold that she had on Reilly's eyes.

Reilly cleared her throat.

"Ready to brush elbows?"

"Let's go, beautiful," said Drew, taking Reilly's arm as they turned toward the car.

The Dinner Party

LOCATED AT ONE OF LOS ANGELES' finest hotels, high on the side of a
hill facing the L.A. Basin, the dinner party wasn't as bad as Reilly had imagined
it would be. The venue was elegant, with tasteful table arrangements and seating
around the pool area. The band was decent, the food was excellent, and most
surprising to her, the other guests, many of whom she knew, were pleasant to talk
to. And she didn't need alcohol to get through it. The evening went by faster than
she thought it would, and near the end, she decided that she was glad that she
had come.

Preparing to leave, Reilly excused herself from Drew and the others seated at
their table. She was on her way back from the ladies' room when she happened to
catch a glimpse of the Los Angeles city skyline casting its world famous sparkle
into a clear indigo sky. She paused at the railing for a moment to appreciate the
scene. A trillion lights bathed the valley floor and surged up the surrounding
hills while the jagged shapes of the downtown buildings thrust up through the
center of it all. A bright moon shone down upon the landscape to complete the
perfect postcard setting.

A soft breeze, cool from the winds sweeping in from the distant coast blew
Reilly's loose hair back in gentle gusts while it skimmed the bare skin of her arms
and shoulders. She took a deep breath and closed her eyes.

Without turning, she felt Drew walk up the path behind her.

The impact of the moment and Drew's arrival sent a small shiver through
her.

"Cold?"

Reilly felt soft hands run down her arms and then back up to rest on her
shoulders. If it was a gesture meant to chase away the cold, it worked better

than a warm coat. Where Drew touched her, waves of heat began, spreading in radiating pulses through every inch of Reilly's body. It did more than just erase the cold. The caress electrified every nerve in her being.

"No, I'm not cold," she managed to say, afraid that Drew would remove her hands. But Drew didn't take them away. They traveled back down her arms and then moved around her waist. Reilly's heart raced, and she dared to lean back into the embrace. They stood like that for several minutes, enjoying the view, but Reilly's attention was focused on the new feeling of Drew's body pressed against her back.

"Thanks for bringing me with you tonight, Reilly. I've had a great evening."

Drew's voice was close to Reilly's ear and her warm breath tickled Reilly's sensitive skin. The faint scent of cinnamon drifted by.

"It's me who should be thanking you. You made it possible for me to be here tonight," said Reilly, trying to sound calm even though Drew could surely feel the pounding of her heart. Reilly tried to distract herself by playing with the charm on Drew's bracelet. She called upon the silver ohm symbol to give her the peace that she needed so that she wouldn't fly apart from the tsunami of sensations that whirled within her.

"Why's that?" asked Drew, resting her chin on Reilly's shoulder. The soft length of Drew's throat rested on Reilly's bare skin. The gesture was intimate in its simple casualness, and Reilly had never felt the kind of connection it elicited in her.

"Being near you grounds me," confessed Reilly, though in that moment it was doing the exact opposite. "You exude a sort of peace. I felt it the first time I saw you. This is the first public event I've attended since…" Reilly shrugged her shoulders to finish the sentence and it caused Drew to adjust her position. Reilly felt soft lips glance across her shoulder before Drew's chin settled back in place.

"Then I'm honored that you asked me."

"Everyone in this town seems to think they have the right to know everyone else's business," continued Reilly. "When you're around, I don't feel that pressure."

"Has anyone made you feel uncomfortable tonight?" asked Drew. Her voice was calm, but Reilly heard a protective tone in it that made her feel safe and cared for.

"No," said Reilly, surprising herself with her next words, giving voice to a feeling that she had only felt deep within her own self. "Though I wonder what's worse."

"Worse than what?"

"Worse than knowing that I don't deserve protection."

Drew brushed her chin along Reilly's shoulder, and Reilly could sense that Drew was thinking that comment over.

"You think that people are protecting you? And that you don't deserve it?"

"Some of them, yes," answered Reilly, after a half a moment's consideration. "Some of the others avoid the issue to make sure that they keep getting invited to these things. They don't want to rock the boat. But give them enough to drink and they'll start to say what's really on their minds." Even as she spoke, Reilly thought that she sounded bitter. That's not how she wanted to come off. She tried to smile. "But I signed up for it. It's all part of the game of who gets to take down the reigning kings and queens of Hollywood. It makes it easy when we do it to ourselves."

"Hmmm…"

"God, that sounds so cynical, or, worse yet, self-important." *And I've turned a perfect moment into a downer*, she added in her head. She needed to shut up.

Drew's arms tightened around Reilly's waist, and Reilly dropped her gaze to them, wondering what Drew was thinking. She could feel every curve of the woman behind her. The warmth of the firm softness felt better than she had ever imagined. She waited for Drew to pull away.

Without removing her arms from Reilly's waist, and in a single graceful motion, Drew slid around so that she was standing between Reilly and the railing. They were face to face. The distant city provided a canvas of twinkling lights around the beautiful face before her, and Reilly watched a single strand of hair flutter across Drew's smooth forehead. Drew's silver gray eyes shone in the reflection of the lights from the hotel as they searched Reilly's. Neither woman spoke.

Reilly reached up and smoothed the loose hair behind Drew's ear, and her fingers lingered against the long length of Drew's neck.

"I'm going to kiss you now," whispered Drew, as her eyes swept down over Reilly's mouth and then moved back to Reilly's eyes. She paused, which had the effect of making Reilly's lips begin to burn with the ache of wanting that kiss more than anything she had ever wanted before.

"Yes," she heard herself say as Drew moved closer. When Reilly felt Drew's mouth claim hers, the electric current that she always felt buzzing between them became a rush of energy that pulsed, heightening every one of her senses. The kiss was different—better—than anything she had ever imagined.

It was gentle at first, as Reilly learned the texture of Drew's lips. Every fantasy she'd had about kissing Drew paled in comparison to that kiss. Reilly's breath caught, and a small groan escaped her as she closed her eyes and sank into the sensations coursing through her. Every inch of her reacted to the feel of Drew's body pressed to hers. The hand that had been on Drew's neck slid, almost of its own accord, behind Drew's head, and she pulled Drew to her, deepening the kiss. Reilly's mouth opened and she shivered as Drew's soft tongue met hers. An almost desperate intensity crept over her, as an internal voice told her to slow down before she lost control. She had already lost that battle, though, and she leaned into Drew, trying to close any distance left between them.

Reilly felt like they were just getting started when Drew eased away and rested her forehead against Reilly's. Her eyes flashed with an intensity that Reilly had never seen in them, and then they closed. Reilly felt like she was in that moment of suspension before falling from a cliff.

"I'm—" began Drew, in a low voice.

"Don't say you're sorry. Please, don't say you're sorry," whispered Reilly, out of breath, her voice deep with the feelings that welled up within her. It terrified her that Drew might already regret their kiss.

Drew opened her eyes and smiled.

"I was about to say that I'm relieved to have finally kissed you. I've wanted it for so long. It's been killing me."

Reilly released the breath that she had been holding and pushed her fingers into Drew's hair, releasing more of it from the clip.

"I'll bet you say that to all the girls," said Reilly, resorting to glib humor, afraid of the truth.

"Nope. Just you," said Drew, which was the perfect answer. "And now that I've done it, I want to do it again."

Drew stroked Reilly's back, and Reilly closed her eyes as Drew lowered her head to kiss her again. Their hands and lips revealed the desire that each of them had been holding onto. Unable to resist it, Reilly brushed her lips down to trace a path across Drew's jaw and down her throat, wanting more, needing more. Drew lifted her head and bared the full expanse of her neck, a gesture that sent Reilly reeling. She ran her lips along the pulse that ended just above Drew's collarbone, breathing in the scent. Reilly continued to kiss and taste along her path of discovery. She couldn't get enough and there was so much left to explore. Her fingers sketched the trail that her lips meant to travel, and when she ran into fabric, she pushed it away. She was surprised when gentle hands guided her head back up. Through half-closed eyes she met Drew's gaze, and Drew moved back in for another long, slow kiss. A dazed smile trembled across Drew's beautiful face when they parted.

"Sorry, but I was just about to let you get us into trouble out here," murmured Drew. "If I let you keep going where I think you were going… where I hope you were going…"

Reilly blinked, and Drew's words filtered through the haze enshrouding her brain. The tips of her fingers were still inside the top of Drew's silky shirt, resting between Drew's breasts. If Drew hadn't stopped her, Reilly had no doubt that she would have had one of Drew's nipples in her mouth, and her lips tingled at the thought. She sketched small circles in the heat between Drew's breasts, while her eyes searched the silver ones locked onto her.

"Do you want to get a room?" she asked, hearing how that sounded but not caring. She took Drew's hand, ready to find the registration desk. Drew nodded her head but didn't move. Reilly took a step back, pulling Drew with her. But Drew didn't follow. Reilly's heart swelled at how beautiful Drew was in the wind and the moonlight.

"Come with me," she whispered, tugging Drew's hand.

When Drew shook her head, Reilly felt like she would shatter. She didn't know how she had gotten it wrong. A knot formed in her throat.

"Um… I… god, I'm sorry. I just got carried away." Reilly stammered, and she contemplated Drew's fingers, which were still clasped in her hand. She let go, but Drew held on. Instead, Drew pulled Reilly back to her and kissed her again. None of the heat had left them, and Reilly returned the kiss like a drowning woman gasping for air.

When they parted again, Drew brushed Reilly's hair back and ran her thumbs along the line of Reilly's high cheekbones. Reilly felt those beautiful eyes study her face. She closed her own eyes, wishing that she knew what Drew wanted.

"We have houses nearby and a driver to take us."

Reilly opened her eyes and smiled with relief. Drew tilted her head toward the front of the hotel.

"Are you ready to leave?"

Reilly nodded, and this time when she took Drew's hand to go, Drew followed.

Walk Me to the Door

THE CAR ROLLED TO A STOP at the curb in front of Drew's house, and
Reilly was about to tell Alison to take the rest of the night off when Drew beat
her to the punch.

"Walk me to me door, Reilly," said Drew, sliding across the backseat toward
the door.

The side of her that had been pressed against Drew on the short ride home
felt cold when Drew moved away, and Reilly wondered what Drew meant.
Maybe she didn't want to be obvious about what was about to happen. So full of
expectation and desire, Reilly took no note of the walk to the porch. With every
step, she fought the urge to stop Drew for more kisses.

When they arrived at the door, Drew pulled Reilly to her.

"I love the way you feel. I could do this all night," whispered Drew into
Reilly's neck.

Reilly wanted nothing less, and she arched into the circle of Drew's arms
as Drew caressed her bare shoulders and trailed her fingers over her back.
The touch made her insides expand and contract, almost as though Drew was
already inside of her, filling her, claiming her. Then they kissed. The heat that
they had held in check during the drive home rushed back like a tidal wave. In
the semi-privacy of the surrounding vegetation and the low lighting provided
by the porch lamp, their kiss was unbridled, and as her mouth responded to the
warm sensation of the tip of Drew's tongue teasing her lips open, Reilly's hands
found the opening in the back of Drew's tunic. The tips of her fingers pulsed as
they wandered over the smooth warmth that met them. Reilly pressed further
into Drew as her body burned with a fever that felt like fire in contrast to the cool
night air. Goosebumps rose on her bare skin.

Reilly slid her lips across Drew's sculpted jaw and she tasted a path down the column of her throat. The faint scent of vanilla and sage mixed with the smell of Drew's warm skin made her dizzy. "Drew, I want you so much," whispered Reilly against the pulse at Drew's throat.

"I want you, too. So much," said Drew into Reilly's mouth as she lifted Reilly's chin and they kissed again. Reilly melted even further into the moment, desire wrapping her tightly, and she almost missed the breathless words that were whispered against her lips. "But… but I think we should wait."

Reilly's hands were slipping under the waistband of Drew's pants when the words broke through the fog of passion clouding Reilly's mind.

She leaned her head back, but kept the lower parts of their bodies pressed together. She wasn't ready to let any distance come between them.

"Did you just say—?"

"I'm sorry. I know what I said at the hotel… but… I wonder if we should wait."

Reilly slipped her fingertips out from under the edge of Drew's waistband, feeling as if ice water had been poured over her. Her insides were still flaming with desire. It was all she could do not to beg Drew to let her stay, to try to sway her back to the need that she was sure they both still felt.

"I'm certain that's not what I want. But if that's what you need," said Reilly. She ran her hands along the arms that were around her and caught Drew's fingers in her own. She had to stop the hands that continued to wander across her shoulders, causing her skin to tingle. She hoped that Drew couldn't hear the frustration in her voice. She stepped back, and though she held Drew's hands, the separation of their bodies felt like a loss.

"I don't want it, either. But I think I need it," said Drew, stepping forward to caress Reilly's face. "I want to see you tomorrow. Are you free?"

Drew kissed her and Reilly wanted to melt. When Drew pulled away again she thought that she would scream.

"I'll be at the studio until 7:00 tomorrow night, but I'm free after that," said Reilly. She wished that she didn't have to work the next day. When Drew moved toward her again, she stopped her by taking another step back. "I won't be able to stop if you kiss me again."

Drew paused, but her eyes roamed over Reilly like a caress.

"I'll make dinner."

"That sounds great," said Reilly, breathless, backing down the steps. She wanted more, but she wasn't sure she would survive Drew's pulling away again. The mere sight of Drew leaning against the porch post, glowing with desire, her lips swollen, made her head swim with need.

"Okay then, it's a date. You, me, and my world famous lasagna."

I Love This Time of Night

REILLY STOOD ON DREW'S FRONT porch the next evening, dressed in
a soft cotton blouse, well-worn jeans, and flip-flops. She rang the doorbell
for the third time and shifted a bottle of her favorite cabernet from one hand
to the other, wondering if it had been a mistake to send Alison home. In her
impatience to see Drew again, she was an hour early, so the unanswered bell
didn't worry her too much, just frustrated her. She had rushed through the first
of her two Saturday afternoon meetings and, to the director's frustration, with a
vague complaint of not feeling well, she had rescheduled the second meeting for
Monday. Finally free, she'd rushed home, got ready and had come over without a
thought to the time.

Reilly hadn't slept well at all the night before, and she hadn't been able to
concentrate on anything throughout the day. Her thoughts were filled with
Drew's lips against hers and Drew's skin under her fingertips. She had replayed
every moment from the night before in an endless loop in her mind, and a
delicious tingle ran through Reilly every time she remembered Drew throwing
her head back on the hotel balcony. With that first real kiss, Reilly forgot about
not being good enough for Drew. Nothing outside of holding her, kissing her,
touching and tasting her made it into Reilly's consciousness. A shiver raced over
her with the thoughts that preoccupied her mind, and she wondered how she
was going to behave herself when Drew answered the door. If Drew wanted to
take things slow, she'd honor her wishes. It would be hard, though.

She rang the bell one more time and then checked her messages again. Drew
still hadn't responded to the text Reilly had sent when she left her house. Lights
were on in the studio, and Reilly wondered if Drew was back there. Part of her
itched to go find out, but she didn't want to snoop, so she stood on the porch

with her bottle of wine and a bad sense of timing.

She walked to the edge of the porch, placed the bottle of wine on the rail, and leaned against the corner post that Drew had been resting against last night when Reilly left. Reilly sighed at the memory of the beautiful woman, loose strands of her black hair blowing gently in the breeze, the soft light of the porch lamp casting a gentle glow around her. Her belly rolled at the thought of Drew's full red lips lifting in a smile with promises of dinner, hinting at more, as her eyes painted Reilly with the heat of their gaze. Reilly's eyes wandered over the fairytale yard. The soft sound of water from the small stream in the rock waterfall near the porch drew her eyes, and she followed its path as it flowed beside the walkway to the yoga studio, where it turned and wound its way down to the small koi pond. Dusk was falling, and the solar path lights hadn't yet switched on. The shadows amid the drooping peppertree branches appeared alive with the magic of early evening. Reilly closed her eyes and took a deep breath of the spicy fragrance in the damp night air.

Listening to the water, she let her mind wander to the night before. The sensations were still so fresh on her skin. She could almost feel Drew's body in her arms.

"I love this time of night."

It was only a whisper, and Reilly might have thought that she had imagined it, if not for the gentle touch of a hand on her lower back. She turned, and words of greeting paused on her lips, unsaid.

Drew stood before her in nothing but a towel. Without a word, Reilly's eyes traveled every inch of Drew, from her damp black hair and beautiful eyes to her long legs and bare toes. Reilly soaked up every detail before her eyes returned to the silver gray ones in front of her. Even in the low light, Reilly saw them gleaming, dark with desire.

"You can't look at me like that," whispered Drew, taking a step toward Reilly. An inch of expectation and vibrating need separated them.

"Like what?" asked Reilly, focused on the lips that she had been thinking about since the night before.

"Like you're going to make love to me. Right now. On my porch."

In Reilly's mind she had already bridged the gap of desire and was inside of Drew. She watched a drop of water make its way down Drew's collarbone, and her lips felt the heat as if she were already tracing its path with her tongue.

"Is that what you want?" she asked, short of breath.

"It's what I need."

"Then kiss me," said Reilly. She reached out and pulled Drew toward her by the hips.

"You're dangerous." Drew smiled as she slid her arms around Reilly's neck.

"You have no idea," murmured Reilly as she leaned forward.

When their lips met, Reilly lost all sense of where they were. When their bodies met, her ability to think at all fled. Her hands found the opening in the towel and they smoothed across the silky sway of Drew's waist. The towel came undone and fell to Drew's feet. Reilly caught her breath and wrapped her arms around Drew, relishing the soft compliance of the body that she sheltered with her own. The kiss was slow and deep, taking up where the last one had ended the night before. Reilly's fingers swept across the expanse of Drew's strong back, charting the topography of toned muscles under Drew's soft warm skin. Drew arched into her with a moan, causing a cascade of tremors to slide down Reilly's spine.

Without breaking the kiss, Drew backed toward the house, pulling Reilly with her. Reilly's world was nothing but the woman in her arms, the kisses that they shared, and the frantic beating of their hearts. As soon as the door shut and they were inside, Drew pushed her against the wall, and pressed into her, making quick work of the buttons on her blouse. Warm hands wandered over Reilly's stomach and back, and her shirt dropped to the floor. Reilly wore no bra, and when Drew touched her breasts, she gasped into Drew's mouth. Their heaving bellies moved over each other in a soft dance that left them both breathless.

Reilly continued to kiss Drew as she ran her palms along Drew's sides, pausing as she brushed along the sides of Drew's full round breasts. Reilly moaned and cupped the pliant flesh. Drew's breasts were warm and firm in her hands, her nipples hard and small, straining under Reilly's fingers. Reilly wanted to put her mouth on them, but she was lost in the kiss that inflamed an agony of desire in her.

Drew's thigh pushed between Reilly's legs, causing her to groan at the pressure that drove her mounting need. Reilly slid her hand to Drew's lower back, settling in the soft arch, and pulled Drew more tightly to her. She threw her head back as the seam in her jeans rubbed against her clit. Her hips worked in an urgent gyration as she lowered her head to take one of Drew's nipples between her lips. The velvet surface of the tight flesh was warm and soft, and Reilly swirled her tongue around the tip before sucking it into her mouth.

"Yes," sighed Drew, arching into her, almost setting Reilly off with the thigh moving between her legs. "You're going to make me come if you don't stop that," whispered Drew, voicing Reilly's own thoughts in a raspy voice as she eased Reilly's head away from her breast.

The pressure from the thigh between Reilly's legs eased and Reilly tried to catch her breath. She had been a fraction of a second from release. It had happened so fast. She wanted to make her first discovery of Drew's body last. She wanted to lie Drew down, learn her landscape, and then fill her up. She wanted to fall into her and never come up. Her hands wandered over Drew's bare back and she ran her tongue along Drew's collarbone.

"You feel, taste, sound… so good… so good…" Reilly could hear the desire in the low tones of her own voice.

"You do too, but I want to feel all of you, taste all of you," said Drew lifting Reilly's head to kiss her. The words made the backs of Reilly's knees tingle.

Reilly felt a tug at her waist, and without breaking their kiss, Drew stepped back just enough to unbutton Reilly's jeans and push them, and the damp silk panties Reilly wore beneath them, down and over her hips. Loose-fitting, they slid with ease down to Reilly's ankles and she stepped out of them, kicking the garments aside. Reilly then switched positions with Drew, holding her against the wall. She held Drew's arms to her sides, and kissed her slowly, breathing her breath, tasting her mouth, feeling the tremble of Drew's body beneath her. She molded herself to Drew's curves, pinning her to the wall in a way that told Drew that there was no turning back. The heat between them surged, and Drew spread her legs, straddling Reilly's thigh, the fragrance of their need mingling. Reilly let go of Drew's arms, rested her hands on Drew's hips and pulled her close, spreading Drew's wet desire across her thigh.

"Touch me, Reilly. I need you," moaned Drew into Reilly's mouth, as she rocked.

Reilly skimmed her palm across Drew's hip, swaying with Drew, caught up in the dance of their bodies, and just as her hand slipped between them, she had one last thought about how she should slow down for their first time. But Drew's kiss and the hand around her wrist guiding her told Reilly that slow was not an option.

"Please," breathed Drew into her mouth, and the plea drove away all remaining thoughts of slow beginnings.

The tips of Reilly's fingers pressed into hot, wet silk and found the firm knot of flesh that pulsed under her touch. She drew slow circles around it, grazing it every so often as she fell into the rhythm of Drew's desire.

"God, yes," whispered Drew, clinging to Reilly. They moved together in a slow, rocking rhythm. "I need you inside," groaned Drew. Her hips became insistent.

Reilly's center contracted at the whispered cry, and she plunged into Drew's hot slickness, lost to the increased tempo of Drew's passion. Drew set the pace, and Reilly moved with her, applying pressure as she felt Drew nearing release. It wasn't long before Drew cried out and her mouth stilled against Reilly's, as she ground down on Reilly's hand, driving Reilly deeper. Reilly felt a strong contraction grip her fingers. Drew's motions stilled as she shuddered, and a warm gush filled Reilly's palm. Drew's legs buckled, but Reilly held her up, still deep inside, and she marveled at the strong pulses that grew fainter and further apart, until they were just small waves, tickling her fingertips. Reilly held onto Drew until her breathing became less ragged, soothing her with soft kisses, reveling in the sensuous heat that wrapped around her hand.

Drew's trembling calmed, and she buried her face in Reilly's neck. Reilly felt Drew's chest heave as Drew took a deep breath. She eased from the warm depths of Drew's body and wrapped her arms around her, holding her close. As they relaxed, Drew's feet slid along the floor, and her back moved down the wall until they both came to a rest, sitting on the hardwood floor.

Reilly was in Drew's lap with her legs wrapped around Drew's waist. The smell of their sex filled the air, making Reilly light-headed with a new surge of desire. Her core clenched and she moved against Drew, trying to get closer. Drew lifted her head and gazed into Reilly's eyes. Reilly felt herself fall into the beautiful silver current that swirled within them. They kissed again, and Reilly felt warm caresses traveling along her back and down her legs in a languorous exploration that sent electric shocks out along each of her limbs. Reilly's stomach rolled as Drew's hand slid down and teased at the sensitive warmth between her legs. She gasped as Drew ran her fingertips around her clit and then slid into her.

The pressure that filled her was immediate and exquisite. It expanded to fill every inch of her, pulling the edges of her skin tight with expectation. Her hips rocked against the fingers that touched her deep inside, and the urgency built until she was writhing, on the very precipice of release. Never before had she let herself go so easily, so freely. She threw her head back and Drew held her as she arched into the mounting need that pulsed inside, expanding with each smooth thrust. Then Drew's mouth was on her breast, her warm tongue circling her nipple. Soft lips wrapped around the taut peak and sucked. The sensation was all it took to send Reilly over the edge. A loud keen rushed from her and she shuddered uncontrollably. Cascading light and heat spread from her, igniting her, shattering her, spreading her, releasing her, as wave after wave of incandescence spilled from her. She collapsed against Drew, her chest heaving as she tried to catch her breath and the last of her orgasm shook through her, leaving her incapacitated and spent. Reilly's body continued to move slowly, almost of its own accord. She was only aware that she was doing it because of the unbelievable feeling it continued to spread through her, but it was not a conscious motion. Slowly, the fury within her subsided, and when Drew eased her fingers out, Reilly wrapped her arms around her, burying her face in Drew's neck, trying to retain the closeness of their bodies. She felt like crying and laughing at the same time, though the wordless murmurs of the woman beneath her calmed the unexpected chaos of emotion that tucked itself back into her chest, under her ribs, safe against her heart.

"Did that just happen?" asked Reilly, feeling drunk. She kissed her way up the side of Drew's neck. As exhausted as she was from the most shattering orgasm she'd ever had, she couldn't hold still. She couldn't stop her lips from claiming Drew's skin, her hands from wanting to own her. She was consumed with want, overcome with the need to preserve the feelings that roiled within her.

"It did," replied Drew, groaning as Reilly's lips grazed over Drew's jaw and found her mouth.

"Wow," sighed Reilly as they parted to catch their breath, and Reilly reached up to push Drew's hair behind her ears. The simple gesture tempered the almost blinding craze of desire that swirled within Reilly, and she relaxed in Drew's embrace.

"Wow, indeed," said Drew.

"You are so beautiful," said Reilly lifting her head to capture Drew's gaze. Her hands fluttered beside Drew's face, pushing the damp hair back. Her voice trembled with emotion, but she didn't care.

"I feel beautiful when you look at me like that," replied Drew.

Reilly kissed her again and explored all of the skin within her reach. They were quiet as they absorbed what had just happened between them.

"What's this?" asked Reilly, running her fingers over a flat scar on Drew's hip.

"Oh… just a thing I got when I was a kid. It happened so long ago," said Drew, shrugging.

"It might just be my favorite part on you," said Reilly.

"Why is that?" asked Drew, a furrow forming in the middle of her normally smooth brow.

"Because it proves that you aren't perfect. If you didn't have that, I'd have to worry that you're too good to be true," teased Reilly, only half-kidding.

Drew smiled at Reilly's remark and kissed her again. Reilly moaned and felt the tumult of craving surge inside of her again. She would never get enough of Drew's warm lips.

"Reilly?" whispered Drew.

"Hmmm?" asked Reilly, tracing the edges of Drew's lower lip with her tongue.

"I wish I didn't have to, but I have to get up. My butt is asleep."

Reilly laughed and, with great reluctance, left the warmth of Drew's lap. Standing, she offered Drew her hand.

They both laughed as Drew rose with stiff legs, but the laughs died in their throats as Reilly caught Drew's eyes roaming over her with a visible hunger. When Drew's eyes met hers, Reilly saw the irises constrict into a thin ring around the unfathomable dark depths, and she wondered what Drew saw in her eyes.

"You are breathtaking, Reilly. Breathtaking," whispered Drew. She stepped closer, taking Reilly's arms and wrapping them around her waist.

"I never want to stop touching you," said Reilly, and she threw her head back with a deep groan when Drew's lips left hers to kiss a path down her neck.

"That would be paradise," murmured Drew, moving back to Reilly's mouth.

Several minutes later, when Reilly's hand had made its way back to the moist apex between Drew's legs and she was about to suggest they find a bed, a persistent bell broke through the fog of their desire.

Drew gave a frustrated moan and made to move away, but Reilly held her.

"I have to get that," laughed Drew, even as she relaxed into Reilly's arms.

"Get what?" asked Reilly, intent on continuing her exploration.

"The oven," smiled Drew, kissing Reilly one more time, as she eased away.

"Oven?" asked Reilly. Intoxicated by the feel of Drew's body, she didn't understand. She felt their separation with acute awareness as Drew stepped out of reach. Reluctance to leave was written in Drew's eyes even as she smiled and disappeared through a doorway behind her.

It was only when Drew's naked body was no longer distracting her that Reilly finally comprehended why Drew was walking away. Dinner. She followed the delicious smells and the sound of the oven timer toward the door Drew had disappeared through and found herself in the kitchen. Drew was already turning off the timer and opening the oven door. Steam billowed out, and Reilly's stomach growled at the promise of food while her heart clenched at the sight of the beautiful woman standing in her view.

Reilly stood near the doorway and watched as Drew donned oven mitts to take a shallow pan from the oven and place it on the counter. Her eyes traced the long lines that defined the toned curves of Drew's naked form as she performed the task. The muscles in Drew's arms flexed as she handled the pan while browned cheese bubbled at the edges, and the fragrance of simmering red sauce filled the room. Drew picked up another pan containing freshly risen dough that had been sitting on the counter, and slid it into the hot oven, and Reilly thought about skimming her fingers along the swaying roundness of Drew's breasts. Drew caught Reilly staring as she closed the oven and gave Reilly a slow smile. She took off the mitts and reset the timer. With great appreciation, Reilly watched the smooth ease with which Drew accomplished each motion, seeing Drew's grace from the yoga studio reflected in even this domestic demonstration. The fact that Drew was still nude, her body flushed with their recent activity, fanned Reilly's desire.

"Lasagna's ready and the bread will be done in a few minutes. I hope you're hungry," said Drew, setting the timer and placing it on the counter.

"I'm ravenous," replied Reilly, moving closer to Drew, slipping her hand over her silky hip. "For more of you. I could use some food, too."

"There's enough of both, believe me," said Drew. "But food first. You'll need your energy."

Drew covered the pan she had removed from the oven with loose foil and pushed it to the back of the counter, while Reilly snaked her arms around her from behind and kissed a line across her shoulders. Drew groaned and pressed back against her. Reilly's core pulsed.

"Does that need to cool down? Can I help with anything?" asked Reilly, hopeful. When Drew nodded and turned her head, Reilly took an earlobe between her teeth, and she felt Drew shiver. She slid her hands up and down Drew, stopping to cup a breast in one palm as her other hand went south and grazed the soft hair between Drew's thighs. Drew spread her stance just a little, to allow Reilly's fingers access to stroke the swollen flesh. Drew groaned, but Reilly only made one pass through the silken folds before she traced a path down the front of Drew's leg, and then drew her fingertips back up. Drew leaned forward against the counter and pressed her ass into Reilly as Reilly repeated the motions while returning Drew's press from behind. When Reilly's fingers lingered in the soft curls, and then moved more deeply into the depths between them, Drew gasped and grabbed Reilly's wrist, stopping Reilly from continuing her exploration.

"I'm afraid that if we start again, we'll never get around to dinner," said Drew.

"Too late," whispered Reilly, releasing Drew's breast and dropping her own arm to wrap Drew more tightly against her. At the same time, her fingers slid deeply into Drew, her palm brushing against Drew's swollen clit.

"Oh," moaned Drew, her nails pressed into Reilly's wrist. She lowered her head to the counter, and Reilly felt the slick folds of Drew's center wrap tightly around her fingers, which moved so easily into the wet warmth. Drew swayed in front of her, and Reilly watched the muscles dance along Drew's back. Reilly's sex clutched and pulsed as she watched Drew move before her, and she wanted Drew inside of her again. Reilly's fingers slid in and out of Drew as she leaned over and kissed the soft skin in the middle of Drew's back.

"God, I want—" Drew moaned, bucking under Reilly's breasts, which were now pressed into Drew's back. "I want—"

Reilly's core pulsed at the sound of Drew's voice straining, and Reilly thrust more deeply into her, taking her, filling her. Drew's cries grew louder, and Reilly had to control herself so that, in her own excitement, she didn't break the rhythm that Drew kept with her hips. Without warning, Drew spun to face Reilly, and Reilly's hand was pulled from its tight sheath. But Drew held her gaze and pulled Reilly's hand to her again. Reilly was once again deep within Drew, who leaned back against the counter and spread her legs, pulling Reilly close to her, kissing her, devouring her. Reilly straddled Drew's thigh and ground against it as her fingers slid in and out of Drew, faster and harder. Drew was so close. They both were. Reilly pressed down on Drew's thigh and felt the fire start to spread in her belly, felt the first ripple of what she knew would soon become a brilliant rush of release. The muscles in her thighs tightened. She felt strong and powerful, and she wanted to fill Drew with that feeling.

"I want to see your eyes when I come," panted Drew. She held onto the counter behind her and her eyes penetrated Reilly as her brows rose and her lips parted.

"Come for me now, Drew," demanded Reilly, held by the power of Drew's stare.

"Oh god. Soon."

Drew's hips moved frantically against Reilly, and Reilly pressed her aching clit against the firmness of Drew's thigh. Drew's breaths started to shake between her low groans. She felt the steady contractions of Drew's depths pull at her fingers. Drew let go of the counter and wrapped her hands around Reilly's waist, pressing Reilly down upon her thigh, never breaking the gaze that felt like a physical tether between them.

Reilly wanted to watch Drew come before she let herself fall over the edge, but the sounds that Drew made as she teetered on her own ledge kept driving the tension in the center of Reilly's belly higher. She tried to hold back.

"You're so close," whispered Reilly, as she concentrated, projecting her own imminent release upon Drew, as her fingers moved in the rhythm that Drew had set.

"Yes," moaned Drew. "Can you feel what you're doing to me?"

Reilly felt the contractions of Drew's core grow stronger, saw the flame of passion burn in Drew's eyes, and she wanted Drew to come. But the feel and look of Drew so close to release ripped open the gates of Reilly's control, and Drew's low-timbered question was the final thing that sent Reilly to the point of no return. She opened her mouth in a silent cry when she felt the first rush of bliss erupt inside of her.

"Yes, yes, yes," chanted Drew, holding Reilly with her hands and her eyes. Reilly thought that she would explode with the sensations that rolled within her, radiating like electric waves to the edges of her skin. Reilly writhed against Drew, unable to determine where her body left off and Drew's body began. Her breaths came out in hoarse shudders, and Reilly collapsed against Drew, though their eyes remained locked.

"That was beautiful," said Drew, holding Reilly to her, pressing against her, rolling her hips in the rhythm that she had kept going, even as Reilly had lost control during her powerful orgasm. Reilly should have been spent, but the waves of heat that she felt rolling through Drew's center and the intensity in Drew's eyes kept her moving. "That was the most… the most…"

Drew's mouth opened wide and Reilly moved in time to Drew's motion. Reilly could see the erupting desire filling Drew's eyes, the silver almost completely obscured by her dilated pupils. The cords of Drew's neck stood out as every part of her grew taut. She started to shudder, and Reilly felt a flood of moisture fill her palm. The fingers grasping her waist clutched at her. Drew's breathing grew jagged, and her hips began to pump again. Wave after wave of warm contractions swept across Reilly's fingers, and Reilly felt herself swept away again, as the thigh between her legs pressed against her. Her orgasm, unexpected and sudden, was like a gunshot, and she cried out. She wanted to close her eyes and fall into Drew, but she held on and maintained the eye-lock that seemed to ratchet the intensity between them higher.

Reilly held onto Drew and their movements became less frantic. As Reilly caught her breath, she continued to stare into Drew's eyes, which were now soft and unfocused. Carefully, she eased away from the thigh between her legs, knowing that she would come again if she stayed where she was. She didn't move far though, and she leaned her forehead against Drew's. Their breathing slowed to normal, but her fingers remained inside of Drew as Reilly enjoyed feeling Drew's flutters of pleasure grow fainter. When Reilly began to slide out, Drew groaned and squeezed her thighs together. This renewed Reilly's passion, and she pressed into Drew again, immediately ready to see Drew climb to even higher pleasure.

With a smile, Drew wrapped her hand around Reilly's wrist, stopping Reilly's motions. Slowly, she eased Reilly's fingers out of her. "I might have a heart attack if you do that."

"I think I already had one," laughed Reilly, blowing out a breath and finally breaking their gaze to kiss Drew's neck. Drew groaned and pulled Reilly against her. Reilly wrapped her arms around Drew and the feeling of their breasts pressed together sent Reilly's pulse racing again.

"That was the most intense thing that I've ever experienced," sighed Drew, next to Reilly's ear. The vibration of Drew's voice so near made her shiver. Every one of her senses was on high, and the sensation threatened to send her toward the precipice again. She wondered if she could come simply from hearing Drew speak.

"I'm not sure I've ever had so many orgasms so close together," admitted Reilly.

"It wouldn't take much to send me over the edge again, either," said Drew. Hearing an invitation, Reilly slid her hand over Drew's hip and grazed the damp heat between Drew's legs. Drew laughed and guided Reilly's hand back around her waist. "Oh, no you don't. Heart attack, remember?"

"Then we better get some clothes on," said Reilly leaning back, and moaning with a shudder as Drew's nipples grazed hers again. "Otherwise, I won't be able to keep my hands off of you."

"Good idea. I'll meet you right back here," said Drew, sliding from between Reilly and the counter with a lingering kiss. Reilly swiveled to watch, but didn't move as Drew slowly walked backward through a doorway that led to the back of the house. She almost followed her, but part of her was in shock. Nothing had ever felt more right, and she took a minute to let it sink in. The euphoria that filled Reilly was better than any drug. She couldn't control her smile as she finally went to get her clothes.

Reilly was just slipping a foot into one of her flip-flops when arms wrapped around her from behind.

"You make that pair of jeans look sinful."

Warm lips kissed her neck and Reilly lost herself in the sensation.

When Drew's lips moved away, Reilly turned in her arms.

"Hey, don't stop."

Drew wore a simple, flowing top and drawstring pants that went down to mid-calf. Dressed all in black, and with her black hair, Drew's silver eyes stood out like beautiful stars in a velvet sky. Reilly wanted to kiss her again.

"I already warned you that you can't look at me like that."

"Like what?" asked Reilly, unable to take her eyes from Drew's mouth.

"Like that. Like you're doing right now."

Reilly smiled and kissed Drew slowly.

"I refuse to take all of the blame," she said, when they finally parted. "You just make me feel so—" Reilly leaned back in for another kiss, but Drew captured her face in her hands before she could land it on her smiling mouth.

"No more kisses until after dinner, and then I promise there will be many, many more. Do you think you can manage?"

"I'll try," groaned Reilly, letting Drew step back from her embrace. Then she remembered the wine that she had brought. "Oh, I forgot—" she said as she opened the door and came back with the bottle she had left on the porch railing and the towel that had been completely forgotten. "I brought wine… and your towel."

Drew took both from Reilly and thanked her with a lingering kiss.

"I thought you said—"

"That's it. The last one until after dinner."

Reilly laughed and let Drew pull her into the kitchen, where Drew immediately placed her on a barstool on the other side of the counter.

"You stay right there. I only have a couple of things I need to finish up," said Drew.

"Let me help."

"The kind of help you provide is a little counterproductive, wouldn't you say?"

"I can keep my hands to myself."

"Yeah? But I'm not sure I can. That's why I need you on that side of the counter."

Reilly did as she was told, swinging a leg over a high stool that she pulled from beneath the counter. Her eyes were still glued on Drew as she leaned forward, resting her elbows on the smooth granite countertops, but the smell of Drew on her fingers made her mouth water. Drew must have had the same reaction, because just as she was about to dump a bag of salad into a bowl, she looked at Reilly with a grin and then turned on the faucet to wash her hands. Reilly grinned back and slid from her seat to join her. Reilly couldn't help herself and leaned over to kiss Drew as she was rinsing the suds from her hands. The timer for the bread was the only thing that brought them back to the task at hand. Drew pushed her away, and Reilly flicked water at Drew, but she dutifully went back to her seat to watch Drew make a salad and put the finishing touches on the bread in the oven. Drew took down dishes and wouldn't let Reilly help set the table.

"At least let me open the wine," said Reilly, when the enticement of kissing Drew's neck became almost undeniable.

"That would be perfect," said Drew reaching into a drawer to get the corkscrew. "You didn't drink last night. I wondered if you had quit."

"I don't drink nearly as much as I used to, but I didn't drink last night because I was afraid that I would say something stupid."

"Ah," said Drew, handing Reilly the corkscrew. When Drew didn't press for more detail, Reilly realized that, for once, she wanted to share more about herself.

"I was also worried about being around you. I haven't been very… well behaved with you in the past. Plus, I was nervous. I wanted to prove that I could do it without chemical assistance," admitted Reilly, searching Drew's eyes and body language for signs that the topic made her uncomfortable. "Are you okay with me telling you this?"

"I'm glad you told me," said Drew. She placed two glasses next to the wine bottle that Reilly had just opened and wrapped her arms around Reilly's neck. "I'm not much of a drinker. Most of the time I can take it or leave it. But I do like a nice glass of wine with dinner sometimes. So, you pour and I'll serve up the food. Dinner's ready."

Drew kissed her one more time and they went to the table, where the delicious aroma of lasagna and fresh baked bread made Reilly's stomach growl in anticipation.

As they sat down to eat, Reilly realized that they had broached a few things that she had been worried about discussing with Drew. And none of them had resulted in rejection. The evening was going well on several different levels.

"This is delicious," moaned Reilly after her first bite.

"Thanks. It's my mom's recipe," said Drew with a bright smile.

"I can't remember the last time I had a home cooked meal," said Reilly.

"And I can't remember the last time I cooked one," said Drew. "Cooking for one isn't very fun, so I eat out a lot."

"I know that feeling," agreed Reilly. "Besides the fact that I can't cook."

Drew smiled at her and took another bite. They were quiet as they ate and watched each other, and Reilly started thinking about satisfying another hunger when dinner was done.

"I have to ask," began Reilly as she paused in her eating to take a sip of her wine. Her eyes danced as she gazed over the rim at Drew.

"Yes?" Drew asked, mirroring Reilly's posture.

Reilly smiled and put her glass down.

"Do you often greet your guests on the porch in a towel?"

Drew laughed.

"Only my special guests," she said as she put her glass down. "You know, the UPS woman, the landscaping guys, my towel service—"

"I think I need to join the service industry then," deadpanned Reilly.

Drew laughed and Reilly's heart melted when she saw a shy smile replace the gleam in Drew's eyes.

"I was coming in from the studio. I was so nervous about you coming over that I went out there to burn off a little energy. I was a little… preoccupied about some of those kisses you gave me last night." Drew paused and her eyes darkened, making Reilly squeeze her legs together. "Anyhow, I took a shower out there and forgot to bring a change of clothes with me. I was trying to sneak back to the house, and there you were, so pretty in the light. I had to pass you to get into the house, and, well, I just—"

"Had to seduce me?" teased Reilly, finishing Drew's sentence.

"I don't think I so much seduced you as it was that I couldn't stop myself from touching you," said Drew, her face changing from bashful to serious.

Reilly had a hard time swallowing her wine. Drew's eyes were boring into her and she wanted to go to her.

"I know the feeling," said Reilly, absently trailing her fingers over the lip of her glass.

"Do you?" asked Drew, staring so deeply into Reilly's eyes that Reilly finally understood the meaning of hypnotic pull.

"I do," replied Reilly. "There's something about you that I can't resist. I couldn't wait to see you today, so I ditched my last meeting and came over early. I'm never early."

"Ah. I thought I was just running behind."

"I almost came back last night."

"I wanted you to come back last night. I stood on the porch watching you walk away, and I wished for it. And then I went into the house and I wished for it. I climbed into my bed and I wished for it."

Reilly thought about Drew in her bed wishing for her to return and Reilly imagined Drew doing what she had done when she had been in her own bed thinking about going back.

"Why did you send me away, then?" she asked.

"I don't know," replied Drew. Drew's eyes flitted away, and Reilly felt like she was holding something back. "When we were in the car, and Alison was there, and I didn't have your kisses to short circuit my brain, I started to think that maybe we shouldn't—"

"But we did," said Reilly. She felt her sex clench at the memory of what they had just done.

"Yes, we definitely did," said Drew in a low voice that made Reilly shiver. "It was inevitable."

"Do you feel it, too?" asked Reilly, talking about the electricity she felt when Drew was near.

"Yes. I felt it the first time I saw you."

"You did?"

"Yes. I felt it. And then you kissed me."

"I was such a jerk," Reilly admitted, ashamed at how she had acted, but relieved to get it out in the open. Jerk or not, that kiss had haunted her all this time.

"But a sweet jerk. Not like Sylvia."

"Sylvie," laughed Reilly, remembering the conversation that had made her cringe so long ago in the bathroom.

"You're nothing like her."

"I used to be," said Reilly.

"I don't think so. And I admit that I don't have much to go on, but what I've experienced with you, is that you're nothing like her. She's a…"

Drew paused to search for a word and Reilly tried to help.

"Player?"

"A predator," said Drew.

Reilly frowned. She'd never thought of Sylvie in those terms.

Concern fell over Drew's face and she leaned forward.

"Oh. I've stepped over a line, haven't I? I'm sorry. That was insensitive. I've never asked you about how you two ended."

"She dumped me just after… what happened," explained Reilly.

"*She* dumped *you*?" asked Drew, sounding incredulous.

Reilly hesitated. They were on the edge of talking about what had happened. She wasn't sure that she could bear to know what Drew really felt about her past, but she was already in a place where rejection would feel like death. Not knowing could be worse.

"Yes. She was embarrassed about what I did. She couldn't be with me because of it. It was too much for her," admitted Reilly. She thought about the last time she had seen Sylvie, that day in her mother's living room when Sylvie had told her that she couldn't be with her. Reilly had been close to killing herself that morning. She had decided not to when she realized that she had lost everything because of her selfishness, and that it was time for her to take responsibility for it.

Drew was silent and Reilly could feel a question in her eyes. She wished that she had changed the subject several minutes earlier.

"She couldn't stand the public scrutiny?" Drew finally asked.

"We never discussed the details. Maybe some of it was because of that. But I think that she saw me as a monster. And I don't blame her."

"She made you feel like that?" asked Drew. She sounded angry. "She did that to you, when you were going through all of that?"

"I don't blame her," repeated Reilly.

"You should," countered Drew, picking up a crumb from the table.

"I should what?" asked Reilly. She didn't understand.

"You should blame her. She should have supported you," replied Drew, shifting her gaze to Reilly.

"I don't… didn't… deserve that, Drew," said Reilly. She was surprised at Drew's response.

"Why wouldn't you deserve that?" asked Drew.

"I've taken responsibility for what I did. I couldn't ask her to do that for me. It's my own load to carry."

Drew searched Reilly's eyes. Reilly fought the urge to look away, but the intense gray eyes held hers. Drew reached over the table and took one of Reilly's hands.

"Oh, Reilly. Have you gone all this time thinking that people shouldn't love you because of what you've done?"

Reilly pulled her eyes away from Drew's and concentrated on their intertwined fingers. Fear welled up in her heart. She didn't want to lose Drew so soon, but she needed Drew to know who she really was.

"That's how it works, Drew."

"That is not how it works, Reilly. People make mistakes. Love should not be based on perfection."

"But actions define people, Drew," said Reilly. It was tempting to let Drew believe that she deserved to be loved no matter what, but she knew that some mistakes set some people apart from others in ways that couldn't be ignored. She met Drew's eyes again. "I killed someone."

"Oh god, Reilly," said Drew, tears welling up in her eyes. "And I believe that you have regretted that and everything that led up to that with all of your heart. I also know that you would change it if you could, wouldn't you?"

"Of course I would," said Reilly and her voice cracked. "I'll spend the rest of my life making up for it."

It hurt so much to say it out loud, but at the same time, a great weight seemed to lift from her. Guilt that she was thinking about herself when she didn't deserve it tried to sweep in, but she ignored it, greedily soaking up a little relief. In a way, the discussion they were having now was more intimate than the sex they'd had.

"That's all anyone can do, Reilly. Some mistakes are bigger than others. And it takes time to put things back once they've been knocked out of balance. But you have to forgive yourself first. That's the very first thing you have to do."

"But I killed a man. I killed a husband and a father, and nothing I do will ever fix that," whispered Reilly. She kept her eyes on Drew, though her eyes swam with tears.

"No. You're right. You can't fix that," agreed Drew. "But you can forgive yourself. Accept that your actions have become part of who you are, but you can and should move past it. From what I know about you, what I feel in my heart is that you're a fundamentally good person. You might be surprised at the forgiveness of others. Maybe his wife and kids will forgive you if you ask. But it won't matter if you don't forgive yourself."

Reilly was silent for a moment as she took it in. If Drew could see past her sins, she should try to, too. She wondered if she was even capable of it. The judge and jury in her soul told her no. But Drew was telling her yes. It was so confusing. She shut her eyes and saw the faces of Matt Traynor's family staring back at her.

"They have," she said in a quiet voice.

"What do you mean?" asked Drew.

"His family has forgiven me. His wife, Lydia, came to the prison and told me that she forgave me," said Reilly, opening her eyes to gauge Drew's reaction.

"She did?"

Reilly felt the memory fill her mind like it was happening right then and there. She had never told anyone about that day, and the days after that. She had tucked them away and walled them off, not knowing what to do with them, how to feel about them. The words emerged from her mouth in a torrent.

"She came to the prison. When they told me who had requested to see me, I almost refused to meet her. I was afraid. Afraid of her words. Afraid of her eyes.

Just afraid," explained Reilly, who still remembered how none of the Traynor family would look at her during the trial. She stared into the middle distance of the room, seeing nothing but the gray visiting room of the prison, and how hot it had been the day that Lydia Traynor had come to visit her. At the time, she had still been numb. She'd known what she should have felt—fear, shame—but it had never made it through her skin. "I accepted the request, but when she showed up, I almost told the guard to send her away. If it wasn't for the fact that I felt like I deserved to face anything she had to say, I would have sent her away. She surprised me, though. She asked me how I was doing. She asked if I needed anything. I couldn't speak. I just started to cry. And she cried too. She told me about him, then. She told me about Matt. She told me what a good father her husband had been. She told me about the Little League team he had coached and his Sunday school class. She told me about the award he had just received at work for some sort of sales thing. She told me what his favorite cereal was and how he always put the shoe and sock on one foot, before he did the other, and that his daughters put theirs on the same way. She told me all about him.

"And then visiting hours were over and she had to leave. But she came back the next week and told me more things about him. She told me that he would never cut his toenails until she threatened to do it for him because they scratched her at night. And that he left fast food cups in the cup holders in the car, which drove her nuts. She said that their biggest arguments were over the fact that he couldn't tell his mother to stop telling them how to discipline the kids. She told me that he could fly a kite even when there was no wind, and that he could fold the fitted sheets better than she could."

Reilly paused for a moment, remembering. She thought how Lydia had sat on the other side of the table in the visiting room telling her these things and how tears had streamed down Lydia's face, even while her bright eyes watched Reilly. And the stories had made Reilly feel like she knew him. The loss had hit her then. The loss of a man who had been so much more than just a jogger with one shoe missing. More than a man with a list of attributes that described him in an obituary. Pain lanced through her chest, remembering that day in the visitor's room when she'd realized that Matt was not just a regret. Matt could have been her friend. The pain had felt like it would cut Reilly in half as she listened to Lydia draw the portrait of her husband's life. But Reilly knew that Lydia needed to pass his history—their history—to her, and she took it. And how it still sat like a ten-ton rock in her chest, at first a burden and then, like a familiar ache, it had become a comfort to her.

Reilly told all of this to Drew. The words spilled from her and she had no control over them.

Then she was quiet for a moment as the memory receded.

"And when she was done telling me about him," Reilly said, stopping to swallow the sob that rose in her throat, "she told me that she forgave me. She told me that it was hard, but that she forgave me."

A few tears slid down Reilly's cheeks then, as she sat at the table with Drew and she wiped at them, embarrassed. She didn't deserve pity or forgiveness, and she didn't want the tears to buy any of that for her.

Reilly didn't tell Drew that Lydia Traynor had intentionally come all the way out there to tell her just that: that her forgiveness couldn't be bought. She was there because Reilly had set up a trust fund for both of the girls and for Lydia, and Lydia hadn't wanted any of it.

Reilly's mother had been against it, too. Melissa had been convinced that Lydia would sue Reilly anyway, and that giving them money would be the same as admitting guilt. But Reilly had still done it. And Lydia hadn't sued. Reilly wouldn't have cared if she had, either. But, even as Reilly had been setting up the trusts, Lydia had sent a registered letter to Reilly, via their lawyers. The letter inferred that Reilly already had enough on her soul, and that no amount of money would bring back her husband, so she wouldn't accept money as a payoff for having her daughters' father stolen from them. Reilly had set up the trusts anyway. And, at first, Lydia had refused the money. That was why she had come to the prison—to tell her in person. But, instead, Lydia had ended up forgiving Reilly.

Reilly didn't tell Drew any of that. It didn't matter.

Reilly couldn't forgive herself.

"She forgave you, Reilly. You should forgive yourself," said Drew, accurately guessing Reilly's thoughts.

"I'm not sure I can," said Reilly staring at her wineglass, thinking that Matt Traynor would never have another nice meal. That thought pattern, listing the things that had been robbed from Matt Traynor, was as natural to Reilly as breathing now.

They sat in thoughtful silence. Reilly didn't get the sense that Drew was using the time to figure out a different angle to get Reilly to accept her words. Drew simply seemed to be comfortable with silence. Reilly didn't know many people like that, especially in Hollywood.

"Do your shoulders hurt?" asked Drew, after several minutes had passed.

Surprised by the randomness of the question, Reilly abandoned the scrutiny of her wineglass and looked up at Drew.

Drew must have seen the question in her eyes.

"You're rubbing your shoulders."

Reilly realized that she was kneading the muscles where her neck met her shoulders. She stopped.

"Thus the reason I need your yoga," said Reilly, with a weak smile, trying to lift the mood.

"Thus the reason I am going to give you a massage," responded Drew with a wink. She stood and pushed her chair back from the table.

"A massage, huh?" Reilly asked, her dark thoughts had retreated, but the mood they had created was still there.

"Come with me, beautiful lady," said Drew. She walked around the table and extended her hand to Reilly.

Reilly took her hand, and Drew led them out of the dining room. They walked down a hall toward the back of the house, and Drew opened the first door but didn't enter. Dim light from several tea light candles on a tall dresser illuminated a simple, low bed with a fluffy duvet and many pillows. The room was large and open. The gentle smell of an earthy fragrance wafted from the room. It was sensual, something that Reilly would have expected from Drew.

"My bedroom."

Reilly took a step forward, craving to lie down on the bed, to sink into the circle of Drew's arms, but Drew pulled her back.

"Soon," Drew promised with a small smile that made Reilly's insides flutter. Drew turned to a door directly behind them and opened it.

"Doctor's office."

"We're going to play doctor?" asked Reilly, raising an eyebrow, and glancing around the room.

"I'm going to play doctor, and you are going to play satisfied patient," said Drew, walking into the room. Though the words were playful, her tone was not.

Reilly trailed Drew into the room and watched as she turned on a soft lamp and took a folded sheet from a nearby shelf. She walked to the head of a sturdy, cushioned massage table that stood in the middle of the room and snapped the sheet out over it, so that the white fabric floated down and covered it. Drew reached under the table for a cushioned ring with two prongs attached to it, and slid it into the table so that the ring extended from the end of the table. She worked with an efficiency that told Reilly that she had done it a few times.

"What other secrets and talents are you hiding?" asked Reilly.

"Wouldn't you like to know," replied Drew, her voice was light, but her eyes were serious. She moved toward the wall with built-in shelving where she had found the sheet. She gave Reilly another sheet and nodded toward the table. "Take off your clothes and lie down on your stomach. You can drape this sheet over you."

"Yes, Mistress," joked Reilly as a slow roll danced in her belly. Drew had her full attention, and the cold place that she'd gone to while telling Drew about Lydia Traynor started to recede.

Reilly did as she was told while Drew took a few bottles out of a cabinet and mixed the contents into a small bowl. The soothing scents of lavender, lemon, and sage soon filled the air.

On the table, face down in the cushioned ring with the sheet draped over her, Reilly closed her eyes and anticipated Drew's touch. She had almost left the sheet folded on the end of the table, thinking that they were beyond modesty after what had happened between them before dinner, but she still felt a little exposed by the recent conversation. She sensed Drew's nearness and shivered as the sheet was pulled down to just below her hips.

"Cold?"

"Just the opposite," replied Reilly.

Drew chuckled, and her soft hands brushed long slow circles over Reilly's back, before they began to knead her muscles. Drew's hands were stronger than she anticipated, and Reilly was soon transported to a place of bliss.

When Drew finished her back, she asked Reilly to roll over and then she worked on Reilly's upper chest and neck. When Drew cradled Reilly's head and rolled it from side to side, she was a relaxed woman. And when Drew cracked her neck, Reilly was surprised, but enjoyed the huge release of pressure up and down her back.

"How did you learn to do that?" asked Reilly. "It's magical."

"A magician never reveals her secrets," said Drew cryptically, as she walked to the other end of the table, trailing a hand down the length of Reilly's body. When she got to the end of the table, she rolled one of Reilly's legs and then pulled. Reilly felt a pop in her hip and then a feeling of relief where she didn't know she needed it.

"Don't get me wrong, that feels like heaven, but aren't you afraid of doing something like that?" asked Reilly.

"Don't worry. I know what I'm doing," said Drew, and Reilly could hear a smile in her voice as Drew adjusted the other side of her hip.

"You could give massages and adjustments for a living," said Reilly, sighing with the pleasure of relief.

"Yoga is what I do," replied Drew after a pause, and she moved again to the head of the table and ran her hands through Reilly's hair.

"Yes. And you do that well, too," said Reilly. Her eyes were closed, but she sensed Drew's smile through the hands that were massaging her scalp. "I'm so glad I picked it up while I was—in prison." She still had a hard time saying it out loud.

"Is that when you first tried it?" asked Drew.

"I'd gone a few times before. And I liked it. But there was something missing. It felt so—plastic," said Reilly, trying to figure out a way to describe the pretense she had sensed in places where she had hoped to find peace. "When I took my first class in prison, I didn't expect much. It was just a way to fill the tedium and to stay out of the way of some of the other inmates. But the instructor was amazing. She was one of the guards. To see her in uniform, you would never imagine the grace and poise she possessed when she was teaching a class. She was my favorite instructor until I took your class."

"I'm flattered," replied Drew. Reilly opened her eyes to find Drew studying her face. The scrutiny would have felt uncomfortable from anyone else, but not from Drew. She reached up and pulled Drew down by the front of her shirt and kissed her. When they broke for air, Reilly took Drew's hands and put them on her breasts.

"I think you missed a couple of spots."

This Marking You Have

SHAKING RAIN FROM HER HAIR, Reilly stood on the porch outside
of Drew's yoga studio and watched fat drops splash down into the koi pond,
showering the lawn and making the yard glisten and dance among the impossible variations of the shade of green. The smell of earth and vibrant plant life filled
her senses, and she cupped her palm to catch a stream of water that ran from the
sloped roof above her head. The heavy rain, so rare in Southern California, felt
enchanting. She smiled at the cool water that splashed out of her hand and ran
in a rivulet over her wrist and down her arm to drip from her elbow onto the
wood planks beneath her sandals. The cool air of the summer storm made her
thoughts return to waking up that morning, wrapped in blankets, pressed against
Drew's soft body naked against hers, the sound and scent of steady rain coming
in through the open window. She wanted to be back in that moment right now
and was counting the minutes before she could see Drew again.

It had been raining for two days, forcing the postponement of the scheduled
location shoot at Malibu. Reilly was grateful for the unexpected time off, but
Drew still had her classes to teach. Reilly was impatient to see her. She wanted to
be with her every minute of every day. She wanted to touch her, talk to her, know
her, and breathe her. She just *wanted* her. Reilly had never felt that way before,
the constant need, the absolute desire that she felt for Drew.

Taking one last breath of rain-scrubbed air, she went into the studio to wait.
The place was deserted, but she was early. She had considered making a detour to
Drew's house before coming to the studio, but she had to prove to herself that she
had control—at least over her base desires. She didn't know about her heart. Her
neediness for Drew was so unlike her. By forcing herself to stay away, she was just
playing a mind game with herself, but at least she knew it.

She stored her stuff, unrolled her mat in her usual spot, and then, to kill time, she wandered down the hall to examine the framed black-and-white photos that hung on the walls. She'd glanced down the hall at them a few times, but in her preoccupation with Drew, she had never had a chance to really look at them. In each one, Drew stood with someone new. There were individuals, groups of people, celebrities, and public figures. She'd even had a photo taken with the Dalai Lama.

In one picture, Drew stood in a yoga studio between two familiar-looking women. All three of them were glistening with moisture as if they had just completed a hot yoga class. Reilly studied Drew, who was beautiful and toned in a skimpy yoga outfit that consisted of tight running briefs and a sports bra. The abs that Reilly had worshipped during lovemaking stood out in defined symmetry, and Reilly vowed right then to work on her own. She studied the picture, a low thrum of lust rising in her, unbidden but always there these days. Her eyes followed the edges of the skimpy outfit and noticed that a couple of dark lines extended out of the front of Drew's low-rise shorts on the right side. Reilly squinted to inspect the marks. She smiled when she realized that the scar she often kissed was not a childhood injury as Drew had said, but the results of tattoo removal. She wondered what childhood insanity Drew was embarrassed about enough to remove. An old lover's name? An outgrown cartoon character? The little mystery titillated Reilly.

The door to the studio opened. Without looking, she already knew who it was. She wondered if Drew felt the same electric charge that always rolled over her skin when they were near each other. In another test of her control, Reilly resisted the urge to go to her.

"Hey, beautiful," said Drew, moving in behind her. "I saw you walk up. I was hoping that you'd come up to the house. How was your day?"

Reilly leaned into the embrace that Drew gave her from behind and smiled as warm lips brushed across her neck. Most of her control fled the moment Drew touched her.

"It was good but I missed you," purred Reilly, closing her eyes, enjoying the warm mouth making its way up her neck. "Mmmm… You feel unbelievable. I didn't go up to the house because I had to prove to myself that I could survive more than an hour without this."

"I missed you, too. We have fifteen minutes before class. We could slip into the back room and…" murmured Drew, letting her words trail off as she pressed her lips to Reilly's sensitive skin and her hands roamed over Reilly's bare midriff.

"We could," agreed Reilly, thinking the same thing. "But then your students might hear their favorite yoga instructor screaming out the name of a deity, thus shattering the illusion of their Zen Master."

"Hmmm… so true. It's hard to practice the serene art of nothingness when you have your head between my—"

With regret, Reilly moved her neck away from Drew's searching kisses and playfully slapped at the arms that held her tight.

"Okay, okay! Enough, or I won't be in a position to protect your reputation," laughed Reilly.

Drew kissed her neck again, and Reilly, whose restraint was weak already, was a kiss away from dragging Drew to the back room anyway. In a last effort to be strong for both of them, she tried to redirect Drew's attention. She pointed to the photograph in front of her.

"Who are these women with you in this picture? They look familiar."

"That's Misty May-Treanor and Kerri Walsh Jennings, the women's gold medalists in Olympic beach volleyball," explained Drew, resting her chin on Reilly's shoulder.

"Who are they to you?"

"They were my lucky break when I first went into business for myself. The short story is that they found me through a friend of a friend. Because they enjoyed my classes, they spread the word about my studio with the other athletes. And then I was mentioned a couple of times during the Olympic telecast when the announcers commented on their focus and someone mentioned that they'd been using yoga in their training. That was all it took to get some celebrities to come check the studio out. It was all luck."

"Luck, my ass. You're good. They provided the advertising, but it was karma. Your energy, your hard work," said Reilly tracing a finger over Drew's glistening abs in the photo and landing near the mark that had caught her eye moments earlier. "And what, pray tell, is this marking you have almost covered up here, Miss Oh-that's-a-childhood-scar? Is it a heart? The Olympic symbol? Boobies? What embarrassing skeleton have I found with my sleuthing skills?"

Reilly laughed, but the arms that stiffened around her told her that the question had hit a nerve. A small stone lodged in Reilly's gut.

Drew studied the picture, but Reilly got the feeling it was more to buy time than to see what Reilly was pointing at.

"I was just teasing—" began Reilly, but Drew cut her off.

"It was stupid. I'm sorry that I misled you. I had it removed. It was a scribbled piece of shit." The shame in Drew's voice made Reilly wish that she hadn't brought it up. Reilly turned in her arms and saw that Drew was about to cry.

"Hey. Hey. Don't be sorry. I was just messing with you," said Reilly, stroking Drew's face. "I'm not mad. You can retain some mystery. I don't need to know everything."

"It's not mystery, it's regret. And it's not cool that I lied to you," said Drew, lowering her head. Shame was something that Reilly never would have expected from Drew. She was always open, confident, and serene.

"I know, babe. Don't worry about it," said Reilly, squeezing Drew and searching her eyes. She wanted to kiss the uncomfortable moment away. "I still love the scar. It's one of my favorite places on you, aside from—"

The door opened and they reluctantly stepped apart as two women came in. Reilly had seen a glimmer of the happier Drew come back, though, and she felt a little relief.

What a Small World

"NAMASTE," SAID DREW, AS THE SESSION came to a close an hour and a half later.

"Namaste," murmured more than a dozen voices from around the studio.

Reilly stood and stretched like a sated cat, even while her eyes sought out Drew. It wasn't hard to find her. Her body felt her, could locate her without fail, anytime she was near. She was standing near her mat, talking in a low voice to one of the students. One of her hands rested on his elbow. Reilly took a moment to watch and smiled at the way that Drew always made whomever she was talking to know that they were the center of her attention.

Though anxious to reconnect with Drew after the weirdness between them before class, Reilly was respectful of Drew's need to nurture her business, so she took her time with stowing her mat in its bag and retrieving her things from the cubby where she had left everything before class.

On most days, the studio cleared within five or ten minutes, as the quiet peace that prevailed in the session held the yoga students' desire for socializing to a minimum. But on this day, a few students stopped to chat with Drew, and when Reilly turned with all of her belongings in hand, Drew was talking to another one. With a sigh, Reilly decided to wait for Drew on the porch, but something familiar about the person Drew was talking to caused her to pause. Part of her wanted to walk away, but she couldn't.

"Fergie?" she asked, as she approached the tall woman from behind. When the woman turned around at the sound of her name, Reilly was suddenly standing in an entirely different yoga classroom. Warm wood accents and open windows disappeared, and the ghosts of grey walls and sparse furnishings surrounded her. She immediately wanted to shrink away for approaching her former guard without permission.

But Fergie returned her greeting with a smile, an expression that Reilly had never witnessed from the woman. Dressed in a tight tee-shirt and yoga pants, her demeanor was unexpectedly informal, but the loose hang of her shoulders conveyed a lightness that made the moment almost surreal. Reilly realized that seeing a reminder of the lowest time in her life wasn't as bad as she would have predicted. Running into the guard out in her real life was like seeing a teacher at the grocery store when you were in elementary school. The realization told her more about herself than anything else ever had.

"Hi," breathed Reilly, unable to think of anything else to say. She was surprised even more for the urge she had to hug the woman. She stopped a respectful foot away, though. Some things were too hard to unlearn in a moment.

"I thought that was you in the back of the class when I came in," said Fergie. "How are you?" Reilly remembered the deep voice well, but it now held a new degree of warmth.

"Fine. Great, actually," said Reilly. "I always set up in the back. I didn't see you until now. I'm oblivious once class starts. Drew is a phenomenal instructor."

Reilly rambled, surprise stealing her poise.

"Drew is one of the best," agreed Fergie, glancing at Drew with a smile.

Reilly switched focus from Fergie to Drew and saw that some of the tension from before class was still there. And though it was an unexpected pleasure to run into her guard and protector from prison, she was anxious to be alone with Drew to make sure things were right between them. Whatever had transpired between them before the class was deeper than she had imagined if Drew was still so tense after an hour and a half of yoga. She didn't want to be rude to Fergie, though.

"So, you know each other? I haven't seen you here before," said Reilly.

"She's somewhat of a regular," offered Drew, answering for Fergie, who just smiled and nodded.

"Oh," responded Reilly. She struggled for words, absorbing the fact that Drew knew Fergie. "Um, I guess it really is a small world."

Fergie nodded her agreement and the three women looked at each other for a minute and Reilly felt the need to break the silence.

"Fergie is the instructor I told you about," she said to Drew. "No wonder she's so good if she learned it from you."

Reilly hoped her smile and the compliment would help Drew relax. It didn't. In fact, it seemed to worsen it. She turned to Fergie, hoping that the insecurity she felt, causing her to second-guess everything she did, didn't show. Between Drew's unfamiliar tension and how Fergie's presence brought up so many old and uncomfortable memories, Reilly struggled to find confidence. Facing it directly was all she could do. "This is so weird. I feel like I'm supposed to be careful about what I say, how I should talk to you. Is it okay if I ask you what you're doing so far from… home?"

Fergie smiled like she understood and Reilly wondered how many prisoners she ran into outside of work. "Home is close by. I live in Venice Beach when I'm not working. I commute."

"That makes sense. I always wondered how anyone could live out there in the desert full-time," said Reilly.

"Me too," Fergie laughed. "But few of us do. There isn't much housing out there, and what there is is pretty dismal. I grew up in the house I live in. When my shift is over, I can't wait to get out of there and get back to the beach."

Reilly felt her uneasiness begin to abate, even as it felt strange to find out that Fergie was a real person. Aside from hearing the guard bark out orders, calling out yoga poses during class, or the one time they had talked about the prison library, Reilly had never heard Fergie speak more than a few words at a time.

The feelings and memories that played in the back of Reilly's mind as they spoke coalesced into one particular memory that was more vivid than the rest.

While at Ral-Rutherford, Reilly had fast learned that the guard schedule was forty-eight hours on, forty-eight hours off, and that the guards slept in dorms in prescribed rotations during their shifts. The schedule had been disorienting at first, as Reilly had tried to predict which guards she had to be wary of and which were more laid back. The interesting thing was, at first, she had been most wary of Fergie. The Amazonian guard had always been the one to catch Reilly doing something wrong—the time she had sneaked food into her cell, the handful of times that she had more than the allowed number of books in her cell, every time she tried to go barefoot through the dayroom to go to the latrine. Any time Reilly caught eye of the towering guard, it had seemed the intense blue eyes were on her. And for a while there, Reilly had been sure that Fergie had been gunning for her. But soon enough, Reilly realized that the same eagle eye that caught all of her screw-ups had also been the thing to save Reilly from many of Twist's sick games. For that, she had come to value the guard's unwavering attention to detail.

Now she suddenly realized that she wanted Fergie to like her.

"I told Drew what a great instructor you were," said Reilly. She had already said that. She was gushing, a little intimidated from being around one of the people who had seemed so untouchable to her for so long. She wondered if it was a feeling her fans felt when they met her. It was a strange juxtaposition.

Reilly saw Fergie glance at Drew, and she suspected that Fergie was weighing her response, probably because she didn't know how much Drew knew about Reilly's incarceration.

"It's okay. Drew and I are… close. We've talked a little about RR," said Reilly, referring to Ral-Rutherford in the way of inmates and guards who have done time there.

It seemed that Fergie was about to say something when Drew spoke.

"Didn't you tell me that you were in a hurry to get home, Ferg? We can catch up later."

"Yeah, I need to get on the road. I have a shift tonight," said Fergie, nodding her head. "It was a great class, Drew, as always. Nice to see you again, Rans… Reilly."

Reilly noted the name correction and, in a way, it was a kind of closure, as if the short meeting had validated that Reilly was a real human again.

"It was nice to see you, Fergie. I hope to see you around," said Reilly stepping aside to let Fergie pass on her way to the door.

Fergie smiled and waved as she shut the door behind her. The rest of the students were long gone.

Reilly turned to Drew, who didn't seem as tense as she had just moments before. She wanted to ask her about it, but wasn't sure how to bring it up. Drew would probably tell her in her own time, but Reilly needed to feel connected to her again.

"That was a surprise, huh?" said Reilly, testing the waters as she moved closer to Drew and put her arms around her waist.

"Yes, it was," said Drew with a small smile, putting her arms around Reilly's shoulders and searching her eyes. "I suspected you two would run into each other before too long. Maybe I should have said something."

The stiffness was almost gone from Drew's stance. So, Fergie was the cause of the renewed tension, and not the earlier conversation. Reilly could deal with that.

"It was nice running into her. Weird, though."

"I can imagine. I didn't…" began Drew, but she just shook her head and let the sentence hang. "Never mind."

Reilly was determined to assuage Drew's agitation. She didn't like the weirdness that had settled between them.

"You didn't what? Know if we knew each other?" asked Reilly, guessing at what Drew was about to say. She wanted Drew to know it was okay to talk about her past. And if Drew had a hard time with it, it would be good to get it out in the open sooner, rather than later. "How could you? But it's okay to ask. I'll tell you anything you want to know about it."

"Okay," agreed Drew. Reilly thought that she still saw a question in her eyes. But she didn't ask. So Reilly asked her own question.

"Has she been attending your classes for long?"

"Since the beginning, off and on. Her schedule makes it hard for her to attend regularly," said Drew, and Reilly felt her loosen up. She almost seemed like the Drew that she was used to.

"I'll bet your classes are a little expensive on a prison guard's salary."

"Guards working out in the desert make more than you'd think for the hassle of having to commute so far, but I also give her a discount. She's been coming here since the beginning. You have to reward loyalty. And she sends referrals."

"Karma, huh?" Reilly gave Drew a light kiss. She hugged Drew tighter.

"Yeah, karma," agreed Drew, hugging Reilly back.

"Will I get karma points for washing your back if we take a shower?" asked Reilly, wiggling against Drew and eliciting the smile she was after. She was desperate to feel their connection again.

"Washing my back will definitely get you karma points," said Drew, kissing Reilly, and the connection was there.

"Can I trade my karma points for other stuff?" asked Reilly. She nuzzled a path down Drew's neck, tasting salt, and then slid her hands into the back of Drew's yoga pants to cup her ass.

"What kind of other stuff?" asked Drew. She tilted her head back so Reilly had access to more of her neck.

"I'll show you in the shower," said Reilly biting Drew's neck, which produced a low moan from Drew.

Heat rose in Reilly's body when Drew went to lock the doors to the studio and she followed Drew into the back room.

That's Tonight?

"ARE YOU GOING TO TAKE DREW to the thing tonight at the Marmont?"
asked Cray, stopping in the studio parking lot near Reilly's car. It was noon and
they were already done for the day. The days of long shoots were over and they'd
been called in for a few voice-overs.

"The Marmont? That's tonight? Oh, jeez. I forgot about that," said Reilly,
lifting her phone to check her calendar. "So the publicity junket begins."

Salsa Nights II was in post-production and, though it wouldn't be released for
at least six months, the studio had started to ramp up the schedule of publicity
events. By the volume of them, Reilly suspected that the studio was making up
for all the interviews and events she'd missed during the dark days after the accident. Reilly still wouldn't do interviews, but she had at least two appearances per
week scheduled over the next month, and it would just get busier the closer they
got to the film's release date. The press so far had been positive. The event at the
Marmont wasn't required, since it was just a private party for the stars and crew
of the movie, but Reilly had privately committed to making as many appearances
as possible for this movie since she had done so little for the previous one.

"Drew has a yoga thing in Santa Barbara today. I'm not sure she'll be back in
time to go. But I'll check," said Reilly.

"If she can't, let's go together. Hank is at some sort of fashion week thing in
New York."

"He's busier than we are these days," laughed Reilly, happy for her old friend.
"And so much for his aversion to fame. He's sucking it up like oxygen."

"He says it's different being famous for what he makes rather than how he
looks," said Cray, with a shrug of his shoulders that said he didn't understand but
accepted it.

"I get that," said Reilly remembering some of the talks she and Hank had had when he had quit acting. Even back then, when they were still so young, he had been more mature than most of the other young actors she met and worked with. Although she respected his decision, she hadn't really understood. He'd tried to explain to her how the industry valued the right look more than the person who wore it, how it had made him feel like he was disappearing in full sight of everyone. She'd seen the effect that it had on him, but it had taken her a few years to finally understand what he meant. And it had never really bothered her as much as it did him. It was only in the last few years, when she wasn't so immersed in the whole Hollywood scene that she'd started to feel some of what he had described to her. Then she wondered if anyone really even knew her. Whether anyone really cared about Reilly the person, rather than Reilly the actress. She'd even questioned whether acting was what she should be doing. Was it enough to offer the world ninety minutes of cinematic escape for a small fortune? Should she be doing more? But who was she to think anything about a better purpose? She was the quintessential fuck-up. When she got to that point in her introspection, she always had to stop. She didn't know what the next step was, didn't have any answers. It was too hard to think beyond that.

"Okay, so let me know," said Cray, walking toward his red Porsche, reminding Reilly of where she was. "I can have my driver pick us both up."

Alison held her door open and snorted.

"Or Alison can drive us," said Reilly, swatting Alison's shoulder as she turned toward the car. "I'll call Drew and let you know."

At the Hotel Marmont

"WHAT PART OF *NO COMMENT* do you not understand, mister?" asked Cray, stepping between Reilly and the heavyset man with the camera who had popped up out of nowhere as they exited the car at the Hotel Marmont. Drew's Santa Barbara trip had her making it back to the city a little later and she had promised to meet Reilly after she showered and changed. Reilly had already called ahead and left her name at the door, and was currently glad that Drew didn't have to deal with the invasive paparazzi that was now accosting her and Cray.

"Is this the start of your new party phase, Reilly? Where have you been all of these months? What have you been doing since you got out?" asked the persistent man in the bad suit, even as Cray blocked his approach with his own body.

"Dude, this is a private party. Now get out of our way or I'll call the—" Cray's eyes landed on a point over Reilly's shoulder, and his words stopped behind a relieved smile. She turned to see a man approaching them wearing a suit jacket over a black tee shirt. She recognized him and his vast beard from her past visits to the hotel bar that was popular with celebrities.

"Hey, Miss Reilly. Someone bothering you?"

"Hey, Trent," said Reilly, pulling Cray's sleeve to lead him away. "That guy just needs to be taught some manners. Be nice though, okay?"

"What're you talking about? I'm always nice," smiled the giant man as he moved past them.

Reilly and Cray stepped around the reporter and walked toward the garage entrance of the Hotel Marmont. Alison had let them out in back instead of on the street to a avoid some of the paparazzi. It appeared that the plan had backfired.

"Hey, jerkwad! Take a hike!" said the huge doorman stepping between them and the man, who was still snapping photos. "You really should wear the strap around your neck. Otherwise your camera might… Oops!"

Reilly heard a scuffle behind her and the sound of something hard hit the cement, but she didn't turn to see. She just held onto Cray's arm and followed him up the steps and down the ornately tiled pathway that led to the hotel bar. She stopped for a moment to ask another door guard to get the pushy reporter's address and what kind of camera he'd been using. There was a line of people waiting to go in when the private party wound down later in the evening, but the doorman nodded and ushered them in through the closed side door.

"No problem, Miss Reilly. Nice to see you here again," he said as he lifted the rope.

"Thanks, Nick," she said, surprised that she remembered his name.

They headed toward the far side of the room where some of the other actors from *Salsa Nights II: Dare to Dream* were congregated.

"Does that happen everywhere you go?" asked Cray, his mouth close to her ear, shouting to be heard over the loud music and the wall-to-wall people as they pushed past the bar.

"Not since I first got home. But then again, I don't go anywhere much—other than the studio and Drew's place."

"You've got your priorities right, then. And you're not missing much," sighed Cray, sounding bored with the fame machine all of a sudden. It was a side of Cray that Reilly hadn't seen before, and she was about to ask about it when a woman stopped them before they made it halfway across the floor.

"Reilly! I haven't seen you in forever!"

Reilly struggled to place her. She snuck a furtive glance at Cray, who raised his eyebrows to tell her that he didn't know who she was either.

"You look fantastic! How are you?" asked the woman, flipping back her shoulder-length blond hair with two fingers and a raised chin.

Then Reilly remembered. The woman had a distinctive diction that was almost a parody of a California Valley Girl, but it was that in combination with the almost obsessive hair flip that triggered her memory. The woman—her name started with a T or maybe an R—was a development executive at one of the studios that Reilly hadn't yet worked for. She'd gone home with her and Sylvie one night after a benefit auction. Reilly had fallen asleep, fully clothed, on the couch in her room while Sylvie and the woman had fucked. Reilly cringed on the inside, while she continued to smile on the outside.

"I'm fine, Tasha," said Reilly, remembering her name and peering over Tasha's shoulder, searching for people she knew. Anyone she wanted to see was still all the way across the bar.

"What projects are you working on?" asked Tasha. She flipped her hair again.

Before she could respond, someone touched Reilly's shoulder from behind. She turned but didn't recognize anyone. Suppressing irritation, she returned her attention back to Tasha, but a guy she didn't know pushed in front of Tasha, even as Tasha tried to move him aside. Another man approached her from another direction and jostled for Reilly's attention. Someone else picked at her arm.

"Hey, Reilly!"

"Looking good, girl! Come over here, let me buy you a drink!"

"Wait! Reilly. I have a project you might—"

Feeling claustrophobic, Reilly turned to Cray, who stepped in front of the small crowd that had suddenly appeared and put his arm around Reilly. He led her toward the back corner, away from the grasping hands.

"Holy shit, girl. That was sudden and intense. I don't know how you do it," said Cray, as they entered a cordoned-off corner to join the people they knew from the movie. Reilly shook her head. The bar was small, and the space was still crowded, but she was relieved to be out of the throng.

"Honestly, I don't, either. Sylvie always played defense for me, I guess."

"Maybe it's just worse than usual because you've been away so long," suggested Cray.

"Maybe. Or maybe I was just too high to care before," said Reilly, wondering if that was more true than anything else.

"Do you want a glass of wine? Or should I just get you a Diet Coke or soda water or something?"

His attentiveness was sweet—and another aspect that she hadn't seen often. She wondered if his relationship with Hank was settling him down.

"Wine sounds good, but I think I'll stick with water tonight. This isn't going to be a late night for me."

Cray deposited Reilly with the people they knew from the movie and went to fetch their drinks.

It was strange to be out and about after having been away from the scene for so long, especially at a place where she had partied so many times before. If any bar could be considered her bar, the Marmont was it. But the once exciting energy that had filled the room for her was no longer there. Part of it was the lack of chemical courage, but most of it was the feeling of separateness that Reilly felt. It seemed so contrived, all the cheerfulness and camaraderie, and she wondered if she would ever get comfortable with it again.

The evening wasn't a complete hassle, though. She enjoyed talking to the director's assistant, Jackie, who had run lines and played rummy with Reilly during her breaks between shooting. And the director was a genuine, nice man, just as passionate about travelling as he was about his work. He had a million interesting stories to tell, and Reilly sat riveted, listening to every one. She was glad that the bar was packed. She took that as an excuse to stay where she was, to watch people from afar, and to enjoy the people she had come to meet.

When Cray still hadn't come back after more than what seemed to be an adequate amount of time to retrieve a couple of drinks, Reilly began to scan the room. She spied him near the bar holding her bottle of water in one hand and sipping a drink from the other. He was talking to a handsome man whom she remembered from the first movie she and Cray had done. She was pretty sure that the guy had been one of Cray's many conquests. To her irritation, they seemed to be getting along really well. Almost too well. She loved Cray, but she was loyal to Hank.

"What's the matter, Rye?" asked Jackie, following Reilly's gaze.

"Oh, nothing. I'm thirsty. I'll be right back," she said and decided to brave the crowd to go see about Cray.

Reilly had almost made it through the sea of people, ignoring those who tried to stop her, when she saw the man Cray was talking to put his hand on the back of Cray's neck and pull him in for a kiss. Reilly's heart sank, and she was about to turn around and go back to the table when she saw Cray remove the man's hand from his neck and take a step back. Reilly watched as Cray said a few words while shaking his head. When he headed back toward the table, Reilly started toward him. They met a few steps later.

"Sorry that took so long, Rye," said Cray, smiling at her in apology. He gave her the bottle of water and hooked a thumb toward the bar where he had been standing. The other guy was still there, frowning into his drink. "I ran into an ex—if that's what you'd call a prolonged one night stand. He's smashed. Poor guy just got dumped. He tried to hit on me."

"He was in the last movie, wasn't he?" said Reilly, pretending that she had just seen the guy when Cray pointed him out.

"Yeah. But he slept with the wrong person, or something, so the director blackballed him from this one."

"Well, like they say… it's not what you know, but who you do, am I right?" asked a familiar voice from just behind Reilly.

Cray frowned and his eyes flicked to someone behind her. Reilly turned to see the sandy-haired production assistant from a movie that she had starred in several years earlier. He was also the personal drug dealer for half of Hollywood's film industry.

"How's it going, Reilly? Cray? Long time, no see."

"Hey, Torrance," said Reilly, surprised to see him at the party. He knew everyone, but due to the nature of his lucrative side job, he wasn't usually a guest at the parties he supplied. Reilly was surprised that he hadn't gone to jail by now.

"Sorry, I'm not sure we've met," said Cray offering his hand, seeming to take Reilly's greeting as a sign that Torrance was a friend. Reilly wanted to correct him, but the old anticipatory tingle in her gums took Reilly by surprise. A feeling of panic followed in its wake. She wanted to be anywhere but where she was standing in that moment.

"I have to use the ladies room. Excuse me," said Reilly. She headed for the women's bathroom.

She made a line through the crowd, turned the corner toward the restrooms and, by virtue of a miracle, the large, single occupancy women's restroom was empty. She hurried in and shut the door behind her. Across from the door was an ornate sink with a large mirror. She leaned with her back against the door and locked eyes with her reflection. She looked good. Aside from the scowl on her face, there was no sign of the feeling of terror that had seized her when the unwanted body memories of her past had inundated her. She took a deep breath and, feeling better, she smiled. It had been a visceral memory brought on by familiar people and surroundings, she reminded herself. That was all. She was fine. She moved toward the sink to wash her hands.

The door behind her opened and, in the reflection of the mirror, she saw Torrance enter behind her.

"What are you doing? Get out of here!" she ordered, spinning to face him.

"Relax, Reilly. No one saw me come in."

"I don't care about that. What the hell are you doing in here?"

"I came to deliver," he said pulling a baggie from an inside pocket of his jacket.

The baggie was about a quarter full of white powder, and this time, Reilly had no physical reaction other than anger over Torrance's invasion of her privacy.

"I'm not interested."

"Hey, I'll give it to you for the old price. You were a good customer. I still provide for Sylvie."

"I'm not interested," repeated Reilly, feeling an odd serenity. She really wasn't interested, and knowing that made her feel strong and in control.

"Okay. Okay. Tell you what. I'll give you a little, just in case you change your mind," he said, folding the baggie so that most of the powder fell to one side, but a small amount the size of a thimble remained in the bottom corner of the other half. He twisted it until the corner broke free, placed it on the vanity counter, and then tied a knot in the larger bag. He slid the bag into his jacket pocket and gave her a half-smile. "That's on the house. Call me when you need some more, okay?"

Reilly watched him leave the bathroom and shook her head. She walked over to the counter and picked up the conical little packet of cocaine. She held it up between her forefinger and thumb. Not even a tingle. She felt nothing. She reached for the faucet.

The door behind her flew open and hit the wall with an echoing thud.

"Reilly?" asked Drew, as she strode into the bathroom.

The noise startled Reilly and the packet of powder fell from her fingers. She tried to catch it, but only succeeded in hitting it so the powder scattered and flew across the vanity. A fine dust filled the air in front of her. In the mirror, she saw Drew's startled face behind her.

"Oh," said Drew.

"You scared the shit out of me," said Reilly, grabbing some paper towels and wetting them to wipe down the counter. She watched Drew in the mirror and the noise from the bar was muted once again as the door clicked shut.

"I was standing at the door, and I saw that guy follow you in here, and the doorman took so long to find my name on the list…"

Drew stood just inside the door and Reilly watched her eyes wander over the dust-strewn vanity as she talked. Reilly turned to face her.

"He's just a presumptive asshole," said Reilly, searching Drew's face in an effort to determine what she was thinking.

"Who is he, Reilly?"

"He used to be my connection," answered Reilly, truthfully. It didn't even occur to her to lie or minimize it.

"Connection?"

"You know, for drugs. Coke, mostly." Reilly saw Drew trying to process the information.

"Oh."

"He isn't anymore." Reilly threw the damp paper towels on the counter behind her.

"Oh." Drew's eyes roamed the vanity again.

"Drew. I said he isn't anymore. I swear it."

"You don't need to explain to me, Reilly. It isn't my business."

Drew didn't believe her. Reilly felt panic expand within her chest. She needed Drew to believe her.

"Drew. I didn't ask him to give it to me. I didn't use any of it," she said, leaning back against the counter, grasping the edge. "He gave me that little bit to try to get my business back. I didn't want it. I don't want it."

"Reilly, seriously, you don't have to—"

"I know I don't have to do anything, Drew," said Reilly, but the panic surged in her gut. "It's important to me that you believe me. I was just about to wash it down the sink."

"Reilly, I don't—"

"Let's go."

"Okay, but—"

"I'll prove it to you," said Reilly.

"Reilly. You don't have to prove anything to me."

But Reilly took Drew's hand and led her from the bathroom and out of the bar, so intent on her mission, that she took no notice of the dense crowd that she had to push through. A line of taxis stood on the other side of the winding, hillside street, and she got into the first one they reached. She couldn't wait for Alison, who wasn't expecting her to call so soon. Reilly knew that she was frightening Drew, but she had to show her that she hadn't taken any of the drugs. Reilly's heart beat like a drum and she gave the driver her address. Then she shot Cray a quick text telling him that she'd gone home sick.

When the cab rolled to a stop in front of Reilly's house, she waited for the driver to run her card, impatient. She didn't wait for the receipt. She got out of the car and pulled Drew along with her. She keyed her gate code and led her up the long driveway, the landscaping lights casting an eerie glow over the plants and pavement. She never let go of Drew's hand, afraid that Drew would leave her if she did. Camille let her in, surprised to see her, since she had told the housekeeper that she'd be spending the night at Drew's when she'd left earlier. She didn't try to explain. She took Drew upstairs to her bedroom and headed straight for her bathroom. She took a sealed drug testing kit from one of the linen cabinets in the large room, and only then did she finally let go of Drew's hand, so she could tear it open. The test kits were an artifact from the time that she had spent between being charged with vehicular manslaughter and the time she was sentenced and sent to prison. The tests had been a condition of being released on her own recognizance. She had to buy them herself, and once a week, she had to take one with her to the testing facility, where she pissed in a cup while a female officer watched.

When Reilly unbuttoned her pants, Drew backed toward the door.

"No, stay. I had to do this in front of an audience so many times before, that I'm numb to it," said Reilly.

"Reilly—" Drew pressed against the doorframe. Reilly saw that Drew was uncomfortable, and probably a little scared, but Reilly couldn't let her leave.

"No, stay. Please."

Reilly started to squat, and then she remembered that the cocaine had spilled all over the place when she had hit the little packet with her hand. She didn't want it to contaminate the sample.

"Fuck, I have to wash my hands first," she said, throwing the cup on the floor, pulling up her pants, and moving toward the sink. She caught a glimpse of her reflection. A streak of white was smeared across her forehead.

"Fuck. Fuck. Fuck," she said grabbing the towel beside the sink and wetting it from the spigot. She leaned toward the mirror and wiped her forehead until it was pink. "Fuck."

"Reilly—"

"Fuck." Reilly knew everything that she was doing was odd, but she couldn't control it. What if the coke had seeped in through her skin? What if she had breathed it in when the powder was floating in the air after she spilled it in the bathroom? She thought that she could taste the chalky tang. Her heartbeat hammered in her chest. Was it the drugs?

"Reilly," said Drew, taking a step forward. She stood behind Reilly and put her hands on Reilly's shoulders. Reilly watched her in the mirror, watched the silver eyes find hers. They held her stare, open and understanding. "Reilly, you don't have to do this."

"I do, Drew. I do."

"Why?"

"Because I need you to believe me."

"Reilly, I—"

"No. Wait." said Reilly, taking another test kit from the cupboard.

She ripped it open, sat it on the counter beside the toilet, and took her pants down. She filled the sample cup, placed it on the counter, and then adjusted her pants. She sealed the test and tipped it into the stand. She was an old pro at the piss test.

She washed her hands again and held her breath as she waited for the results to show.

"It takes about five minutes," she said to Drew. "If it turns color, it's negative. If it doesn't, it's positive.

Drew turned Reilly away from her sentry duty, staring at the test, and forced Reilly to meet her eyes.

"Reilly, baby. I don't care," Drew said, shaking her head. "I know who you are. I know you aren't the irresponsible woman that you seem to be afraid that I think you are. I know that you didn't take any drugs tonight."

"How do you know that? You just walked in on me with cocaine smeared all over my face and spread all over the counter."

"I saw it fall and spill. You got some on your fingers when you were cleaning it up. I saw you smear it on your face when you were talking to me in the bathroom."

"How do you know that I hadn't just taken some? How do you know that I wasn't just about to take some more?"

"Because I know you. I can see it in your eyes. I can feel it in my heart," said Drew, holding both of Reilly's hands in hers. She pressed them to her chest. "And if you had taken any, or had planned on taking any, I know that you would tell me. "

Reilly's heart stopped pounding so hard, and the spinning, out of control feeling that had taken hold of her eased. All of the energy drained from her at once. She dropped her arms. Her legs felt like a rag doll's. She was so tired. She rested her head on Drew's chest, unable to lift her arms to reach around Drew's waist. Drew held on to her instead. Reilly timed her breathing with Drew's and inhaled her familiar smell. The fog in her head started to drift away.

"Reilly?"

"Hmm?"

"If they turn color it's negative, right?"

"Yes," said Reilly lifting her head to see the test. All of the test strips had color on them. She had known they would. Sweet relief filled her just the same. She sank to the bathroom floor and held her head. "Thank god."

"You were worried that some might have been absorbed through your skin, weren't you?" asked Drew as she slipped down next to her and wrapped an arm around Reilly's shoulder, pulling her close.

Reilly nestled her forehead into the curve of Drew's neck, and Drew ran her fingers through Reilly's hair.

"Yes, how did you know?"

"You have a very pink mark on your forehead where you tried to rub your skin off, and your hands are almost scrubbed raw."

Reilly raised her hands and saw how pink they were. She started to cry.

Drew tightened her hold on Reilly and held Reilly's head against her chest.

"Baby, what's wrong?"

"I'm such a fuck-up."

"Why do you say that?"

"Because I can't get away from my past. I can't do anything to change what I've done and I don't know how I will ever learn to live with it."

Reilly cried in jagged sobs and she clung to Drew as if it would save her from falling. Drew rocked her.

"Hush now. You've just had a rough night. That's all. It's one of your first real nights out since everything happened. You came face-to-face with an old demon and you won, honey. You won."

"I don't deserve you, you know," said Reilly, trying to calm her sobs.

"What does that even mean?" asked Drew. "If you're trying to say that you're not good enough for me, then you're wrong," Drew said as she blew out a mirthful breath. "If anything, it's the other way around."

"I know when I'm being placated with bullshit," Reilly managed to laugh, and she wiped her nose.

"Well, I do have one thing up on you," said Drew, capturing Reilly's eyes. "I'm better than you when it comes to bullshit detectors. Because I'm dead serious when I say that it's me who doesn't deserve you. And that is no bullshit, Reilly."

"How did I get lucky enough to find you?" asked Reilly, pressing her face back into the warmth of Drew's neck.

Drew was quiet for a minute, and Reilly thought she wasn't going to answer. It was just a rhetorical question, anyway. But Drew finally cleared her throat and breathed out a long sigh.

"That, my love, is something I don't have an answer for. Because I've been thinking about that a lot myself, lately."

It's Not You, It's Me

REILLY WOKE UP THE NEXT morning feeling disoriented. She was in her own bed—the bed that she hadn't slept in since she and Drew first made love. And although she was alone, she knew that Drew had been next to her all night, because she remembered waking up periodically and reaching for her. The feel of Drew's arms wrapping around her, pulling her close, was the only thing that helped her to fall back to sleep.

It was morning now, and Drew was gone. A knot of apprehension formed in Reilly's chest as she lay there, staring across the expanse of the empty bed. She'd been a basket case the night before. She wondered what Drew thought about that.

Judging from the amount of sunshine filling the room, most of the morning was gone. She hadn't slept this late since the days of inky depression that had followed the morning that she had awoken to learn she had killed a man. When, for several weeks, she had abandoned life for the nothingness of sleep. That blackness tried to enfold her, but she refused to close her eyes.

She listened for signs of Drew's presence. The house was big, and Reilly wouldn't necessarily hear her, but Reilly could feel that Drew was near. She was relieved about that, but nervous about having to face Drew in the stark light of day.

As if summoned by her thoughts, Drew walked into the room. Reilly rolled onto her back and watched Drew move toward her.

"You're awake. I thought that you'd sleep all day." Drew was smiling, and she looked happy to see her. The knot in Reilly's chest eased. "You have absolutely no food in this house. I didn't expect you to have tea, Ms. Coffee Addict, but you don't even have the makings for coffee. How do you live?" asked Drew. She placed a cardboard tray with two cups nestled in it on the bedside table and opened a paper bag as she plopped down on the edge of the bed. "And since you kidnapped me last night, I was forced to take a cab halfway across town to fetch us some breakfast burritos from Manny's. I'd never been. I like that place. I did find it hilarious that they have one named the Rocking Reilly Ransome. Menu item number ten. It made it easy to order for you, though."

The reminder of her mad rush out of the bar the previous night and her subsequent breakdown flooded Reilly with hot shame.

"I was expecting to stay over at your house again last night, and Camille has her own living area. She wouldn't know to cook for me. She would have if I warned her. But since I didn't—" Reilly stopped herself. She knew that she was rambling. This was Drew's first time at her home, since she preferred the homier feel of Drew's place, and she was ashamed at her ineptitude as a host. "Manny's is good. I've gone there a few times," said Reilly, pushing herself into a seated position against the headboard. The smell of the food made her stomach growl, but she pulled the covers up to just below her breasts. She grimaced at the reminder of her behavior the night before. God, she'd nearly pulled Drew's arm from the socket dragging her out of the bar. Drew's cheery demeanor was taking away some of the shame, though.

"I know. I've seen the wrappers you've thrown away right before some of the morning yoga classes. That's why I went there. I had to get something I knew you would eat." Drew stopped rustling around in the paper bag. "That makes me sound creepy, doesn't it? Examining your garbage? I swear it's just that the wrappers are so easily identified and I take out the garbage at the studio."

Reilly laughed at the look on Drew's face.

"It's no creepier than me studying the pictures on the walls in your studio to find out more about you."

"Well, now I know that you like tofu and avocado on your burritos, wrapped in whole wheat tortillas. No cheese, though? That's a sin."

"Believe me, I dream about cheese. But such is the life of a person with a public image to uphold."

"Is that why you have no food in the house? You don't eat?"

"I eat. I have food," Reilly argued, adjusting the pillow that propped her up. She didn't want Drew to think an eating disorder was among her list of flaws. She had plenty without that.

"Dried fruit. You have dried fruit and protein bars. I'm really going to have to help you with your diet."

The casual conversation made Reilly feel much better. She could almost forget about the way she had acted the night before.

"Offer accepted," said Reilly, taking the wrapped burrito Drew held out to her and reaching for the coffee on the bedside table. She peeked at Drew from under her lashes. "I'm sorry for stranding you. There's a car service I use when Alison isn't here. Did you make it in time for your class this morning?"

"No. I wanted to be here when you woke up. Hunger pangs drove me out, though. You looked too peaceful to wake."

"God, I'm sorry. I'm such an ass," said Reilly. Guilt swept through her at the mention of the night before. Now she had caused Drew to miss her class. She wanted to bury herself under the blankets, but her hands were full.

"No biggie," said Drew, biting into her burrito and groaning with pleasure.

"No biggie? That's your livelihood and I—"

Drew stroked Reilly's leg.

"No. Really. It's okay," she interrupted. "I called Fergie last night, after you fell asleep. She taught my classes."

"Classes? As in plural? Shit. I hope you told her that it was my fault. I'll pay her." Reilly grimaced with guilt.

"Of course I didn't tell her anything like that. And don't worry about it. I wanted to be here with you," said Drew, leaning closer to stroke Reilly's face.

"I'm such a loser. You're too good to me," said Reilly closing her eyes at the touch.

"It's easy to be good to you," said Drew, and something in Drew's voice made Reilly open her eyes. The way that Drew's eyes pierced her made the skin on Reilly's neck tingle. "I need to tell you something, though."

Just like that, the mood switched, and a knot of apprehension tied itself around Reilly's heart.

"What? Should I be scared?" asked Reilly, when Drew didn't begin to speak immediately. Was she about to get broken up with? It had happened to her before, but she had never cared for anyone the way she cared for Drew. She couldn't imagine that her life was about to cave in, that she was about to lose her.

"Scared? Of me? I hope not," said Drew, with a nervous laugh.

"Are you having doubts? About us? I was a mess last night, I know—"

A look of comprehension fell over Drew's face. She leaned toward Reilly and stroked her cheek.

"Baby, no. Last night has nothing to do with it. Well, other than making me see that I haven't been… that I haven't… What I'm trying to say is that any doubt I have isn't about you. It's about me."

Reilly, who had begun to believe that maybe Drew wasn't about to give her the brush off, couldn't believe that Drew had just said those words to her. Everyone knew they were *the* segue into a break up.

"Whoa, 'it's not you, it's me,'" said Reilly. She tried to swallow around her tightening throat. She wanted to cry, and she felt vulnerable sitting there with sleep-tousled hair and the forgotten food in her hands. Her stomach churned.

Drew took a sip of her tea and paused like she was gathering her thoughts.

"I don't know how to begin," she said, breathing out with a loud puff and running her fingers through her hair with what looked like anxious dread.

Reilly wanted to scream with the anticipation roiling in her. It took everything in her not to get up and pace to burn off some of her anxiety.

"I've lied to you, Reilly," Drew finally said. Her eyes were downcast and she rolled the take out cup of tea between her hands. Reilly watched the strings from the teabags with the paper squares flare out.

"About what?" prodded Reilly when Drew didn't continue, even though she didn't want to know.

"About a few things. The tattoo—"

"We already covered that, Drew," interrupted Reilly. "I don't care about that."

"I know. But you asked me how I knew Fergie, and I let you believe that she was just one of my students."

"How is that a lie? She's been coming to your class for years."

"I started out as her student."

"Okay. I'm not sure I get it," said Reilly, a little surprised, but not sure why that would be a big deal. "Anyway, so what? What does that have to do with anything?"

"Prison, Reilly. She teaches yoga in prison," said Drew, finally meeting Reilly's eyes.

"I don't understand."

"That's where I met her. I was in prison, too. In Ral-Rutherford. Same as you."

"What?" asked Reilly. Her growing impatience turned to confusion. She put her untouched burrito and cup of coffee on the table next to the bed.

"I should have told you. But I didn't. And I had so many chances," said Drew dropping her eyes to her lap again. "But I didn't. Not when you saw Fergie in my class that day. Not when I was telling you that you needed to forgive yourself. Not last night… Not when it could have made you feel better to know that you weren't alone with everything. There were a thousand opportunities, but I didn't say anything, and then it got to where it seemed too hard to bring up, since I hadn't earlier."

Drew searched her eyes, and Reilly didn't know what to say. She didn't know how she felt about Drew's having been in prison. She certainly didn't feel like she had any right to be appalled about it. And she wasn't. It seemed so implausible, but even if it were true, Drew could never have committed anything as awful as what Reilly had done.

"When were you in?"

"I got out about a year before that night I first saw you at the club." Drew met Reilly's eyes and then dropped her gaze again.

"What were you in for?" asked Reilly, still unable to imagine Drew doing anything that would land her in jail.

"Drug trafficking," replied Drew.

The answer surprised Reilly almost as much as it would have if Drew had admitted to murder.

"What kind of drugs?"

"Hash."

"Hash," repeated Reilly, trying to envision Drew as a drug dealer. She couldn't see it.

"How long were you in for?"

"Almost two and a half years."

"For hash?" asked Reilly unable to hide her incredulity. That was a year longer than the time she had done for murder. It didn't sound right. "How much did you have? Was it a lot?"

Drew blew out a sigh and pushed her hand through her hair.

"I honestly don't know what a lot is, but I do know that two kilos is enough to get you up to five years for a first offense."

"How did they catch you?"

"They caught me coming in from Mexico. Bringing it over international borders made it a federal offense. Otherwise, I might have gotten a lighter sentence," said Drew, talking to the cup that she continued to spin between her hands. With a quick glance at Reilly to judge her reaction, she continued. "I had to research all of this after I was arrested. Before that, my experience with drugs consisted of a single line of coke at a college party and a few hits of pot in high school. I didn't even know what hash was until I looked it up. I mean, I knew it was a drug, but... God, listen to me. I can't just say that I was in jail, too, and leave it at that. I'm not going to give you excuses. Anyway, I'm not exactly the person you probably think I am, Reilly. I'm not a drug dealer either. I'm not trying to defend myself. I just don't want you to think I'm a terrible person. God, this isn't coming out right."

Drew spoke in a torrent. Reilly had never seen her so insecure. The confession was shocking, but most of all—and she felt guilty about it—she was relieved that Drew wasn't breaking up with her. She felt selfish that she focused on that, since Drew's secret seemed have been eating away at her, but it was true. She tried to suppress her own relief so that she could just be there for Drew.

"I already know that you are the least terrible person I have ever known, Drew," said Reilly. She remembered how much better she had felt after telling Drew about Lydia Traynor coming to visit her in prison. "I'd like to hear about it, if you want to talk about it. I know how much better I felt after telling you about some of my stuff."

Drew's shoulders relaxed a little. She was quiet as she seemed to gather her thoughts. At first, she spoke in short bursts, but then it started to flow. Reilly laid a hand on her leg, but otherwise she just listened to Drew's story.

"Amy was my girlfriend. We met at school, in college. I fell for her the first time I saw her. She was the popular type. The kind who had both girlfriends and boyfriends. The kind who would flirt with anyone and everyone. We lived in the same dorms, so before we got together, I would see her around all the time. Everyone responded to her. Her professors, other students, baristas—Amy got so many free coffees, it was unreal." Drew laughed at her memory, and then shook her head. "Later, I saw how many undeserved passing grades she got, as well. She was such a player. And a user. She used people to get what she wanted. But she did it just for fun, too. Just to see how far she could take it. Sometimes she would sleep with them, sometimes she wouldn't. It depended on the person, or what she needed at the time. I had no clue back then, though. She enthralled me from the first minute I saw her in biology class. I had a crush on her for an entire semester before she even acknowledged me.

"I was still kind of figuring things out. Even though I was pretty sure that I was gay, I had only dated men, and it wasn't doing much for me. I was taking a break from all of it and was trying to come to terms with things. But then I saw her and it cemented it for me. Still, months went by, and then one day she chose me. I still don't know why she did, but she did. I didn't have anything that she needed. She'd already slept with the professor for her grade in biology. She just seemed to notice me one day, and then we were together.

"I told myself that I knew what I was getting into. She never promised to be my girlfriend, and I never asked. I just knew that I was more attracted to her than I had ever been to anyone before, and that I felt it more and more every time we were together. I told myself that I was in it for the fun—and the sex. She helped me to figure out who I was. It was liberating and powerful. And for a little while, I felt like I was the special one, the one who might get to keep her. She never said it, but she acted like it, talked all around it, and I thought that she was starting to have real feelings for me. It was a wonderful, chaotic time."

Reilly remembered her own experience of coming out and understood how consuming just the thought of kissing a woman could be—well, Imelda had been a girl just like her, not a mysterious co-ed, but she knew the feeling just the same. She squeezed Drew's leg to let her know she was listening.

"The whirlwind made it easy for me to ignore a lot of things that she did. Drugs for one—it was mostly just recreational, so I justified it as youthful experimentation. Besides, I had smoked a few joints myself. Then there was the irritating fact that sometimes she had sex with other women—but we never declared that we were monogamous, so I ignored that too. She lied sometimes—but they were always little lies, never anything important, so I let that slide." Reilly watched Drew's eyes focus on an internal past as she paused. "The thing was, when she focused her attention on you, she made you feel like you were the only other person in her world. It made you forgive all the little things. I thought that I was in love with her. And like a fool I thought that she loved me, too.

"When she bought us tickets to Mexico to celebrate our graduation and my acceptance to graduate school, I was so certain that it meant that we were going to be together forever. It was a great time. We moved in together when we got back. I was ecstatic. We were together for a few years, all through grad school, and life was perfect. She was an awesome girlfriend—if I pretended that all that other stuff didn't matter. So, we built our little life and things were great. When I passed my licensing exam, we went back to Mexico to celebrate."

Drew paused for a moment, and a small smile softened her lips. Reilly saw that Drew was lost in the time that she spoke of. She had also heard the tone of old hurt in Drew's voice, and it made her want to hold her. But she didn't know if Drew wanted that, so she just sat and listened. Drew began again a moment later.

"We went down to San Carlos, Mexico. It was just as beautiful as I had remembered it. She knew some people down there and we stayed with them for a few days, just like the last time, but we traveled a little, too. While we stayed with her friends, she left me for a little while, but when I asked, she told me the less I knew, the better. I suspected that she was maybe sneaking off with one of the women we were staying with, and while I didn't like it, she always came back to me, so, in a weird way, I thought that she was kind of protecting me. I pretended not to care.

"The day that we were to return to the States, we were at the airport about to check in. She said that she had left her wallet in the hotel room that we had stayed in the night before—"

"Oh," said Reilly, suspecting she knew where Drew was going with her story.

"Yeah," said Drew nodding her head. "The hotel was just down the road from the airport, but we were already cutting it close, so when I turned to leave with her, she convinced me to stay and check in for the flight, while she hurried back to the hotel. She left her bag with me so it wouldn't slow her down. When I said that I would wait, she reminded me that I was starting my new job the next day and that I couldn't afford to miss the flight. I had to agree. She told me that if she missed the plane that she would just get on the next one. Well, she didn't make the plane."

"I can totally see where this is going."

"I'm taking too much time to tell the story, aren't I?" asked Drew.

"No. Not at all," said Reilly quickly, hoping that she hadn't made Drew self-conscious.

"When I got off the plane in the States, I should have known something was up. I noticed several canine cops and guys in stereotypical plainclothes, trying to fit in. You know, khakis and navy blue polos."

Reilly nodded though she had never given a thought to plain-clothed cops.

"I had seen enough television to look around me and wonder who on my flight had swallowed balloons of heroin. I was such an idiot. I never once thought that it was me they were looking for. I was clueless when the agent grabbed my arm as I lifted Amy's bag from the belt—the bag that I had checked in as my own when Amy didn't show up. I got a big clue when they sat me down in the interrogation room and pulled the two bricks of hash out of the bag, though."

"I can imagine the shock you felt," said Reilly, thinking how she had felt when she realized that there was a dead man under the sheet that morning on the beach. She could still feel the arctic chill that had filled her head and had made a slow descent down her body at the realization that she was involved in the death. She shuddered away the memories. It wasn't the same thing, but she knew how it felt to have your world implode in an instant. "How much is two kilos?"

"About five pounds. It was compressed into the size of a couple of large bricks," said Drew, holding her hands out to indicate how big one of them had been.

"You had no idea at all that it was in the bag?"

"None. I didn't believe it, even when they took the drugs out of the bag right in front of me. It was the same bag Amy had carried on her back all through Mexico, but nothing in it was hers. Except the tee shirts, which we had bought at an outdoor store the day before we left. They were wrapped around the drugs. She was so adamant that I check the bag and not take it with me as a carry on.

"At first, I didn't tell them it wasn't my bag. I didn't want to get Amy into trouble. I thought that there was some sort of mistake, that the drugs must have been put in the bag after I checked it in. But, when the prosecution's first exhibit was a trail of time stamped videos showing the bag through check in all the way until I picked it up, I knew that I was screwed. Then there was the whole way that Amy just disappeared."

"Disappeared? You never saw her again?"

Drew shook her head.

"I was actually worried that something had happened to her, and for whatever reason, she couldn't contact me. At first, I agonized over the thought of her showing up on a later flight and not knowing where I was. It was worse when I imagined her in some jail cell, being subjected to the same things I was, and her not knowing that the reason that I wasn't coming to see her was because I was locked up, too. It seems stupid to me now. I called her mother and left a message to tell her where I was. That wasn't a fun conversation, but at least she could have done the same. But she didn't, and there I was, worrying about her."

"How long did it take before you realized that she set you up?"

"I don't think she intended for me to get caught. It was more that she let me assume all of the risk. But it wasn't until I saw the video during the trial that it dawned on me. She had definitely let me take the fall. Up until then, I was certain that someone else had planted the drugs. I told my lawyer what had happened then, and he told me that it would do more harm than good to change my story halfway through the trial. That it would kill my credibility. Now that I look back, I don't think that he believed me. Or he just didn't care. He was court appointed and I was so young, stupid, and scared that I was just grateful to have a lawyer. I didn't question his advice."

"How could he not do anything? Didn't he check into it? He just let your—Amy—get away with it?" Reilly was upset about the injustice of it all.

Drew shrugged her shoulders. Reilly couldn't believe how accepting Drew was about the whole thing. It would have eaten her alive.

"They had someone to pin it on. I have no idea if they ever checked her out."

"That's incredible. And so messed up," said Reilly. She was enraged for Drew and all that she had gone through. "So you did two and a half years after taking the fall for someone else?"

Drew nodded her head.

"Twenty-nine months, three days, and nineteen hours."

"Have you ever tried to find her? Don't you want to… to…" Reilly struggled to find the right word.

"Settle the score? Get revenge?" offered Drew.

"Yeah, settle the score," said Reilly.

"At first, it kind of ate me up. I had fantasies of retribution. But, you know how prison is. You have a lot of time to think. And I realized that she already knew what had happened to me, and that she already felt whatever it was she was going to feel about what she had done to me—whether it was guilt, or relief at not having been caught—whatever it was. Nothing I could ever do or say would make what I went through go away. So I decided to not put any more negative energy into it."

"I'm not sure I could have done that. You're a better person than I am, Drew."

Drew shrugged as if she didn't quite believe her.

"I'm sure that you came out of prison a little more self-aware than you were going in."

Reilly had to think about that a little. It was true. She had done a lot of soul-searching, mostly about how she wanted to live her life when she got out. "I guess I did."

"Prison certainly gives you a lot of time to think."

"You said that you were in for twenty-nine months, three days, and nineteen hours. I counted the time down to the hours, too. Minutes actually."

"Time is different inside."

"It is," nodded Reilly, feeling a little surreal about bonding over the concept of prison time with Drew—something she would never have guessed that she'd be doing.

It Was Survival

REILLY STRETCHED ALONG DREW'S SIDE and smiled when Drew hugged her close. Once she had finished telling Reilly the story of how she'd gone to prison, Drew had visibly relaxed, and while they both seemed to be lighter for having talked about it, a tired heaviness had fallen over both of them. Drew had put her empty tea cup on the bedside table, crawled over to Reilly, stretched out beside her, and they'd simply held each other for several minutes, absorbing the information.

"You don't have the feel of someone who's been in prison," said Reilly after a while.

"You don't either," said Drew.

"Sure I do. I have an edge… a wariness that wasn't there before," said Reilly, recalling some of what she had read about herself in the press. She'd agreed with what she read.

Drew surprised her by laughing.

"Honey, I hate to tell you, but you don't own that particular swagger. You might have an edge that you didn't have before, but no one would mistake you for a hardened convict."

"Despite the fact that the entire world knows otherwise, I'm glad that I don't show the effects of my stay," said Reilly, feeling a weird mix of relief and disappointment at Drew's observation. The emotional and psychological scars were a part of her, and that part wanted the world to see the evidence of having survived them. Reilly tilted her head to look up at Drew. "Look at you, though. You don't look damaged the way that people who have done time do. You're too gentle. Serene. How did you survive in there like that? The other inmates sniff that kind of thing out and take advantage of it."

"I haven't always been this way," said Drew, and Reilly could tell that she was thinking back to a time long before they met. "I've searched a long time for it, and some days, it's still hard to find. But when I first entered prison, I wasn't even close to gentle or serene."

"I don't believe it, but I won't argue with you. You had to have done something right to get out of there in one piece," said Reilly. She wondered if Drew had dealt with her own version of Twist, and a band tightened across her heart.

"I didn't give anyone the opportunity to get at me. I found the toughest woman there and struck an alliance."

"What kind of—" Reilly started to ask, but when Drew raised an eyebrow, she knew. "Oh."

"Does that disgust you?"

"No," said Reilly. She meant it, too. It was still hard to imagine Drew in prison, but she knew how it was. You did what you had to do to get through it. "At one time it might have. But having done my own bit, and having learned how to sleep with one eye open and always keeping your back to the wall, I think it was smart. I never even thought of doing that. But then again, the toughest woman in my bay was a psychopath, so I'm not sure that would have worked for me."

They were quiet for a moment, each of them lost in thoughts from a time that no regular person would want to revisit.

Reilly had witnessed various types of alliances while she was in prison, and while she had somehow been successful at remaining a loner, she had still developed a few of her own, although none of them had been sexual. She might have gone that route had circumstances been different—or had she had no choice.

Of the alliances Reilly had entered into, the first had been one of the most unlikely. She remembered how it had started.

Reilly had been in the infirmary for a week after the attack in the chow hall by Twist and her goons. She'd sustained two concussions in less than a month, and the prison doctor had wanted to monitor her before they discharged her. A week after being discharged, she no longer had to work the kitchen detail, and her new job in the library had been going well. Being a half-hour late for chow every day after taking a late shower meant that the only food left after the rest of the population had gone through was the stuff that even the hardiest of inmates wouldn't eat. Her semi-private shower time had been worth it, though.

Her damp hair had hung down her back, and she'd grabbed a tray, placed the rubber spork and cup that she'd been issued at in-processing on it, then pushed it down the stainless steel counter. She'd frowned at the remains in the steam table trays. A fresh loogie dripped down the Plexiglas sneeze guard over the almost-full tray of creamed lima beans and she'd held back a gag.

"I see Tiny Tanya showed Bird what she thought of the lima beans, huh?"

chuckled Bren, one of the women who did laundry detail, and who, like Reilly, also came to dinner late after showers.

"I was trying to ignore that," laughed Roberts, Bren's laundry detail partner.

At the time, Reilly didn't know Bren and Roberts very well. All she knew were the well-defined muscles she saw in the showers. So, that day, she'd just stood behind them listening. She remembered the smell of laundry soap that wafted from their work shirts, which was a nice change from the everyday scents of too many women living too closely together. They'd waited for Bird to come back to the line and serve them. The inmates that worked chow had already loaded their trays and had been eating among the others.

"What's it gonna be, ladies?" Bird barked as she came out of the back storeroom and approached the serving station. She wiped her hands dry on the front of the stained apron she wore.

"Is that bacon in the greens, Bird?" asked the one called Bren, a tall, short-haired brunette.

"Yup."

"Fuck me," mumbled Bren. "Got anything without pork in it?"

"The eggplant and lima beans don't got any. But I'm pretty sure that the Jew god can't see through these cinderblock walls to see who's keeping kosher."

"I'll pretend that I didn't hear that, Bird," sighed Bren. "I'll take the lima beans and eggplant."

"I'll take a little of whatever you got, Bird," said Roberts, tossing back damp blonde curls with a shake of her head.

"I guess everything she eats ain't kosher, if she don't care about you eating the pork, eh, Roberts?" Bird laughed at her own crude joke and spooned a generous amount of food onto each of their plates.

Reilly felt a kinship to her late-shift companions when she heard Bird's reference to Bren and Roberts' possible romantic relationship. Compared to others on the inside, they seemed more—real. And that gave Reilly a weird sort of hope.

"Funny lady," said Bren wryly as she and Roberts took their trays into the dining area.

"I guess I'll take a little of everything, too," said Reilly, and she pushed her tray down the rail.

"Here you go," said Bird. She handed Reilly a ready-made plate of food that she had pulled from under the counter.

"What's this?"

"Food. What's it look like?"

Reilly stared at the plate that Bird had given to her. On it was a little of everything that had been served that night, even the food that had been finished off. There was even a cookie. Reilly was unsure how she should react. A gift was never just a gift. She hadn't been there long, but that was one of the first things she'd learned. Either Bird had done something to the food, or she was going to ask for something in return.

"Don't worry," nodded the crusty old woman, tossing the over-sized serving spoon she'd been holding into a steam dish that contained the remnants of canned green beans. She put one hand on her hip and adjusted her hairnet with the other as she considered Reilly's expression. "You earned it. You back up your words with your fists—even though you can't take a punch."

"I don't under—"

Bird had stopped her with an impatient sigh.

"It's not hard to process, princess. You'll have a plate waiting as long as I'm galley queen. You got rid of some shit for me. That's all."

Reilly hadn't seen Twist or her minions since she'd left the infirmary. She'd kept her eyes open, but she'd noticed that the three women who had put her down hadn't been around. Since her new job meant that she didn't have to do yard time or communal showers any more, she'd figured that they just weren't crossing paths as much.

"Get the fuckin' lead out, princess! Dining hall closes in five minutes, even for you."

That had been the first alliance Reilly had made. Shortly after, she had made one with Bren and Roberts, too. In the beginning, Reilly had been wary of the laundry dykes—the endearment bestowed on the two women by the rest of the inmates—and kept out of their way. Aside from the regular gym time, the heavy work of hauling laundry made the muscles stand out on their arms and shoulders, and they were both tall and intense. But, one day, Bren had asked if Reilly would reserve a book on appliance repair for her, and soon she was taking their library requests and giving them first shot at the new books Reilly had started to receive after finding out there was a budget for the languishing library. In return, they would replace her worn clothing with new, so that she didn't have to spend the paltry amount of money she earned doing her library job on replacing her state issued uniform.

Reilly's alliances seemed to happen gradually and without anyone being on the losing end of an unsavory agreement. Alliances involving sex were different, though. Reilly didn't know how they were brokered, and she assumed that most of them were coerced. She couldn't imagine Drew being a part of something so demeaning—or more aptly, she didn't want to. In her mind, Drew wouldn't force it, and almost worse, she hoped that it hadn't been forced upon her. She had to know, but part of her was reluctant to find out. She asked anyway.

"How does that work? Did you just go up and tell her you wanted to… to…?"

She couldn't finish the question, and when Drew hesitated, Reilly wondered if she had crossed a line.

"The woman had her sights set on me already. So rather than wait for her to turn me out, I approached her. It was the only way I could think of to be safe. I found out that she branded people—"

"That must be a common thing. There was a woman in my wing that did that too," interjected Reilly, shuddering at the memory of Twist telling her that she would put her mark on her.

"Twist," said Drew

"Yes, Twist. You knew her?" asked Reilly, surprised.

Drew didn't answer immediately, and by the time she did, Reilly had started to put it together.

"You mean—?" Reilly couldn't say it.

"Yes, Twist is how I survived my time there."

Reilly felt the realization hit her hard. It was almost physical.

"Holy shit… how could you… I mean… she's so…" struggled Reilly, trying to get out of bed feeling confined. Drew loosened her embrace to let her go, but then Reilly didn't want to get up. Instead she sat up so she could face Drew.

"It was survival."

"And she branded you?" asked Reilly, her heart folding in on itself, knowing that Drew had born the pretzel shaped image that Twist had called her mark. She remembered the childish drawing she had seen on Twist's hip in the shower that first day.

"Not the way you think," answered Drew, and she must have read the confusion on Reilly's face, so she started to explain. "Rather than have her and her goons—"

"Thing One and Thing Two," said Reilly. She heard the contempt coat her words.

"That's a good description of them," said Drew, but she didn't smile. "I found out that she had her eyes on me. Let me rephrase that: she *told* me that she had her eyes on me."

"So you just—" Reilly couldn't finish the sentence. Echoes of being called fish as she fled the showers whispered in her memory.

"Rather than wait for them to jump me and leave the mark, I had my cell-mate put it on me. It was the only thing I could think of. So Sal took a stickpin and a ballpoint pen and gave me the mark. I let Twist see it in the shower. I figured she couldn't mark me if I did it to myself."

"That was pretty smart. Did it work?"

"Kind of. At first, I think she thought that I was some sort of stalker. I think I scared her. But she still liked it and, well… I didn't have to… it didn't happen very often," explained Drew, appearing to be unable to elaborate on her half of the alliance. "It turns out that when Twist doesn't have to force herself on someone, she loses interest. Plus, I think that being the one to beat everyone else to the new fish was enough for her. So it sort of worked out for me. Fergie's yoga class helped, too. At first it was just a place to go where Twist couldn't get to me, but it wasn't long before I immersed myself in it. It changed my life. Maybe even saved it."

"I don't know what to say," said Reilly, vacillating between awe and distaste after hearing what Drew had been through. Drew's experience made hers seem like a cakewalk. Drew may have avoided the beatings, but she had had to endure Twist and her goons for two and a half years. Reilly knew that she would never have come out alive if it had been her. She wanted to make Drew feel better, but she of all people had learned that you couldn't undo your past. All you can do is manage your reaction to it and keep on living your life the best that you can. Drew seemed to have found the secret.

"Some things defy a response," said Drew with a small laugh, shrugging her shoulders.

"Your experience deserves more than just a response. Look at you. Prison breaks people. You managed to survive prison on your own terms," said Reilly. "Now, you have a great business, and you're the most serene and balanced person I have ever met."

"It wasn't always on my own terms. Twist felt the need to remind me who was in charge once in a while. I still have nightmares about some of the things that she did to me," said Drew with a shudder, and Reilly wished that she had done more than leave a scar on Twist's face for what she had done to Drew. "But worse than that, I lost my license."

"License?" asked Reilly, relieved to turn the conversation away from Twist.

Drew didn't answer immediately, and Reilly saw strong emotion play across her beautiful face.

"I had just passed my medical exams," said Drew.

"Medical exams, as in medical doctor?"

Drew nodded.

"I'm a chiropractor. At least I have the degree. I can't practice, though. Never got to start."

"Wow," said Reilly, having no other words. She remembered the massage and the adjustment that Drew had given her. "That explains a few things."

"Yeah." Drew just nodded again, seeming to read Reilly's mind. "That's why I don't do massage professionally, either. I tried. It's too close to working with patients and I can't bear to be reminded. My mother is the one who suggested that I try instructing yoga after I got out of prison. Yoga saved my life. I was living in the converted garage behind her house, filling my days with gardening and attending yoga at the YMCA. One day she suggested that I become an instructor and convert my place into a studio. She gave me the money to do it. I had received my certification and was almost done with the remodel when she died."

"I'm so sorry, baby," said Reilly, entwining their fingers and squeezing.

"It was sudden. She was so healthy. She had a mole removed from her back, and the incision got infected. The antibiotics couldn't treat it and she died when the infection spread to her lungs. It was a freak thing and turned my life on its head, probably more than prison did."

"I had almost given up on pursuing the yoga studio when I ran into Fergie at a farmer's market. It was such a shock to see her away from the prison. I barely knew her, but she was so relaxed and friendly. It was weird, but it helped. We went to get a cup of coffee, and I told her about how inspiring her classes had been for me and about my plans for the studio, but that my mother's death had sort of taken the wind out of my sails. She listened and then gave me encouragement to keep going. We've been friends ever since."

Reilly fell silent for a moment as she absorbed the information and couldn't help thinking about her relationship with her own mother. It made her wonder if she should try harder with her own.

She was in deep thought when Drew pulled her back to the conversation.

"I'm sorry if what I've told you is too much. Fergie is a good friend. I shouldn't have—"

"No. No, it's not too much. It's a lot to take in, but not too much. That last bit about your mother. It just got me to thinking about mine. We've kind of grown apart over the last couple of years, but I'm not ready to lose her. As much as she drives me crazy, she's still my mom, you know? I'm glad that Fergie re-entered your life when she did."

They were quiet for a few moments and Reilly moved back to her position close to Drew, resting her head on her chest.

"You said earlier that over time it got too hard to tell me. I kind of get that, but why didn't you tell me any of this before then? In the beginning?" asked Reilly.

"It was six years ago, and I don't talk about it much. Then, after a while it seemed like I'd waited too long to tell you some of it, and then it had felt impossible to bring up." Drew shrugged and glanced up at Reilly. Her eyes were bright with tears. "But honestly? I guess I was just afraid that you'd think less of me. Or not want to see me anymore."

"What? I was in prison, remember?" reminded Reilly. She was offended. She didn't know where the sudden anger came from, but it was there, and she moved away a little, pounding her own chest. "I would get it, Drew, me of all people."

Drew gave her a bitter smile and wiped away a tear.

"You can't even forgive yourself for the time you spent in there," she said quietly.

"Why would that matter?" asked Reilly.

"I can just imagine what you think of other people who have been inside. People like me."

Reilly's anger shifted to empathy when she realized that Drew was just as afraid of not being good enough as she was.

"God, Drew. No. Prison isn't what I'm ashamed of. It's what I did to get sent there. I killed someone. That's what I have a problem with."

Reilly wanted to tell Drew that, if anything, she thought more of her, knowing that she had come out the other side as a stronger, better person. But no words would ever say it the way she wanted Drew to hear it.

"I'm ashamed of that, too."

"But, you were set up."

"I let myself get set up. I was an idiot," said Drew. "I'm smarter than that. There were signs all around me and I ignored them."

"Well, you can't fault yourself for loving someone, and you can't fault yourself for trusting someone. It's those who abuse the trust that should feel the shame. Prison breaks the strongest women. You're not broken. You're far from broken," said Reilly.

Drew rested her head again on Drew's chest. Drew kissed the top of her head. Reilly sighed while Drew held her closely, seeming to need the closeness that Reilly craved, too. Most of the tension that had ebbed and flowed during the course of their conversation was gone.

"We have a few scars between the two of us," said Reilly. She fingered the faint mark that she still had on her forehead from the stiches she had received when Twist had head-butted her in the kitchen fight. The one behind her ear had all but disappeared. The scars that she spoke of were not physical, though.

"True," agreed Drew.

"Are you okay?" asked Reilly, looking up at Drew. "Are *we* okay?"

Drew returned Reilly's stare, searching her eyes. Reilly reached up to stroke the soft skin of Drew's strong chin.

"I'm okay," said Drew. "I *hope* we're okay. I do have one more thing to confess, though."

"Should I be nervous?"

"Not nervous. But I honestly don't know how you'll take it."

"Then just tell me. Nothing you've told me has changed my opinion of you."

"That's a relief," said Drew. "Okay—"

Reilly waited for Drew to continue. When she didn't, Reilly bounced a leg against her.

Drew blew her breath out.

"I asked Fergie to watch out for you when you went to prison."

Things began to fall into place in Reilly's mind. The way Fergie had always seemed to be there, watching; the library job that had gotten Reilly out of communal showers—and away from Twist's predatory ways; the way Twist and her goons had been moved to the other wing, just when things seemed to be coming to a stand-off. She wondered if the guard had even been the one to suggest to the warden that Cray was visiting her under an assumed name.

"Did she report back to you?" asked Reilly.

"No! Nothing like that," said Drew, sitting up to face Reilly. "Once in a while, I would ask her if you were okay, and she would always say that you were doing as well as could be expected. Nothing more than that. I wanted to know more, but she wouldn't have said anything if I had asked, and I didn't. I understand how it is. When you're in, everyone knows what everyone else is doing, right down to the schedule of bodily functions. I wouldn't spy. I wouldn't want you to think—"

Drew was crying, and Reilly couldn't stand to see her so upset. Their emotions, raw from the discussion, were pulled so tight. Reilly felt a wave of something more powerful than she'd ever felt wash over her.

Reilly sat up and shifted to face Drew. She reached over and held Drew's face between her palms. She waited until Drew's eyes found hers.

"I love you," she said.

"You probably don't believe me," said Drew. "Why would you believe me? I know it sounds—"

Reilly pulled Drew toward her and held her tight. She smoothed the hair on the back of Drew's head and felt an unbearable rush of emotion for having uttered the words that had been stuck in her throat for days without her even knowing.

"I love you," she said again, trying out the feel of the words on her tongue again, and feeling them even more.

"I know that it wasn't my place, and that I didn't have the right, but I knew that Twist was still there, and there was a fifty-fifty chance that you would be assigned to her wing."

"Shut up already, Drew. I don't care. I love you," said Reilly again, reaching up and turning Drew's face toward her.

Drew's silver eyes shimmered.

"What?"

"I love you," said Reilly, loving how much loving Drew felt. It was a feeling that she had never experienced, and it made her feel strong and almost whole again. "Not just because you asked Fergie to take care of me, but because of the person that you are. The woman that I know," said Reilly, stroking Drew's face.

"I love you, too," said Drew. Reilly watched her face and could tell she had more to say, but all she felt was a surge of bliss and a great relief that Drew felt the same way. The next words from Drew surprised her. "I've known since the night on the hotel terrace. I almost told you then."

"What stopped you?"

"Knowing that I didn't deserve you. That you'd leave when you found out about my past."

"I'm sorry for not making you feel safe. I thought that you understood—"

"You never talked about it."

"I didn't want anyone to forgive me."

"I'm sorry for not trusting you enough to tell you. Are you mad that I spied on you?" asked Drew, touching the fingers Reilly rested on her cheek.

"Come here and let me love you," said Reilly, lying back as she kissed Drew, pulling her down on top of her.

Randy Candy's Website Survey

DREW STEPPED OUT OF THE BATHROOM and leaned against the doorframe, drying her hair. Reilly sat against the pillowed headboard on the bed that they had barely left in the last 24 hours and let her eyes wander over the nude woman standing across the room. She pushed her laptop to the side and opened her arms, inviting Drew to lie down. Drew came to her immediately, and Reilly's chest filled with excitement when she saw the unguarded look of loving desire that darkened Drew's eyes. The difficult discussion from the day before seemed like it had taken place an eternity ago. Reilly felt closer and more at ease about their relationship—and her life—than she ever thought she would. It was a good feeling.

"Mmmm… you smell so good," purred Reilly, as she wrapped her arms around Drew's waist and pulled her down on top of her. She buried her face in the clean smell of Drew's neck and kissed it. Drew groaned, her hips pressing against Reilly's thigh.

"You're such a bad influence on me. You make me not want to go teach my class. I just want to stay here in this bed and make love to you all day."

"You don't have to convince me," murmured Reilly, nuzzling Drew's neck. "Let's put a sign up. Tell them you have the kissing disease. Because I do. A bad, bad case," she said, biting down on the sensitive skin below Drew's ear. The shiver she felt in the woman above her inspired her to give Drew another gentle bite. And another. "And it's highly contagious. The best cure is to stay in bed all day. "

"I wish it were that simple," sighed Drew, but she made no move to get up. Instead, she let Reilly nibble her neck a little longer and then began kissing her way down Reilly's chest.

"Oh, but it is that simple. I promise," coerced Reilly, lifting her tee shirt to expose her breasts to Drew's attentions.

"It wouldn't be fair to my students," said Drew, licking Reilly's nipple and then taking it between her teeth, eliciting a hiss from Reilly. Drew made a trail to the other nipple, talking between kisses. "Besides, it's easy for you, Miss I-can-stay-in-bed-with-my-laptop-and-look-at-fuzzy-kitties-all-day. Some of us have to work for a living."

"Hey, I work," said Reilly, groaning as Drew took the other nipple into her mouth. Her center clenched as she watched Drew's beautiful lips wrap around her tender breast.

"Yes, you do," agreed Drew, pulling Reilly's tee shirt back down and snuggling into the circle of Reilly's arms. Her hand cupped the rigid peak that her mouth had just left, and Reilly wished that she'd move it lower to take care of the ache that she'd caused. "And when you're doing a movie, you work longer hours than most. You deserve to take a break today."

"I'm working right now. Well, I was, until a temptress wandered into view and captured my attention," said Reilly playing with Drew's long damp hair. She watched the black strands snake through her fingers and thought about how lucky she was to have Drew in her bed. In her life.

"Surfing the net is not working," laughed Drew, batting away Reilly's other hand, which was tickling its way up Drew's inner thigh.

With one hand Reilly turned the laptop that sat beside her on the bed so Drew could see the screen. She moved the cursor between tabs that she had open on her browser to show her what she was doing.

"I have to keep my social media sites current. I have to answer my email. I have to keep up on the gossip about me."

"So, you post and chat and watch gossip about yourself?"

Reilly nodded and showed Drew the number of unread emails she had to go through. She had fan club managers who dealt with most of it, but there was still much to address outside of that. As much as her mother had vexed her, Reilly really missed the way that she had taken most of the administrative work out of her day-to-day.

"When my mom managed me, all of that was her job. Now I have to do it. I think I'm going to have to get another assistant. I don't know how she did it. I hate it."

"What's that one?" Drew asked, as Reilly navigated with one hand to a garish webpage that blasted a techno riff before the page even finished loading. Reilly pushed the mute button.

"Randy Candy's column."

"You seriously read his crap?"

"There is nothing serious about him, but the stuff he talks about is actually pretty spot on. Although he can be a bit dramatic," said Reilly, laughing as Drew rolled her eyes and shook her head. "I know. But he knows everybody, and everybody knows him. He doesn't care if people don't like him, either. He still gets invited to all the events because he keeps people in the news. My mother adores him. They exchange holiday gifts."

"Ugh! Maybe you'd change your mind if you read some of the stuff he wrote about you after your accident," said Drew.

"Ha! Busted!" said Reilly, tickling Drew and laughing when she squirmed. "That means that you read his blog! None of that means I like the guy. And my mom shielded me from all of that back then. She didn't even try to show me. I can imagine, though. He'd sell out his best friend for a story."

"What does he have to say today? I have a few minutes to kill before I have to go," said Drew, moving back into her position with her head on Reilly's chest so she could see the screen. Reilly could feel Drew's hot breath on her breast through the tee shirt, and she had a hard time concentrating. She'd rather spend these few minutes doing something else.

"I don't know," replied Reilly, forcing herself to focus on the screen. She followed links on the page to get to that day's blog. "I just pulled it up. It's about me, though. His blog came up when I Googled myself."

"Narcissist much?" laughed Drew, as she hooked a finger into the V-neck of Reilly's tee shirt, inched it down, and kissed the valley between Reilly's breasts.

"Hmmm?" asked Reilly, the laptop now forgotten and her concentration shattered, as she peered down at her naked lover, loving the sensation of Drew's mouth on her skin.

"I asked whether you often Googled yourself."

"Oh… I know… self-absorbed," said Reilly. She had a hard time focusing on the conversation, but Drew helped when she pulled the shirt back into place and smiled at her. "It's an unfortunate side effect of being an actor."

"I was just kidding. About the narcissist thing."

"I know," said Reilly, but she wanted to explain. "I need to stay informed. To stay on top of things."

"What does Mr. Rancid Candy have to say about you?"

"Rancid. I like that."

Reilly dragged the computer back into her lap, and navigated to Randy Candy's blog. The post started off about a television star that had driven his Porsche into the side of a house after leaving a club the night before. The accident had put an eight-year-old boy, who was in the house when the car rammed into it, into the hospital with some serious, but not critical, injuries. The actor had been taken into custody after blowing four times the legal limit on a Breathalyzer. The real kicker was that the actor was known as the face of a well-known anti-drunk driving campaign.

Near the end of the post, Randy posed a question asking whether the actor would survive the scandal. He then recited a long list of actors who had never bounced back from scandal, and then a short list of those who had. At the end of the list, he cited Reilly as the poster-child for survival, and he asked his followers what they thought her secret was. Reilly scrolled down to the comments section and saw several hundred posts. The blog was only a few hours old. She scanned the most recent.

@dreamGyrl: beauty and brains, the woman isn't a survivor, she's a woman in charge of her own destiny! #reillyrocks

@deantoo: Who says she survived? The man she killed sure didn't. No more RR movies for me! #boycottrr #rehabwarrior

@Redondo137: Who cares? She's awesome!#reillyrocks

@classicFilmy: It's like it was just a role from one of her movies. It just doesn't seem real. Who knows? Maybe it wasn't. She's never said anything about it.

@sicpuppy: evrybdy nos it wuz jst uh pblcty stunt

@classicFilmy: I never thought about that

@sicpuppy: gurl nvr sed nuthin bout it she prbly jst wantd uh vcashun cant bleev the news

@deantoo: Hey @sicpuppy. Read the obituary. http://tinyurl.com/jmovnj3 A man DIED. Idiot.#boycottrr #rehabwarrior

@twelvelongsteps: No matter how far down the scale we have gone, we will see how our experience can benefit others. #easydoesit

@SalsaCaliente: I LOVE YOU REILLY RANSOME!!!!!!!<3 FOREVER!!!!!!

@dragonscale: Have seen some of her movies many times. RR is this generation's Meryl Streep/Marilyn Monroe. Hope she does a remake of GI Jane.#reillyrocks #dragonscalegamer

Reilly stopped reading after the first few posts. She knew better than to read that stuff. She could read a thousand positive things, but she only remembered the bad things. The comment about the whole thing not being real because she never talked about it rolled like thunder through her head. Was that how people saw it? Did they really think that she could just forget all of that?

A video was embedded at the bottom of the blog post and a photo showed Randy Candy standing in front of a cardboard display of Reilly and Cray at a movie theater somewhere in L.A. promoting the soon to be released *Salsa Nights*

II. She hesitated before she turned the volume back up and hit the play button. Randy Candy's nasal whine blasted from the speakers.

"I'm standing here at the Galleria Cineplex asking John and Jane Q. Public their thoughts on why Reilly Ransome has overcome a scandal that would have ruined most of her peers," Randy Candy said in an over-the-top imitation of a news anchor. "You! Sir! What's your take? Has Reilly Ransome literally gotten away with murder?"

The ambushed man passed Randy, dodging the microphone that Randy pushed into his face. He walked away as the cameraman followed him. The view panned back and settled on another man who stopped when he noticed that he was about to walk in view of the camera. Randy rushed toward him.

"Has she, sir? Has Reilly Ransome gotten away with murder?"

"She went to jail, right? That doesn't sound like she got away with anything to me." The man cast a nervous glance between Randy and the camera.

"What about you two?" Randy asked a middle-aged couple passing in the opposite direction. They laughed but just kept walking. Then he turned to a man who followed behind them.

The man shook his head and smiled, but continued to walk, too.

Randy jumped up and down, acting like a child about to throw a tantrum. His trademark high-water pants with funky socks and red Converse helped complete the image.

"Come on, people, I know you have an opinion on this!" he shout-whined. "Why did Reilly Ransome literally get away with murder?"

"That's bullshit," said Drew, reaching over to stop the video.

Reilly grabbed her hand and held it, intent on watching people answer the question. Randy thrust his microphone at a man walking by holding a half-eaten tub of popcorn.

"She's a good actress. We shouldn't care about her personal life," the soft-spoken man offered as twin splotches of red stained his cheeks.

A crowd had started to gather.

"What do you think?" asked Randy, holding the microphone toward a girl standing behind the popcorn guy.

"I don't know. There's something about her," said the teenaged girl after pausing to consider the question.

Randy swiveled and shot his microphone out to another person.

"Duh. She's hot," said a platinum-haired surfer dude, who flashed the hang loose sign with his fingers before he continued on his way.

Randy, who had walked backward to keep up with the surfer dude, stopped to chase down two women who passed going the other way.

"I like her because she just doesn't give a crap. She just moves on. Shit rolls right off her back. A true survivor," said a young woman sporting several tattoos and piercings, glancing at her companion who vigorously nodded her head and chomped on a wad of gum.

"She, like, showed me how to not care about what other people think about me, you know? She doesn't talk about it. Like, it was her business. Not ours. She's, like, eff the people who want to get all up in her business! And I think that's, like, super-badass. Totally."

"Fuck yeah!" said the first girl, and they did a fist bump as they walked away.

The camera followed the two girls, zooming in on the tattoos that showed on their lower backs between the top of each of the young women's low-rise jeans and their short black tee shirts.

"Those two young women are an example of why I don't go see her movies anymore," said a voice off-camera. The camera swung over to a woman holding the hands of two young children. "She takes no responsibility for her actions and she makes her carefree and immoral life seem glamorous. We're raising a generation of selfish children because of people like her."

"Well, there you have it, folks," said Randy, as the camera came in for a close up on him. When it zoomed in on his face and took the focus off of the ridiculous clothing and strange hat, Randy almost passed as normal. Until he opened his mouth. "It seems that all you have to do is pretend that it didn't happen. Easy peasy. Just take a lot of drugs and drink like a fish, and chances are you won't remember it, anyway!"

And in trademark fashion, Randy Candy laughed at his own terrible joke, the bray of it absorbed into the techno grind as the music played over the credits. Reilly turned the audio all the way down.

"Wow. That was pretty harsh," said Drew, curled up against Reilly, tracing a circle on her stomach.

Reilly stared at the frozen last frame of Randy Candy's video.

Had she been wrong in refusing to speak about the accident all this time? Had her silence sent the signal that she just didn't care, or that she was afraid to take responsibility for her actions? Reilly had spent the last three years feeling just the opposite, and she knew that she would spend the rest of her life feeling that way. The last thing she wanted to do was to gain publicity over it. It wasn't fair to Matt Traynor, and it wasn't fair to his family. But if people were getting the wrong impression, thinking that she thought that she was impervious to what she had done, she needed to let them know that wasn't the case. She wondered how she could make it right without making it about herself.

I Don't Think You're Going to Like It

REILLY STEPPED INTO THE LITTLE restaurant, and after a short pause to let her eyes adjust to the dimmer light, she spotted the back of a familiar blond head over the top of a booth seat. When she arrived at the table, she tossed her bag and phone onto the cushioned bench and slid in.

"Hey, Trip. What's up?" she asked her agent, Michael "Trip" Trippletorn, fighting the urge to muss his perfect hair. Instead, she took a sip of the water that was already waiting for her and held back a smile. She was in a good mood, having just left Drew's place. They both had late starts for the day, since Drew worked in Santa Barbara that afternoon, and she didn't have any morning classes scheduled. Even so, Reilly had barely had time for a shower after one last kiss had left them in a sweaty tangle on the already-made bed.

"Well, hello, Miss Ransome. I'm just fine, thanks for asking. How are you?" teased Trip, flashing his dimpled grin, looking just like the Ken doll Reilly had always thought he resembled.

"Oh, jeez. Sorry," laughed Reilly, falling into the easy kidding around that she and Trip had always enjoyed together. "I am delighted that you are fine, Mr. Trippletorn. And I am, in turn, equally fine. Nay! Better than fine. Perhaps exquisite is the better word. Outstanding weather today, is it not? How are the husband and kids?"

"Paul is doing great. He sends his love and told me to ask you over for dinner some night soon. Lovey and Gerard are doing well. They had mani-pedis at Paws and Claws this morning. I just dropped them back at the house, and they were prancing around like they were the stars of "Terriers and Tiaras" or something," he said, turning his iPhone around to show her a picture of his identical, perfectly groomed Pomeranians posing with him on the fourth step of a sweeping staircase.

"Hey! I was just kidding, but I should run that idea by the studio. "Terriers and Tiaras". Maybe Jane Lynch will produce it. That's my idea. Don't steal it!"

"Don't worry. I won't. So cute! I love the bows," exclaimed Reilly leaning over to look at the picture. She was a little disgusted by the way Trip allowed them to lick inside of his mouth and surprised that he had taken a picture of it. But to each his own she thought. He loved those dogs as much as he loved his partner of fifteen years, and husband of three. Anyone with that kind of heart was good in her book.

"I wanted something a little less Dorothy and more Lady Gaga, but they were out of black netting," he shrugged, as he took a last peek at the photo on his phone display, blew it a kiss, and then pushed a couple of buttons on the display before he spoke into the speaker. "Terriers and Tiaras". A hybrid reality show that crosses that "Toddlers" horror with "Best in Show". Try the studio or A&E. They'll show anything."

Reilly raised an eyebrow.

"Sorry, doll. Gotta move on inspiration. It evaporates if you don't."

Reilly only shrugged. She was used to Trip's rapid-fire shifts of attention.

"What's going on? We have our bi-weekly meeting scheduled for Friday. Not that I don't love seeing you, but couldn't this have waited until then, or possibly have been handled over the phone?" she asked.

They were sitting in their usual spot in the back booth of Scippio's, an upscale Italian deli a mile away from her house. She put her water down and absently traced the drops of condensation that rolled down the sides of the glass. Trip was like family to her. Her mother had hired him when she landed her first role, and he'd been her agent ever since. She tried not to show how put out she was, but it was her first full day off in a couple of weeks and she had been planning on flopping down on a beach with an umbrella, a non-fat mocha frappe, and a good book. And when Drew got back from Santa Barbara, they had planned a quiet dinner. It was going to be the perfect day. She needed the break from the constant publicity circuit she had been on for the new movie.

"I have something to show you, and I don't think you're going to like it," said Trip, taking a large manila envelope out of the worn leather bag sitting next to him on the cushioned bench seat.

"No good conversation ever started out like that," she said, sitting back, tapping her fingers on the white tablecloth. He pushed the envelope toward her.

"What is this?" she asked, opening the envelope. It was addressed to both Trip and her, and had been sent to his office on Wilshire. "A book? I don't understand."

Reilly pulled the book out of the envelope and noticed the word *REVIEW* stamped in red on the sides and cover. The picture on the cover was familiar and when she turned the book right side up, bright anger warmed her face.

The background picture was the one of her parents and her standing near the Santa Monica pier when she was much younger. A bench that should have been in the shot—THE bench—had been removed somehow with the miracle of digital photography. The original picture, the one with the bench still in it, was hanging on the wall in her parent's family room. Reilly scanned the rest of the cover. A montage of thumbnail-sized photos that chronicled Reilly's transformation, from child television star to award winning actress, marched across the top of the cover in a narrow strip. The one in the top right corner was a shot of her accepting her first Academy Award. It was chronologically out of sequence from the rest, and she supposed that it was because she had missed the second award ceremony, which had gone on as planned while she had been sitting on a cold metal bench in a holding cell at the Santa Monica police station.

"*Growing Up Reilly* by Melissa Tyler-Ransome" was printed in large letters across the bottom of the cover.

"Holy fuck!" said Reilly. Holding it up for Trip to see. "What the—?"

"That's exactly what I said when I opened it this morning."

"She can't do this. Not without my permission. I told her no."

"Apparently she can. It's her story, Reilly. So, I take it that she didn't tell you about it?"

"She told me about it several weeks ago, but I said no. I assumed that she would honor that. Did you know about it before now? Who sent it?"

"No, I didn't know about it and I don't know who sent it. Maybe someone who didn't want it to be a surprise. What are you going to do about it?"

"God, I don't know. I suppose I should talk to my mother about it," she said, opening the front cover to look at the inside dust jacket. A picture of Reilly when she was four or five took up the bottom third of the page. She remembered that day. She and her parents had gone to a local amusement park called Hee Haw Valley and she was sitting on a burro that was wearing a huge straw hat, his long ears pulled through the brim on either side. Her mother was posing next to her, standing to one side, holding her securely in the saddle. Both of them had long strands of straw sticking out of the corners of their mouths. Her father had brayed like a donkey to get them to laugh as he shot the picture.

"Good luck with that," said Trip, and she could tell by the sympathetic look on his face that he suspected it wouldn't go well. But before she talked to her mom, she was going to read the book. It looked like she would get the reading in that she had planned, although it wouldn't be the science fiction novel in which she had planned to get lost.

"She's the one who'll need the luck," she said, tucking the book under her arm as she gathered the rest of her stuff to leave.

Growing Up Reilly

REILLY WENT HOME AND SETTLED down under an umbrella by the pool. She didn't want to be caught in public reading about herself. The book rested in her lap before she got started, and she gazed out over the arroyo behind her house. Although she'd envisioned the day on the beach being soothed by the sound of waves marching across the sand and the briny scent of the ocean on the wind, she had to settle instead for the smells of chlorine and fresh cut grass, which wasn't that much of a disappointment when she thought about it. She had the sun, a cool breeze, and a great view. All of that, along with a tall glass of iced tea, and she was set.

She was finished with the book by late afternoon. To her surprise, it was very well written. Between the first draft that she had started and the finished product, it was evident that a good editor had helped Melissa through the revisions. The embarrassing *me-me-me* point of view that the first draft had been steeped in was gone, and most of the clunky ways that events had been strung together before had been smoothed out. Her mother was a smart and witty woman, and her voice was clear and evident in the final version. And, even as Reilly resented the intrusion into her life and the lack of respect that her mother had demon-strated by going against her wishes in publishing it, Reilly found herself deeply engrossed in the story. She laughed in several parts, grew sad in a few, and even felt the expectation building as the tale unfolded. It was hard to remember that it was her own life that she was reading about.

When she finished, she closed the book and rested it on her chest while she thought about what she had just read. She had to give it to her mother; she had talent. And to Reilly's surprise, the entire book was true. Nothing in it had been overly embellished or made up. Her mother had even managed to make the events that had led up to Reilly's firing of her into a heartfelt saga: the story of a daughter trying to find her own way while the mother has to let go and allow her to figure it out. In a small step showing evolution, Melissa had even referred to Reilly as her *gay* daughter, a minor adjective, but one that provided the acceptance that Reilly had craved all of her life. She had stared at the word for several moments as the words on the page shimmered through her tears, and she had to wipe her eyes in order to continue reading.

As the warm wind blew the scent of wisteria and chlorinated water to her, an unexpected sense of understanding dawned on her. Having been an observer to her own life and seeing herself through someone else's eyes, it made her think that all that she had been—what she had been remembering as a wasted journey—wasn't as wasted as she had come to see it. Not everything had been a write off. And her mother hadn't been as inattentive as she had thought. Not really.

There were some things that her mother had brought up in the book that mystified Reilly, though—the odd, inconsequential moments that her mother had chosen to include when Reilly would have left them out—who cared about Reilly's angst over the dress she had worn to her first Kid's Choice Awards? Or what she had eaten for lunch the first day of shooting the television show that had made her famous?

More confusing, were the moments that her mother had left out. Reilly's father was a prominent subject in the photos on the dust jacket and in the photo inlays at the center of the book, yet in the book he was mentioned only a handful of times, and never in any detail. Her mother had blasted out the fact that he had once had a young mistress, but she hadn't gone into any detail about it. It just hung there, just like it had all of Reilly's childhood. The book was mainly about Melissa and Reilly. Everyone else were just supporting characters. Reilly had to admit that the depiction, at least of her father, was accurate.

When she got to the end, where Melissa sat down to re-write the manuscript, after having just left the studio where she and Reilly had agreed to go their separate ways, Reilly realized that a very important event had been left out. The accident and Reilly's subsequent prison stay weren't even mentioned. Her mother had left out the most defining moment of Reilly's life. It hadn't been merely skimmed over. It was missing completely.

Reilly sat there thinking about the book, and she tried to understand her mother's motivation for writing it and why she had picked and omitted what she had.

As her thoughts skittered from place to place, trying to fold together her life and her relationship with her mother, Reilly wondered if she had been harsh in expecting her mother to play a less invested role, when Melissa had woven all of what she was into the fabric of Reilly and her career. It was a difficult rumination for Reilly, because she had to accept that her life and career were important, even while she struggled with the way that it made her feel. Was she inflating her own importance? If she assigned value to what she did with her life, was she a narcissist falling for her own fame? If she minimized her importance to the people in her life, was she not taking her impact on other people's lives seriously enough? Did she even have a responsibility to acknowledge that?

Reilly rested an arm over her eyes and tried to settle her thoughts. She was just an actress, for Christ's sake. She wasn't a doctor who saved lives, or an activist who fought for them. She memorized words and repeated them in front of a camera. Why should anyone give a crap about her? She was honest enough to accept that a book about her was probably going to be purchased by her enormous fan base, even as she wondered what real importance it held for them. Regardless of all that, she felt that the book should contain her worst moments, too. She didn't want people to think that she didn't acknowledge the life that she had extinguished because of her irresponsibility. But she and her mother had never even spoken about it. How could she have written about it?

Reilly picked up her phone and dialed. The call dropped into her mother's voicemail and she was both relieved and disappointed.

"Mom? Call me when you get this, okay? I read your book. It's very good," she said, and was about to hang up, when she remembered that it had been several weeks since she had last spoken with her mother. "And I miss you. Call me."

The Morning Show Again

"**HOW ON EARTH DID YOU** get me booked on *The Morning Show* again? I thought that they blacklisted me after the last time." Reilly's voice was a loud whisper, and she made sure that they were alone before she hurried toward Trip, whom she had just spotted down the long linoleum-floored hallway behind the show's studio on Rockefeller Plaza. She was relieved to see her manager, but she grimaced as her black and white Converse squeaked on the heavily waxed floor in her eagerness to meet him. The noise was enormous in the pre-show pause, before caffeine kicked in for the staff and guests, before orders started getting barked by the studio manager, before the frenetic energy that fueled the whole operation could almost be seen in the air. Trip looked fresh, despite having just arrived via cab after catching the red eye from L.A. In contrast, Reilly had just come from makeup, where the studio artist had spent extra time trying to conceal the dark circles beneath her eyes. She blamed Trip's last minute call the night before, asking if she would appear on the show.

"How, you ask?" replied Trip, laughing at the greeting from Reilly and acting surprised at Reilly's question. "Charm, persistence, being outstanding at my job… plus they called me to see if you were available. I was just as surprised as you, to be honest. They nearly begged me to have you when they found out that you were in town. Tristan and Melinda's people offered you a lot of money to have first interview rights. You're hot, baby! What can I say? Everybody wants a piece of you."

"Whatever," Reilly said in a whisper as they passed the open door of her hosts' dressing room. Unlike last time, when she had wanted to stop in and say hello before the broadcast, this time she was a little apprehensive. "I'm sure he's gonna flay me with his big old Chiclet teeth. I don't know why I think I deserve it."

"You don't," said Trip, stopping her once they had passed the open door and were a safe enough distance away not to be overheard. He turned her toward him and locked eyes with her. "So, don't let him. No matter how nice he pretends to be. Remember they begged to have you. Everyone would kill for a piece of you right now. You've been out of circulation for four years. Your movie is slated to be the hottest thing out this season. He needs you more than you need him, all of which I told him. Now you make sure that he behaves. I know you can."

"I'm not the same—"

"Hush," said Trip, putting a finger over her lips. "No excuses. Release your inner Reilly!"

Reilly sighed, took his hand, and headed toward the green room where they could wait together for her stage call. She estimated that she had about twenty minutes to get her head straight before facing the first interview she'd given since the accident. It was time to talk, she knew that. And she was ready. Well, at least as ready as she'd ever be. Her head had raced with responses to possible questions all night long—hence the dark circles beneath her eyes. She just hoped that it all came out right.

The short jaunt to New York was supposed to have been an easy re-immersion into doing promotional appearances. Her schedule was already crazy, but she and Trip had deliberately scheduled only minor appearances and dinners for this whirlwind visit. There had been no one-on-one interviews planned—not until Trip's phone call, that is. And before *The Morning Show* booking, she could have probably handled most of it on her own, but the last minute request for an interview had thrown her for a loop. It was her first televised interview—her first personal interview, period, since she had gone to prison—and even though it was just *The Morning Show*, where the interaction rarely went too deep or got too serious, she was still going to be on the spot to answer questions. And she hadn't forgotten the last time she had been there. She'd pushed it pretty far by kissing Melinda. She wouldn't blame Tristan for retaliating in some way.

The first thing she had done when she had hung up the phone with Trip the night before was call Drew, who had immediately started to make plans to fly out so she could be with Reilly. But when Reilly found out that Fergie was on rotation at the prison and was unavailable to take classes in Drew's absence, she tried to dissuade Drew from coming. It was only because Trip had texted Reilly saying he had already purchased a ticket to meet her that Drew decided not to cancel her classes and come out. Reilly's heart had swelled at the show of support, which helped her more than she could express. It was because of it that she knew that she would be able to deal with this part of her job again.

Reilly and Trip sat on the couch in the green room and watched the show on the closed-circuit monitor while they waited. On the enormous screen, a woman with two toy poodles demonstrated their skill at building towers out of plastic cups. Reilly barely absorbed it; she was busy remembering how she had behaved the time before, but more acutely, she was worried about how he would bring up the accident. She'd gone over what she would say in her head a thousand times. What could Tristan really do? Tell her that she was a terrible person? She already knew that. She lifted her chin and breathed out. She kept the rhinos in her stomach calm, remembering that no one would judge her as brutally as she already judged herself. She might never stop beating herself up over her past, but she couldn't change it, so she had to learn to deal with it and keep moving on. How could she convey that without coming off as unaffected by her terrible mistakes?

The door to the room opened a crack, and a young woman with an iPad in the crook of her arm poked her head in and put a hand to the side of her head over an earpiece.

"Ms. Ransome? You're on in five."

Reilly stood. Trip followed suit, straightening her collar.

"There you go, kid! Give them the Reilly smile!" He picked something from her shoulder and she tried to smile as she smoothed the front of her outfit. Another Hank original—a fitted black women's business suit with two dancing skeletons stenciled on the left breast pocket. An almost translucent purple blouse under the jacket and a pair of chunky heels that she had swapped out for the Converse gave the outfit a feminine touch. She felt good in the clothes. They gave her confidence, even though she still felt like throwing up. Taking a deep breath, she headed for the door.

Reilly followed the stage manager down the short hall and took a place in the shadows just off stage. Her arms rested at her sides, and she clenched and unclenched her fists to relieve the itching as she wrestled with the wildlife in her belly. She stood next to the stage manager, who seemed oblivious to Reilly's nerves. With intent focus, the woman watched the iPad waiting for the signal, and then with a dramatic flight attendant's gesture, she signaled for Reilly to follow the dashed line around the backstage curtain. On her cue, Reilly shook out her hair, pulled her shoulders back, smiled, and started walking. The dusty smell of the television stage under the bright lights and the sound of the studio audience gave her a visceral memory of filming her first sitcom, a time and place when her future held unlimited possibility and her past wasn't tied around her neck like a noose. She remembered those perfect moments when she had been happy, excited, ready for anything. A little bit of her old confidence returned.

Reilly pushed past the curtains into the bright light and remembered not to squint as her eyes adjusted. Tristan and Melinda stood near the seating area to greet her, clapping and smiling at her as she approached. She gave each of them a hug before she followed their lead and moved to her own chair. Tristan's hug was warm, but when she embraced Melinda, the crowd went wild. Melinda seemed to enjoy the reaction, and when Reilly loosened her hold, Melinda held tight, extending the hug a few seconds longer.

"Sorry about last time," said Reilly into Melinda's ear, her mouth obscured by the co-host's hair so viewers couldn't see what she was saying.

"I'm not," said Melinda, squeezing Reilly's arms as she stepped back from the embrace.

Reilly glanced over at Tristan with a questioning smile. She knew that she appeared confident, but inside, she was worried about his response. She wasn't in the mood to spar with him on national television. Tristan dropped his chin and shook his head, but his wide smile indicated amusement, which filled Reilly with relief.

Reilly stood in front of her seat and scanned the audience. They were on their feet and the energy was far more powerful than the last time she had been there. The clapping swelled when she waved to them.

"We love you, Reilly!" shouted a woman in the back. Tristan nudged her shoulder. When she looked at him, he was making a puppy face and forming the shape of a heart with the fingers of both hands over the left side of his chest. Reilly laughed at the adolescent gesture and blew a kiss in the direction of the woman's voice.

"Here she is! After a four-year interview hiatus! Two-time Academy Award winner! In all her salsa hotness—Reilly Ransome!" introduced Tristan over the din.

Melinda took her seat, and Tristan's trademark bright smile sparkled as he seemed to drink in the crowd's response to Reilly, which continued to build until Tristan had to signal the crowd to settle down. When the noise subsided, Reilly and Tristan took their seats.

"Wow! What a reception. Listen to all that love! Welcome back, Reilly! Welcome back!" shouted Tristan, clearly enjoying the audience's response to his guest. He slid a cup of coffee toward Reilly as if they were sitting down to chat. It was something that Tristan did with his favored guests. Reilly had never been one of them. This detail was not lost on her, although she wasn't quite sure what to make of it. "Let's chat over coffee, why don't we? Thank you so much for being here with us today, Reilly. It's always so nice to have you on the show." He turned toward the audience and lifted his eyebrows, and then turned back to Reilly. "But I hope you don't mind if I keep a protective eye on Melinda!"

The crowd roared. Despite the reference to her last visit, Reilly was pleased with the playful way he approached it. She laughed.

"I'm happy to be here! I promise to behave this time," she said with a genuine smile. And she discovered that she *was* happy to be there. She swung her smile Melinda's way. She just couldn't resist. "Although it may be difficult. Melinda, you just get more ravishing every time I see you."

Tristan laughed and leaned to the side to put his hand on Melinda's knee. Unlike last time, Reilly didn't see it as a misogynist's gesture, but as a sign of insecurity. She wondered if the edge between Tristan and her had always been from the subtle tension she now knew was between her and Melinda. She had never acknowledged it, even though she had accidentally exposed it when she had kissed Melinda the last time there.

"I can see why both ladies and men adore you," he said with a smile, as he glanced at his blushing wife and then shifted back in his chair to get down to business. "Now, let's talk about your second Academy Award, the one you received for *Angel's Flight*. If I'm correct, this is the first interview you've done since you were released from prison?"

"That's right, Tristan." Reilly swallowed but continued to smile. Publicly acknowledging her time in prison for the first time wasn't as hard as she thought it would be.

"And the last time we spoke you were up for the Best Actress award, which you ended up winning. Congratulations, by the way!"

He clapped and smiled as the audience applauded again.

"It was such an honor," said Reilly, and she guessed at what was coming next. She struggled to keep her hands loose along the arms of her chair, even as all of her muscles wanted to clench. She vacillated between hoping he would—and hoping he wouldn't—go there as she worked to maintain her smile.

"The director of the film accepted the award for you that night."

She decided to beat him to the punch.

"Yes. I was down at L.A. County being booked for manslaughter. I wasn't released on bail until the next day, so I missed the awards show."

Tristan paused for a beat, and Reilly wondered what he would say next. The silence in the room was deafening. She prayed that he wouldn't ask her how she felt. It had never been about her. His next words were a surprise.

"Well, the speech that Peter gave on your behalf was fabulous. Did you work with him on that?"

"No. As a matter of fact, I hadn't even watched it until a month or so ago. He was quite inspiring." Reilly remembered watching Peter's speech in an internet clip, his tears flowing as he talked about the movie, only skimming over Reilly's situation, but bringing them together by talking about the need to overcome obstacles. She thought at the time that he had been too generous in his regard for her, but in the past few weeks she had come to understand his capacity to see the strength in people through trying situations, which had ultimately been the secret to making an award-winning movie along that theme. A surge of emotion rose in her at the memory, and she was unable to elaborate on her comment through the lump in her throat. Thankfully, Tristan pressed on.

"It's no wonder that the film swept the awards that night. The story of four young women, escaping wretched lives to become nuns, only to find that their mortal savior was worse than what they'd fled. It's brutal. And you were exquisite in the role as the street smart heroine."

"Thank you, Tristan. It was a difficult movie to make," replied Reilly, relieved that her voice didn't betray her internal turmoil.

"I can imagine. And then you immediately went on to make *Salsa Nights*. A blockbuster, but hardly Academy Award fodder."

Reilly's relief at the tangent was huge, and she wondered if it was visible.

"Don't be so sure about that, Tristan. There are some dance numbers in the next one that I think might just blow some minds."

"And that brings us to my next question: the upcoming *Dare to Dream*, the sequel to the blockbuster dance hit, *Salsa Nights*. We hear it's set to open up to the same, if not larger, opening weekend sales. And by the trailers I've seen, I think they're right. How did you ever learn to dance like that, Reilly?"

"The same way everyone does," began Reilly, casting aside her earlier emotion and remembering the grueling schedule of dance classes and the fun but exacting dance coach that the studio had hired to teach her.

"Tequila?" suggested Tristan, interrupting her response.

"I was going to say a personal dance coach," laughed Reilly, going along with the joke, though the mention of tequila seemed in poor taste considering the topic that she knew they would eventually address.

"Well, you and Cray sure heat up the screen as you play the underdog contenders in the International Salsa contest, not just once, but twice. Who would have thought that two Southern California beach bums would break that mold?"

"Not me, that's for sure," said Reilly. Words started to flow more easily. "When I read for the role… what, five years ago? Has it really been that long? Wow! Anyway, I did it against advice from my manager, my agent—my friends even. But I did it on a lark. I wanted to try something other than the dramatic teenager or the girl next door. I love those, too, don't get me wrong, but the dance movie seemed fun. And I'm so glad I did it. It allowed me to expand my repertoire and show a different side of me. Plus I met some great people. I'm glad it works. Cray Layton is the one who should get all the credit, though. He makes it work for us. That man sure knows how to shake his tail feathers."

"You're telling me," said Melinda, waving her hand in front of her face like a fan. "Aye carumba!"

"It appears Reilly isn't the only one I have to watch out for," laughed Tristan, playfully swatting at Melinda before he turned back to Reilly. "You're being modest, though."

"Not at all. Cray is the secret to the *Salsa Nights* success. I believe that one hundred percent," said Reilly with full sincerity. She started to think that Tristan was going to avoid a direct conversation about the accident, and part of her was grateful to put it off for a while longer. Maybe *The Morning Show* wasn't the proper venue for it, anyway.

"Well, you'll have to convince the rest of the world," laughed Tristan, leaning forward to rest his chin on his fist. "So, Reilly, tell me your secret then."

"My secret to dancing?" she asked, confused. "I had an awesome dance coach."

"No. The secret to rising above it all," said Tristan, leaning back in his chair and lifting his hands in the air for emphasis. "The secret to plunging into the abyss and coming out unscathed. The secret to being untouchable."

The switch took Reilly by surprise. She was immediately reminded of the interviews on Randy Candy's website, and she felt sick. The strength that she had so diligently established in order to open up about the accident slipped away. Did the entire world think she was so cavalier?

"I'm not sure how to answer that, Tristan," said Reilly, as she tried to retain her poise at the sudden re-introduction of the topic that she had stupidly thought that they had already skimmed through.

Tristan's eyes searched hers for a moment, and Reilly saw something there that she had never noticed. Depth. And because of that, she couldn't be upset by the dramatic change in topic. Uncomfortable, yes. But upset, no. Tristan was asking what the rest of the world wanted to know.

"Let me rephrase it then, how do you go through what you went through, and not have it stick to you? You killed someone, Reilly," said Tristan, leaning forward. He whispered the last three words as if they were in a private conversation. Then he leaned back and tented his fingers beneath his chin with his elbows resting on the arms of his chair. "Yet you're more loved and more in demand than ever before. We hear that you have movies scheduled for the next six years. How did you do it?"

Reilly hesitated. Not because she didn't want to answer the question, but because she wasn't prepared for the feelings that came up when it was finally asked of her. It seemed no amount of anticipation would make it easy. She wanted to talk about. She needed to talk about it. But it deserved to be approached with more respect. A man had died because of her terrible decisions, and she couldn't discuss that immediately after a skit containing toy poodles, a reference to tequila, and a joke about infidelity. Most of all, it couldn't be brought up in context with Reilly's continued success. Her decision to hold off was supported by Tristan's next comment. "It must make you feel invincible." She hoped that he couldn't see the cringe that his statement induced in her. She felt the exact opposite of invincible. "Some people think your silence on the subject gives you a mystique, and therefore a power. You haven't done a single interview about that fateful night."

"You're right. I haven't spoken publicly about it, and I was wrong to wait so long," Reilly said, hoping that her voice didn't shake with the emotion that was swirling in her head, thudding in her chest.

"It must be so hard, having all of that locked inside," offered Tristan when Reilly once again paused and tried to compose herself.

She wanted to say that she didn't deserve to whine about how broken she was, that she thought about the man she had killed almost constantly, that not long ago, she hadn't thought about him for an entire day, and the guilt that she had over realizing it had almost consumed her. She wanted to explain that if it weren't for the love of Drew—the best thing in her life—that she'd probably still be sequestering herself to her house, only to leave for work and required engagements. She didn't deserve to whine about that, because Matt Traynor would never get to say his share. And for that, she deserved to suffer without comfort. That was her lot in life. She needed to let people know that she wasn't impervious, that she didn't deserve to rise above it all, seemingly unscathed.

Reilly watched Tristan search her eyes again, and she hoped that he didn't see the storm inside of her, the chaos that was her private hell. He saw something, she could tell. But she had no idea what he was thinking. Part of her was grateful for that.

"Tristan, Matt Traynor deserves..." she paused, trying to give words to what she needed to say. But all of the words that she had rehearsed seemed to fall flat. This wasn't the place to talk about a man who deserved more. How did she tell Tristan that she didn't think that his show provided the respect that Matt Traynor deserved? That she didn't have the words to express it adequately. All of her thinking, all of her meditation, all of the growing that she had thought she'd done came down to this one minute, and she realized that nothing had changed. "I killed Matt Traynor. He was a good man. And because of my bad decisions, his family has to live with that loss. I think he deserves every bit of respect that I can give him when I tell his story. Because it's his story. Not mine. I will discuss the accident and what I have learned about him. But not right here. Not today. Soon, though. Okay?"

Tristan watched Reilly as she tried to hide the tears that threatened to come, but she wasn't able to stop a few from slipping down her cheek. She wiped them away with a finger and raised her eyebrows in a silent plea for some understanding.

"Well, when you do decide to add to that story, please remember your friends Tristan and Melinda." Unbelievably, he didn't push. Reilly was grateful.

"I will Tristan, I will," said Reilly with a smile that she could not feel.

"So, about those rumors about you and Cray Layton…"

Just Breakfast

"DID DAD ENJOY EUROPE?"

Reilly slid into her seat at the Ova Café, finding it interesting how nervous she felt about meeting with her mother. It was just breakfast, but it was the first time they'd gotten together since the day five months ago when she had told her that she couldn't work with her anymore. They had spoken on the phone a few times, and those conversations had all gone well, but it felt different face to face. Reilly pushed her hair behind her ears and took the menu from the waiter as she waited for her mother to get settled at the table.

"You know your father. If there is wine to be swilled or beer to be drunk…" answered Melissa with a smile and an accepting sigh. "For a while I thought that you took after him in that regard, but you seem to have grown up a little faster than he did."

Reilly took in the comment and decided that, in her mother's way, it had been intended as praise toward her and not a slam on her father. She smiled back and watched her mother lower her sunglasses to scan the menu that the waiter had just handed to her. They were seated at their usual table on the patio. It was still crowded, even though most of the plastic covers were pulled down around the deck to block the November chill. It was a little strange joining her mother for breakfast like this and not having work to discuss. The meeting felt like old times, but different.

"Yeah, he does like his beer and wine," said Reilly, even as she thought that she really didn't know her father very well anymore. Not since the accident happened and he had withdrawn from her. He had withdrawn from everything, really. As far as she knew, all he did was work and golf. But she hadn't seen him in so long she didn't know what he did to fill his time these days. She'd been surprised that he'd gone to Europe with her mother, though. Surprised that either of them had gone, actually.

"We had fun. He geeked out on the architecture and I got my fill of shopping for a while."

Reilly raised an eyebrow at her mother.

"I'm not sure I completely believe you. Dad and architecture? That, I can see. You, tired of shopping, though?"

"Seriously. If I see the inside of another dressing room, I will run," laughed Melissa, putting down her menu.

"I never thought I'd hear you say that."

"Even old dogs can surprise you once in a while."

Reilly was happy to see her mother so relaxed. It looked like the vacation had done some good. When she had called her mother a few weeks earlier, after reading the book, Melissa hadn't immediately returned her call. She had surprised Reilly by calling a few days later, though, from a bistro in the south of France. That was how Reilly had discovered that her parents had gone to Europe. It was the first vacation that the two of them had taken since Reilly had been a little girl. And Reilly surprised herself by feeling a little left out, and a lot hurt, for not knowing about their plans. Her mother's call from the bistro had been short, but a start at rebuilding their relationship. She decided that she needed to spend more time with her parents. She didn't want to find out that they'd left the country after the fact again.

When the waiter returned to take their orders, they asked for their usual egg white omelets. Reilly ordered coffee, while her mother ordered a pomegranate mimosa.

"I saw you on *The Morning Show* earlier this week," said Melissa, picking up her napkin.

"I wimped out," Reilly didn't even pause before she answered. She'd been thinking about it all week long. Over and over, she had gone through that interview in her mind. All along she had insisted on not making it about herself. Now she realized that it had just been a ruse. She hadn't avoided talking about it out of respect for a man's memory. She'd avoided it because she hadn't really taken responsibility for it. Taking responsibility for it was so much more than admitting to having done it. She had to also understand how she had allowed it to happen. That's where she'd failed. She still didn't have any answers, but she could have said that. She could have talked about it and released some of the mystery. Given Matt his due. So many times, she had picked up the phone to ask Trip to schedule a do-over.

"Wimped out on what?" asked her mother, looking up from spreading her napkin over her lap.

"Not talking about the accident," replied Reilly, expecting her mother to change the subject. Her mother surprised her.

"I thought you were brave."

"Brave? Really? How was I brave?" Trip had said the same thing when she had returned to the green room after the show, where he'd waited. She had been numb and exhausted from overthinking what her other responses could have been. She hadn't believed him, either.

"Reilly, you admitted to the entire world that you killed a man."

"How is that brave? I went to prison for that. I just said what everyone else already knows."

"Well, for starters, it's one thing to be convicted of a crime, Reilly. It's an entirely different thing to own up to it. To face it directly. You didn't learn that from me, I will be the first to tell you. And you were right not to go into it with those two that morning. The tone of the show was too… too… irreverent up until then. And then he goes and gets all Barbara Walters on you. Only Barbara Walters has the class to pull that kind of emotional switcheroo and get away with it. I can't wait to hear the interview when you do decide to discuss what happened in its entirety. I've had an onslaught of calls from journalists who want that interview, by the way. I've sent them all to Trip."

The waiter delivered their beverages and Reilly busied herself with doctoring her coffee while she digested all that her mother had just said. She wondered then, why she'd found it so hard to talk about. They were talking now and it wasn't hard.

"What's the other thing?" she asked after she took a sip of the hot beverage.

"What other thing?"

"You said 'for starters.' That infers there's more. Is there?"

"Oh, yes. The other thing was when you told Tristan that the rumors of your sexuality were none of his business, but that if he did insist on spreading them, he should get it right and stop pairing you up with men. I think that Melinda was hoping for another kiss to prove it," Melissa giggled at the last, and though Reilly wanted to talk to her mother about the other thing, she was beyond surprised at her mother's broach of the subject that had sat between them for so long.

"Who are you, and what have you done with my mother?" asked Reilly.

"What?"

"Where is the woman who insisted that I act straight in public? The one who 'leaked' rumors of my romantic interest in men so that I wouldn't sink my career? The one who ripped me a new one after the kiss you're now giggling about? Giggling!" Reilly was amused, but her amusement was tinged with anger. Where had this mother been when she needed her? Instead she'd been left with a mother who had been controlling and judgmental.

"I still think that you're playing with fire. And if one of these movies that you're scheduled to star in flops, and they blame it on your inability to authentically play the female romantic lead across from the next Mr. Hollywood, I will have a hard time not saying 'I told you so.' But since I am no longer responsible for your career decisions, I admit that I feel a lot more accepting of your lifestyle. It's kind of liberating, to be honest."

Reilly was incredulous.

"Wow. I'm not sure what to do with that."

"There's nothing to do. I do reserve the right to be a mom, though. I still disapprove of that Sylvie creature. Not because she's a woman, but because she's absolutely not good for you. I never see her in the papers with Parker anymore. I hope to god that you haven't picked back up with her. If you have—"

Reilly interrupted her.

"I haven't seen or heard from her since before I went to prison, mom. You have no worries there."

"Thank goodness for small blessings. I'm glad that you decided to remain single for a while."

"Well, there is someone else."

Her mother sighed.

"Why am I not surprised? Is it a man? A woman?"

"Woman, mom. It will always be a woman," Reilly responded with an angry glare.

"Sorry. I will never again assume, or wish, otherwise."

Reilly paused a moment, knowing that the strength of her anger was because of old triggers. Her mother seemed to be trying, and she needed to meet her at least halfway.

"Her name is Drew. She owns a yoga studio in West Hollywood. You saw her one day at the studio, but you probably wouldn't remember." Reilly didn't want to remind her that it was the day that she had fired her.

"How long have you known her?"

"I met her right before the accident, and we were friends for a while, but we just recently started seeing each other as more than that."

"Is it serious?"

"I love her, mom."

Her mother studied her.

"I can see it on your face. Is it mutual?"

Reilly nodded.

"I can't wait to meet her. What are your plans for Thanksgiving? Will you bring Drew to dinner?"

Reilly was shocked. Her mother had never invited one of Reilly's girlfriends to the house, let alone a holiday event. In the past, it had never been an issue, since Sylvie had always gone home to her own parents' house for the holidays, and Reilly and her parents had always celebrated with a small dinner. That was all before she had gone to prison, though, and before she and her mother had had the falling out, so Reilly hadn't counted on anything being the same this year. She hadn't even expected to be invited over herself.

"Drew and I are having some friends over for an early Thanksgiving dinner this afternoon, actually. We don't have plans for Thursday, though. I wasn't sure you were planning on doing dinner this Thanksgiving."

"Of course I was. We do it every year. You'll bring Drew, then?"

"Sure. I'll ask her," said Reilly.

"Good. It will be nice."

Their food was delivered and they were quiet for a few minutes while they got everything situated. When the waiter left, Reilly caught her mother looking at her and she smiled. Reilly liked the new ease she felt with her mother, and she hoped that it would last.

"Hey. By the way, here's to your new book," said Reilly, picking up her water glass and tipping it against her mother's champagne flute. Her mother smiled and returned the gesture. The insecurity Reilly saw in her mother's eyes touched her.

"Thank you, Rye. I'm nervous. What if it flops?"

"It won't flop. I told you that when you were still in France. It's really good."

"You're sweet. I'm still worried, though. I've been thinking, you're right about leaving out the whole accident. I really thought that it was your story to tell. But people are going to wonder."

"I thought you took care of that by putting in an epilogue."

"I did. But I'm thinking now that I rushed it. What if it was a mistake?"

"It will be fine."

"But—"

"It will be fine."

Reilly smiled back at the look of gratitude she received from her mother as she took a bite of her omelet.

I Don't Think They Meant to Record This

"HANK! YOU'RE EARLY!" SAID REILLY, a couple of hours after brunch with her mother, but still an hour before she'd expected anyone to arrive for the early Thanksgiving gathering she and Drew had planned for their small group of friends. Hank, who was standing on the porch with a cardboard box held to his chest, shifted the box to look at his watch.

"Is that a veiled jab at my very intentional efforts at being fashionably late? It's ten after two. I can go wait in the car for another fifteen minutes," offered Hank with a laugh.

"You were supposed to be here at three."

"Cray said two."

Reilly stepped to the side, realizing that she was being rude by keeping him on the porch. "It doesn't matter. Come in! It feels like I haven't seen you in ages!"

"Because it has been ages," said Hank over the burden he carried, leaning to the side to kiss her cheek as he passed her on his way into the house. "You look awesome! All glowy. Love suits you, my dear."

"Thank you. And right back at ya. Where's Cray? Is the dessert he raved about in the box?" asked Reilly, looking down the front path for signs of Hank's partner. She couldn't wait to see what he had made. Cray had been very mysterious about what he was going to bring, but promised it would be a culinary masterpiece.

Reilly was excited about the gathering. She'd never really been much of a hanging-out-with-friends kind of person and the gathering was a new thing for her. It seemed so "normal", whatever "normal" really meant, and she liked how it felt. Even the fact that everyone she'd invited had offered to bring something to add to the festivities promoted a quaint ambiance of intimacy around the whole thing. Fergie and her partner Serena were going to be there, bringing a pumpkin pie. And Alison and Lisa were coming with a vague promise of "some sort of side dish". Trip had declined the gathering, having already made plans to be in Aspen with his husband, but they'd sent over a couple of bottles of wine with a request that the group text them a group photo during the first toast so they could join them virtually.

"Cray's just a few steps behind. He's bringing in the wine and the Black Forest Trifle that he whipped up this morning."

"What's with the box, then?"

"This," he said, glancing over his shoulder at her and nodding to the box in his arms, "is the box of stuff the police took out of your car, plus a couple of things that they had left that I cleaned out of your car before I sold it. You can open a store with the number of sunglasses and hoodies you left in there. Not to mention how much I could have gotten on eBay for the leopard print thong I found in the back seat. I know. I'm a good friend. You're welcome."

Reilly tried to see into the box over his shoulder, but only saw a mound of sweatshirts. She wondered what else was in it but figured it couldn't be too interesting if she hadn't missed any of it over the last four years. The thing she didn't want to see in the box was the check for the sale of the BMW. She'd told Hank to keep it for the trouble of dealing with the car since he got it out of impound all those months ago, but he'd already tried to give the check to her twice. She decided that if she saw it in the box, she'd give it to charity this time.

"I gave the check from the sale to the Human Rights Campaign, by the way. I did it in the name of that vile representative from Minnesota, though it pains me to speak that woman's name aloud."

"You didn't! That's awesome!"

"That's me. Awesome Hank. Now where can I put this? I'm getting a cramp from holding it."

"Just put it there. I'll go through it later," she said with a laugh, motioning to the credenza that stood against the wall in the entryway.

"Hell-oooo, gorgeous! Help a girl out? Take this bottle of wine," called Cray, shifting a large glass bowl in his arms to hand Reilly a bottle of wine as he came up the walk. It never failed to surprise her when Cray dropped the butch movie star façade and showed his campy side. He didn't do it often, just around Hank and close friends. She wondered how much effort it took to keep the two sides of him separate.

"Oooh, that's beautiful—and probably very fattening!" said Reilly, eyeing the gorgeously layered dessert. She tried to dip her finger into the dish, but missed her target of thick whipped cream sprinkled with chocolate curls when Cray swiveled away from her, keeping the dish out of her reach.

"Down, girl! You only get to admire it until after dinner."

"I told you, he worked on it all day," explained Hank, then he turned to his lover. "Hey, Cray-Cray, Reilly said we're early."

"No, we're—Oh my god! That's right! You told me three and I told Hank two so we wouldn't be an hour late and ruin this fabulous dessert. I forgot my own lie! I can't believe I did that! How the hell did we get here this early? We're always late!"

"Because you wouldn't let me—"

Cray put a hand over Hank's mouth. "Hush, shnookums! Reilly doesn't want to hear about our raunchy sex life."

Reilly laughed so hard she snorted. Hank rushed over and hugged her from behind, tickling her sides.

"Laugh all you want, woman, but I'm surprised we didn't interrupt you two mid-cunnilingus since we're early. Talk about nymphos."

Reilly laughed harder and spun away from him, getting ready to launch her own attack, when Cray rolled his eyes and waved the dessert just under her nose. Then he turned toward the kitchen.

"Only a hundred and thirty-five calories per serving, and fat-free. You may have two helpings if you're a good girl," said Cray, looking at her over his shoulder and down his perfect nose.

She gave Hank a warning look, closed the door, and followed them down the wide hall toward the kitchen where she hoped that Drew was fully dressed again. Hank's remark hadn't been far off.

"Yes, Daddy," laughed Reilly.

"That's my line!" joked Hank. "Let's crack open that awesome bottle of wine we brought and watch Drew get her Rachael Ray on! I know that Reilly had nothing to do with the fabulous smells wafting through this house."

"Hey, I'm helping with the cooking, too."

"Did you open a box of crackers? Slice some cheese?" asked Hank.

"Yes. And I arranged pickles and olives on a relish tray."

"What? Was there a shortage of caterers this year or something?"

"Drew likes to cook. I even went shopping with her. It was fun."

"Watch out world, Reilly is gonna take over the Food Network next!"

Reilly pinched Hank's arm as they entered the professionally appointed kitchen that Reilly had never cooked in. Drew's head rose from a cloud of steam issuing from the oven that she had just opened. The scent of roasted vegetables filled the room.

"Hey! The boys are here!" she called out as Hank laughed and she saw them. She pulled on a pair of oven mitts. "Hugs in a minute, I have to turn the veggies."

Reilly smiled at the scene. Drew cooking always reminded her of their first night together, and a tremble pulsed low in her belly. The fact that they had just finished a quickie when the doorbell sounded didn't diminish the blaze that swept through her once again. Drew smiled at her, and Reilly saw post orgasm softness in the beautiful silver eyes.

"Said boys are present and accounted for, ma'am," responded Cray, as Reilly envisioned herself vaulting the counter separating her from Drew. She dragged her eyes away from her lover and laughed at Cray's sharp salute. He was filming a World War II movie and the skater-talk that she had so despised had been replaced with soldier-speak. She preferred the soldier-speak.

"Tell me one of you has some music with you. Reilly and I don't have anything worth listening to around here," came Drew's voice from below the countertop. The smell of roasted bell peppers and onions intensified as Drew stirred the vegetables. She closed the oven door.

"All the Zen Master over there has on her iPhone is yoga and meditation music," explained Reilly, hooking a thumb at the two identical phones lying on the counter. "And I haven't had a chance to download all my stuff onto my new phone since I dropped the old one during that impromptu salsa you and I did for Ellen last week, Cray."

"Fret no longer. Cray will save the day," said Cray, setting the trifle dish on the counter with one hand and sliding his phone out of his back pocket with the other.

Hank rushed over waving his phone and tried to push Cray's phone back toward his pocket.

"Uno momento, mi amore! At the risk of being asked to hand in my gay card, I have to say that I am not listening to 'It's Raining Men' tonight!"

"Well, I'm not listening to that brain rattling skater music tonight," countered Cray, flashing a mean frown and devil-horn hands.

Reilly smiled and looked at Drew, whose eyes widened, and she pointed to Reilly's chest. When Reilly looked down, she saw that her shirt was buttoned askew. She turned away and fixed it while the boys were bickering. She tossed Drew a knowing smile and blew her a kiss as she turned back, a rush of body memories from the frantic sex they'd just had against the island counter flooding her senses.

"Boys, boys. Have we discovered trouble in paradise?" asked Reilly, fixing the last button and moving to stand between them.

Hank winked at Cray with a smile.

"Don't worry, Sweet Reilly. The beautiful music we make together surpasses all obstacles—even Cray's unfortunate taste for all things disco."

Cray returned the smile and reached around to swat Hank's ass.

"You guys make me a little sick with all this sweetness," Reilly said with a roll of her eyes. "Just hand me one of your phones."

"Hey! That reminds me. I found an old phone in your car when I was cleaning it out," said Hank heading toward the foyer. "I charged it with the cord I found in the console. But there's a password on it, so I don't know if it still works or not."

"Let me see. I'm sure there's music on it, and I probably remember the password," said Reilly, hoping it was her old phone just for the photos she had on it.

Hank retrieved the box he had brought in and set it on one of the dining room chairs. The first thing he held up was a light blue hoodie with rhinestone and sequined applique of a puppy on the front.

"Classic barf," he said as he held it up to his chest.

"That is hideous and not mine. I have no idea where that came from. Are you sure you cleaned out the right car?" laughed Reilly.

"Do these ring a bell?" asked Hank holding up a leopard print thong, which she did remember.

"They do. But also not mine," she said, offering no details, although she saw his eyes begging for more of the story. "The phone?"

"Here we go. The high tech LG Dare," announced Hank. He held the phone next to his face and waved his other hand under it, a la Vanna White. "If I remember correctly, they were the shit back in the day. You always have had the latest gadget."

"They were and I do," agreed Reilly. "But that's not mine. That one was Sylvie's. We had the same phone, but she had the red case. Mine was silver."

"So much for music, then," said Hank dropping the phone back into the box. "It's password protected."

Reilly had mixed feelings of curiosity and avoidance about peeking into a past that she normally didn't want to visit, but she held out her hand.

"I think I remember the password. She had some good music. Let's check it out."

Hank pulled the phone out of the box again and tossed it to Reilly, who tried a couple of passwords before unlocking the touch screen.

"Success," she said as an image of her and Sylvie appeared. She immediately regretted succumbing to her curiosity. A confusing mix of emotions swirled within her. In the picture, she and Sylvie appeared to be having the time of their lives. There was a party in the background and Sylvie kissed Reilly's neck, while Reilly smiled for the photo. Typical for that time in her life, Reilly remembered posing for the shot but not much more. She scrolled through the files on the phone, searching for more of what she suspected would be there but worried about what she would find. Sylvie had a habit of taking naked snapshots of people—which is why she knew the password. When they had been together, she had routinely scanned for and deleted them. At the time, she justified it as being cautious, just in case Sylvie lost her phone. But she now knew that it was because she hadn't trusted her. And for good reason.

She wasn't ready for what she found. The first was of Sylvie with her hand up Parker's dress in the backseat of Reilly's car. Parker must have been holding the camera. The angle of Sylvie's arm and the half-lidded expression on Parker's face indicated that Sylvie's hand was up something more than just Parker's skirt. A third person's arm was draped along the back of the seat behind them. Reilly knew whose arm it was before she saw the next photo of herself passed out, curled up, her head resting on her arm that was lying across the back of the seat. The photo featured Parker smiling into the camera beside her, sticking out her tongue. Yet another picture showed Sylvie kissing Parker, and Parker was cupping Sylvie's breast.

Reilly felt sick. She recognized the green dress that she had on.

"Reilly, what's wrong?" asked Drew, wrapping an arm around her waist.

"These are pictures from the night that I… that I… of that night," said Reilly, her eyes never leaving the images that rotated across the screen of the phone in her hand.

"What kind of pictures?" asked Drew, peering down at the phone.

"Just pictures of me passed out in the backseat of my car, while my former girlfriend fucks another woman right next to me," said Reilly. Her words were wooden, but there were three sets of startled eyes before her.

Despite her words, the content of the photos didn't bother Reilly, not really, not after all the time that had passed. She and Sylvie had had an open relationship and Reilly had known that Parker had joined them on occasion, so there was no surprise there. It was the fact that she had absolutely no memory of that night. Nothing beyond the party at Cray's house. For all she knew, she was looking at the very moments of decision that had altered hers and so many other people's lives, and it looked like she had been sleeping right through it. She wanted to reach back and shake herself, to wake herself up, to warn herself.

"Let me see," said Hank, holding out his hand.

Reilly gave the phone to him, and she watched as he flipped through the pictures.

"What a filthy whore!" said Hank. The words made Reilly felt a little better, if for nothing more than they were predictable. "And I touched those panties with my bare hands. There's a video. Should we watch it?"

"I don't care what you do," replied Reilly. "Go in the other room or something, though. I don't want to see or hear anything."

Reilly moved closer to Drew, who tightened her embrace. She watched Hank pull a set of headphones out of the box, and he and Cray, each with one ear bud in, began to watch a video that probably featured her ex-girlfriend having sex with another woman. Drew kissed the side of her neck and squeezed her. Reilly shut her eyes and leaned into it. It was nice to know that all of that was behind her. She liked who she was now. She didn't even know that Reilly anymore.

"Reilly, you should watch this." Reilly opened her eyes and saw Hank riveted to the screen.

"Hank, I don't really want to—'

"No, Reilly. You really need to watch this," said Cray, waving her and Drew over. Hank pulled the headphones out of the phone so that the audio played into the room, small and tinny.

"There's no video," said Reilly, glancing at the screen and then at Drew, relieved.

"There is, but I think the phone is in her pocket or something. I don't think they meant to record this," said Cray, pointing at the screen. "The video is still playing, though. See the lights every once in a while? You can still hear stuff."

Reilly nodded her head as she heard the sounds of rustling coming from the phone.

Then she heard Parker's voice, muffled and far away, but clearly Parker's voice.

"…*stupid bitch. Out like a baby every time.*"

"*Stupid, yes, but never a bitch. She's just a wet blanket,*" came Sylvie's very familiar voice from a distance. Then there was laughter. "*Unlike you, who are a bitch and will do anything, anyone, anytime…*" The rest was unintelligible until Parker could be heard again.

"*It's the only way to get a job in this town. Don't knock it, baby.*"

"*I don't know how you get any jobs when you wear shit like that,*" laughed Sylvie.

"*What? You don't like my doggie hoodie? My niece gave it to me.*"

The sound of dull rustling and whooshing as the phone, wherever it was—in the pocket of the hoodie being discussed?—was tussled by casual movement.

"*Let's just say I wouldn't go out with you in public if you had it on.*"

"*Good thing I have other plans for you, then.*" There was a pause. "*I think she's totally out. Let's dump her and then go back to your place so I can fuck your brains out.*"

The next words were unintelligible under a knocking noise, and then it was quiet for a few seconds before Sylvie spoke again.

"*How much did you give her?*"

"*Just a few drops in her drink. Check it out.*" Reilly wished that she could see what Parker was doing. There was a thump and a moan. "*We could light fire to her hair and she wouldn't even know."*

"Just as long as you didn't give her too much. She was out too long that first time after we gave her a second dose because it wasn't working fast enough. That was scary," said Sylvie, again from a distance, and Reilly had to struggle to hear it.

"They drugged me?" asked Reilly, incredulous. "I can't believe they fucking drugged me."

"Do you know what this means?" asked Hank. He was excited and tugged at Reilly's sleeve.

"Shh!" said Reilly. She wanted to hear the rest. "Rewind it. I missed that last part."

Hank ran the recording back.

"—that was scary."

"People don't O.D. on this shit. Otherwise there would be a lot more frat boys in jail for murder. It's not like she'll ever know, anyway. No one ever tests for it," said Parker.

"I don't know—"

"Stop overthinking things. We're just having fun. Now let's do it."

"Hold on. Make sure no one's around," said Sylvie.

There was a pause.

"Now?" asked Parker, and Reilly heard the impatience in her voice.

"Yeah. There's no one. It's too cold even for the hobos tonight." Sylvie laughed.

"Is this some sort of forties movie? Who says hobos?"

"Bums, then. Jeez," said Sylvie, and Reilly could hear the impatience in Sylvie's voice now.

"There's one over by the garbage bins. He's probably passed out cold on his Thunderbird, though." Parker laughed. *"Get it? Out cold?"*

"Yeah. Very funny. Just like his fucking dancing Snoopy blanket. Who the hell has Snoopy anymore?"

"Um, people who take what they can get?"

Reilly blew out an impatient sigh, thinking about the irony of Parker schooling anyone on being more sensitive.

"Well, it looks like he's zipped all the way in. Who's he going to tell anyway?"

"Should we put a jacket on her?" asked Parker.

"No. Hopefully the cold will wake her up so she's not out here all night. We want to fuck with her, not give her pneumonia."

"Are you sure? We could put my doggie hoodie on her."

"She'd never wear something like that over this dress. It's Marlo Leechy. She'd know something was up if she woke up wearing it. Okay, let's go. Let's knock the movie queen down a notch or two," said Sylvie.

"Remind me not to act like I might want to break up with you, okay?"

"It's more than that. Three years together and I don't have so much as a toothbrush at her place and she's been in my house exactly once. She's never even brought up living together. She doesn't care if I fuck other women. She didn't even care when I brought you around. That alone should have set her off."

"Is that what this is? You were using me to piss her off?"

Reilly pictured Parker standing there with her hands on her hips and her hip thrust out in the defiant pose she struck at least once in any movie she made. She was known for that posture. It was part of her B-movie charm.

"Payback's a bitch."

"Ouch. It's a good thing that I'm not in love with you, then."

"What are you talking about?"

"You using me to piss off your girlfriend."

"Hey. You told me up front that you only wanted to be fuck-buddies."

"True. But still…"

"Just shut up and grab her feet. No, leave her shoes on. We'll just put her on the bench—" Sylvie said something else but Reilly couldn't hear her over the noise in the background. Her head spun. Had it all been because Sylvie thought that Reilly was going to leave her? Reilly didn't remember having thoughts about leaving. Sure, she had been getting a little irritated at Sylvie for small stuff, and there were the feelings that she had for Drew, but she didn't remember having any focused thoughts on breaking up with her. Sylvie had broken up with her, in fact. Had it simply been a game of revenge gone horribly wrong? Had Sylvie's fast retreat after everything had happened been an act of guilt for putting Reilly in a position to harm someone?

The sounds of rustling got louder, and Reilly huddled with the others around the phone in Hank's hand. There were grunts, as the two women in the recording exerted some sort of effort. Reilly imagined that they were having sex.

"We don't need to listen to—" she started to say before voices issued from the phone again.

"Fucking cow," complained Parker, her voice strained. "This is hard to do in a dress. We should have changed our clothes."

"You're just weak. We're almost there. That sweatshirt goes great with those heels, by the way," teased Sylvie.

"Fuck you."

"Promises, promises."

A thump sounded, and a moan floated from the phone's tinny speakers.

"Shit, Syl. Gentle. That's going to bruise. Besides, you'll wake her up."

"My hand slipped. Anyway, a train wouldn't wake her ass up right now. We've done this before. She'll have no fucking idea what happened to her. She'll wake up on the bench and think she had another blackout. I can't wait to hear what she says *this time."*

"*She tried to hit me the last time we did this,*" said Parker.

"*That's why you gave her more of the stuff. She woke up when we were fucking that woman we met at the bar.*"

"*She kept calling her Drew.*"

"*Yeah, I think she thought it was the Ice Queen you brought to the party tonight. What's with you bringing her to the party, by the way?*"

"*I know her from yoga. Cray invited her, but I think she has a thing for Reilly. She didn't say anything, but I could tell. Drew's nice, but totally not into having fun,*" said Parker.

"*I'm sure I could warm her up.*"

Reilly felt the old jealousy rise in her and she tensed. Drew squeezed her, as if she knew what she was feeling, and the jealousy went away.

"*So, are we gonna do the same thing? Just leave her here?*"

There was a pause, and Reilly could see Sylvie's expression as she considered their options.

"*Let's do something different. Since this will probably be the last time, let's do something to remember.*"

Reilly heard Sylvie laugh and wished that she were there so that she could hit her, or worse. They were having fun, totally unaware that a man was going to die. A silent rage burned inside of her even as anxiety mounted within her. How had it happened? Would she finally find out?

"*A trash can or something? Like she ran into it?*" Parker asked, sounding like she was moving around.

"*No. I have it. Let's drive her car up the pier a little way. Leave it out there. That should be interesting. The cops will have a field day.*"

"*Those metal poles are in the—*"

"*We drive around them, idiot. Like the lifeguard Jeeps do it.*"

"*Okay. Okay. Let's do it.*"

The sound of laugher and footsteps preceded the sound of car doors opening and closing, then the sound of the car starting.

"*Jesus, Syl! Turn the headlights off. You'll attract attention. Besides, you're shining them right on her. She's moving.*"

"*Shit. She's going to fall off the bench.*"

The seatbelt warning bell sounded.

"*What do you care? What are you doing? Get back in the car! She's fine. Let's just get the car up on the pier and get out of here. I have plans for you,*" Parker laughed.

"*Is that all you ever think about? I can't see anything in the dark with the lights off.*"

"*That's why we come here—Stop the car! Someone's coming. It's a jogger and he's headed right by here. Who the fuck jogs at this hour? What if he sees her? Get down!*" Parker giggled.

"*Shut up! And get your hands off of me. I swear you've got problems. Can you see? What's he doing?*"

There was a lot of background noise as Reilly imagined both women slumped down low in the car, trying not to be seen.

"*He slowed down and he's standing right in front of the car. He's looking at her.*"

"*If he asks, we say our friend just needed some fresh air.*"

"*Get down! He just looked at the car.*"

Sylvie just laughed.

"*He can't see us, it's dark as shit. Besides, he has his back to us. Why's he just standing there? Go away, runner man. Ow! He can't hear me. Okay! Okay! Don't fucking hit me!*" laughed Sylvie.

"*Is the car moving? You took it out of gear, right? It feels like…*"

"*Oh fuck!*"

A loud thud sounded and a loud keen that sounded like it was coming from an injured man far away filled the air making the skin on Reilly's body crawl.

"What was that? Oh my god, was that—?" Reilly couldn't bear to finish the sentence. She knew what it was. She had just heard Matt Traynor die. She ran to the sink and threw up.

"Turn it off! Turn it off!" demanded Drew behind her, and although Reilly couldn't hear any more of the recording, she was grateful that Drew was there, taking care of her. She finished heaving and rinsed her mouth out with the glass of water that someone handed to her. Gusts of cool air soothed her as Drew gently held her hair back and blew on the back of her neck. "Are you okay, baby? I'm sorry that you had to hear that."

"Was that—?" Reilly started and then looked up at Drew with her head still hanging over the sink. Drew just nodded. Reilly dropped her head between her arms resting over the edge of the sink. She closed her eyes and wiped her mouth with the back of her hand, not sure if she was finished. Her stomach was churning with the knowledge of what she had just heard. Her mind flew back to that early morning when she had awakened on the bench with a dead man just feet from her. The scene made more sense to her now.

"Is there more?"

Hank nodded.

"Rye, you don't have to—"

Reilly squeezed Drew's hands, which grasped hers, but she had to know.

"Can you rewind it? I don't want to… I can't hear… that last part again. Rewind it to right after that."

"Are you sure? I can listen to it and—" began Hank.

"Yes. I'm sure. I have to know."

Reilly moved back to the place where she had been standing before they had paused it. Drew slid in next to her and wrapped an arm around her waist. Hank put the headphones on and, with Cray holding him from behind, he rewound and listened until he had the recording at the place where Reilly asked. Then he removed the headphones and placed the phone on the counter rather than hold it like he had been, as if he couldn't bear to touch the conduit of such an event. He pressed the play button.

"*Oh, shit! Shit! Shit!*" screamed Sylvie's voice.

"*What the hell just happened?*" asked Parker, her voice low and tremulous. There was a short silence and the sound of muffled and jagged breathing issued from the phone that now sat on the counter.

"*I don't know!*" screamed Sylvie. "*You were leaning on me and my foot slid off the brake and onto the gas. We hit the parking barrier. At least I hope that's what we hit. Fuck! Go check.*"

"*You're coming with me.*"

The distinct sound of the seatbelt chime chirped into the room again, and then the sound of doors opening. Noise obscured the next few words and then Parker screamed.

"*Holy shit, Syl! What the fuck is that? Is that—?*"

"*Oh my god, Parker! Oh my god! Check—*"

The next sounds were unintelligible until Parker spoke again.

"*Stop clawing at me! I can't feel anything. So much blood. He's not breathing. What are you going to do?*"

"*What do you mean, what am I going to do?*"

"*You were driving—*"

"*No! This is your ass as much as it's mine, Parker! We need to get out of here. Give me your sweatshirt.*"

"*Why?*"

Loud sounds of rustling and breathing obscured all other sounds.

"*Just fucking take the stupid thing off! I need to get my fucking fingerprints off of everything in the fucking car. Shit! We were in the back seat, too. Shit! Shit! Shit!*"

The sounds of rustling sounded and then the video portion picked up for a few seconds as the phone appeared to fly out of the pocket in which it had been stowed and landed on the driver's seat. They all had had a fleeting look at Sylvie hurriedly wiping down the steering wheel before, from what Reilly could tell, the phone slid between the front seat console and the driver's seat. Then the recording stopped.

Reilly stared at the phone. She expected to feel anger or relief over what she had just learned, but she didn't feel anything except hot pressure behind her eyes and in her ears.

Drew pulled her close and held her. It wasn't until she hid her face against Drew's chest that she realized that she was crying.

Here on HardCandy

REILLY HIT THE PLAY BUTTON on the video box that appeared on her screen. The vertigo-inducing camera angles and rapid in-and-out, now-we're-close-up, now-we're-not focus of the video that began to play almost made Reilly slam her laptop closed. At least she'd had the forethought to turn down the sound before she'd hit play. The annoying and discordant techno riff still blasted through the speakers even at minimum audio. A still image of Randy Candy's face imitating the *Home Alone* kid's classic hands-on-cheeks expression started to swell, filling the space in the player window.

Reilly and Drew sat in bed staring at the laptop, their backs propped up by a pile of pillows. Reilly relaxed into Drew's side, pulling her arm around her. Drew was her rock, her safety, her sanity. It had been Drew who'd calmed down a revenge-seeking Hank who'd been ready to storm over and do physical damage to the two women who'd nearly ruined Reilly's life, and it was Drew who had her call her lawyer who, in turn, had advised them to go to the police station with what they'd found. Drew was the one who repeatedly helped to protect her from the swarms of persistent paparazzi that always knew where she'd be. Drew was there every night to comfort her when the nightmare of Matt Traynor's scream echoed in her nightmares. It had even been Drew who'd carried the conversation at the Thanksgiving dinner at her parents' house when Reilly was mostly silent. Drew had done all of that and more, and she protected her now, by checking in to see if she should be watching even more press about the still unbelievable turn of events that had found her innocent of a crime that she had willingly taken full responsibility for.

"Baby, are you sure—?" began Drew, but Reilly just stroked the arm that held her and she continued to watch the video. Drew sighed, but relaxed beside her.

Reilly knew that she was being slightly obsessive about seeking out news about Parker Stevens and Sylvie Simonson ever since she'd turned them in for what they'd discovered in the recording, but she needed to hear what the world was saying.

Reilly turned the volume up just enough to hear what Randy Candy was saying.

"All I want for Christmas is my free-ee-dom, my free-ee-dom, my free-ee-dom!'" Randy Candy's surprisingly good tenor voice sang the butchered and mercifully short version of the classic holiday song to open his latest installment of his video blog. The still image shattered into a thousand smaller images of the larger picture, which spun in a circle, and then shot off the screen to reveal the man standing in front of UCLA Medical Center. He was wearing what for him was a fairly plain outfit: neat jeans, a pressed shirt buttoned all the way up, and a brightly colored sweater vest. As always the red Cons were on his feet. Randy's daily vlog had been posting new segments several times a day to keep up with the amazing details that kept turning up in the breaking news of Reilly's innocence. His website view rate was probably through the roof.

"Okay, so technically, Reilly Ransome has been free since last March, but now it turns out that she never should have gone to prison in the first place. I'm going to say it," crowed Randy into the camera. "I told you so. And I'll keep saying it. I told you so. I told you so. I told you so. I always said that there was something mysterious about how Reilly Ransome never seemed to be affected by the murder she supposedly committed. Now we know why. It's because she didn't do it! I still can't believe it. But it's true. You heard it here, almost first, folks! And you'll keep hearing it here. After CNN, after MSNBC, after Cocks—I mean, FOX—puts their spin on it. I tell you what really happened. Here, on HardCandy. When the others tell you about new evidence, I play you actual recordings. When the others tell you that two other suspects have been identified, I tell you that they're actress Parker Stevens and entertainment lawyer Sylvie Simonson. When they tell you that arrests have been made and one of them has been admitted to the hospital, I tell you who sang like a canary and which one of them tried to blow her brains out."

Reilly flinched, but she didn't close her laptop.

Randy Candy cleared his throat, and his face took on a solemn expression. The fidgeting was gone. His eyes looked somber. Even the oversized, neon yellow microphone he usually held had been replaced with a standard-sized newscaster field mic.

"Just moments ago, doctors for actress Parker Stevens, who was admitted seven days ago into UCLA Medical Center with a self-inflicted gunshot wound to the head, made a statement on her condition with permission from her family. The actress remains in guarded and critical condition, still in a medically-induced coma following the initial emergency surgery she underwent upon her admittance into the hospital. Since then, she has undergone three additional surgeries to repair tissue, relieve pressure from swelling, and to stem the bleeding. Now, doctors are making predictions on her recovery, which aren't good, folks. If Parker Stevens regains consciousness, she'll likely never progress beyond a vegetative state."

An out-of-focus image came up in the upper right corner of the video. Reilly squinted to see what it might be and realized it was the ivy-covered walls that flanked the delivery entrance to the hospital. A white semi-truck was backed up to one of the large bay doors and next to it was a short set of cement steps that led up to a smaller entrance door. It was the entrance that she'd used to sneak into the hospital when she'd received permission from the authorities to visit Parker Stevens. In the blurry image, a small group of people was descending the steps, and she recognized them as herself, Drew, and the two detectives she'd been speaking to almost every day since the discovery of the recording.

"How do they do that? There were security guards all over the place."

"Who knows? I've stopped trying to figure out how those insects get into places they shouldn't be."

"We have exclusive footage of Reilly Ransome and her posse leaving the hospital after paying a private visit to Parker Steven's room in ICU just this morning. I'd pay money to hear any of the conversations that went on while she was there. I'm not kidding. Real money. If there are any recordings out there, I'm interested. HardCandy will pay cash money."

"Good luck with that," mumbled Reilly. Even if she had wanted to talk to Parker, she hadn't gotten closer than the doorway to her room because of all of the equipment and attendants in the room. She hadn't said a word to anyone while she was there. She merely held Drew's hand and looked at the unrecognizable person in the hospital bed.

Randy continued. "Sources say that Reilly was visibly shaken during the visit. I wonder what the real story is. So far—and this is the recap for any of you who have been hiding under a rock for the past week—what we do know is that last Sunday, Reilly Ransome discovered a cell phone recording that inextricably and directly links Parker Stevens and Sylvie Simonson to the accidental murder of jogger Matt Traynor. The video, which has been verified as authentic, also shows how they set Reilly Ransome up to take the blame. When the evidence was turned over to the authorities and they approached the suspects for questioning, Parker Stevens tried to take her own life, while several blocks away at her own home, Sylvie Stevens surrendered without incident."

The picture changed to a split screen with Sylvie Simonson on one side, looking ten years older than Reilly remembered. The footage showed her being led into the Los Angeles Police station, flanked by two police detectives, and her hands were cuffed behind her back. The other side of the screen displayed hectic televised news coverage of Parker Stevens on a gurney being wheeled into an ambulance as emergency medical personnel surrounded her in a flurry of activity. Reilly had seen the scenes many times, but the same feeling of painful confusion and anger washed over her again.

"Why do you keep watching this stuff, baby?" Reilly felt Drew pick up her hand, which was balled into a fist next to the laptop. She looked over to watch her unbend her fingers, and then weave them together with her own.

"I don't know. It's for the same reason I had to go down to the hospital. I just can't help it. You'd think I'd feel some sort of closure, but I don't."

"I guess I sort of understand," responded Drew, kissing the hand she held. "But, maybe you should avoid his stuff. It's not news. It's just screaming and begging for attention."

Randy Candy's image was briefly replaced by a group of video snippets that showed Reilly repeatedly refusing to talk to reporters who tried to ambush her for sound bites whenever she left her house. The words "NO COMMENT" materialized on the screen, spinning until they landed on a still image of Reilly with her head turned away from the camera, her palm predominately displayed on the screen. Randy returned to the video, the main doors to UCLA Medical Center just behind him.

"Reilly Ransome still refuses to talk to the media about the accident that happened four years ago. And now she refuses to speak about the new evidence that proves her innocence. For a person who once flaunted her party girl lifestyle, she's been a virtual shadow since she was released from prison. One can only speculate on what she's trying to accomplish with the whole mystery building thing."

"Not that again. Can't the guy let it go?" Drew sounded angry, and Reilly thought that maybe that's how she should feel, too. But she didn't. Mostly, she just felt tired.

"Let's see what people have to say about Reilly's newly proven innocence," said Randy Candy as his eyes scanned the area around him and he held out the microphone toward a young man trying to enter the hospital. "You, sir. What do you have to say about the new evidence in the Reilly Ransome case?"

Reilly closed the laptop and leaned into Drew's arms.

New Year's Eve

THE SNOW WAS COMING DOWN, fat and heavy. Stuffed from a delicious dinner and feeling mellow, Reilly sipped a glass of wine and cuddled next to Drew on the posh outdoor furniture of the spacious vacation home in Lake Tahoe that they had rented for the week between Christmas and the new year. Hank and Cray were sprawled out on a matching sofa across from them, illuminated by the gas fire that roared in the circular pit between the two couples. Every one of them was worn out—in a good way—from a week of snowboarding and snowshoeing.

Fluffy white powder piled up on the wood railing that spanned the length of the third floor balcony, but the fire and the canvas awning that stretched out above them kept the area toasty. Drew's arm was wrapped around Reilly, and low music drifted from unseen speakers situated around the wide deck. It was a fitting end to an overall perfect day in the Heavenly Ski Resort, in the mountains above Lake Tahoe. Reilly took in a deep draught of the snow and pine-scented air and couldn't think of a better way to ring out the year.

It was only a few minutes after 10:00 pm, but with the low clouds and thin mountain air, the sounds of early New Year's celebrations could be heard from all directions. A party was in full force in the condo next to theirs, though they could only hear the thumping music and laughing crowd when the door opened to admit more guests.

"I'm glad that we decided to stay in tonight. I'm really not up to dealing with a bunch of drunk revelers," said Cray, as another snippet of dance music filled the night. Boisterous greetings echoed from next door, followed by sudden silence with the slam of a door. Cray was lying with his head in Hank's lap, and Reilly smiled at the way his normally perfect hair was sticking up in crazy tufts all over his head, an effect caused from the knit cap he'd been wearing all day. Reilly thought the look suited him.

"Me, too," agreed Hank, refilling Cray's wine glass from the bottle that had been sitting on the table next to him. Cray laughed as he tried to take a sip while lying down, and Hank playfully pulled Cray's hair. "Sit up before you spill that on both of us, lazy ass!"

"Lazy ass is correct. I might not even make it to the magic countdown. This kid is worn out!" sighed Cray, plopping his head back down in Hank's lap.

Reilly was relieved. She had been worried that Hank and Cray were only there out of some sense of duty to keep her company. Part of her—a phantom of her old self—was kind of disappointed that she wouldn't be spending her first New Year's Eve out of prison doing something wild and fun, but most of her was completely satisfied with spending the special night in a more peaceful fashion with the most important people in her life.

Cray and Drew had prepared a late dinner that they all had gorged on— grilled salmon with a pecan crust and a spinach salad—after which, the foursome had settled in on the balcony with a bottle of excellent wine. An over-priced bottle of champagne chilled in the refrigerator, which they planned to open at mid- night—if they made it to the countdown. They could all see a television inside the condo that was tuned into the revelry on Times Square so they could keep track of the impending celebration. The setting couldn't have been more beautiful, with the balcony overlooking one of the main slopes of the resort, which was festooned with twinkling white lights and a view of the dark lake far below. A few party boats, outlined in more twinkling white lights, were out in the middle of the water shooting off intermittent fireworks. The setting was almost magical.

"I'm glad that you two decided to come up here," said Reilly. "Drew and I would probably be in bed by now, if it was just the two of us."

"Hey, if we're cramping your style—" began Cray, pretending to get up.

"That's not what I said—"

"—we can always go down to that bar in the square and come back when you're done. Just leave a tee shirt hanging on the front doorknob until you're finished. That's how they signal they're getting laid in the fraternities, right?" asked Cray, looking up at Hank who shrugged his shoulders. "At least they did in that movie I was in a couple years ago."

"That's not what I meant, and you know it!"

"Uh-huh," nodded Hank with a mischievous grin and a wink at Cray. Then he yawned. "I wasn't kidding when I said I was wiped out. Plus, I'd rather hang out with you guys. If that makes me an old lady, so be it."

"Yeah. What he said," said Cray, parroting Hank's yawn and closing his eyes. "Besides, I can't kiss him when the bell rings if we go out. It would be on the front page of all the rags tomorrow."

"Probably," agreed Reilly. She wondered if her friends would ever go public with their relationship. She knew Hank would be fine with it, but he wouldn't press the issue, and Cray was too worried about his leading man appeal. She didn't judge him for it, but she wished he felt like he could be open about who he was.

Hank made a disgusted sound, bringing Reilly back from her musing.

"Jeez. You would know about the media stalking you, Rye. They've been hounding you non-stop since those crazy bitches were arrested for fucking you over. I'm surprised none of them have scaled the walls to get up here. I'm telling you, if I ever get within ten feet of one of those two cows, they'll have to put me behind bars, too. I can't believe—"

Reilly dropped her head back on the couch and groaned. Not that again.

"Come on. Please don't start," she begged. "Not tonight. I've listened to you rail against Sylvie and Parker for the last month and a half, ever since we found that damn cell phone. I'm grateful for your unwavering loyalty and outrage. I really am. But, just for tonight, I really just want it all to go away."

Hank sat up, jostling Cray's head.

"Sorry, baby," he said, stroking Cray's chin, and Reilly thought that she might have won this round. But Hank looked up, and the adoring look he had given to Cray became incredulous once again. "You want it to just go away? Like it never happened? I don't get—"

"Okay. Okay. I just want you to stop plotting revenge. It's over. Please let it be over? Please?" She'd had to beg Hank not to storm over to Sylvie's and Parker's houses to confront them the day they'd first seen the video. She'd literally had to hold him back when he'd threatened to take his scrawny little body over to go kick their asses. Since then, he'd been excessive in his vitriol. So much so that she was beginning to believe that he was the one who was a bit obsessed. A *bit*? Try *a lot* obsessed. Even she'd stopped watching the news for anything about the case. But Hank was still watching and seething. "The cops have taken care of them, Hank. Sylvie's confessed. Parker tried to kill herself. What's the use in getting angry?" Reilly rubbed her temple. She was so tired of thinking about it. So tired of trying to take the high road. Exhausted, really, from maintaining what she hoped was a dignified silence on the whole subject. She knew that as soon as she said anything to anyone, it would get plastered in the next day's headlines. Best to keep it to herself. She wished everyone would just stop asking her about it.

"I guess you're tired of it," said Hank.

"A little," said Reilly, uttering the understatement of the year.

"Am I making it worse for you? Reminding you?"

"Yes," admitted Reilly. She didn't want to hurt his feelings, but it was true. His tirades were constant reminders. She just wanted to forget.

"Okay," he said. "I'll shut up about it tonight."

"Good boy," said Cray, stroking his face and closing his eyes again. Hank smiled and ran his hands through Cray's tousled hair.

"Dramatic subject change, then. New Year's resolutions. Cray, you first."

"That's easy," said Cray, not even opening his eyes. "My resolution is to take acting classes from Walt Archer."

"*The* Walt Archer?" asked Drew. Even she knew who he was. "The one who coached what's-his-face-Coulsen in *Rage of Man*? The movie that was up against Reilly's for Best Picture this year?"

"Yeah. *That* Walt Archer. I figure if he could get Coulsen an Academy Award nod, it's worth a shot. Besides, Reilly helped me see that I've been typecast. I need to expand my repertoire."

"When did I say that you were typecast?" asked Reilly.

"That day in the studio. The day I called Drew to see if I could get her to come on set to 'teach you yoga,'" Cray said, using his fingers to make air quotes. "You're welcome, by the way. That makes us even. I got you laid and you opened my eyes to expanding my career horizons."

Reilly vaguely remembered the conversation.

"Jesus! That was months ago. I was in a bad mood that day."

"Thus my efforts to get you some somethin'-somethin'."

Reilly was about to tell Cray where he could stuff his somethin'-somethin', but a quick memory of the first time that she and Drew made love filled her mind, so Hank got there first.

"My man, America's Hunkiest Man-slash-Pimp! I'm so proud," said Hank, laughing. "Drew, you go next. I need to hear what the perfect woman wants to improve upon."

"Oh, that's easy," said Drew without any hesitation. "This very imperfect woman would like to be more charitable. I want to find a way to give back this year. What about you, Hank?"

The resolution could have sounded trite and syrupy from almost anyone else, but Reilly knew that Drew's statement was genuine. It made her love her all the more.

"Christ. How can I follow that?" exclaimed Hank, throwing a hand in the air.

"You started it. You must have had something on your mind when you asked everyone else what their resolutions were," replied Reilly.

"Well, I was going to say, double the profits of my company, but Mother Teresa over there ruined that. So I guess I have to give up all my worldly possessions and become a monk?"

"A monk who has sex, right? Because otherwise I'm not down with that, lover," responded Cray, suddenly wide-awake.

Reilly snorted. "Hank wouldn't last a day as a celibate man."

"She's right," agreed Hank. "I'll stick with my profit plan. But I'll continue to source from responsible vendors… and encourage others to do the same. Maybe start a clothing line using hemp or bamboo," Hank was teasing Drew now, mentioning things that Drew had suggested to him that he'd already laughed off. Hank was unapologetically and consciously oblivious to the environment, which frustrated both Drew and Reilly. "Yeah! That's it. Phew! Maybe I can rock that halo after all!"

"If I didn't have the Zen Master image to sustain, I'd kick your ass, little man," Drew said with a menacing growl that they all knew lacked any bite.

Reilly laughed and felt a little turned on by Drew's flare of butchness.

"Does anyone have a tee shirt that I can borrow?" joked Reilly, snuggling a little closer to her lover. "Maybe you two *should* go down to the bar for a bit. It'll be quick."

"I think I might barf," sighed Hank.

"It's your turn, Rye. What's your New Year's resolution?" mumbled Cray, barely awake again.

Reilly had hoped they'd forgotten her. Every time she thought about New Year's resolutions she got all wound up inside, thinking that she needed to do exactly what she'd been begging Hank to do—let go of all of the negative feelings she felt for Sylvie and Parker. Despite her words, she'd still spent a lot of time stewing on it and wondering why she didn't feel more relieved about not being the person behind the wheel. Instead, she couldn't stop feeling the betrayal and, yes, embarrassment about having been played and framed by those two. It felt petty and foolish, horrible to hold on to that shit. But she just couldn't let it go. She shrugged and sighed.

"I don't have one," she said, putting her empty glass on the table beside her.

"Come on," scoffed Hank. "Everyone has one. At least until the first hangover of the year wears off."

"Not me."

"I guess you don't want to push it, huh? What with getting the biggest break of your life already, huh?" Hank said. Reilly got up, grabbed the empty wine bottle, and made to leave to get another bottle of wine. Not because she wanted more wine—just the opposite, actually—but because she suddenly wanted to cry. She didn't know where it came from, but it was just there, ready to flow.

"Hey!" called Hank after her. "Where do you think you're going? You have to tell us your resolution. We told ours."

"My resolution?" She stopped at the glass door leading in to the house and turned back to him. She had almost escaped.

"Yeah, your resolution."

"Um, okay. To get in better shape?" she threw out there. That was as good as any resolution.

"Try again. You're in perfect shape thanks to G.I. Jane over here." Hank hooked a thumb at Drew sitting on the edge of the couch, watching her. Reilly saw the look of concern on her face. Drew knew something was getting to her, and Reilly had to admit that she'd been more and more thin-skinned since the discovery of the cell phone. The look of concern from Drew was starting to get familiar, yet she hadn't pushed Reilly to talk, and Reilly was grateful for that.

"Okay! Okay! Forgiveness. I'm going to work on forgiveness," she said, trying to get Hank off her back. It was close. He should buy it. She was tired of the resolution game.

"Now who's trying to be Mother Teresa?" asked Hank. His voice held no playfulness in it.

"Come on, Hank." Cray sat up and tried to distract him, but Hank was leaning toward Reilly with such an earnest look on his face that she didn't know how to feel—angry or sympathetic. How could she be mad at someone who so consistently had her back? But she was getting mad, and she tried to tuck it down like she always did.

"What does that even mean," she asked wearily.

"You told that guy on E! a few weeks ago—the one who ambushed you by the hospital? You told him how much you've already forgiven those two cows that set you up. I know you don't want to talk about it—you never want to talk about it—but I have an idea. How about *you* start plotting your *own* revenge? Figure out how to fuck them over. If you won't, I will. I hate them for doing what they did to you."

So, they were back to Sylvie and Parker. Reilly shrugged her shoulders, outwardly dismissing the subject, while inside she felt the coil of tension tightening to a critical level. She tried to summon some of Drew's zen.

"I'm not claiming to be some sort of saint, Hank. There's just no use expending any more energy on them. That's all."

"What the fuck, Reilly? How can you be like that?"

"Because there is no use in perpetuating that kind—"

"Hey, Rye. News flash. You aren't the Dalai Lama."

"I never said—"

"You don't have to say it. I just don't see why you can't just admit it, that they fucked you over and they deserve whatever comes to them. How can you just stand by?"

"Because I have to!" she screamed, dropping the empty bottle at her feet and stepping forward. The bottle didn't break on the wood deck, but she kicked it hard enough that it rolled and shattered against the rock side of the fire pit. Drew got up and came to her, but Reilly barely felt the hands that brushed against her arms. She focused on Hank's indignant face and blasted all of the rage she felt toward him. Not at him, because he wasn't the source of all of her pent up anger, but he had triggered it, and it had to go somewhere.

"Don't you understand? I have no choice! Because if I don't hold it in, if I say what I really feel, it gets printed in some newspaper and it will be taken in the worst possible way, and I end up in the same prison I was in before. Only this one is one of my own making. People watch and they wait. Waiting for me to do or say anything that they can print. I can't say anything I feel. Parker is lying in a hospital after trying to blow her brains out, and if I say anything bad, I'm the insensitive monster. Part of me is glad that they didn't let me actually talk to her at the hospital when I went to visit her. When I went to tell her that I forgave her, like Lydia did to me in prison. But I wasn't allowed to speak to her. And I'm glad. Glad, because I don't forgive her. And who knows what I would have said?

"Don't you think that I'm angry? I'm fucking raging inside! I want to get even! I want to punish them in the worst possible way. I trusted them. At least I trusted Sylvie. I trusted her and she fucked me over. My head," she said grabbing the hair at her temples, "wants to explode thinking about it. I spend countless hours stewing on how they treated me, how they took away my dignity, how they made me believe that I was insane. I went to prison. Prison! Where I was beaten and raped." She noted the shock that flashed across Hank's and Cray's faces, and Drew's arm tightened around her at the statement, but she couldn't stop now. Her words were a flood that she couldn't hold back any longer. "Where I feared for my life every goddamned fucking day. Where I lost the will to live. I was taken down to nothing there, and I have struggled every day since then to try to regain some sort of semblance of… of… of who I think I should be. But I can't find it. I don't even know who that is anymore. Everyone else seems to know who I am, but I don't. Don't you see? Everyone sees what they want to see. I can't give them more. I just can't."

Hank had risen. Cray was sitting on the couch and they were both watching her. Tears were pouring down her face and snot streamed from her running nose. She wiped it with the base of her palm, but she didn't look away. She stood her ground, shaking and tense. There was so much to say. Now that she'd let some of it go, the words, trapped in the pit of her stomach for so long, were rushing like a flood through her mind, ready to begin another torrent. Only the grounding touch of Drew kept her from flying away.

"Oh Rye," began Hank, his voice breaking on her name. Some of the red that tinted her vision cleared. She let go of a rasping breath.

"Tell me, Hank. What's the use in it? Huh? What's the use in getting mad?"

"To get it out, honey," said Hank quietly, still standing by the couch but reaching out for her, even though she was too far away to touch. "Oh, I had no idea."

His face reflected the anguish inside of her, and she felt awful for having allowed the poison she had held onto for so long spill out and infect her friends. She'd tucked it away so securely that she'd almost forgotten how bad it was. But now it was out. She felt like a balloon that had collapsed, tired and weak, but lighter, too.

Drew pulled Reilly into her arms and Reilly sagged in to her, unable to stand on her own.

"I'm sorry," she mumbled into Drew's chest. "I'm sorry."

Drew's hands ran soothing circles over her back and along her cheeks, and Reilly felt soft kisses on her forehead. The contact helped to ease the ache.

"You're fine, baby. It's okay. It's going to be okay."

And Reilly started to believe it was possible. Maybe she would be okay. One day.

Special On-Location Segment
of The Morning Show

REILLY'S MIND WANDERED. HER CLEAR eyes scanned the thick vegetation adorning the deep canyon called Jacaranda Arroyo that ran behind her house. It was the end of February, but all of the green before her, the gift of her beloved California, was almost blinding in the perfect mid-morning sunlight that cast long shadows and painted the world a golden hue. A cool breeze flowed over her, and she pushed an errant strand of blond hair behind her ear. A sense of clarity that she hadn't felt in a long time—maybe ever—had begun to build in her over the last few weeks, filling her, and she took it all in with a deep breath. She shifted her gaze and watched Tristan and Melinda Powers, who were sitting across from her. Their heads were together as they scanned their interview notes one more time before the live portion of the special on-location airing of *The Morning Show* began. She noted with amusement that Tristan's hair didn't move in the slight wind. Melinda glanced up at her, and seeing Reilly's gaze on them, gave her a perky thumbs up. Reilly returned the gesture with a warm smile.

They were finishing up two days of on-location shots for the primetime interview that would culminate in the live sit-down portion that they were just about to broadcast. Reilly had turned down many larger names from the throng of journalists that had approached her over the last months, begging for first dibs on her story. But Reilly hadn't been ready. Now that she was, Tristan was the one she wanted to tell it to. She couldn't explain the strong connection that she felt toward him. All she knew was that even in his seemingly shallow fashion, he'd always seen through her, exposing who she really was—even when it was just to unleash a childish tantrum on national television, or to force her to come to grips with the knowledge that she had been avoiding talking about the accident, not only because she wanted to preserve Matt Traynor's memory, but mostly because she was simply too scared to face it. It struck her as ironic that the façade she had always thought Tristan wore was more authentic than anything that she had ever had to offer. Until now.

The pre-taped segments that they had already filmed were an interview with her parents and a tour of her home and its sprawling grounds. The interview with her was to be a live, in-depth segment that focused on the accident, her time in prison, life since getting out of prison, and, finally, the shocking truth of Reilly's innocence. It had been months since reports of the recording had been made public, and Reilly would have thought that interest in it would have faded a bit by now. But it hadn't. She'd done many interviews but had avoided discussing what she could rightfully call the worst time of her life. Now it was time.

Reilly travelled through a panorama of emotions as she prepared herself for the discussion she was about to have with Tristan and Melinda. She was prepared for them to bring on the tough questions. She'd asked them to. She told them to be direct, that she didn't want to hide or side-step anything. It was time to lay it all out there. But knowing it was coming didn't make it any easier, and she was tied up in knots worse than any stage fright she'd ever experienced.

Reilly tried to distract herself by watching the taped tour of her house that she had given to Tristan and Melinda the day before. The segment was airing right then, and it would segue into the live interview that would begin in just a few minutes. She watched as her on-screen self guided them around her home, surprised at the composure she displayed on the screen. Of course she'd seen herself on film countless times, but this time it was the real her. Still, the on-air Reilly showed no sign of the onslaught of emotions that had battered her from the inside. She studied her own eyes, surprised that they didn't project her thoughts, imagining what her audience was seeing—an enormous structure without personality, without a heart. Would they translate that into who they thought she was? The house was a showcase, she knew, tasteful and expensively decorated. But it had never reflected who she really was. Until recently, she hadn't even known who that was herself. With nothing else to measure her by, would the world assume that she was just the same, a shell that held no soul? She'd changed so much over the last several months. She wanted people to know that.

The pre-taped segment rolled on and she watched as she, Tristan and Melinda entered her kitchen.

"What a great space," the on-screen Tristan declared, as the camera moved into the open room. Both of the Reillys agreed—the taped Reilly and the live one. Aside from the bedroom, the kitchen had become one of Reilly's favorite rooms. Tristan admired the rare Italian granite counter tops, the state of the art appliances, the rich wood inlay of the handmade cabinetry, and the custom wine racks that covered most of one wall. Then there were the new touches, the improvements that Drew had helped her with. A professional cook's rack held an impressive display of pots and pans. A butcher's block held a dazzling array of handcrafted Hattori knives. A small rack of potted herbs basked under a complex system of lights that allowed them to thrive indoors. Reilly enjoyed watching Tristan gush. "I'm not sure if you knew this about me, Reilly, but I love to cook. I could really do some damage in here. This has got to be one of your favorite rooms."

"I did know that about you, Tristan. Your cooking segments are legendary," Reilly watched herself reply. "This is one of my favorite places in the house, but probably not for what you think. Unlike you, I can't cook. This is my girlfriend's domain. I love to sit right here," she said, resting a hand on the back of a stool that was tucked under the counter, "and watch her practice her magic."

"Speak of the devil," exclaimed Tristan. Reilly watched the segment play out and couldn't help but smile when she saw Drew join her on camera. The entire thing had been staged in order to introduce Drew to America as Reilly's partner, but she still felt a thrill when she saw how good she and Drew looked together. When Reilly watched herself wind her arm around Drew's waist and kiss her on the cheek on screen, it struck her that she had officially announced who she was to the world. All of the ambiguity that her mother had manufactured around her love life over the years had been officially obliterated in that one gesture. It was a good feeling.

Reilly watched as they chatted for a few more seconds, closing out the tour, and the screen switched to commercial.

"Ready for this?" asked the flesh and blood Tristan across from her. He handed the paper he had been studying to a woman who walked by wearing a headset. Reilly admired his cool composure. Of course, he was used to broadcasting live to millions of viewers every day.

"As ready as I'll ever be," replied Reilly with a nervous laugh. She looked off to the side just in time to see Drew, her mother, Hank, and Cray emerge from the house and walk toward the make-shift set. They would all join the interview at different times during the live filming, and with the guidance of one of the set managers, they stood by to await their cues. Her mother had already taped a segment where they had discussed *Growing Up Reilly*. At Reilly's suggestion, it had aired prior to the tour. She thought that it was a good way to get things started. Her father had even made a brief appearance.

She found Drew's eyes and she relaxed. Just one look, that lone connection, provided her with the calm she needed.

"In ten, nine, eight—" the set director intoned, signaling rather than saying the last few numbers of the countdown as the commercial ended and the cameras went live—with a five second delay. The network had a long memory. Reilly didn't blame them.

Tristan waited with a dazzling but frozen smile plastered to his face. Melinda sat next to him, calm and composed. When the cameras went live, Tristan did, too, leaning forward in his chair. The energy swelled. Reilly had to give it to him. He knew his job. She wanted it to go well, and she somehow knew that it would. She'd suggested the tour of her house and grounds to provide the lightweight banter that Tristan's fans loved, but she had insisted that they dispatch with the fluff once they sat down to do the actual interview. He had agreed. For what seemed like the hundredth time, Reilly wished that she had done an interview like this long before the startling new information had been found. Before talking about it had become the huge albatross that it now was. But the opportunity for that had passed. It was time to go on the record.

"Reilly Ransome, thank you so much for inviting us into your private world today."

"It's a pleasure to have you and Melinda here, Tristan."

"You have a beautiful home and we're grateful that you chose to share it with us during this special on-location segment of *The Morning Show*." Reilly returned Tristan's smile with an expression that she hoped conveyed her welcome but also showed the audience that the interview was a serious event for her. She was nervous.

"Thank you. I appreciate that you traveled all the way out to California to do it here."

"Are you kidding? We wouldn't have missed it. But now Melinda and I are thinking that we might need to go bi-coastal. It was thirty degrees colder in New York when we left. Spring hasn't quite hit us yet. I can't get over all of this sunshine in winter!" Tristan rested his hand on his wife's leg as his other hand swept the air in front of him, indicating everything around him. Melinda nodded when he looked at her.

"It would take a lot to get me to leave the city, but I could get used to doing laps in a pool like this. It's like being on a private tropical island," agreed Melinda.

"You're welcome to visit any time you like." Reilly was sincere in her offer, and she took in the bamboo and other greenery that surrounded the pool deck. She knew it was lovely and she was happy that her guests appreciated it as much as she did. "To be honest, though, until recently, I never spent very much time here at my house, which has only recently begun to feel like a home."

"It's beautiful, Reilly. What do you mean by saying that it's only recently felt like home?" asked Tristan.

"Things changed when I got out of prison. Before then, when I wasn't working—which wasn't very often—I spent most of my time going to parties, traveling. I never spent much time at my house. When I was released from prison and I finally got to go home, I realized that the house that I called home wasn't really a home at all. It had very little of me in it. That's changed in the last few months. I'm more of a homebody now."

"All of the fresh flowers you have throughout your home are fantastic."

"Thanks. I love fresh flowers," agreed Reilly. "But I think it finally became a home when I met Drew."

"That is so sweet," gushed Melinda, leaning forward to touch Reilly's hand.

"I'm going to have to ask Reilly to give me some pointers on making my wife swoon," said Tristan shaking his head. "But that is sweet, Reilly. It's nice to see you so happy. You are happy, right?"

"Oh, yes, Tristan. I am very happy."

"That is truly wonderful, Reilly. I have to guess that not all of that is due to being in love. Don't blush. It's obvious," said Tristan, smiling at her. Reilly blushed even harder but couldn't argue. "So, you mentioned prison. I have to ask. How has it been since you've been out?"

"Absolutely surreal." Reilly's response was immediate.

"I can imagine," said Melinda.

"How did it feel to find out that you were innocent of the murder that you went to prison for?" asked Tristan.

"Honestly, it took a while to sink in. And I've gone through a lot of emotions through that process. Some of them very surprising," admitted Reilly. Part of her was self-conscious about talking about what happened as if she were the only one who mattered. "But, it doesn't change the end result. A man has died. Nothing can change that."

"Yes. Of course. There is no doubt that the death is still the most tragic outcome of everything that happened," said Tristan, and Reilly saw what she was sure was true sadness in his eyes. "But, you suffered, too. You spent four years thinking that you were the one responsible for his death. You went to jail for something that you didn't do. Being exonerated for that has got to be one of the best things to ever happen to you."

"I admit that there is a huge sense of relief, Tristan. I haven't been exonerated yet, though" explained Reilly.

"Melinda, can you explain this? You're the one with the Harvard law degree," said Tristan, turning to his wife

"It will take a little while to process the exoneration, which can be a lengthy legal ordeal," explained Melinda. "It's a series of administrative actions that offi-cially removes the blame from someone, in this case Reilly, who was previously convicted of this particular crime. But even in a cut-and-dried case like this, it can take several months for the administrative process to complete."

"It's just a matter of time, though," said Tristan, as if the details were of no concern. It didn't slip past Reilly that Tristan seemed to have already dismissed Reilly's guilt in the whole thing. While she was relieved that things had turned out the way they had, Reilly couldn't help feel that he was at least a little wrong. "Reilly, you found an incriminating audio recording of the night in question, which has led to at least one confession by the real killers. There is also a new witness—the only witness that night—who corroborates your innocence. This witness offers new details regarding what happened on that night four and a half years ago when Matt Traynor was killed."

"That's true. Even now I can barely believe it." Reilly shook her head.

"What kind of shock was it for you to learn that Sylvie Simonson, Hollywood entertainment lawyer, admitted to the police that she was the one behind the wheel on that fateful night? She was your girlfriend at the time, is that correct? What a betrayal that must have been!"

"Shock is an understatement, Tristan," said Reilly, remembering the disbelief and sense of disconnection she'd felt as she'd listened to that recording. The same feeling had swept through her when she had heard of Sylvie's confession as soon as she'd been confronted. "The biggest shock, though…" Reilly paused as an unexpected lump took away her ability to speak.

"Must have been what happened when the police confronted Parker Stevens, is that right?" asked Tristan, making a correct guess at what she had been about to say.

Reilly cleared her throat and nodded. She was still unable to speak.

"Parker is still in the hospital after having tried to take her own life, and it looks like she may never regain most of the abilities that were taken away by the bullet that came very close to killing her. She's regained consciousness, but doctors remain skeptical that she'll ever leave her hospital bed, let alone speak or even communicate again."

Reilly tried to push away the image of Parker lying in her hospital bed, half of her head covered in bandages that couldn't disguise that a large portion of her face and head were just missing. Tubes and machines had added to the dissonance of the situation, invading Parker's body, monitoring her vital signs. That was before the doctors had confirmed that the bullet from Parker's gun had irreversibly destroyed anything that had once been the core of who Parker Stevens really was. Reilly had been grateful that she hadn't been able to get close enough to talk to her then. And she hadn't been able to bring herself to go back to see her since. The horror of coming face-to-face with the condition of her formerly beautiful rival was one thing, but the anger that had erupted inside of

Reilly as she had stood outside of the room looking in at the severely injured woman was what kept her away. Reilly tried not to feel guilty about the hate that she felt, the sense of vindication. But it was there. She didn't possess the grace of Lydia Traynor who had been able to grant forgiveness. So Reilly tried to forgive herself instead.

Tristan continued.

"Though Sylvie Simonson has implicated Parker Stevens as an accomplice in the accident that killed Matt Traynor, chances are that Ms. Stevens will never see the inside of a courthouse. You seem visibly upset about all of this, Reilly. We were just talking about how happy you must be, but this terrible topic has put a damper on that."

Reilly cleared her throat and found that she could speak again. She peered beyond Tristan's shoulder at her friends. Drew smiled, and Hank gave her a nod of encouragement.

"Yes. Some of it is very hard to take in," agreed Reilly.

"I can imagine," said Tristan, leaning forward in his chair. Then, leaning back, he turned toward the camera. "We'll talk more about the evidence that exonerates our guest, Reilly Ransome, when we return from a break. This is Tristan and Melinda Powers of *The Morning Show*, on location at Miss Ransome's home in West Hollywood, California. Please stay tuned."

The cameramen stepped back from their gear and the television screen switched to a commercial for pet food. Reilly let her shoulders relax.

"How are you doing? Are you good?" Tristan leaned toward Reilly and checked in with her.

"Just a little nervous. I didn't expect to react the way I did."

"You would never know by looking at you," replied Melinda, with a wink and a pat. Reilly scanned the area for Drew, and found her being led toward the set.

She watched as Drew, Hank, and Cray took a seat in the wide wicker sofa that had been placed next to her chair. The sofa and her chair sat at a slight angle to each other across the table from Tristan and Melinda's seats. If the boom mics and cameras hadn't been lurking over their heads and behind their backs, the setting would have seemed cozy. The others patiently endured the placement of the microphones that were clipped to their clothes, and Reilly was glad to see that Drew, who had been a little nervous in the days leading up to the show, seemed to be taking it all in stride. Reilly wasn't worried about Hank and Cray. They were used to being on camera.

"Back in ten, nine…" the set director started the countdown as the commercial break ended.

Tristan sat up and the energy returned in full force. He faced the camera and spoke.

"Thank you for joining us for this special segment of *The Morning Show* with Tristan and Melinda Powers. We're here with Reilly Ransome, at her beautiful home in West Hollywood, California, doing a special on-location interview for *The Morning Show*. Reilly's partner, Drew Tamrin, has joined us, as well as Hollywood's most sought after leading man, Cray Leighton, and their friend Hank Thomas, who many may remember as Dusty's kid brother from the hit sitcom that launched Reilly's career, *Home Grown*. Welcome, Drew, Cray, and Hank."

The three murmured their hellos.

"So, Reilly, all of you were together when the recording was discovered," stated Tristan.

"Yes. We were having a small get together to celebrate Thanksgiving here at my house," said Reilly.

"That was a day none of us will ever forget," added Cray.

"I'll bet. Which one of you found the cell phone?" asked Tristan.

"I did," said Hank. "It was still in Reilly's car, wedged under the driver's seat belt clip and the center console. I almost missed it." Hank provided more detail on how he had come across the phone when he was getting ready to sell the car. The others added small details about how they had gathered around the phone to listen to the events that had led up to the accident. Reilly even described how she had gotten sick.

"It seems so implausible. Why wasn't the phone logged into evidence? Was the investigation conducted that poorly?" asked Melinda.

Reilly had thought long and hard about that, but she understood why the police hadn't searched her car very thoroughly.

"The police did a great job. I suppose they didn't think they needed to really search the car," she explained. "Even I assumed that I had been the person behind the wheel that night. I entered a not guilty plea at the advice of counsel, but never offered any kind of defense for myself, and my attorneys were more focused on shortening the sentence than proving my innocence. There was no reason for the police to investigate further. For all intents and purposes, they thought that they had the guilty party in custody."

"Do you think that's the same reason the police have for not having interviewed the only witness, Albert Stillman?" asked Tristan.

Reilly was still amazed that Albert Stillman, the homeless man that the police had chased away from the scene that morning, had been able to provide a full account of what had happened that night. Reilly had forgotten all about him until one of the officers mentioned him to her during the interview that occurred when she and Hank had brought the cell phone into the police. His name was listed in the 9-1-1 logs as the caller. She had no idea that it was he who had been at the scene until just a few days ago, when the investigator assigned to the re-opened case called and told her that they had found him, a military veteran with severe PTSD, on the same beach, sleeping near the garbage collection bins. It turned out that he had been arrested for vagrancy during the time of the investigation and had never even been questioned in the case. Four years later, when asked, he provided a full description of what had happened, almost down to the exact dialog that they had all heard in the video.

Reilly thought about the note scratched out on the piece of notebook paper that the investigator had given to her the day before.

I been thinking about you all this time pretty lady. Your heart is good. Things gonna be just fine.

The writing matched that of another note that had been with the rest of the belongings from her car. The note from the coffee shop all those months ago. *Hope comes in unlikely packages.* The original note had seemed nothing more than a thank you at the time. Reilly's mind still couldn't wrap around the synchronicity of certain events in her life. The note was now tucked into the corner of her vanity mirror at home.

"I suspect that a few things contributed to the failure to bring Mr. Stillman in as a witness," offered Reilly. She refrained from going into more detail because, like many homeless people, he was in that position because of a lack of social assistance in treating mental illness. He wasn't a danger to anyone, but some of his idiosyncrasies—such as repeating phrases over and over at a loud volume—were, at times, alarming. Another topic she didn't discuss was that she had set up the help he needed to get off the streets, but his distrust of people made that difficult, and he continued to live out there. He seemed to trust her more than others, and she'd have to play it carefully with him, but she hoped to develop a relationship that would allow him to let her help him some day. She didn't want to bring any of that up on national television, though. "His being homeless probably had a lot to do with it. But yes, I think that since the police already had me in custody, assuming that they had apprehended their killer, there was no need to expend more resources on what they saw as an already solved case."

"It must be frustrating to you, though. If they had just looked a little harder, things might have unraveled differently."

"One thing I've learned is that you can't change what has already happened," said Reilly. "The police did the best job they could with the information they had." Although she knew that what she said was true, Reilly couldn't help but feel resentment about what had happened. She could now talk about it with her friends, but this was one thing she wasn't ready to discuss with the media. Forgiveness took time, and she'd only recently begun to forgive herself. It was going to take time for her to extend that forgiveness to everyone else. She was glad that Tristan didn't try to press it.

"Let's talk about that recording, then. Tell us about what went through your minds when you first listened to it."

Reilly shuddered at the memory that haunted her, and her throat grew tight. The awful sound of Matt Traynor dying in the recording still played frequently through her mind. The old dreams that had contained a single running shoe lying on wet pavement had started to fill her nights again after hearing that sound. She'd woken more than once in the middle of the night, sobbing into Drew's arms. Talking about it with Drew helped. She was grateful that she had been advised not to speak about the content of the recording, as it was the primary evidence against Sylvie in the trial that was scheduled to begin in the fall. Parker's condition had prevented formal charges from being pressed against her.

"We can't discuss those details until after the trial is over," said Cray. "What I can tell you is that it proves beyond a shadow of a doubt that Reilly was not responsible for the accident. She was as much a victim as Mr. Traynor was."

Reilly had an impulse to correct him, but the lump in her throat made her pause, and then Tristan was talking again.

"Well, I'm sure that the rest of the world feels a lot like I do, and I'm just happy that the right people are being brought to justice," said Tristan.

Reilly glanced over at Hank, afraid of how he would respond. He'd reined in his anger since those earlier days, but it still rose up one in a while, and when it did, it made Reilly flinch.

"We are, too, Tristan," said Hank. "We're also glad that they're taking responsibility for it—well, at least Sylvie is." Reilly was proud of Hank for his mild response, and she gave him a little smile.

Sylvie's immediate confession had surprised everyone. Reilly guessed that the guilt had been crushing her all the while when she saw the pictures in the news of a gaunt and haggard Sylvie being booked at the police station. The four years that had passed since Reilly had last seen her had aged her far more than they should have. Parker hadn't been so easy. She had invited the police into her house and had then excused herself to go to the bathroom. Moments later a shot had rung out. She had been in the hospital ever since. Reilly would have never predicted Parker's actions. But then again, all of the other things she and Sylvie had done were beyond her comprehension, too.

As Cray added some of his feelings about the matter, Reilly looked beyond the camera crew and out over her beloved arroyo. Despite the subject of the interview, she couldn't get over how amazing it felt to be outside, to feel the sunshine on her skin and smell the sweet scent of the early season wisteria and honeysuckle on the trellis behind them. Being near Drew and her best friends helped to ground her. She reached over to grasp Drew's hand.

"Reilly, you spent almost two years in prison for a crime that you didn't commit. Aren't you angry about that?" asked Tristan.

Reilly had rehearsed this answer. It was the first question most people asked her. Her practiced response only skimmed the surface of what she really thought, but no one but her closest friends needed to hear her deeper, darker thoughts. And, in truth, she was still trying to come to terms with her feelings about it. In sticking to the script with the public, she was allowed to explore the less tidy part of her healing in private. And, even so, the superficial response was still mostly true, anyway.

"I think angry goes without saying. But anger is so counterproductive. Therapists and enlightened people will tell you that you have to process things to heal, and anger is part of that. But you don't have to dwell there. You can move past that to a more productive place. I can't change what's already happened. And being human, I have resentment about that, but I'm trying to let go of it. You know—leave the past in the past and avoid adding even more negativity to that very awful thing that happened four years ago. The thing is, I am very aware that the effect on me was nothing compared to what happened to the man who died and the family he left behind. So, I'm trying to stay focused on being the best person I can be. And, maybe I'm being trite, but it's what I think is the right thing to do. Forgiving and being a better role model will help me do that."

"Come on, Reilly. I'm not sure that the Pope would be that forgiving."

Reilly laughed and glanced at Hank, who winked back. It was true. She'd heard that more than once or twice, hadn't she?

"I won't say that I've been successful at forgiving everyone, but I'm trying," she said, studying Tristan's eyes. It was important to her that she said what she meant. She owed it to her fans and to herself to be honest about what was going on inside of her. She owed it to Matt and his family to make sure that he wasn't forgotten. She decided to reveal a little more. "It took so long for me to begin to forgive myself for what I thought I had done. I figure that if I could do that, I could at least try to forgive others."

"Still, you must have some sort of anger at having been blamed for something that you had no part in. What do you do with that?"

"Sure, I feel anger. But that's mixed in with a lot of guilt. Ultimately, I lost very little compared to the Traynor family," said Reilly, remembering her last visit from Matt's wife, just a few days ago. Lydia had brought the girls with her. The girls were young and Reilly didn't know how much they knew about their father's death or what they had been told about Reilly's part in it. But they'd been sweet and seemed like normal kids, even with everything that had happened. Reilly had spent the visit in awe over the girl's resilience and feeling wonder over the closeness she saw binding the mother with her daughters. All the while, she wrestled with a tremendous sadness knowing Matt would never be a part of it again. It was hard to feel like she deserved their forgiveness, but she was working on it. Something occurred to her then. A certain clarity filled her and she decided to give voice to it. "I believe it's important to acknowledge that I was not completely innocent in what happened. I need to take responsibility for the kind of person I was at the time. The thing is that it could have very well been me behind that wheel, with the way my life was headed and how I was behaving at the time."

"When you put it that way, it could have been any of us behind the wheel, Reilly," said Tristan, looking a little surprised at her candor, even a little skeptical.

"In some respects, yes. Accidents happen," she said, the realization becoming more solid as she gave voice to it. "But I know the empty person that I used to be. When you don't care, or when you care too much about your own happiness to the exclusion of others, you breed a certain kind of environment around you. I take responsibility for the life I used to lead and the influence I had on others. For a long time I truly believed that I had killed a man. And thinking that I was capable of it has had a profound impact on my life. It's made me think long and hard about the power of intent. It's made me more aware of how I need to focus my own intent and how that impacts others. I know that I didn't have any power over Sylvie and Parker's choices—they were very wrong in what they did to me, and everyone else involved—but, I can't help but think that if I had behaved as a better person, they may not have made the choices that they did. Like I said, I can't change what happened, but I can try to be a better person going forward."

"It sounds like you're taking on a lot of responsibility for other people's actions," said Tristan.

"No more than I should, I guess," said Reilly, hoping that she didn't sound like she had a messiah complex. "I've come to realize that a certain responsibility comes with being a public figure. It's just reality, Tristan. And I think most people naturally live their lives in a responsible way without even trying. I just have to learn how to be that way, too."

"What took you so long to speak publicly about what happened? Was it that you knew all along that you were innocent?"

"Until last November, I genuinely thought that I was guilty. I didn't speak about it because I was a coward. I tried to justify it to myself that I was honoring Matt Traynor by not making the whole thing about me, but that backfired. The longer I didn't speak, the more it actually did become about me," admitted Reilly. "To be honest, I feel like I deserve what I've gone through. I don't think that what Sylvie and Parker did was okay, but I acknowledge that I played a part in what happened. Like I said earlier in the interview, it could have easily been me behind the wheel."

The forgiveness that she'd been searching for started to take hold within her. It felt like a weight was lifting from her and she was glad when Tristan shifted the conversation. She needed some time to digest her revelation.

"Tell me a little about the Matt Traynor Project."

Reilly blushed. Nothing in Hollywood was secret for long.

"With the generous help of my studio, a large portion of the proceeds from *Salsa Nights* will be used to fund the Matt Traynor Project, a grant program that provides support to families who have lost a parent due to drunk or drugged driving."

"By 'a large portion,' don't you mean your entire salary from the sequel, and your full portion of the proceeds?"

Reilly's blush burned hotter.

"She's too modest to discuss it, but her generosity has inspired some of the other actors to contribute to the effort, along with the studio, who will donate a portion of all ticket and other movie sales to the program," Cray confirmed. Reilly wanted to slug him. It was supposed to be anonymous.

"That's amazing. I'm sure his family is pleased. You've turned a terrible thing into a positive thing."

"I'm sure that they'd rather have Matt back," said Reilly.

"True. I'm sure it would have been best if none of this was even needed," agreed Tristan. "But, to paraphrase a saying I've heard, it's not our mistakes that define us, but the way we respond to them. I have no doubt that the project will be successful. So, do you have other plans? What's next?"

Reilly could sense that the interview was coming to a close, and she relaxed a little with the new found peace. She wondered if she would have found it earlier if only she'd spoken out before now. In a way, she felt that, despite all of the changes that she had made, and all of the difficulties that she had gone through over the last four years, she could now start to really move forward with her life.

"Well, *Salsa Nights II: Dare to Dream* is going to be released this summer. My studio would kill me if I didn't mention that," smiled Reilly. As important as the topic of the interview was, she still knew that the show couldn't end on a downer. There was a delicate balance in maintaining a dignity needed to honor the fallen man while keeping her fan base interested enough to watch the interview. It was a responsibility she had learned to accept as part of her celebrity. Her hope was that she could use her public presence to become a better role model for those who looked up to her. If just one person learned to become a better person because of her experience, she would be grateful. "And I have a few movies in the works. Aside from that, Drew and I are working on a yoga-based prison release transition program. But most of all, I'm just going to try to live a more meaningful life, however that might evolve." Reilly smiled. "Who knows? Maybe I'll write a book—give my mom some competition for the top of the bestseller list."

"I've read her book. I loved it. With the list of movie projects that you're rumored to have signed up for, and with all of what you just listed, it sounds like you'll be a busy lady for quite some time. I hope that you'll find room in your schedule to visit us at *The Morning Show* in New York even with all of that going on."

"I don't know, Tristan. I kind of like the idea of taking the show on the road and coming here," chimed in Melinda.

"I'd have to agree with that suggestion," chuckled Tristan, smiling at his wife.

"I'll never turn down a chance to see Melinda," said Reilly with a wink at the blushing co-host. She fought a giggle when Drew squeezed her hand.

Reilly smiled and her eyes shifted to find her mother, who was standing just beyond the boom operator, taking everything in with a calm intensity. Reilly squeezed Drew's hand and smiled at her. When she glanced over, Drew's silver eyes filled with encouragement and love, and Reilly's heart overflowed with emotion. There was so much to do, but now that her life had a purpose, Reilly looked forward to seeing how it would all unfold.

Peace

THERE WERE SEVERAL MINUTES BEFORE class would start and Reilly sat on her mat in her usual place in the back corner of Drew's yoga studio. She'd been early, as was usual on days that she came directly from meetings at the studio, and the room had been empty upon her arrival. Her eyes were closed and she was comfortable in Lotus, pushing away thoughts about the new movie she was just about to start filming, tangled in worry over how she was going to fit in the meetings with the county that she needed to attend regarding the prison release program she and Drew were establishing. Drew was doing most of the work, but Reilly wanted to participate, and when filming started there wouldn't be much time. She juggled schedules in her mind.

Set the intruding thoughts aside, she told herself.

She switched her focus to an image of the beautiful stream in Drew's yard and how the dappled summer sunlight had made the surface look like diamonds tumbling over the pebbled bottom when she'd walked along it on her way to the studio. Reilly imagined that she was smaller and her body was floating along the stream, buoyant and serene. The koi swam slowly below her, sometimes nibbling at her limbs, tickling her skin. Long grasses growing along the sides brushed over her skin. The heat of the sun warmed her, while the water below soothed her. The mat beneath her was liquid, and she was drifting. The sounds of people slowly entering the room and settling around her faded away, became inconsequential outside of her immediate consciousness. Her surroundings blurred and ran together. She was at peace.

It started with a tingle that ran along her arms, through her legs, across the edges of her body. Her chest filled with anticipation.

Drew was in the room.

Reilly was back on her mat. Her eyes were still closed. The light pressing in on her eyelids grew dim as the shades on the wide front windows were lowered.

"Namaste," Drew's low voice floated over the room, caressing Reilly's skin, returning Reilly's being to the life of high definition. She'd learned to stop fighting her inability to remain in tranquil repose. Her life was a blend of both now. It was just the way it was.

Reilly willingly surrendered.

Namaste.

Coming soon *from* Kimberly Cooper Griffin!

Chasing Mercury

Two worlds collide when an airplane goes down in the wilds of Alaska. Nora Kavendash, a retired software developer, finds herself taking care of a mysterious woman with amnesia who she soon nicknames 4B. Weather and rugged terrain work against them as they wait for rescue and Nora worries about a package that she must deliver as a matter of life and death. When help finally arrives, it seems that life was somehow simpler when it was just the two of them against the unknown. Life sweeps in and threatens to break the tenuous tie the two women have forged and 4B is faced with finding out who she really is. More importantly, they both find out that it's impossible to run from yourself.

kimberlycoopergriffin.com/chasing-mercury

www.ingramcontent.com/pod-product-compliance
Lightning Source LLC
Chambersburg PA
CBHW030655120726

47905CB00001B/224